# GOOD BLOOD

## THE DESCENDANTS OF TERNE

BILLY KETCH ALLEN

MOONGLASS
BOOKS

Published by Moonglass Books

ISBN: 978-0-9886365-6-9
First Edition 2018

Thank you for supporting my work.

*To Kyle and our two-man writing group.*

Ghost Mountains

Gorgen

Broming

Severen

Carmine

Clyda

Rune

Temple of the Faith

Hidden Wood

Chamberlain

Tannen

Faatus

Caldesh

Suthra

Sanstar

Mordal

Rockfall

The Endless Desert

Land of Terene

Realms of High Noble Lords

N
W · E
S

# PART I

CASTLE CARMINE

# 1

---

*"One day, when the history of our people is written, it will be said that up until the very end—we did not see it coming."*

---

The boy shook awake, blinking into darkness. The floor moved, bouncing his stiff body up and down. He groaned and hot air escaped his lips, dry as dust. He reached for his burning side and touched ribs shooting in different directions, like rungs on a broken ladder.

The floor shifted with a thump, and he slammed into a wall. Wheels creaked beneath him. Horses galloped somewhere up ahead. He was moving.

*Where…am I?*

It wasn't complete darkness. Cracks of light broke through slats in the wooden box. It was enough light to see the bruises that colored his bare torso like spilled ink. He reached a hand up to his throbbing head, and it came away with flecks of dry blood.

How did he get here? The boy gritted his teeth to block the

3

pain in his head and searched through his memory. Nothing. He couldn't remember how he got into this windowless box that reeked of blood and sweat. He couldn't remember why his body was covered in cuts and bruises. He couldn't even remember—

The boy froze.

"No," he screamed, or tried to, for the plea came out as a broken whisper. Leaning against the wall, he pulled himself to his feet; his muscles cried for rest. As small as he was, the boy still had to duck under the low wooden roof.

"Stop," he groaned and struck the wall. The blow landed with a dull tap. He pounded again and again, his strength returning along with his voice. "Stop…Stop…STOP!"

The clomping horse hooves slowed, and the squeaking wagon wheels settled to a stop.

The boy pressed against the wall, catching his breath. Small clipped breaths so as not to stretch his ribs.

After a moment, he made out the voices of two men.

"I know what I heard. It came from the cage."

"You're still spooked. How is it a big man like you can be afraid of bed-time stories?"

"Cause I've been doing this long enough to know to stay away from this cursed place. This heavy fog. Ghost Mountains that rise up without end. It's not natural. Too many people have ventured this far north, never to come back."

"Right. And you also believe the fog brings corpses back to life?"

"I told you something moved in the cage. You're so certain I'm wrong, go and check it out."

The back of the box creaked and swung open. The boy staggered back, raising his hands to block the light.

"Great Hemo," one of the men shouted. "He's alive."

Two men stared with open mouths. They had tan skin that almost matched their dusty travel coats. The small, thin man stepped back beside his companion, a large brute with a flattened nose. The boy recoiled to the back wall of the cage. The big man raised a club in his oversized hand.

"I thought you checked him," the smaller man yelped.

"We both did," the big man said. "His head was cracked open, and he looked like he'd been trampled under a dozen horses."

"Well, he's not dead," the big man said. "But doesn't look too far from it."

"Please," the boy said. "What happened to me?"

The men exchanged looks.

"Looks like you got beat and left for dead," the smaller man said. "You don't remember?"

The boy reached out. "Help me."

The smaller man smiled, but there was no warmth in his eyes. "You're lucky we found you and hauled you away. Tell me, where is your mark?"

The boy shifted, confused.

The big man turned to his companion. "You think he's…"

"I don't need the test to tell a Descendant. They have a stink to them. Isn't that right boy?"

The boy stared back blankly.

"Not very bright either," the smaller man said. "Generations of breeding left them good for only one thing."

"But how? He doesn't have a house brand."

"Which means he's all ours." He slapped the bigger man on the arm. "The Temple auction is in three days. If we clean him up, I think he'll fetch us a good price. Even for a low blood."

"Don't get your hopes up. When it comes to spending their shrines, Noble lords aren't complete clots."

The boy touched his aching head. Though he understood the words, they didn't make sense. It was like reading a book with holes cut in the pages. He had to get out of here, had to figure out what was going on. He had to remember.

The boy made a break for the cage door. He kicked at the men as he scrambled free, but his legs gave out and he toppled to the ground. The boy clawed at the dirt, using whatever strength he had left to get away from his captors.

"Little beast!" Hands grabbed his legs. He kicked wildly, pain shooting through his body like knives. He twisted in the man's grip.

"What did you do to me?" the boy cried.

The big man swung his club down, smashing the boy's knee.

"Ahhhh," the boy screamed. His leg stopped working.

Hands clamped around the boy's neck and lifted him off the ground. "Don't get wild now, boy, or we'll leave you deader than we found you."

He threw the boy back in the wooden cage. The boy grabbed the back of his ringing head. His fingers discovered a wet crevice, sinking into his scalp as if it were mud. The boy vomited on the cage floor.

"That was a mistake," the smaller man snorted. "It's a long ride to the Temple, and you'll be swimming in that the whole way."

"We're not going to get much for him with those wounds," the big man said. "Maybe we wait until the next auction. Give him time to heal up. Put some color on him. He looks like a ghost."

"And feed and shelter him for a full season? Are you crazy? We're getting rid of this little clot while we can. We either get a few shrines for him or they execute him. Either way, we're free of him."

The men's words were fading like the sunlight through the fog. It took all of the boy's strength not to pass out. What had he done? Why was this happening to him?

A half-filled water-skin slid along the cage floor. It came to rest against the boy's leg, which bent at an unnatural angle.

"That's all the water you're getting. Best not drink it all at once."

The cage door slammed shut, and a metal bar slid into place.

The men's footsteps faded and, after a few moments, the cage started moving again.

The boy sat alone in the darkness, pain everywhere. He didn't understand what was happening to him. It was as if he'd drifted off into some horrible nightmare. He couldn't remember anything. He couldn't even remember who *he* was!

*This isn't real. I'll wake up and it'll all be over.*

But as the cage bounced along the road, his aching body reminded him how wrong he was.

BRITON'S CARRIAGE rolled through the city gates, past statues of Hemo. The Faith had settled on this depiction of their god, long ago. Though the facial features changed from artist to artist, Hemo's beard was constant—pointed and always well-trimmed. As if a god had nothing better to do than manicure his facial hair.

No matter how many times Briton came, he never got used to the sight of the Temple. A series of connected buildings of white stone, each one bigger and more marvelous than the last. The large, golden domes that topped the buildings glowed, even in the sunless morning. Whatever hatred people held for the Royals of old, they had to admit, they could build. The Temple appeared all the more majestic in contrast to the hovels that surrounded it; a marketplace of street vendors and merchant shops. Visitors flocked here from all across Terene to exchange goods or worship in the Temple's outer sanctuary.

The Fathers of the Faith were unprejudiced when it came to taking money.

The carriage pulled to a stop, and Carmine's men began unpacking the carts. Briton threw his empty satchel over his shoulder and climbed to the ground, his old bones cracking from the journey. In recent years, Briton's duties kept him mostly to Castle Carmine. His body was not used to travel, even travel as gentle as this. Jonathan Carmine had been surprised when his advisor had volunteered to oversee the trip, knowing how Briton disapproved of the Descendant auction. But Briton had his own business in the Temple square. He hoped this trip would not be a waste.

"Are you coming to supervise the auction, Master Briton?" asked Typher, Carmine's house Curor. Sarcasm dripped from the title he bestowed on Briton.

"Go on ahead, Typher," Briton said. "I have other business to attend to first."

"As you wish," the Curor bowed, his red robes touching the dirt of the street before sweeping away with a company of guards.

The Temple square was always crowded on auction day. Briton recognized the sigils of other noble houses, some loyal to Carmine, others not. Each was looking for an advantage in the blood trade.

The remaining party of Carmine's men stood, awaiting orders. Briton began with Semus, the castle's gardener. "You have your instructions?"

"Yes," Semus said, tightening his floppy hat to hold in those ever-escaping curls of his. "Lord Carmine has high hopes for this trip. Word is out that the traders have retrieved a blood rose from the Endless Desert."

"And I'm sure he gave you permission to spend a fortune on it."

"It is a rare plant. We'd be the only house in the north to possess one."

"Such a high honor," Briton sighed. "Go, go, you have your instructions. May it be healthy and bring his Lordship eternal happiness."

The rest of Carmine's workers were sent about their business, purchasing everything from food and kitchen supplies to weapons. With everyone about their tasks, Briton crossed the Temple square and followed a small side street to a quieter part of the market. It was here that one could find the more…irregular items.

After winding down some back alleys, Briton stopped before an unmarked building with a faded green door. The Hidden Gem posted no signs or window displays. Patrons did not simply stumble upon it. Briton pushed open the stubborn door with a series of kicks and stepped inside. The shop was empty, the shelves bare, save for layers of dust. Briton would have believed the shop was abandoned had it not always worn this facade. He approached the deserted counter and waited, scratching his bald head and batting the dust from his blue-gray robes.

After some time, the back door opened, and a large woman with curly orange hair squeezed inside. She wore a thin green dress that struggled to hold her substantial body. The top of the dress was further weighted down by a large bosom and a waterfall of colorful necklaces.

"Welcome to the Hidden Gem, sir," she said, betraying a slight smile. "How may I be of service?"

"Is it here?" Briton asked.

"May I ask what you are referring to?" The woman set down a lockbox and opened a ledger. "I have no memory of your order as all our customers and their requests are kept confidential."

"Spare me the act, Barbara, you know very well…" Briton sighed, annoyed at his own impatience, and the advantage it gave the owner of the Hidden Gem. "My name is Briton Moonglass of House Carmine, and I seek the same thing that has brought me into this wonderful establishment two times this past year."

Barbara raised a bushy orange eyebrow, no longer attempting to conceal her smile.

Briton sighed. "Item four-two-four."

"Four-two-four," she repeated, turning the pages in the book. "Ah, yes, here we are. You asked for our services in tracking down a certain book. One year ago next week."

"Is it in?" Briton asked, putting his hands on the counter.

Barbara leaned forward, squishing her bosom on the counter, and whispered one, beautiful word. "Yes."

Briton's pulse quickened. *At long last.*

"My net of contacts spreads wide throughout Terene, but this item proved very difficult to find. Plus, they are not as experienced in searching for such an…unusual item."

"Not many readers among your clientele?"

"This will be reflected in the final price."

"I expect no less from someone of your reputation."

"One hundred and sixty shrines," Barbara said. "Or twenty vials if you prefer."

Briton cringed. This was more than he'd expected. And, as he was paying with his own purse, not Carmine's, it would nearly drain him.

But if the book contained what he hoped…

"If it had taken you another week, I suppose I would have some more bargaining power."

"A bit more, yes."

"And what happens if I refuse your price? The Hidden Gem can't have much of a market for old books."

"Let us hope you do not refuse," Barbara said, the playfulness gone from her face. Briton emptied his coin purse on the counter. Good thing he'd brought it all. To have waited this long, only to leave empty-handed.

Barbara recounted the one hundred and sixty shrines, and then placed the gold coins into the lockbox. She carried the box and the ledger out the back door. Briton's fingers tapped on the counter.

A year ago he had come to the Hidden Gem when his own search for the book proved fruitless. Barbara had boasted her contacts could find anything—as long as it existed—but Briton's hope had diminished as the year wore on. Now, he might finally have answers to the questions that had consumed his studies. The true origin of the Royals' blood.

Barbara slid back into the shop and set a small package on the counter. It was no bigger than an earring box.

Briton scowled. "What is this?"

"Item four-two-four."

His heart sank.

"It is not what you expected," Barbara smiled. "That proved an obstacle for us as well. Based on your description, we searched for some ancient tome buried in the Temple vault or forgotten in the back of a lord's library. We were lucky to find this in the end."

Briton gently tore away the protective paper. It was indeed a book, though small enough to fit in his palm. The cover was faded brown and unmarked. He opened it, and the pages stuck together, warped and colored like dead leaves. Carefully, he pushed the pages back, revealing the first page. Briton bent closer. Written in tiny swirling handwriting were the words, *The Last Writings of King Garian Kovar.*

This was it. What he'd been searching for.

"It came enclosed in a case, would you like it as well?"

"For one hundred and sixty shrines it should come with a carriage."

Barbra smiled and pulled a chain out of the pocket of her dress. On the end of the chain hung a square metal locket. She set it on the table. "Thank you for your business."

Briton examined the case. The craftsmanship was remarkable; an intricate maze-like pattern carved into the metal. He imagined King Kovar wearing the necklace as he went through meetings and Temple feasts, no one knowing of the secret diary within. Briton held a piece of history in his hands.

"I hope it holds what you seek, Briton Moonglass," Barbara said.

Briton locked the book into the necklace and placed it into his satchel. *So do I.*

Briton hurried back through the narrow streets of the market, into the Temple square. Though he hadn't done anything illegal, it wouldn't look proper for the advisor of House Carmine to be seen doing business in a place like the Hidden Gem.

Back at the wagons, Semus and his men unloaded a wooden crate from their cart. "You were successful," Briton said.

"Lord Carmine's garden is now in possession of a genuine blood rose," Semus beamed.

Briton leaned over the crate where a green flower poked up through the sandy soil; its slender green stem was topped with a closed red bud. "It's alive at least, isn't it?"

"It's young. It won't bloom for some time yet and only in warm conditions."

Briton was in no place to chastise Carmine for the frivolous expense when he just spent one hundred and sixty shrines on a book. Briton left the men to their work and moved to his carriage. He opened the door and pulled out the necklace containing the diary of Garian Kovar, last king of the Royals. He ran his finger over the necklace's pattern. This was the king's personal journal, written at the end of his reign.

Briton had read many accounts of the Blood Wars but none written from the perspective of a Royal—the Faith had eradicated almost all of Royal culture. To think, King Kovar had written these pages centuries ago from within the walls of this very Temple. Briton was tempted to lock himself in the carriage and explore the tiny text. But he had waited this long, he could wait just a little longer. He wrapped the chain around the box and slid it back in the satchel, hiding it under the seat. Then, locking the carriage door, he hurried to the Temple.

The statue of General Drusas stood outside the Temple, the leader's sword pointed high in the air. Another artistic interpretation. As great as the general must have been to defeat the Royals, he was not ten feet tall, wielding a sword as long as a man.

Briton entered the Temple's outer sanctuary door, bypassing the saucer of blood wine—he'd accepted his old bones and aching back long ago. Chants and murmurs filled the sanctuary as people prayed to the Lord Hemo.

The sanctuary, like every inch of the Temple, was ornately designed. Complex patterns were cut into every door and painted on every shutter; there was no such thing as mere function. Any tile under Briton's feet could be cut away and hung as a work of art.

Briton walked to the back of the sanctuary where the Temple guards stood watch over the inner door. He held up his ring. "Briton Moonglass of House Carmine. I'm here for the auction."

"You're late," one of the guards said.

"Then best not delay me further."

The guards' armor clinked as they stepped aside, opening the door. The security was for show. Guards in pressed white uniforms. They had probably never even drawn their swords outside of training. No one would dare cause trouble in the Temple of the Faith.

Hurrying through the hallway, Briton had to stop against the wall to catch his breath. Maybe he should have taken some blood. What is the abstinence of one person worth when the whole world is guzzling?

The inner sanctuary was a circular room with a high domed ceiling. The pews were filled with Curors there to purchase Descendants for their noble houses. The red-robed uniforms spread around the room like blood stains. It was a suspicious person that sought to be a Curor. Or any role in the Faith.

*I'm lucky I only have to deal with one.*

Briton made his way to the pew where Typher sat with a pair of Carmine guards. On the stage in the center of the room stood a large shirtless man with the faded letter "S" tattooed on the right side of his face.

"How goes the shopping?" Briton asked.

The Curor frowned at the sight of Briton. "Even poorer prospects than usual," Typher said. "From the crop on display,

I'd swear the bloodline had already run dry. Low bloods and fair bloods; not one has tested under thirty seconds."

"Would be a shame for you blood doctors to be out of a job."

Typher shot Briton a nasty look.

The Descendant from House Severen was sold to House Broming for three thousand and two hundred shrines. Guards in blue escorted the man from the stage.

Voices in the crowd fell silent as the next Descendant was led out. It was a young girl, no more than seven years of age. Long blonde hair fell straight down her back and lit up the room. Her face, tattooed with a "T," was the definition of fright.

"Finally a decent female," Typher sneered. Briton bit his tongue.

The handlers held out her hand, and the auctioneer made a show of drawing out the needle. Satisfied he'd gotten the room's attention, he brought it down, pricking the girl's palm.

Typher's lips moved as he counted the seconds in his head. Around them, people leaned forward in their pews, awaiting the results.

"Twenty-two seconds!" the auctioneer called. He held up the girl's hand, confirming the hole had sealed. "A young prize of good blood, able to breed for many years. We will start the bidding at five thousand shrines."

Shouts and hands shot up from the red robes in the crowd. The young girl's fear seemed to grow with the rising price.

"Not going to make a bid?" Briton asked.

Typher snorted. "I didn't think anyone would sell a good blood anymore. House Tannen must be worse off than we are."

After a few minutes of heated bidding, the auctioneer pounded on his table, and the girl's life was bought for ten thousand shrines. She was led off the stage, tears on her cheeks. The handlers turned her over to guards in purple uniforms who brought the girl to their waiting master. Gorgen had come to the auction himself. The fat lord was all smiles as he patted the girl on her straight yellow hair.

Now Briton remembered why he stopped attending Descendant auctions.

Scoffs brought Briton's attention back to the stage where the handlers hauled out the next Descendant. The source of the crowd's disappointment was a ghostly pale boy of around fifteen years of age. He had short brown hair that was matted down with sweat. His face was all eyes. Big bronze eyes that seemed to take in the world for the first time, and find it a horrifying place. The handlers yanked on chains that secured his wrists; a bad sign that was only amplified by the bruises and scars discoloring his body. The boy looked like a confused corpse who had not been informed of his death.

*Why would someone submit a Descendant in his state for auction? Could he even be a Descendant if he can't heal his own body?*

"Alright, alright that's enough," the auctioneer interjected. "We know not all blood flows pure but each Descendant has some worth."

Grumbles rippled around the room. The auctioneer motioned to the handlers who forced the boy's hand up. A quick jab of the needle and the blood test had begun.

"He's not going to pass," Typher snorted.

Briton shifted in his seat. The strength of the Descendants' blood diminished with each generation. If a Descendant's blood grew too weak, they were no longer of worth. A blood test over one minute was a death sentence.

Briton held his breath as the count grew higher.

*Poor boy must have put up a fight. It may well cost him his life.*

"Fifty-two seconds," the auctioneer called, holding up the boy's hand as proof. Low blood, but still a Descendant. "Let us start the bidding at two thousand shrines."

"Ambitious," Typher said. "If ever one was destined for the Temple dungeons, it was that one."

The room waited in silence.

"Come now," the auctioneer's voice cracked a little. "Even the lowliest of Descendants is worth something. It doesn't take good blood to clean stables or work in the fields."

"That one wouldn't last a day in my fields," a man barked.

There were nods of agreement and laughter.

"Bring out the next one," another voice called.

A curse came from behind the stage. Two men in brown travel coats argued with each other. They must be the hunters that brought the boy in. Had they beaten him? Surely they'd know that such a damaged specimen wouldn't sell. And a Descendant who didn't sell at auction...

"Fifteen hundred shrines," the auctioneer called.

"It'd cost more shrines to bathe him than he's worth," someone yelled.

"Come now," the auctioneer pounded the table. "Fifteen hundred shrines. The boy is young with a lifetime of service ahead of him."

Briton studied the boy closer. There was something different about him; something he couldn't put his finger on. He looked wretched but not entirely weak. His eyes were not the usual dead eyes of a broken Descendant, they bounced around the room, searching. For answers maybe? For a way out?

Briton squinted. "Where is his tattoo?"

"Hmm," Typher scanned his auction pamphlet. "There's no previous owner listed. Odd."

Conversations in the crowd grew louder as the Descendant on stage was ignored. In the upper balcony, men in white robes watched the scene. The Fathers of the Faith. The order who ran the Temple—who ran Terene. If the boy wasn't sold to a noble lord, he would stay here. Locked away in the Temple dungeons with outlaws and rebel Descendants. Never seeing the light of day. Drained of blood until there was nothing of him left.

"Buy the boy," Briton said.

"What was that?" Typher turned to Briton as if he had misheard.

"A thousand shrines."

"That one isn't worth the chains on his wrists," Typher said. "I am Carmine's appointed Curor, purchasing of Descendants is my duty."

"Don't speak to me about authority, Curor," Briton said. "As his advisor, I speak for Lord Carmine on all matters. Now, buy the boy."

"It's a waste of coin," Typher whined. "We've only bought one so far and need all the shrines we have left to fetch a decent female."

Briton's hard gaze ended the discussion. Typher sighed and raised his hand an inch above his head.

"Is that a bid?" the auctioneer called in relief.

"A thousand shrines," Typher mumbled.

"One thousand shrines," the auctioneer said, enthusiasm returning to his voice. "Do I hear twelve hundred?"

Boos echoed in the domed sanctuary. The auctioneer waved for the handlers to remove the boy. The young Descendant squirmed as the men seized him, fighting their grasp. The handlers knocked him to the floor and dragged him away by his chains.

"I hope you're happy," Typher snapped. "We'll be lucky if that one produces good enough blood for Carmine's horses."

Briton knew the act had been pointless. Spawned by guilt, not rationality. What was the life of one boy when a whole race suffered? It changed nothing.

The next Descendant brought on the stage was an older woman. She had the faint traces of an "O" tattooed on the right side of her face from House Octavian. The crowd's energy shifted.

"A remnant of a fallen house with plenty of breeding years left," the auctioneer beamed. "Bidding starts at four thousand shrines!"

Briton rose from his seat; he couldn't watch anymore. Bidding on people as if they were livestock. Families ripped apart so a noble lord could turn a profit. And all under the blessing of the mighty Hemo. Briton stopped at the sanctuary door, beneath the balcony where the Fathers of the Faith stood watch. *How could anyone worship a god who would allow this?*

## 2

The boy lay curled up on the cage floor, his chains rattling with every bump in the road. He'd lost track of the days since joining his new captors, drifting in and out of consciousness. Sleep was the only way to escape this horrendous situation. He woke only long enough to nibble on the tasteless meals and search out the window for a familiar sight.

He found none.

The boy wasn't alone in the cage. A man sat across from him, sobbing into his hands. He wore a sleeveless shirt that revealed arms built to work—or fight. A black symbol marked the side of his face; a "T" that stretched from temple to jaw.

The woman beside the boy had a similar mark, though hers was in the shape of a circle. Or had once been—the symbol was more faded. She slept with her head resting against the cage wall, as if being chained and imprisoned was nothing unusual.

No one had spoken since leaving the city and the strange ceremony.

The boy sat up without a groan. The bruising on his body had all but gone, and it no longer hurt to breathe. He ran his fingers along the back of his head and they came away dry.

His memory, however, had not returned. Not everything was

gone. He knew the names of objects—chains, shoes, the gray sky outside the barred window—he just couldn't remember his life before the cage. Before the two men captured and sold him. *Where had it all gone?*

"You have a question?" the woman asked, awake.

The boy flinched. He'd been staring.

"Sorry." He rubbed at his knee; it still hurt from the blow, but he could straighten it now.

"He's still at it, huh?" The woman shook her head, watching the man across from them. The man didn't respond, his head still buried in his hands.

The boy shrugged, keeping his eyes down.

"Where are you from, boy?"

"I don't know," the boy said.

She gave him a long, scrutinizing look. "How come you don't have a house mark?"

"A what?"

She scoffed and tapped the circle on her cheek.

Again, the boy shrugged.

"Well, you'll get your own soon enough," she said.

So they were slaves. Bought and sold, caged and branded. The boy pulled against his chains. Even with his strength returning, he couldn't break free. He was trapped here in this cage, at the mercy of his captors.

*How could this be allowed?*

The cage darkened. Trees filled the windows on both sides.

"Where...where are we going?" the boy asked.

"Castle Carmine."

"What's there?"

The woman leaned back against the cage wall and closed her eyes. "More of the same."

The boy pushed himself up to his feet, pressing his hands against the wall for balance. He shuffled toward the small window and stared out through the bars. He'd partly expected to see a castle, but there were only trees. So many trees. Enough for someone to get lost in.

The boy gripped the bars and pulled, his bare foot pushing against the cage wall. The bars didn't budge.

"Better rest while you can," the woman said. "You'll need all your strength when we get there."

"For what?" the boy asked.

"You don't know anything, do you?"

The boy released the bars and slid down to the floor. It didn't matter. Even if he escaped the cage, he couldn't outrun these men and their horses. And where would he go? If he had a home he had no idea how to find it. Somewhere, people could be searching for him.

The boy closed his eyes and pushed the panic from his mind. He had a home somewhere, even if he couldn't picture it. It would come back to him. Maybe after some more sleep.

Sometime later, the boy was awoken by a voice.

"There it is."

The boy stood up and followed the woman's gaze out the cage window. On the hill ahead, stood a large fortress. The castle was old but massive, like it was built in times of war. Four towers rose up from within a high wall of dark stone wide enough to enclose an entire town. Trees rose far too high, their canopies stretching over the high castle ramparts. The trees were growing from the castle itself, planted on the rooftops. Archers walking the ramparts waved down. Beneath them, a wide, wooden gate opened like the jaws of a tired beast.

This was Castle Carmine.

"It's amazing what they can build off our backs," the woman said.

The caravan wound along the curved road, climbing uphill toward the castle gate. Men in armor stood at the ready as they passed. Over their chest plates hung red shirts with matching insignias—a bird in flight. The guards stared in at the boy in the cage, disgust on their faces.

The wagons passed into the castle's large inner courtyard, and the horses came to a stop. A tapping noise sounded in the cage. Across from the boy, the man's feet were shaking as he leaned toward the cage door. His chained hands balled into fists.

"Don't you do anything stupid," the woman whispered to him.

Sweat dripped from the man's face, running down the T-shaped mark. Metal clinked against the door as chains were pulled free. The tapping stopped. The boy held his breath.

The door cracked open, and the man sprang forward. He slammed into the cage door, sending the guards toppling to the ground. The man hit the ground and charged across the square toward the castle gate.

"Stop him!" a guard yelled from the dirt.

The man ran for his life. *He's not going to make it.* The two guards at the gate collided with him. Armor clanged in the morning air as all three toppled in a tangle of limbs.

"Noooo," the man screamed, clawing toward the open gate, but the guards had his legs. They held him until more guards arrived. Then they were upon him, kicking and stomping. Everyone at once. The air rang with curses and the crunch of boots shattering bone.

The boy turned his head from the horrible sight.

"Enough," a voice called. "He's not going anywhere now."

An old man climbed down from another wagon. He grabbed at his back, which hunched so that he walked at a slightly forward angle. The guards stepped back from the prisoner's limp body. The old man frowned, shaking his bald head. "Close the gate and take him to the Curor's lab."

The guards did as commanded, hauling up the unconscious man and dragging him away. A trail of blood followed.

The boy exhaled a breath he'd been holding. How could this be happening? What crime had he done to deserve this? Maybe he didn't want to remember.

The old man stopped at the open cage door. Clear blue eyes

moved from the woman to the boy. "I hope this silences any thoughts of a similar attempt."

"This way, new blood," a guard said, pulling the boy's chains. The boy hit the wet dirt. His legs wobbled, but he stayed on his feet. The guards led them across the courtyard toward a door at the side of the castle. The woman marched in silence, and the boy followed her cue. *You'll need all your strength when we get there.* What did she mean?

The boy memorized the layout of the courtyard, counting the steps as he walked. The stone wall stretched all about them, high and unscalable. Archers watched from above, arrows nocked. The gate was the only exit.

The man's beating had been awful, but it didn't silence anything. Stepping through the doorway into the castle, the boy knew one thing for sure. He didn't belong here.

JONATHAN CARMINE LEANED back in his chair and sipped from the crystal goblet. He frowned at the taste of plain red wine. He was the lord of a noble house, and even he felt the tightening of blood rations. That told him more about the state of his house than the mess of finance reports spread out on the table before him.

Carmine flipped through the pages. Even without Briton here to translate the figures, he knew the numbers weren't good. The family's wealth was not what it once was. All the northern houses were struggling under the ever-growing tithes to the Faith. How much longer could he keep this castle running?

The Carmine family crest hung above the wall of his study. A red cardinal in flight. A reminder of generations of Carmines that came before him. What would his father do if he were still around?

A knock rattled the study door.

"Come in, come in," Carmine murmured, grateful for the interruption.

"Lord Carmine," Bennet said with a bow, his guard's armor clanging. "The company has returned from the Temple."

"Excellent. Tell Semus I will meet him in the garden."

Carmine swept the papers away. He'd attend to the house budget later. Right now, he needed some good news.

Built on the rooftop of the throne room by Jonathan's grandmother, the castle garden was now the most magnificent garden in all of Terene. His father had always said the view gave him perspective, looking over the land and the people whose fate he decided. When Jonathan Carmine took over, he expanded the rooftop garden, transforming it into a menagerie of rare plants from the farthest reaches of Terene. Sky creepers hung over the castle's ledges, and an assortment of rare trees and plants decorated the garden in even rows. Jonathan took great pride in showing the garden to visiting lords and ladies. His guests never ceased to be awed by plants whose colors were only thought possible in dreams.

Carmine stood in the middle of the garden, marveling at his newest acquisition. It truly was an extraordinary find. A blood rose retrieved from deep within the Endless Desert. Carmine had never seen one before, only heard tales of the carnivorous plant. A flower that can survive where it does not rain.

"Careful, my Lord," Semus said as Carmine leaned over the blood rose. "Even though it has yet to bloom, the flower can still bite."

"The rose's sting," Carmine smiled, moving even closer to the small flower, its slender petals balled into a tiny red fist. "What a miraculous thing. I'd think it was a fable if I weren't seeing it with my own eyes."

"Such it is with most things, my Lord," called a voice from behind Carmine. Carmine turned toward the soft voice of his long-time advisor. Briton sauntered toward him in the same old robe he'd worn since Jonathan was just a boy. *Why does he still wear that ratty thing? We do pay him, don't we?*

"The world is full of magic," Briton continued. "Only when things become familiar do they cease to amaze."

"And you, Briton, with all your knowledge, do you find the world mundane?"

"I practice a healthy curiosity. There is always more to learn. Even subjects we think we know can still yield surprises."

Briton Moonglass, always the teacher. A lesson hiding in every sentence.

"Thank you, Semus," Carmine said, dismissing the gardener. Semus bowed and walked from the garden, leaving them to speak alone.

"And was your trip a success as well?" Carmine asked.

"Yes," Briton said. "Though our harvest was small this season, we fetched a fair price. We spent a good amount on supplies for the stables' construction. The crops—"

"What of the Descendants?" Carmine interrupted.

Briton sighed as if this was a trivial concern. As if blood wasn't the key to house Carmine's survival.

"Three Descendants. Two males and a female." Briton gazed off the balcony to the courtyard below. "We had an incident with one of them upon arrival."

"An incident?"

"He tried to escape. He was injured during the capture. Typher is inspecting his wounds. He might be unable to produce for a few days."

Carmine scoffed. "Animals. Don't they understand what they have here? Maybe the most civil treatment in all of Terene, and still they disobey. What is the point of all this coddling, Briton?"

"Descendants are still people, my Lord. You can't just lock them in dungeons and take their blood."

"The Fathers of the Faith do exactly that. And see how much blood they harvest?"

"We're better than that." Briton's blue eyes seemed to bore into Carmine. He felt the weight of that gaze. "Your father was better than that."

"Yes, well, my father had the resources to pamper Descendants. Their bloodline continues to dwindle. Good blood is more valuable now than ever. We won't be able to pay the Highfather's price and run this land without increasing production."

"Blood isn't the only thing of value, my Lord. Your family did once make a prosperous living off the land and the people under its governance."

"You've made your stance on the Descendants more than clear, and I've abided much of your council. But these are hard times. The Highfather's demands continue to grow and alliances must be formed in the north. We will not be saved by our wheat."

Briton nodded his head. "You're right. We will be saved by the wisdom of our leaders."

"Do you have more to report?" Carmine snapped. He did not appreciate Briton's tone. He was no longer a boy in need of lectures.

"No, my Lord," Briton bowed his head.

Carmine took a deep breath. He had to remember Briton was on his side. The old man had dedicated his life to the Carmines, forsaking a family of his own. When Jonathan's father had died, it cut a hole in his heart. Still, it was annoying to still be talked to like the scared sixteen-year-old boy who inherited the throne.

"We will defer to Typher's advice on upping the blood draws," Carmine said. "Descendants are quite resilient, after all. I'm sure they will be able to produce blood sooner than you think."

He bent down and hovered a finger over the blood rose's petals. It appeared so tiny, so frail. It looked like any other flower. His finger touched the red bud ever so slightly. The petal stirred like a creature awakened, and latched onto Carmine's skin. Carmine ripped his hand away with a grunt. A drop of blood hung on his fingertip. *Extraordinary.*

26

"As you said yourself…" Carmine sucked the blood from his finger. "Even things you think you know can yield surprises."


"HOUSE OCTAVIAN, EH?" A large man with missing front teeth looked the woman over. She stood stoic as the man traced a dirty finger along the circle on her face. "That'll be a bit of a challenge. Good thing I'm an artist with the ink."

The man smiled as he moved to the boy. "No mark? Where did they find you?"

The boy turned away from the stench of sweat and ale. High windows lit the warm room, yet a small fire burned in the furnace.

"More objections?" asked one of the guards standing behind them. The guard had struck the boy earlier for refusing to undress. It was humiliating. He and the woman had been stripped and forced to stand naked while a man in red robes inspected every inch of them. When the boy demanded to know what was going on, he'd been struck again.

The boy faced forward without a word. His tongue pressed against his swollen lip. *I'm going to make him pay for that.*

The toothless man rubbed his hands on the dark stains of his apron. "Let's do the little one first," he said. "It'll be a warm-up in case my hand slips. Secure the Descendant."

Hands seized the boy's shoulders and pressed him down on a table. Straps ran across his feet, his arms, his waist, and his neck. He was trapped. The toothless man pulled something from his bag. It was a strange device with a thin metal blade sticking out of the top. The man gripped the handle and held the tip of the blade end into the fire.

"What are you doing?" The boy tried to squirm, but hands grabbed the side of his head and held him still. "Wait, stop! I demand you stop!"

"Ha," one of the guards laughed. "He demands."

Hands clamped tighter on his head. The room grew blurry.

It felt like the crevice on the back of his head would reopen, and spill his brains all over the table.

"Please...I beg you...don't do this. Don't."

"The trick with your kind is getting the ink deep enough," the toothless man said. "You need to go down to the deepest layers to make the mark stick. Otherwise, your skin will just heal, and we'll have to do this all over again."

He moved away from the fire and the boy heard a bubbling sound as the hot blade dipped into some liquid. He studied the boy's face for a moment, flashing a toothless grin. "Not every day you get to work on a blank canvas."

He stabbed the blade into the skin above the boy's right eye. Fire burned in the boy's face as the needle melted deeper into his skin.

"Aaahhh!" The boy's harrowing scream started as his own and then turned into something unhuman. He kicked and twisted, trying whatever he could to escape the unbearable pain. But he couldn't get away. The burning blade moved inside him, carving a curved stroke around the boy's temple.

"Keep fighting and you'll lose an eye," the man said. "And you ain't getting that back."

Hands tightened on the boy's head. He tried with all his strength to get away. To move even an inch away from the excruciating pain cutting its way down his cheek. He screamed until there was no air left in him.

Even after the needle came away, the boy's face still burned like it had been set ablaze. The guards released their grip, and the boy rolled his head to the side, hiding his face. Weeping.

The tears stung as they fell into the deep grooves of his face.

Blackness swept over him, and he let it in. Anywhere was better than here. The last thing the boy heard was a voice speaking as if from down a deep stone well.

"You now...belong...to House Carmine."

# 3

Geyer shut his eyes and grimaced at the ringing in his head. It had been a late night at the Moon Tavern. He couldn't even remember the walk back to the castle. Somehow his bad leg worked better when he was drunk. Maybe if he drank while on duty, he'd be a better guard, too. He'd have the drunkard's confidence of a much younger Geyer—before the injury. Back when he was actually called upon to use his sword.

Heavy boots clanged up the castle's stone floor. The voices seemed impossibly loud. Geyer winced and leaned back in his chair, resting his head against the locked door.

"Can you believe they have us running errands like…like… errand boys?"

"A waste of talent is what it is."

Geyer didn't bother looking up from his seat in front of the armory. If the room were a real threat to thieves, Nathaniel wouldn't have assigned him to the post. The captain of Carmine's guards kept Geyer around, but that didn't mean he trusted him with real responsibility. And that was perfectly fine with Geyer. He rubbed his left leg—which grew stiffer every year —and hoped the fog in his head would soon clear.

"What do you think you're doing?"

Geyer opened one eye. Two guards stood over him. Geyer didn't recognize them, but that's not to say he hadn't met them. It was hard to remember every little kid playing soldier. He couldn't even blame the alcohol. Geyer closed his eye and leaned against the door. These two would be smart enough to leave him alone. Certainly, they had something more important to do than bother…

"I said, what are you doing?" the smaller of the two guards repeated.

"Guarding the armory," Geyer grumbled.

"Why are you sitting down?"

"Because I have a chair."

Even with closed eyes, Geyer could sense the two men exchange glances. His mind was already sizing them up—their height, the distance apart, where they kept their weapons. It was an old habit from his fighting days. Something, not even his hangover took away.

"You can't sit on guard duty," the smaller man said.

"I don't think whatever's behind this door minds," Geyer said, wincing. *Why is he talking so loud?*

"It's neglect of duty. I'll have you reported."

Geyer opened his eyes again and looked at the red-faced man. His buddy, the big one with the longer reach, looked down in disgust. Maybe Geyer had seen these guards before. Hard to tell because so many came and went over the years. Good men gone. But surely he would have remembered such an annoying voice.

"He's probably drunk, too," the big one said. "I hear he spends all his off-hours at the tavern, drinking himself sick."

"You both seem very interested in things that are none of your business," Geyer said. He had no tolerance for ignorance. There was an obvious difference between drunk and hungover.

"You do a poor job and it reflects badly on us all," said the smaller man, his voice like a whining child. His sword scabbard swung against the back of his leg as he stepped closer to Geyer. Rear holster. It made marching easier, but it slowed your draw. It also made sitting a challenge. "It's disgraceful they even let a cripple work as a castle guard. You belong in the stables, scrubbing horse dung off the floors."

"Hmm," Geyer rubbed his unshaven face. "Do they have chairs in the stables?"

"I don't know why Nathaniel keeps you around. You're a joke. Sitting around on your ass while real guards like us are running these stairs all day."

"But if you weren't racing all around the castle, you wouldn't be able to tattle on others."

"Let's go," the bigger guard said. "He'll drink himself to death one of these nights. The old coward."

"That's right," Geyer said. "I am a coward. We can't all be heroes like your friend here. Saving the realm from all those who would take a nap."

Geyer was ready for the kick. Even if his head wasn't cloudy from a long night of drinking, he would have seen the clumsy blow coming. He caught the smaller guard's boot and twisted it with a quick jerk. The guard hit the stone floor with a clang of armor and curses.

"See? Isn't sitting more comfortable?"

The big guard grabbed Geyer by the collar and pulled him out of his chair. He was stronger than Geyer expected. Faster too. He landed two punches into Geyer's gut before the old guard could even respond. When he did respond, it was swift and caught the big guard by surprise. Geyer vomited all over him.

"Awww," the big man gagged, throwing Geyer to the ground. Geyer tried to brace himself, but his left leg crumbled. *Fates!*

"Filthy clot," the guard said, rubbing last night's drinks from his eyes.

"Hey, no fair," Geyer wheezed. "I paid half a day's wages for that."

The guard drove his boot into Geyer's side. Geyer heaved, gasping for air.

The little guard was on his feet; he drew his sword. Geyer's hand instinctively touched the hilt of his own sword, with its wheel handle, but he was in no position to draw it. Instead, he coughed for more air, attempting to hold in the remaining contents of his stomach.

"Bastard," the little guard yelled. He raised his sword over-head and brought it down with a grunt, smashing Geyer's chair to pieces. "I'm going to see to it Nathaniel hears about this, cripple."

After a few more kicks, the guards stormed off. "Look what he did," the big guy's voice trailed down the hallway. "Eww…it's in my armor."

When he could breathe again, Geyer sat up, leaning his back against the armory door. He felt for broken ribs. Just bruised. He pulled his left leg straight. It throbbed more than usual, but he could still move it. Nothing a few drinks wouldn't put out of his mind.

Even as out of practice as he was, Geyer couldn't believe he let those two clots get the better of him. There was a time he could have dispatched ten of their kind. When he could breeze through a tournament without taking so much as a dent to his armor. But that was another life.

Geyer wiped his blond-gray hair out of his face. He read-justed his belt and flicked the wheel that decorated his sword pommel. It spun slowly, the spokes moving round and round. Geyer sighed. He still had half the day in front of him. Five more hours before his next drink. Beside him, the chair lay in splinters.

*Well, looks like I'll have to spend the rest of my watch lying down.*

Geyer closed his eyes once again.

THE BOY WOKE WITH A WINCE. Pain erupted on his face. He howled into the darkness and scrambled to break free of his bonds. But he was no longer strapped to the table. He yelped, rolling off a mattress and tumbling to the cold stone floor. Voices yelled at him. The boy got to his feet and raised his fists. He would not go willingly again.

But no one seized him. He scanned the room, but he couldn't make out much for it was dark and…

*Something's wrong.* He twisted his head around. His right eye saw only blackness. *They…they blinded me.*

The boy dropped to his knees and sobbed. Each whimper inflamed his mutilated face.

"Shut up," a voice called. "That's enough."

The boy couldn't fight it. He was helpless and alone. He didn't know how he'd come to be imprisoned and tortured, but he knew there was no escape from this nightmare.

A hand touched his shoulder. It was not the grip of a guard, but small and gentle.

"It's okay," a voice whispered. "The first night is the hardest. You need to sleep, get your strength back."

"Why are they doing this to me?" the boy whimpered.

He looked at the shape kneeling beside him. It was a heavy-set boy, little older than him. Maybe seventeen years old.

"They're doing this to all of us," he said.

The boy let himself be pulled off the ground and set down in a small cot with hardly any cushion. He fell asleep at once.

A hand shook him awake. "You gotta eat something."

The boy opened his left eye. Sunlight streamed in through high horizontal windows, too narrow to fit through. How long had he been asleep?

The room was large and filled with empty cots packed close

together. A pudgy boy sat on the next cot, holding out a tray of food. The right side of his face was marked with a "C" tattoo. "You have work to do today, and then the Curor tonight. You need your strength."

"My…my face…" the boy said. He touched bandages that covered his eye and the surrounding area.

The pudgy boy touched his own tattooed face. "Mine healed in a week. Be thankful you don't have purer blood. Merrick has had to be marked three times now because his tattoo fades."

The pudgy boy shuddered, and then catching himself, smiled quickly. "I'm Chancey, by the way. I work in the kitchen. Obviously." He grinned, holding up the tray of food.

"I…" the boy began, but his name still escaped him. He had one, he was certain, but he still could not bring it to mind. It was as if the details of his life had been stripped away.

The boy sat up, and the room spun. He closed his eye until he gained control. Rows of cots lined the large room. Sixteen in all. The sleeping bodies that had yelled at him last night were gone. Except for Chancey, and another shape sleeping in the corner of the room.

The boy climbed to his feet.

"You really should eat something," Chancey said. "It'll help you heal. Mable says I'm supposed to bring you back to the kitchen with me."

The boy headed to an open doorway at the back of the room. The stench hit him first. The washroom consisted of a bench with three holes in the floor. Flies buzzed around the holes, zigzagging away as if the scent was too foul even for them. There was no mirror, only the dark stone wall that filled the rest of the room.

The boy came back toward Chancey.

"You don't look so good. You really should eat-"

"My face," the boy said. He reached up and peeled away the corner of tape holding the bandage. Scared as he was, he had to know what they'd done to him.

34

He blinked back the light. Then he opened his right eye fully. *I can see!*

"Hemo!" Chancey gasped, staring at the boy's uncovered face.

"What is it?"

"It's already healed."

The boy frowned. There was no pain in the movement. He ran his fingers along the C-shaped scar on his face. The skin was still sensitive, but yesterday's pain had subsided into an awful memory.

"Don't let them see it," a soft voice carried through the room. The older woman he had traveled to Castle Carmine with lay in the corner cot. Bandages wrapped around her own face. The boy passed Chancey and crossed the room to her side.

"Put your bandage back on," she said, leaning his way. Her voice was weak but direct. "Don't let them know what you are."

"What am I?" the boy whispered.

"More than they think," she said. "They'll find out eventually, but in the meantime, it'll go better for you if they think you're a lower blood."

"Lower blood? I don't understand."

She gazed at him with her one, uncovered eye. "Your bruises. A day ago it looked like you had been beaten to death."

The boy lifted his shirt. His skin had returned to a pale white, the bruising gone.

"Never let them know what you can do," the woman said. She winced as she lay back and closed her eye.

The boy sighed. Low blood, Descendants, house brands… nothing made sense. Why couldn't he remember?

The boy re-applied the bandages to his face before walking back to his cot. He picked up the tray the kitchen boy had brought. Porridge and an apple. It wasn't much, but at this moment, the boy was willing to eat anything. He bit down on the overripe fruit and hunger flooded through him like a burst dam. He cleaned the apple to its core and then dug his fingers into the porridge.

The boy finished his meal and licked his fingers, catching every last morsel. Chancey was right, the boy felt better with food in his belly. Stronger.

"I won't tell anyone," Chancey said. "I wouldn't do that."

The pudgy boy had been by his side during the night. He was the closest thing to a friend he had in the world.

Chancey took the empty tray. "We need to go. You've been assigned kitchen duty with me. It's not a bad job really. It's better than working in the fields, and sometimes there are leftover scraps." Chancey blushed and pulled his shirt down over his belly.

"Thank you for the food, Chancey."

The kitchen boy smiled. "There's more of that. I deliver food all over the castle, to Lord Carmine even. Sometimes people don't even touch it. And Mable doesn't mind if I polish off the plates. It saves the dishwashers time."

The room had stopped spinning and the boy felt almost whole. He didn't know what awaited him, but he wasn't going to get any answers staying in this room. He pulled himself to his feet.

"Let's go."

Chancey beamed. He stood and led the boy through a large metal door. The boy studied the lock bar on the outside. With that shut in place, there would be no escaping the sleeping barracks.

They walked down the stone corridor, and the boy felt his strength returning. It was as if the food had lit a fire in his belly that spread through his body, bringing his muscles to life.

High horizontal windows brought dim light into the hallway. But again, the windows were too narrow to fit through. At the end of the hall, they passed a door with a faded heart symbol painted in the color of dried blood.

Turning the corner, the hallway grew brighter. Noises

carried; the shuffling of feet and banging. A woman's voice barked orders.

"You ever worked in a kitchen before?" Chancey asked.

"No. I don't think so."

"Nothing to it. Just keep your head down, and don't let her catch you taking breaks."

They stepped into a large kitchen where people scurried this way and that, carrying dishes and plates of food. Unlike Chancey and the boy, most of these workers did not have "C" tattooed on their faces. In the center of the chaos, a dark skin woman towered over the others. Her black hair was tied up in a cream-colored cloth, and her apron stopped short revealing long brown pants, not a dress like the other women in the kitchen.

"Chancey!" the woman yelled at the sight of them. "In Hemo's name, what took you so long?"

"I'm sorry Miss Mable," he said, hurrying to her side. "I came as soon as I could."

"Next time I'll send a turtle. This is the new Descendant boy?"

"Yes, ma'am."

"Well, fetch him a broom." Chancey scampered off to the kitchen closet. "And don't get lost on the way!"

She looked down at the boy. "Do you come with a name?"

The boy lowered his head. A pile of potatoes rested on the counter beside Mable. The boy's stomach groaned for more.

"Luckily, you don't need a big vocabulary to sweep," she said.

A moment later, the boy had a broom and was sweeping the kitchen floor, dodging cooks and servants. The boy didn't fight the assignment. Sweeping the floors beat being tortured and stuck in a cell.

"What, you never held a broom before?" Mable yelled across the kitchen. The boy looked down at the broom in his hands. He didn't know the answer.

The tall woman dropped her knife among the potatoes and stalked over to the boy.

"You're just spreading it around." She snatched the broom from the boy's hands. "You gotta sweep it all into a single pile. Like this."

She bent low and swung the broom in crisp strokes, collecting a pile of dirt and kitchen scraps. "See?"

She threw the broom back to the boy. Without thinking, he lunged to the side and caught it in one hand. The wood handle felt at home in his hand. Strong. It could do some damage.

"Well go on," she barked.

The boy grabbed the dustpan and began sweeping up the collected scraps and dumping them in the trash bin. Then he continued on, mimicking the woman's quick strokes. Kitchen work was new to the boy, but he caught on quick. Whatever job Mable gave him only had to be demonstrated once. Though work was made difficult by the use of only one eye, the boy got the hang of it. As he cleaned, he studied the other workers, and what their jobs entailed—from the dishwashers to Mable herself. The good news about not remembering your past is there is plenty of space for new information.

The work itself was mindless and gave the boy time to piece together the puzzle of this new world. He had been sold into labor, that much was clear, but what were *Descendants*? What set them apart? Why were he and Chancey tattooed while the other servants were not? And, most importantly, how was he going to get out of here?

As he worked through the day, the boy was amazed at how much work went into feeding a castle. Servants raced in and out the kitchen doors, gathering food or cleaning pots and pans, which were then turned around and re-used. Everyone moved with expert efficiency as if they had performed their routines for years. And then there was the food; roast lamb and buttered potatoes, bread fresh from the oven. The lords and ladies of the house were not living on rotten apples and porridge. The hole in the boy's stomach grew with each whiff of the kitchen's aroma.

A bell chimed somewhere outside, and its sound reverberated through the kitchen. A Descendant woman beside the boy shut the pantry door and headed out of the kitchen. But the rest of the kitchen servants continued their work.

"Clean your station before you go," Mable yelled to him. "You don't leave a mess in my kitchen."

The boy winced as he got off his sore knees. He rang the wet towel in the bucket and carried it to the closet. He was about to follow the Descendant woman out of the kitchen when that commanding voice stopped him.

"Boy," Mable called.

The boy crossed the kitchen to the counter where Mable chopped carrots in quick succession. She waved the boy closer. The boy pressed down on his bandage, making sure it was secure. Then he crept around the counter, his eye on the knife in her hand.

"Here," she slid him three pieces of carrot across the counter. "Best have some food in your belly beforehand."

The woman's face softened. Was there pity in her eyes?

The kitchen door burst open, and Chancey rushed in panting for air.

"Sorry…Miss Mable," he said, setting a tray of dishes in the sink. "Those…blasted stairs."

"Chancey, you snail," she snapped, back to her usual tone. "You better be here extra early tomorrow. Now take your friend here and hurry along. You won't find the Curor as forgiving of tardiness."

Chancey waved to the boy as he rushed from the room. "Come on, we're going to be late."

The boy met Mable's eyes. What was he to make of these people? Some seemed nice, others were downright evil. Could he trust any of them?

The boy pocketed the carrot pieces and hurried down the corridor after Chancey. So far, the boy had only seen a small portion of the castle between the sleeping barracks and the kitchen. Chancey, on the other hand, seemed free to move about where he pleased, delivering food all over the castle. There must be some more defenses to stop someone from escaping, the boy thought. Otherwise, why else are they still here, working as prisoners?

They turned a corner to find a short line of people waiting in the hall. The line formed before the door with the painted heart symbol. Each person had a "C" tattoo on their face. *Descendants.*

The boy moved closer to peer inside the door.

"Get back in line," a guard at the door snapped. The boy slipped back against the wall beside Chancey.

"What are we doing here?" the boy asked.

"Were you raised in the woods or something?" Chancey asked, shaking his head at the boy. "This is the Curor's lab."

A sickly man trudged out the door, barely able to stand. The guard shoved him out of the way, and the next person entered the room.

"What's wrong with him?" the boy asked.

Chancey leaned in closer so the others in line couldn't hear. "You act like you've never worked for the Raw Bloods before?"

"I don't..." the boy began and then thought about it. His memory wasn't completely gone. He knew what most of the items in the kitchen were called and what the carrots in his pocket would taste like, but there was so much that was unfamiliar. Especially his role as a Descendant.

"It's okay." Chancey shrugged. "There's a lot I wish I could forget."

"Where are you from?" the boy asked.

"Here. Castle Carmine. Most of us are. It's only a few that are traded here from other houses. Mostly runaways."

"Runaways?"

"Escaped Descendants. Those that survive recapture, anyway."

The door opened and another Descendant staggered out. The woman in front of the boy walked inside, leaving only the boy and Chancey.

The boy's legs grew heavier as he stepped closer to the door. No sounds came from within the open door, just a chill. The guard at the door sneered at the boy. A birthmark marked his forehead with a splash of red. This hadn't been one of the guards who stripped him and scarred his face. But he didn't look like he'd object to the behavior.

The boy turned back to Chancey. More questions raced through his mind. "You say Descendants, but descendants of who?"

"You really don't know?" Chancey lowered his voice so the Guard wouldn't hear. "Those of us born with special blood."

"Special blood?"

"Yeah, like how your face healed from the branding in less than a day. Raw Bloods can't do that. They need us."

"And Raw Bloods are…"

"Everyone else. Miss Mable, the guards, Lord Carmine—the Highfather himself."

Special blood, Raw Blood. The boy scratched his head, taking it all in. It didn't make sense. How were the ones *without* special blood in charge?

Before he could ask more, the woman stepped out of the door; her face was pale and her eyelids hung heavy as if she were walking in her sleep.

The guard looked down at the boy. "Well?"

Chancey nudged the boy forward, but the boy stopped in the doorway. His gut told him to run. The memory of yesterday's branding flashed through his mind, and he froze in fright.

"Little clot," the guard grabbed the boy by the hair and yanked him inside and down the stairs. The boy shivered, surprised by the sudden drop in temperature. It was like he'd suddenly been transported into a snowy cave, each step the air grew colder and colder. He reached the bottom of the stairs and stepped into a square windowless room. Lamps hung from the ceiling, giving the room plenty of light.

Shelves of bottles, both empty and full, adorned every wall.

A large wooden chair was in the center of the room, its base nailed into the floorboards. Beside the chair was a table covered with strange tools and instruments. A man in red robes stood hunched over the table, sealing a bottle of red wine. He examined the red liquid and put it on the wall with the others.

"Come on, I haven't got all night," the red-robed man said, his breath streamed out like a cloud. He swept around, his lip curled into a snarl. "Oh, great, it's Briton's boy. Get in the chair."

The guard shoved the boy forward. The boy did as he was told, climbing into the solid wooden chair. The guard held the boy's wrists and snapped down the metal cuffs on the armrests. "This one's a slow learner."

The red-robed man snorted, looking down his hooked nose with beady black eyes. "Let's get this over with."

He grabbed a small metal blade from the table.

"Wait," the boy stammered. "What are you doing?"

His uncovered eye moved from the blade to the instruments on the table. A yellow tube stained with a dark substance, a tray of small knives and needles.

"Let me explain how we do things here," the red-robed man said. "You hold perfectly still, and I don't spill any more of your dirty blood than I have to. Got it?"

The boy squirmed, but the bands held his arms tight. *No, not again. I won't let them cut me anymore.*

"Get his legs."

The boy kicked out, driving his feet into the guard's armored chest. "Stop! Let go of me this instant!"

The guard slammed his fist into the boy's stomach. The air flew from the boy's lungs, and he folded forward. Hands seized his feet. Metal bands clicked around his ankles.

"You're going to regret that," the guard said, breathing hard.

"Not yet," the red-robed man snapped. "At least let me get the brat's blood first." The man's second hand seized the long tube from the table and fed one end into an empty glass bottle. His head grew dizzy, and he felt a sickness well up in his stomach. The red bottles of liquid that lined the shelves around the room. *That's not wine.*

This was what they did to Descendants. They stole their blood.

"Alright," the red-robed man said. He held up the tube and a small blade. "Let's find a warm vein."

# 4

―――――――

―――――――

*"We believed it was our right, not by deed or naming, but by the very blood in our veins."*

―――――――

A eilus Haemon, Highfather of Terene, and the most powerful man in the world, winced over his chamberpot. Red-tinted urine dribbled out in painful bursts. Vorrel warned him about consuming too much blood. But let that Curor get to Haemon's age and see how long he lasted without a drink.

Haemon set the chamberpot down and pulled himself out of bed. His old bones cracked with every movement as he reached for his bedpost. It was in the mornings that he felt his age the most, when he'd gone hours without a sip of blood. His feet strained under the weight of even his gaunt frame. After catching his breath, the Highfather let go of the bedpost. He gritted what teeth remained and straightened his knees as best he could. This was his test. Was he still strong enough to get to his feet on his own?

Today he was. *Praise Hemo.*

Haemon snatched a vile of blood from the cold-cabinet and

drank, his hand shaking. Drops spilled down his pointed chin. The effects were immediate. A flood of energy washed through his body. His muscles awakened, bones hardened. He stood straighter and more alert. Aches and pains didn't disappear completely, but were reduced to that of a man decades younger.

Time took its toll on everything, eventually. But by the gifts of Hemo, Aeilus Haemon was allowed to continue his work. His leadership was needed. What clearer sign could there be?

He rang the bell on his table, and a servant came to help him dress. Haemon dawned the ceremonial white robes with red stitching that marked a Father of the Faith. The servant then opened the chest and placed the red miter, crown of the Highfather, on Haemon's head. For most of his early life, Haemon had dreamed about being Highfather of the Faith. Would he still have longed for the position if he knew all that it entailed: the power struggles with the noble houses, the threat of Descendant rebels, even the discord within his own council?

*Yes!*

No one else could be relied upon to do Hemo's will. No one else had the vision. And, after all these years, Haemon was so close to solving mankind's problems and bringing peace to Terene. Hemo would grant him the strength to see this through.

Haemon checked that everything was in place and then strode from the room. His legs were stronger with the Descendant's blood coursing through him, but he didn't push it. He walked through the hallway at a slow pace, taking in the majesty of the Temple.

On the walls hung tapestries depicting the history of the Faith, the Blood War, General Drusas leading the assault on the Royals, the Faith's rise to power, and the eventual salvation of Terene. Haemon was proud of his role in that history; the longest Highfather reign ever. And, once his work was finished, he'd be remembered alongside Drusas as mankind's greatest champions.

Reliance on the Descendants will come to an end. Terene will finally know peace.

A guard pushed open the doors and the Highfather entered the inner sanctuary. The great round room was in the center of the Temple and lit by the dome's glass ceiling. Centuries-old wooden pews circled around the sanctuary's center where the council table now stood. The Fathers rose upon his arrival. Haemon took his time moving to his seat at the head of the council table. In the art of high politics, battles were won with etiquette and gestures. Everything played a role, and no one knew the game better or had played longer than Aeilus Haemon.

Reaching his chair, Haemon waved a hand. "Be seated."

Around the table sat the seven Fathers of the Faith. From all over Terene, these men and women rose through the ranks to reach the Temple's high council. Now, they determined the future of the world.

"Highfather," Father Turney began. "I have an important matter to bring before the—"

Haemon raised a hand, cutting him off.

"We shall begin with prayer, Father Turney," Haemon said. The room fell silent, heads bowed in individual prayer. The young Father shifted in his seat but obeyed. Haemon prayed to Hemo for the prosperity of the realm and wisdom for the council. The prayer came with the ease of decades of recitation, but Haemon still believed every word. The heart is what matters to Hemo.

With the prayer and a few minutes of silent reflection over, Haemon opened the floor to Father Turney. "Edmund, you have something you would like to address?"

"Yes, Father," Edmund said flatly. "I wanted to discuss the use of the Temple's Curors for needs outside the Faith."

Haemon held a stony expression. One bonus of old age; emotions took too much effort. "What are you referring to, specifically?"

The young father cleared his throat and threw back his black hair with a twist of his head. Haemon reflected on his own hair, lost long ago. Blood didn't heal everything.

"It has come to my understanding that a certain sect of Curors have been working in secret. With blood alchemy."

"That's preposterous," Father Kent snapped. "Everyone knows the manipulation of blood is impossible. Transforming normal blood cannot be done."

"Not to mention it is heresy to even attempt transubstantiation," Father Claudia said. She raised a sharp eyebrow to Father Turney. "These are serious claims, Father Turney. I hope you bring us more than rumors."

Descendant blood was a sacred gift from Hemo. Tampering with it was punishable by death.

"Edmund?" Haemon cocked his head, feeling the weight of the Highfather's miter. "You have evidence of blood alchemy performed by the Temple's own Curors?"

"I bring you information," Father Turney said, some of the excitement slipping from his voice. "A room was found within the inner temple. Judging by the equipment found there, it appears to have been used for blood experiments and other pagan rituals. I was not able to ascertain the identities of the Curors responsible, or if they have been tasked to commit such heresy by a higher authority. But I did not want to hide such evidence from the council."

The room fell silent. The faces around the table held the nervous expressions that came whenever an accusation arose. The most powerful people in the world and they were still scared of one another's shadows.

"You did right, Edmund," Haemon said. "These matters must be looked into. The Temple's Curors have much work to do in preserving the health of the realm. Their attention must not be diverted, whether by their own greed or...under the orders of outside elements."

Haemon let this sentence out like a fisherman's bait before a pool of trout.

"What outside elements?" Father Shanon asked.

The Highfather shook his head, sighing. "Noble lords are always quibbling to grow their own station in Terene. It is not hard to imagine they would even go against the Faith's doctrine if it were of benefit to them."

The Fathers nodded in agreement, happy the attention was drawn outside the council room.

"But until we know more, Fathers, we can only practice vigilance." The Highfather gestured a wrinkled hand toward the young Father. "I'll ask you to look into this further, Edmund. Bring what findings you can to me, personally."

"Certainly, Father," Edmund smiled.

With Father Turney's concerns addressed, the council turned matters to the most pressing news of the day. Yesterday's attack on the Curor's shop.

"These Descendant rebels are getting bolder," Father Jessen said. "The Curor shop they raided was at the edge of the city!"

"I heard they didn't even take the blood," Father Shanon said. "They just smashed the shop. A wealth of blood just poured into the street."

"Heresy on top of theft," Father Claudia said, shaking her head.

"Highfather Haemon," Father Thomas said. "Is it true that this rebel leader is uniting the Descendants and orchestrating the attacks?"

Haemon steepled his fingers and sighed. "The Temple Guard has yet to catch the Descendants responsible, but it is only a matter of time." Haemon coughed into his hand. His chest burned from the effort. His strength was already slipping. He needed blood.

Father Kent snorted. "We've all seen the Descendants and what they are capable of. For one of them to be able to write their own name is a stretch…that this—Spade—is some military genius is preposterous."

The Fathers nodded in agreement. Such a fearful group.

Taking comfort in fooling themselves. It was easy to turn a blind eye when you slept safely within the Temple walls. For them, the Descendant rebels were somebody else's problem. *Hemo give me strength. What will happen to Terene when I am—*

"Say what you will," Father Turney broke in. "But Spade and his band of rebels have caused acts of destruction and terror for over a year now, and we've not had so much as a clear report on his appearance, let alone come close to capturing him. Not to mention the strain it puts on our nobles who own Descendants. Remember House Octavian."

The Fathers shivered at the mention of House Octavian. A noble house that had fallen at the hands of its own Descendants. A cautionary tale, warning what happens when you give those beasts too much freedom. *They'll seek to kill Raw Bloods, just like their ancestors.*

"Fathers, calm yourselves," Haemon said. "We have the full strength of the Temple army at our command. We will take care of this rebel problem, I assure you. You must have faith."

There was nodding from across the room, except for Edmund, who remained still, his eyes studying the others. *What game are you playing, Edmund?*

"Now, if there is nothing else, we all have our work before us. Go in Faith."

"Go in Faith," the others repeated. They stood as Haemon pulled himself to his feet, masking the pain that flared through his body. *Don't let them see how much it hurts.*

They needed his strength as much as he did. They had grown needy, feeding on his leadership like piglets on a sow's teat. He needed to show them the fruits of their faith.

Outside the council chambers, a servant waited with a glass of blood wine. Haemon drank, feeling the restorative properties fill his body. Vorrel be cursed; he needed the blood.

At least, for now.

He set the empty glass back on the servant's tray. "Find Bale," Haemon said. The servant boy nearly dropped the tray at the mention of the Blood Knight's name. "Tell him I have a mission for him."

WHEN THE MORNING bell chimed through Castle Carmine, the boy found it difficult to rise. He had not slept well after the previous night's horrors. His blood had been taken from him— an entire bottle drained from his arm. That this violation was common practice at the castle...it was unthinkable.

All around him, Descendants rose from their beds to begin the day's work. The boy closed his uncovered eye to the spinning room.

"Come on." A hand patted him over the blanket. "We have to go."

"I can't move," the boy said, biting down and squinting tight. Maybe if he willed it enough, he'd wake from this nightmare.

"You must," Chancey said. The kitchen boy shook him. "If you don't report to work, they send the guards for you. You don't want that, trust me."

"I feel so weak."

"Once you eat something you'll feel better."

The boy took a deep breath and opened his eyes. With Chancey's help, he was able to sit up in bed. His hand reached down to the carrots in his pocket. After leaving the Curor's lab last night, he hadn't had the stomach to eat anything. He had barely made it to his cot before passing out. The boy chewed, fighting back nausea.

"Keep it down," Chancey said. "You must regain your strength."

The room cleared. Descendants headed out to work in the fields or the stables or other parts of the castle. These were the low bloods. Tasked with slave labor as well as blood draws. Apparently, those with purer blood were somewhere else in the castle, kept under strict guard. Their blood taken twice a day.

The boy didn't know what was worse—being forced to work or being trapped in a room.

The image of the red-robed man with the hooked nose came to the boy, and his blood stirred to life. "That Curor is evil."

"It comes with the job," Chancey said. "I've met hundreds of Raw Bloods in my time. Some are good, some are bad. But I've never heard of a good Curor."

"Why don't people escape?" the boy whispered, slipping on the worn shoes—his toes poked out of the right one—but it was better than walking the stone floor barefoot. "There are so many of you."

Chancey raised an eyebrow. "Where would we go?"

"Move it you two," a guard called from the doorway. "Or you'll get a booting you won't forget."

Chancey helped the boy up, and the two of them moved out of the barracks under the guard's watchful eye.

"I thought you were a fast healer," Chancey whispered as they moved down the hall.

"Apparently not." The boy's head was still cloudy, but with every step down the hallway, he felt his balance return. Chancey had endured a blood draw every night for his entire life. The boy couldn't imagine. He didn't have that kind of strength.

When they entered the kitchen, the staff was in full swing. Chancey left the boy's side and hurried to the sink just as Mable's voice rang out.

"You're late...boy!" the tall woman's voice rattled the kitchen plates, or at least the nervous hands holding them. "I don't even know what name to curse! Get the broom and do not stop sweeping until the floor is clean enough to see your one-eyed face!"

The boy hurried past her, fear doing its part to restore his movements. He swept the kitchen floor. Then he swept the hallway. Then he swept the kitchen floor once more. He worked until his hands were too sore to grip the broomstick.

And so went the boy's day, sweeping up after each new mess,

pausing only to nibble on the food provided and to relieve himself back in the barracks latrine. The day was long and silent as no one spoke to him besides Mable's occasional yelling, and that was mostly out of habit since the floors were spotless. The boy chased dirt down the hallway, switching his grip to avoid the growing blisters. Staring at the stone floor for so long, he fell into a sort of trance.

His mind roamed elsewhere. Outside the castle walls to the image of trees. A forest of great pines. The boy did not press, he let the vision come, afraid he'd scare it off. Something about this picture was...strange. He saw the trees from high above—as if he were a bird looking down on the forest.

"Boy!"

The forest dissolved at the sound of Mable's voice carrying through the hallway, somehow losing none of its power. The boy scampered back to the kitchen, trying to hold onto the vision of the treetops.

Mable was leaning over a tray of food, arranging roasted potatoes on a fine plate. "That fool boy Chancey isn't back yet, and I have more meals to deliver," she said, shaking her head. "How that boy runs errands all day and returns even fatter than before is a mystery."

She looked up at the boy, frowning at his general appearance. "You think you can deliver food without messing that up?"

"Yes, ma'am," the boy said, eager to do anything that didn't require holding a broom handle.

"Take this to the library then. And hurry back!"

The boy nodded, taking the tray and hurrying out of the kitchen before she could change her mind. The smell of the cooked meat wafted up into his nose, bringing his hunger to life. What he wouldn't give for a bite.

The boy reached the end of the hallway before he realized he had no idea where the library was. He turned to go back to the kitchen, but he imagined the scolding he would receive, or worse —Mable would hand the task to someone else. This was the boy's chance to explore the castle. He had to be trusted outside the kitchen if he were to have any hope of escape.

So, the boy continued up a flight of spiraling stairs in search of the library. The stairway led to a second-floor hallway much wider than the bottom floor. Instead of blank walls, paintings hung every few feet. One painting depicted the castle and rolling green fields stretching from its walls. Another, an old man with a pointed beard. Another, a red bird shooting like a flame across a blue sky.

The boy slowed to a stop in the middle of the hallway. There was a chance he'd find the library on this floor. Then the search would be over. The boy turned and took the stairs higher.

Coming to the third floor, the boy's stomach growled, begging for the meat just below his nose. This was its own form of torture. *Would whoever he was delivering this to miss a single bite?*

Something caught the boy's foot. He tripped, barely catching the plate of food before it fell to the ground.

"Watch where you're going!" a man barked. The boy looked down to see a castle guard on the floor, leaning against a door. He grabbed his leg, though the boy hadn't hit him that hard.

"I'm sorry," the boy said. "I…I didn't see you."

"Well maybe you shouldn't walk around with your eye covered," the man was old for a guard and didn't wear a helmet; his long, uncombed hair and graying beard grew wild and untamed. *Why was he sleeping in the hallway?*

"I…I was looking for the library," the boy said.

"Well, you found my foot."

"Do you know where I can find it? The library."

"Try the room with all the books." The man leaned back and closed his eyes.

The castle was enormous, and the boy had only covered a small portion. The food would be cold by the time he got it to whoever it was for.

"Please, what direction—"

"Kid," the guard's eyes shot open. "I'm guarding a highly important area of the castle, and you are distracting me from doing my job. Now, unless you want to be held responsible for the theft of the Lord's trophy room, you better leave me be."

The guard leaned back against the door and yawned.

The boy walked back toward the stairs. He'd just have to return to the kitchen and ask Mable. But, he'd already been gone so long. She'd never send him out again. This could be his only chance to see the castle. The boy took a deep breath and hurried up the stairs to the top floor.

The stairs ended in an arch that led to the roof outside. The boy stopped, taking in a breath of the open air. Plant life surrounded him. It was as if he had stepped from the castle into the forest of his imagination. Ivy hung from the stone arch. Trees and plants of every color were arranged in wooden boxes. Forgetting his task, lost in the strange beauty of the plants, the boy moved farther through the green maze.

He'd never seen anything like it. Such a variety of plants in one location. The afternoon sun poured orange light through the clouds, baking the plants in a warm glow. Walking farther, the boy came upon a tall glass shed. Inside the glass shed stood a large wooden box with a single red flower. *What's so special about you?* The boy set the tray of food down on the edge of a nearby box and opened the door to the glass shed. He stepped inside to a wave of heat. The temperature was much warmer inside the shed.

There was nothing on the surface remarkable about the red flower. The boy couldn't see why it warranted such attention with the big glass shed all to itself. He bent over the crate and leaned down to smell the flower. The petals stirred. It smelled of—

A hand grabbed the boy's shoulder and yanked him back. He gave a startled leap and almost went through the glass wall.

"Careful now!" shouted a man in dirty work clothes. "You want to lose what's left of your face?"

Self-consciously the boy pushed the bandage back into place. "I'm sorry, I didn't mean to…I was just…"

"Snooping around the Lord's garden? You're lucky it was me that found you and not Lord Carmine. If the Blood Flower didn't kill you, he certainly would have."

"Blood Flower?" the boy asked, looking at the small plant. "How can a flower harm someone?"

The man gave the boy a hard look. "What's your name, son?"

The boy's eyes fell to the ground. This was it. He'd be locked away forever, his blood taken and bottled every night.

"I'm Semus," the man said. "What were you doing here in the garden—besides attempting suicide?"

"I'm looking for the library. I'm supposed to deliver food." The boy pointed to the tray as proof.

"The library." Semus sighed. "I know who that's meant for then. Come on, I'll show you where to find it." He stopped and gave the boy a serious look. "This is the last time you set foot in the garden."

The boy nodded.

"Then I guess no one needs to hear about it." Semus walked back toward the arch doorway. The boy stole one final glance at the red Blood Flower and then hurried after Semus. Caught in the Lord's garden, how had he been so careless?

Semus pointed him to the second floor, and the boy walked the rest of the way, following the gardener's directions. The man had seemed nice for a "Raw Blood" as Chancey called them. He had likely saved the boy another beating from the guards. And, although the boy had promised never to visit the garden again, it was not a promise he was likely to keep.

The library entrance was even bigger than Semus described. The boy knocked on the two enormous wooden doors, balancing the tray of food with his other hand. There was no response. Had the person already left? The boy tapped louder until a muffled voice called from inside.

"Open it already, Chancey. I'm starving."

The boy pressed his bandages firmly onto his face and then shouldered his way into the room.

The library was bigger than the boy could have imagined. The roof rose above the highest floor to make room for the high bookshelves that covered each wall. Dust danced in the streams of light from the glass ceiling and the high arched windows. The room was silent and stale as a crypt. Long tables with benches and chairs filled the center of the room, but only one chair was occupied. An old man in faded blue robes. He turned around, and the boy recognized the inspecting blue eyes.

"You're not Chancey," the man said.

"No, sir," the boy said. He stepped forward, his feet echoing in the empty room. He set the tray on an open part of the table. They both looked down at the meal which was now quite cold. "I got a little lost."

"More than a little, I see," the man said with a frown.

The boy prepared for a lashing, but instead, the man turned back to his work. Books lay open on the table along with scattered pages of notes. Closest to the old man was a tiny book with writing so small, the boy couldn't even make it out.

"What are you reading?" the boy asked.

"History," the old man sighed, rubbing his eyes. "Yours, actually."

*Mine?* The boy leaned over the small book.

"Careful," the man said. "It's rather old and delicate. Plus it cost me a great deal. Something I'm beginning to think was a mistake."

From the way he ordered the guards around, the boy knew this man held some important role in the castle. It was not his place to speak to such a man. But he had to know.

"What do you mean it's about my history?" the boy asked.

"It's an account of the Royal bloodline. From which your kind all descended." The old man scribbled notes on a parchment as he spoke. "I'm trying to trace the bloodline back to its source. To where the Royals got their blood in the first place."

"And?" the boy asked, once more leaning over the book.

"*And*, this book is old, but it says nothing about the source of the Royals' power." The old man closed the book and rubbed his eyes. "It doesn't mean the answer is not out there. It just means I've wasted a lot of shrines."

The boy was squinted with his uncovered eye. The script was tiny. Faded.

"There are no pictures, I'm afraid," the old man said, poking his fork into the meat. "If you want to see some drawings, Chancey enjoys the early Cossarts…"

"Our walls will not hold…" The boy stopped, catching himself.

"What was that?" the old man asked, following the boy's gaze to the open section of the book.

The boy stepped back. The Descendant woman's words rang in his head. *Don't let them know what you can do.*

"Wait," the old man said, pointing to the book. "You can read this?"

"I…I have to go," the boy stammered. He turned and hurried to the library's door.

"Wait. What's your name?"

But the boy was already out the door, running down the hallway for the stairs.

## 5

---

Bale rode Smoke up the hill. The great gray horse tore through the night. The chilly air was lost on Bale, for his chest burned beneath his black armor. Over the years, the disease had crept from his heart over his left shoulder in poison veins. The wound that should have killed him long ago finally was. Unless the Highfather made good on his promise.

Up ahead, the Temple guards waited at the edge of the forest, their white shirts glistening in the moonlight. Bale scoffed. Whatever fool designed the uniforms had obviously never done battle at night. Bale had his armor painted black the moment he'd been turned into a Temple guard. It was allowed because Bale got things done. It was allowed because there was no one to stop him.

*Blood Knight.* That was the name people whispered as he passed. It started as an insult, criticism of the ex-assassin's reputation for violence. Bale didn't mind. After years serving as personal-sword to the Highfather, he had certainly earned the title.

Bale pulled Smoke's reins, and the horse slowed to a stop in front of the waiting party of Temple guards.

"You found them?" Bale asked, looking down to Copher and

the bloodhound at his side. The beast's eyes were fixed on the trees. Drool dripped from its jaws.

"They set up camp in the forest," Copher said, his long, braided pony-tail hung down his back like a whip. "We don't know how many, but they're in there."

Copher wore the white Temple guard uniform, he just never had it washed. His shirt was stained with dirt and hard travel. He was an expert tracker and head of Bale's own men—a hand-picked crew that carried out the Highfather's most challenging assignments. Like their leader, most had former lives as assassins and cutthroats. Bale liked to surround himself with people he could trust.

On top of Bale's six men, fifteen more Temple guards stood outside the forest, awaiting his command. Bale had seen the training of most guards, so he didn't expect much from them. But it was always good to have the numbers on your side, especially with an unknown enemy. Besides, if the Descendant rebels had any archers, those clean white shirts would attract the attention away from his men.

"Did you get a look at the camp?" Bale asked.

Copher shook his head. "We risked alerting them if we got too close. But I know these woods. It's only about three-span deep before the cliffs."

Bale nodded. Descendant rebels usually stuck to shadows, attacking small targets before scurrying like rats back to their hideouts. But this band of rebels had attacked a Curor shop only miles from the Temple. That meant they were armed. "Spade's rebels" were growing confident. It was time Bale sent a message.

"Spread out," Bale ordered. "We move in as one. Avoid head wounds if possible. The Highfather's Curor wants us to bring some back alive."

Bale's men grumbled.

The men moved into formation. The Temple guards following the lead of the six seasoned killers.

Bale climbed off Smoke but didn't bother tying his reins.

The horse would wait for his master's return. Bale's gloved hand moved to his collar, pulling the armor away from his neck where the disease made his skin raw. The burning put him in a foul mood. Fortunately, he had some Descendants to take his anger out on.

The men formed a wide line at the forest's edge. Bale drew his long sword from his saddle and held it up, the dark blade invisible in the moonlight. At his signal, the guards crept into the forest.

Bale's keen eyes searched through the darkness for signs of movement. The rebels began as a group of escaped Descendants, hiding in the woods and running from bloodhounds. Then came word of this…Spade. Bale assumed there was more myth than fact to a Descendant rebel leader, but the group *had* grown more organized. They eluded the Temple guard and were now committing acts of crime and destruction that were gaining the attention of the High Counsel. So the Highfather had called upon Bale to end it.

There was a choked gasp to Bale's right. He squatted low, sword ready. Footsteps raced through the brush, farther into the darkness of the forest. Bale surged toward the noise. He found a guard on the forest floor. Throat slit.

The one who killed him was racing back to warn the others.

"Charge," Bale yelled. The Temple guards rushed forward, no longer hiding the sounds of their footsteps. Bale's long, armored legs leaped over bushes. When they reached the camp, the Descendants were scrambling out of tents, weapons in hand. Bale counted only five rebels. Pity. He'd hoped for more of a fight.

Then he saw the Descendant rebels move. It looked like the Temple guards were caught in mud by how easily the rebels passed them. Their crude weapons cut through the night like lightning. One rebel slashed a Temple guard three times before the man got his sword up. The guard fell to his knees, his face confused. He didn't know he'd been killed.

This was not a rugged band of looters. These were trained soldiers. Bale squeezed his sword handle and grinned. He would get his fight after all.

A rebel's sword clashed against Markas's. Every swing met with a block. Markas was a strong swordsman; it might have proved a good battle. Bale got there in three strides and rammed his broadsword through the Descendant's back. Markas stumbled as the sword came at him through the man's chest.

"I had him," Markas said, but Bale was already moving ahead.

Metal on metal echoed through the forest. A guard screamed in pain as his leg was cleaved at the knee. He fell to the ground, useless. The Descendant rebel turned to face Bale, his eyes wide. It wasn't fear in there, but a wild appetite. *Fools.* They actually thought they had a chance.

The rebel swung his sword up toward the taller Bale. Bale blocked the first blow. Then the second. It was more than mere speed. The man swung his blade in efficient strokes. But Bale had a lifetime of experience—a lifetime of killing. Their swords met in the air, and Bale rammed his pommel down into the man's face. Blood fountained from his shattered nose. Valuable blood. The man staggered back in blind pain. Bale took his head.

It rolled along the forest floor.

The fight was soon over. Though the rebels had done more damage, they were too outnumbered. The Temple guards closed in on the one remaining Descendant. The thin rebel swung his sword in wild arcs, trying to ward them off. The Descendant's eyes fell upon the bodies of his friends, and his look changed. He screamed and hurled his sword at the closest guards. Then he turned and ran.

"After him," Bale yelled. "Don't let him get away."

They chased after the fleeing Descendant. Again, Bale was amazed by the man's speed as he increased his lead. He was fast, but he couldn't hope to outrun the Temple guards with their horses. Copher would track him, even through the night.

Then Bale remembered Copher's words. The forest was shallow.

Bale called out to Tesher who ran ahead of him. "Don't let him reach the cliffs!"

The guard unslung his bow and nocked an arrow as he ran. Up ahead the tree line ended, and the ground dropped into darkness. The Descendant rebel charged while the guards slid to a halt. The Descendant reached the edge and leaped off into the air. He floated there in the moonlight for a moment—long enough for Tesher's arrow to find its mark. The Descendant lurched as the arrow drove into his back. Then he fell.

Bale joined Tesher and Copher at the cliff's edge. Trees hid the ground far below. There was no sign of where he landed. The fall would be near impossible to survive. But he had seen the impossible too many times.

"Find the body," Bale said. "No Descendant is counted as dead until his body is strung up and drained by a Curor."

Four of the Temple guards broke off, descending along the cliff's edge. Bale returned to the rebel camp. The guards had already tied up the Descendants' bodies. All but the decapitated one. Bale nudged the headless body with his boot.

"I don't think that one's healing," Copher said.

"Not likely."

"The Fathers will be upset you wasted one."

"They can hunt them down themselves next time." Bale waved to the body. "Bottle what blood you can and then bring the body back to the Temple with the others. Vorrel likes to play with the bodies."

Markas frowned. "I'll never understand the appetites of that Curor."

"They're not paying us to understand," Bale said. "Where's Hilman?"

The men looked around. Hilman was missing. Bale thought

back through the raid. The ax-man had been on his far left...he attacked a rebel.

"There," Copher said, pointing. Temple guards dragged a body from the bushes. Dried blood covered the right side of his face. His arm dangled from his body, nearly severed from the large gash that ran between his shoulder and neck. Shame. Hilman had been with Bale since back when he was an assassin for hire. He would be hard to replace.

"He's gone," Markas said. "Nearly cut in half. Poor bastard."

"Take his ax," Bale said.

Markas sighed and took the weapon, leaving the body. His men didn't object. They knew what to expect when their time came. No ceremony, no prayers. They'd seen too much death to believe it still held any mystery.

"Copher," Bale said. "Stay here and see what you can find that might lead us to the rest of them."

"Yes, sir," Copher said. His pony-tail whipping around as he turned to examine the rebel camp.

"The way these ones moved," Silas said, shaking his head. "I've never seen anything like it."

"They still die," Markas said. "Just takes a few more swings."

"You think one of them was Spade?" Tesher asked, nodding to the bodies.

Bale looked at the head covered in dirt and blood; the eyes wide, frozen in surprise. "No."

Outside the forest, the guards hauled the Descendants into the cell cart. The rebel Bale had run his sword through was conscious and already moving around. *Descendants,* Bale shook his head. No wonder the Faith suppressed them and took their blood. Even these pale versions showed amazing abilities. Bale could only wonder what fighting against the Royals of old had been like.

Smoke trotted over, and Bale petted the horse's gray mane. *Good soldier.* He climbed on with more effort than he wanted to show, aware of the pain in his chest now that the surge of battle had passed. He needed blood.

The Blood Knight rode south to the Temple of the Faith. It was time to have a discussion with Haemon. It was time for the Highfather to fulfill his end of the bargain.

THE FIRE that burned in Bale's chest added to his temper as he stormed up the Temple steps. He pushed past two guards who raised their hands in salute. Things had been much simpler when Haemon had first hired him, working as an assassin. There were fewer games to play when you worked outside the Faith. Now, he had no choice. His disease was a leash, tying him to Haemon and his blood supply.

The wound poisoned his heart, never fully healing. It felt like his heart was held together by a single string, melting away until his next dose. The only thing that kept him alive, lay behind that door.

The guard outside the Highfather's study turned to Bale, his hand instinctively going to his sword hilt.

"Out of the way," Bale said. "I need to speak to him."

"The Highfather is not to be disturbed," the guard said, eyes darting from Bale to the broadsword on his back. There was recognition in the guard's eyes. *Now, to see if he had any brains.*

"I'm going through that door. You can stand aside, or I can use your head as a knocker."

The guard gulped, removing his hand from his sword. He knocked on the door himself. A gentle rap.

"What is it?" Haemon called from within.

"There's a...someone here who..."

Bale pushed open the door and entered the Highfather's study. Haemon sat hunched over a desk, his clean white robes in contrast to the room's darkness. Haemon scowled, his withered face lit by the candles on the desk.

"I'm sorry, father," the guard said, scrambling to the door. "He blindsided me."

"It's alright," Haemon said, spinning his face into a confident grin. As if Bale's sudden arrival had been his plan all along. "Leave us."

The guard shut the door, leaving Bale alone with Aeilius Haemon, Highfather of the Faith.

"Why, Bale," Haemon said. "I pray you've come with good news."

Without his uniform and ceremonial hat, the Highfather could be mistaken for a sickly old man. He bent over as if his bones could hardly support him anymore. The few thin strands of hair that were left, hung from the sides of his head with all the weight of a spiderweb. But Bale knew better than to be fooled by appearances. The Highfather was the most dangerous man in Terene.

One of them, anyway.

"We found the Descendant rebels," Bale said. "Captured four alive...somewhat alive. None of them gave up anything about this so-called Spade."

"So you don't believe in a great rebel leader come to save the Descendants?"

"The reports I've heard have the flimsy details of myth. I think the Descendants have built up an idea in order to give themselves hope. Or, to scare your noble lords."

"Well, it's working," Haemon said, leaning back in his chair. "You should know the power of myth. I've heard Bale the Blood Knight moves as a shadow. That no sword can pierce him. That he can sniff out a Descendant's blood a mile away."

"I wouldn't worry about a single Descendant. The reason we haven't caught Spade is that he doesn't exist."

"Don't let your prejudice blind you. While most Descendants have had the fight beaten out of them over the generations, there are always a few capable of causing trouble." Haemon pulled a second glass from his drawer and set it beside his own, filling both with blood wine. Bale's hands shook at the sight of the dark red liquid.

"Leave the captured Descendants to Vorrel," Haemon said. "If they know anything about Spade, he'll get it out of them. He is as patient as he is cruel. Your value is in the field."

Haemon held up a glass, and Bale snatched it. He sat down in a chair opposite the Highfather's desk and drank. The blood filled his stomach and immediately went to work, soothing the burning in his chest and neck. The disease pulled back its tentacles. The string holding his heart together grew tighter. This was good blood. Sitting safely within their high stone walls, the nobility always got the purest blood. While those who needed it most—soldiers in the field—went without.

"I lost one of my men in the raid," Bale said.

"A valuable one?"

"He'll be difficult to replace. With the army of proper guards your men keep churning out, it's hard to find a real soldier who can actually fight."

"A real killer you mean?"

"Someone who gets things done. Like me."

"While your specific skills have been of great value to me, you can understand why we wouldn't want an army of Bale's roaming Terene."

Bale spun the empty glass on the desk. It wobbled, threatening to fall over before coming back to rest. "You promised me a cure, Haemon. I've done your missions—for longer than we agreed. I'm losing my patience with these temporary fixes."

"Vorrel and his Curors are close to something big. Something that will end the world's reliance on Descendant blood."

"I don't care about your political moves. I want to be cured and done with this." Bale tapped his chest. Haemon owed him. For it had been performing one of his missions that Bale had taken a sword to the heart. If the Highfather couldn't fulfill his promise…

"Hemo has deemed our work worthy," Haemon said. "You must have faith."

Bale scoffed, looking around the Highfather's study. The large room with its vaulted ceiling, the ornate furniture and jeweled lamps that could feed a family for years. "Save the propaganda for the masses, Haemon. I'm not blind."

The Highfather's face darkened. He reached to a cabinet beside his desk. A stream of cold air wafted out. The Highfather removed a wooden box and closed the cabinet door. He unfastened the lid and revealed sixteen vials of blood. Enough to last Bale for weeks. Haemon's spidery finger plucked a vial from its slot and held it up, examining it in the lamplight.

"It's such a curious thing, blood. It is found in all of us, in every animal in the world. Yet for some reason, Hemo has chosen to bless only some of it. Some blood saves lives while other blood is worthless."

Haemon dropped the vial. Bale gasped as the glass shattered on the floor. The precious blood pooled out on the marble floor. Wasted. Haemon pulled another vial from the box. His eyes moved from the blood to Bale's. "I am the Highfather of the Faith. Ruler of Terene. You will not blaspheme in my presence."

Bale took a deep breath and gave a slight nod. He still needed Haemon. For now.

"Find me the one called Spade and stop these terrorists once and for all," Haemon said. "This distraction must be dealt with if we are to focus our efforts elsewhere. Such as your cure."

"Yes, father," Bale whispered.

"Good," Haemon returned the vial to the box and slid it across the table. His face grew solemn. "Go in Faith."

Bale flung the study door open. The guard flinched as Bale stormed down the hallway, the box of blood cradled tight to his chest. He would do as Haemon ordered. He'd kill these Descendant rebels and anyone else he had to, to get his cure. And when he did—the Highfather would finally get what was coming to him.

## 6

R uling a realm is not as glamorous as it sounds. In fact, aside from the lavish food and clothing, Jonathan Carmine found the duties of a noble lord quite tiresome. He longed for the days of his youth when he was free to run about the castle or ride through the Hidden Wood. Now, he sat in the throne room for hours, hearing the appeals of his subjects. Had his father found it this boring?

"I think two vials should do, my Lord," Briton's voice snapped Carmine from his daydream. Seated beside the throne, the old advisor shot him a disapproving look.

"Yes," Carmine said, turning back to the ragged farmer kneeling before the throne. "Two vials it is."

"Thank you, Lord Carmine," the farmer rose and bowed again. "You are most gracious. My family will make it up with this year's harvest."

Carmine waved a hand, and a guard escorted the man out of the throne room. He would be granted his two vials of blood. Being but a farmer, it would be the lowest blood they had.

When the farmer had cleared the room, Carmine turned to Briton. "Are we done for the day?"

"A few more yet, my Lord," Briton said, looking up from the

meeting log. "This is an important part of your rule. Do try to stay awake."

"I wish you could do this, Briton. I grow tired of the constant complaints and tales of woe. They think being in charge of a bean field is tough, they should try running the province. And who do *I* have to complain to?"

"I believe that honor falls on me," Briton said with a sigh. "It's important for people to know their Lord listens to them and cares about their lives. Leadership fosters loyalty in—"

"Yes, yes," Carmine cut him off. He'd heard it all before. "Who is next? A tailor who's run out of thread?"

"Lord Ballard has returned," Briton said, reading from the log.

"Lord Ballard?" Carmine twisted his short beard, trying to remember their previous business. Ballard was a lower lord, so he couldn't have been given much aid. He was probably coming back to complain. "What was he here for again?"

Briton flipped back through his log. "Last week…his wife was sick." Briton's finger stopped on the details of the previous meeting. He frowned. "Gray Fever."

"Gray Fever! Then he's come back to hold us responsible for his wife's death. I don't want to see him."

Before Carmine could rise, the door opened, and Lord Ballad strode into the throne room. Ballard was a tall, gaunt man whose brisk stride covered the distance to Carmine's throne in no time.

"Lord Ballard," Carmine said, sinking back into his chair. "How may House Carmine aid you in so somber a time?"

"Lord Carmine," Ballard said, his voice weak. In fact, the thin lord looked hardly able to stand. His eyes were circled with the dark rings of a man who had not slept in days. He collapsed and buried his head on the marble floor. Carmine glanced to the location of the nearest guard. Hammond stood in the corner of the room, eyes alert. When Ballard finished his blubbering, he rose to one knee, his hollow cheeks wet with tears.

*Here we go.*

"My Lord," Ballard said. "I come as your humble servant. House Carmine will forever have House Ballard's allegiance."

Carmine glanced at Briton. His old teacher was as shocked as he was. His log must have been in error. No one survived Gray Fever. Especially not with the low blood Ballard had been given. "I take this to mean your wife..."

"Healed!" Ballard said. "Completely. It's a miracle."

So, Lady Ballard had been misdiagnosed. Carmine wasn't opposed to reaping the benefits of such a mistake. Let the story of House Carmine's power and generosity spread around Terene. Lord Carmine the Miraculous!

"The good blood you gave us," Ballard continued. "I've never seen anything like it. The color returned to her instantly, the sores melted away within minutes. My wife stood on her own strength for the first time in weeks."

Carmine scratched at his beard. Sores and paralysis? What could this have been if not Gray Fever? Something did not add up.

"I'm happy for your wife's recovery," he said, shifting to a smile. "This truly is wonderful news. Is there anything else House Carmine can help you with, Lord Ballard?"

"We only wished to come and thank you in person. Most high nobles would not treat a...newer lord such as myself to the pure blood from his supply. Lord Carmine, your generosity has saved my family. My wife would like to thank you personally."

"Of course, Lord Ballard," Carmine said. "Whenever she feels up to it I would be honored..."

But Ballard was already striding to the throne room door. A guard pulled the door open, and a woman stepped inside, taking Ballard's hand. She was nearly as tall as Lord Ballard and wore an elegant white gown. There were no signs of sickness, in fact, her skin seemed to glow in the warm afternoon light.

"Lord Carmine," Ballard said, raising the woman's hand. "Lady Ballard."

*It can't be.* This woman was the picture of health, not a dying husk of Gray Fever. Was someone playing a joke at his expense?

"Lady Ballard," Carmine said, composing himself. "We are happy to find your health returned."

"Thank you, Lord Carmine," the woman said. A tear streaked down her rosy cheek. "I owe you my life."

"Your fortunate news is payment enough. Go in peace and with further blessings."

After more bows, Lord and Lady Ballard backed out of the throne room. Carmine sat puzzling over what he had seen. Had it been an act? And if so, to what possible purpose?

Briton seemed to be working this out himself. The old man's bushy eyebrows hung in a puzzled scowl.

"What do you make of it, Briton?" Carmine asked.

"Strange indeed," Briton whispered. "I've never heard of someone surviving Gray Fever. Nor did Lady Ballard appear to have any symptoms at all. Yet, their performance seemed...genuine."

Carmine nodded, almost happy that his old teacher had no answer. It was a rare occurrence to see the great Briton flummoxed.

"Hammond," Carmine called. The guard approached, his armor clinking with each hurried step.

"My Lord?" the guard bowed.

"Visit Lord Ballard's estate. Talk with neighbors and the local Curor. Find out more about Lady Ballard's illness. I want you to find out what these two are up to."

"Yes, my Lord."

"In plain clothes," Carmine added. "We do not need a Carmine guard spotted spying on other lords."

Hammond nodded and crossed the throne room. The door opened, and a guard led in the next visitor. An old woman, hunched like a beggar. Carmine held up a hand, and the guard pulled her back out of the throne room.

"You believe the Ballards are planning something," Briton said.

"What else could it be?" Carmine asked. Ballard was a lesser lord, desperate to raise his standing. And House Carmine's financial troubles were no secret—Ballard must see them as a vulnerable noble house. But why this rouse about Gray Fever? What could he be plotting?

Carmine could tell Briton wasn't satisfied. "Well?"

"I'll talk to Typher," Briton said. "Find out what batch of blood he sold to Ballard. You're likely right about this being a ploy, but if it turns out there's truth to their story, we need to know where that blood came from."

Carmine nodded in agreement. He leaned back in his chair, his mind racing through the possibilities. Something strange was going on. A mystery to solve. Lies, plots, miracles. This day had proven not so boring after all.


THE BOY HOPPED down the stone stairs, carrying the empty tray as a shield against the hall's suit of armor. The decoration dwarfed his thin frame, but what the boy lacked in mass, he more than made up in cunning. The knight stood bewildered as the boy ducked and swung the shield at the knight's knees. Though the boy stopped before impact, both adversaries knew who had won the duel.

The boy bowed to the imaginary crowd and then spun the shield back into a tray as he hurried down the stairs. His promotion to food deliverer was much better than being in the kitchen all day. The boy had explored much of the castle over the past week, and each day held more secrets to discover. In fact, Descendant life at Castle Carmine could almost be tolerable if not for the one thing.

At the thought of the Curor, the boy slowed to a walk, his fingers absently scratching at the week's worth of cuts on his upper forearm. Forget the imaginary knights and beasts, the real enemy was the man in red.

The process of the nightly blood draws had gotten faster as the boy found obedience the easier path in the end. But it had not helped the severity of what he felt. Each night, the boy watched his blood flow from his arm into bottles for the Curor's shelf. Afterward, he'd hobble to bed weak and drained, as if his very life had been stolen from him.

And no amount of glances into the castle garden or treats stolen from Mable's cupboards could ever make that right.

Walking into the kitchen, the boy set the tray down on the counter. His friend was busy at work over the sink. Chancey's head hung so low it almost dipped in the dirty water.

"They got you on dishes," the boy said, coming to Chancey's side. "What'd you do now?"

"Nothing," Chancey mumbled, his face missing its usual liveliness. He turned back to his dishes and continued scrubbing.

"You'll never guess what Lady Royce was wearing," the boy whispered to Chancey. "Or rather, not wearing. Who gets their supper brought to them in the bath?"

"Very funny." Chancey said no more as he dug out a handful of silverware. That was strange, Lady Royce was one of Chancey's favorite subjects.

The boy grabbed the next tray of food to deliver and raced out of the kitchen and up the stairs. He'd never once seen Chancey in a foul mood. Even stumbling to bed after the Curor took his blood, Chancey was able to crack a weak smile or make a half-hearted joke. This was unlike him.

The boy raced around the castle on various kitchen errands. He moved faster and with fewer accidents now that he could use both eyes. The dirty bandage no longer stuck to his face, so the boy got rid of it. It had been long enough for his face to heal, so no one seemed to notice. The boy stole a glance in a mirror. The scarring was gone and all that was left was a black "C" shaped tattoo on the right side of his face. The boy thought seeing his reflection might restore some of his memories. It hadn't. The haggard shape with sloppy brown hair and deep set eyes looked like a stranger. The boy had run his hands over his skeletal cheeks just to make sure it was really him he was seeing.

He looked like any other Descendant prisoner. What more had he expected?

Later that day, when the bell chimed, the boy caught up to Chancey in line for the Curor. The nightly line was a dreary affair. Whatever small tastes of happiness were found during day eroded as the Descendants waited their turn to have their blood drawn. Each night, the boy held out hope for some divine intervention. A fire. A landquake to crumble the castle walls.

With Chancey hanging his head in silence, the boy lost the only thing that made this tolerable.

"Chancey, what's wrong?" the boy whispered.

"I'm just tired," Chancey sighed. "I must have washed ten thousand pieces of cutlery the last few days, and it never ends. I swear that sink has no bottom."

"Tomorrow I'll help with the dishes. And we'll split the meal runs between us."

"You think you can tell Mable what to do?" Chancey scoffed. "I'm off food delivery for good. She said she must have been out of her mind to ever let a fat boy run errands in the first place."

"That's not right," the boy said. "I'll tell her I want to go back to kitchen work."

"Forget it," Chancey said. "We can't control anything here. The sooner you learn that the better."

The boy left Chancey to his gloom and stepped forward in line. Chancey was right, of course. There was nothing they could do. They were worse than slaves. Mistreated and worked through the day and then harvested for their blood at night.

Just because they healed, didn't make the pain any less.

When it was his turn, the boy descended the stairs to find

the Curor's lab in a complete mess. It looked as if there *had* in fact been a landquake. Bottles that once lined the shelves in straight rows were now scattered on counters and tables. There were three other men in the room, counting bottles and marking notes on sheets of paper.

"Come, come, let's get on with it," the Curor shouted from the waiting table. His usual clean red robes were covered in dust, and dark craters formed under his eyes. Perhaps he was sick, dying of some incurable disease. The boy could dream.

The large guard with the splotchy birthmark eyed the boy as he crossed the room. The boy climbed into the chair and waited. He didn't want to receive another beating. The blood draw took enough out of him.

The Curor reached for a bottle but an oily man with fine-combed hair grabbed it first.

"Who's this?" the man asked, holding up a pen to the bottle.

"The new boy," the Curor said. "He's a stray, he hasn't a name."

"He needs a name, Typher," the man said, tapping the point of his pen on the glass bottle. "We wouldn't be in this mess if you kept decent records."

"Call him Stray for all I care. Let's get on with it. You won't find what you're looking for here."

The man dipped the pen in ink and scribbled on the bottle's label. The Curor snatched it back with a heavy groan and inserted the tube into the top. He set the bottle marked "*Stray*" on the table and brought the other end of the tube up to the boy's arm.

"Your scars have healed quickly," the Curor said, squeezing the boy's forearm until the veins rose to the surface. "Perhaps we can take more from you than we thought."

The boy swallowed under the gaze of the three men. The Curor made a small incision on the boy's arm. Then he jammed the tube into the open wound, tightening the clamp on the boy's bicep. Blood flowed through the tube, and the boy felt the usual nausea as his head fogged over.

Behind the Curor, men examined the bottles, arguing and taking notes. They were looking for something. The boy lost focus and his vision blurred. He shivered, feeling the cold of the room more and more. How had Chancey handled this for so long? The boy ran circles around the pudgier kid all day, but how was it that Chancey could stand the Curor's touch while he could barely walk after?

"Next," the Curor called as he ripped the tube from the boy's arm. The boy grabbed a dirty cloth and held it to the cut. Staggering to his feet, he shuffled to the stairs and started the slow climb. Chancey passed him on the way down. The boy tried to offer a smile, but Chancey didn't see. He marched head down into the Curor's lab, hiding tears.

The boy's legs melted like warmed candle wax. He stopped twice in the hallway to steady himself on the stone wall. His mind was still in a haze. He thought he heard voices coming from the Descendants' barracks. Nights after the blood draw were always silent as Descendants recovered from having the life drained from them. But the boy stepped through the heavy metal door to find...talking.

Heads turned his way. While a few Descendants slept, a group gathered on the middle cots. The boy crashed on his mattress like a broken branch. But he was still close enough to hear their conversation.

"I've seen this before," said Jako, an older man who worked in the cellar—his fingers permanently black. "Someone has stolen blood."

"Impossible," Amond said, shaking his head. The man was a large field hand with a flat shovel of a nose. "Who would dare steal from the Curor's lab? No one's getting down there without Typher's key."

"Then why do you think they're suddenly taking inventory

of all the bottles? Something's up. Typher looked even meaner than usual."

"Could it have something to do with the rebellion?" a soft voice asked. The boy turned in his cot to see the speaker. A young, mousy woman lay on her side. He'd never heard her speak before.

"Descendant warriors?" Amond scoffed. "That's just a fairy tale."

"Oh," the woman's eyes lowered, and she sunk deeper under her blanket.

"Don't listen to him," Jako said. "Just because he's lost hope doesn't mean there's nothing to it. Amond's never been outside the Carmine border. Shows what he knows."

"And you're an expert on Descendant rebels and free borns?" Amond asked.

"Free borns?" The boy was surprised to hear himself speak. It just popped out.

The others studied him but didn't seem taken back by his question.

"Descendants born in the wild, outside of Raw Blood control," Jako said. "No owners. No blood draws."

"It's the dream fed to gullible Descendants," Amond said. "They think they'll run off to freedom and join the rebels. That they'll fight back against the Raw Bloods." Amond shook his head. "But all those stories do is give people bad ideas. They get people killed."

"She knows," Jako said, pointing across the room. The heads turned to the far wall, to the woman who'd come to Castle Carmine with the boy. "She's from House Octavian."

A hush fell over the room.

*What was House Octavian?* The boy leaned his head to get a glimpse of the woman. She lay in her cot, staring up at the ceiling. The boy hadn't spoken to her since that second morning after the tattoos. Her "O" tattoo was now covered up by the fresh thick lines of the Carmine "C."

"Well?" Amond asked, calling to the woman. "What do you know?"

"About what?" she asked, not taking her eyes off the ceiling.

"The Descendant rebels," Jako said. "Are there really Descendants out there, living free and fighting the Faith?"

The woman took a tired breath. The topic seemed to bore her. "There's no such thing as a free Descendant," she said. "We're all prisoners, some just have bigger cages."

This sunk the mood in the room. The boy didn't mind. He was too weak to focus. It was a struggle to keep his eyes open. He pulled up his hole-riddled blanket and turned back to the door. Chancey hadn't returned from the Curor's lab. The boy's muscles tensed and the pit of his stomach twisted into a knot. *What was taking so long?*

The boy *would* talk to Mable, no matter what Chancey said. He'd convince her to switch their jobs back, even if it took a tumble or two down the stairs and some dropped meals. He would set things right. He owed it to Chancey.

The boy fell asleep and dreamed once again of flying. He saw the tops of the trees from high above and even felt the wind whipping against his face. The world lay before him, shrouded in clouds. From up high, all felt right. He felt free. Then the clouds blew away and the trees with them, and the boy saw a face. A man with a pointed brown beard. The man was speaking, but the wind was too strong and carried his words away. The boy reached for the face to pull it into the light to see it clearer, but the man fell away, dragged by the wind. The boy was left all alone.

Hands seized his shoulders, waking him from his dream. Even had the boy strength to resist, it would have done little against the strong arms that pulled him from his bed and carried him toward the door. He went without a fight, dazed and weak. Barely aware of the muffled sobs behind him—someone crying into a pillow.

"What's going on?" the boy groaned. His captor slung him

over his armored shoulder and carried him down the hallway. "Where are you taking me?"

The boy felt the cold armor on the man's back. A Carmine guard. What had he done?

The guard pushed open a door, and they stepped out into the courtyard. The night air swirled against the boy's uncovered skin. He shivered, twisting to get a look where they were going. No stars were visible in the cloudy darkness.

They passed the stables and walked beside the high wall to the other end of the castle. Guards looked down at them but did not speak; their faces as blank as the night. They reached a door leading into one of the castle's four towers. The guard opened the door and carried the boy up a spiral staircase. The guard didn't slow, carrying the boy as if he weighed nothing. This wasn't far from the truth. The boy's ribs threatened to snap as they pressed down against the guard's armor; he could hardly breathe. He twisted away and was met by a punch in the side that took all his air.

"Move again and I'll drop you head first down these stairs," the guard said. Gasping for breath, the boy went limp and let the guard take him higher and higher. The boy had never been to this end of the castle. There were no doors to other floors, just the narrow stairs. They must be higher now than even the rooftop garden.

The spiral staircase finally ended at a thick wooden door. The guard set the boy down with a huff. The guard's face under his helmet was red. A spotted birthmark. It was the guard from the Curor's lab. The boy's heart raced. This couldn't be good.

The guard pushed open the door and swept the boy into a small bedroom. In the darkness stood a figure. Dark as blood.

"Thought you could hide from us, did you?" The Curor stepped forward, shaking his head. His eyes were wide—hungry. "When will you people understand? The only reason you exist is to provide for us." He opened a case on the bed, revealing his instruments and eight empty vials.

The boy's knees gave out. The guard caught him by the shirt, suspending him off the ground as the Curor approached. The Curor twisted the boy's wrist and plunged a needle into his palm. The boy flinched, but the guard held him still. He couldn't get away. He couldn't even hold himself up.

"Ha!" the Curor exclaimed, looking down at the boy's palm. "It's true!"

The small needle hole had sealed in a matter of seconds.

The Curor bent down, his hooked nose only inches from the boy's. The eyes that stared into his were utter darkness.

"Hemo has blessed us with a miracle. From the most wretched comes the purest blood ever seen." The Curor's face contorted into a crooked grin. "Welcome to your new life."

# 7

---

*"In order to survive, the Raw Bloods have learned to overcome their natural weaknesses. Their fragility became their strength."*

---

B riton Moonglass fidgeted as he re-read his way through *The Last Writings of King Garian Kovar*. The journal traced the lineage back through the ages to early Royals in the Kovar line, but it said nothing about their origins. What had been the source of the Royal's blood? What gave them that power? And, could it be found again?

The modern history of the Royals he found in the journal was still fascinating. He'd always seen the Royals as an alien race, stronger and faster than mortal men. They lived for hundreds of years. But reading King Kovar's own words, these were the thoughts of a man. Flawed and full of doubts. A man who felt the weight of his throne.

The Blood War Briton knew—the one taught to kids and sung in taverns all over Terene—was shaped by the Faith and generations of hero-worship. When mankind rose up from servitude and wiped out the Royals. Led by the great General Drusas. King Kovar's account was much different. Briton was surprised by how candid the king was as he came to realize his people's mistreatment of the so-called "Raw Bloods." He seemed nothing like the evil tyrant of history. From reading his account, Briton actually felt compassion for the king as he tried to bring about change in those final days. But, even Kovar understood it was too late.

Now, all that was left of the Royals was the Temple and the remnant of their blood that runs through the Descendants' veins.

Briton set aside the book and locked it in its travel case. He had more pressing matters to attend to than his own studies. House Carmine needed to make this season's tithe to the Faith, and the castle's crops were not overflowing at present. And the blood stores had hardly grown. It was an impractical resource, after all. Even in Typher's cellar, the quality did not last more than a few weeks. And after rationing and the purchase of the new Descendants, House Carmine was still not ahead of its debts.

Briton leaned back in his chair, the cracking of his old bones filled the empty library. Whatever stress he was under, Jonathan Carmine was under heavier. The poor boy meant well. Briton believed that.

Behind him, the library door opened. Nathaniel, head of the Lord's guard, stood in the entryway.

"There you are," Nathaniel said, striding into the room.

"Nathaniel. I hope you come bearing good news. A gold mine discovered in the hills. A lost Royal treasure unearthed in the Hidden Wood." Briton stopped when he saw the serious expression on the guard's face. "What's wrong?"

The guard reached Briton. His eyes scanned the castle's accounts scattered on the table. "Then you haven't been informed."

"Informed of what?"

"Lord Carmine is waiting in the garden. We have the source of Lady Ballard's miraculous recovery."

"What? Hammond is back so soon?"

"No. It's Typher. He discovered it late last night."

Briton raised a bushy eyebrow. "Did he now?"

"So this is it?" Carmine asked. He held up the vial of blood in the morning light. "It doesn't look special."

"As with low blood and good blood, there is no difference to the eye," Typher said.

"There must be something," Carmine said. "For this to rescue Lady Ballard from her deathbed." He shook his head. "And you say this came from the new Descendant boy."

"My records traced the blood back to him. Plus, the kitchen boy came forward to report him. He was trying to pass off as a common low blood. Apparently, his scar healed after the first night."

Carmine pondered this news as he looked at the red liquid. Such a simple thing, blood. Found in each and every person. While one type was only valuable to the individual, another could build a kingdom. Or overthrow one.

Carmine walked through the garden. It was a particularly bright morning in the north; a few thin rays of sunlight stabbed through the gray cloud wall. He stopped to watch a night cereus open its white blade-shaped petals and point its pistil at the hidden sun. Carmine felt more at ease among the plants of his garden than trapped in his dank study. It was here that he was truly free to think.

"Lord Carmine," Briton's voice called. The old man hurried toward them, his faded-blue robe held off the ground. He stopped, catching his breath. "There is news of Lady Ballard?"

"Yes," Carmine said. "Typher has tracked down the blood's source. It belongs to the new Descendant boy."

Briton's mouth hung open. Carmine relished the stunned expression on his old master's face.

"And we know for sure it was the blood that healed Lady Ballard?" Briton asked.

"We've already gone over it, Briton," Typher said. "It is the new boy's blood."

Carmine ran his other hand against the purple leaves of the koboto tree and gently touched its fist-sized fruit. A koboto tree produced only one fruit in its lifetime. Carmine's mother had planted this tree before he was born. He had looked upon this fruit for most of his life—watched as it changed from green to dull red. It would soon be ready.

"The timing makes sense," Briton said. "The boy coming to the castle when he did. It's just…surprising."

"A fortunate pick, Typher," Carmine said. "The boy could have easily fallen into someone else's hands."

Typher and Briton exchanged a look. There had always been animosity between the two men. They had different views on how to treat the Descendants. Carmine couldn't remember the last time they agreed on anything. This would be no different.

"If the blood could cure Gray Fever, then it is like nothing we've ever seen," Typher said. "It's a true gift from Hemo. We must get all we can from the boy."

Briton gazed out into the distance. Toward the northern mountains. "The blood is indeed special. Though I disagree with Typher's proposal of what to do with the boy."

Carmine almost smiled.

Briton turned to him. "If his blood is indeed pure enough to cure Gray Fever, then he is perhaps the most valuable person in all of Terene. He could provide so many answers. We should learn from him, not lock him away and bleed him dry."

"The blood is the value," Typher countered. "Not the boy. We should get as much as we can before word spreads of what we have. There's no telling what the other lords will do to get this blood."

"Or the Faith," said Briton.

Typher frowned. "I know Master Briton has a great interest in studying the Descendants and their lineage," Typher said. "But surely his…hobby…does not outweigh the needs of House Carmine or the realm."

"It's not a matter of personal interest," Briton snapped at the Curor. "It's a matter of morality. We already treat these people as livestock. What right do we have to impart a life of torture? Especially on a boy with blood that has not been seen since that of the Royals!"

"Your pagan ideas blind you, Briton," Typher said. "You forget the blood is a gift from Lord Hemo to his chosen people. If it was against his will for us to use the blood, he would not have blessed us with it."

Briton's face darkened. If Carmine didn't know better, it almost looked as if the old man would take a swing at the Curor.

"Enough talk," Carmine said. He left their quibbling, walking deeper into the garden. *Talk* is all it was. *Action* is what separates a leader from a philosopher, Carmine's father had said. Carmine stopped at the glass house that encased the Blood Flower. His newest treasure. Or, it had been.

Without another thought, Carmine uncorked the glass vial and drank.

"My Lord!" Briton stammered in shock.

But it was too late. The blood flowed down his throat and lit a fire in his belly. Warmth shot through him, to his toes, to his fingertips. It felt as if life itself coursed through his veins. Carmine gripped the ivy as he leaned over the roof's edge. The view of his realm was much clearer, even the village miles away came into focus—bent wooden buildings and thatched roofs. Carmine looked down to the castle's courtyard far below. Part of him believed he'd survive the fall.

"Lord Carmine?" Briton touched Carmine's shoulder. "Are you alright?"

"Yes," Carmine said, turning around. Both Briton and Typher wore their concern on their faces.

"It's true," Carmine gasped. "The boy's blood is stronger than any I've ever tasted."

Even Carmine's mind felt clearer. As if the petty problems of his province were now beneath him.

"Briton, you may attend to the boy. Learn what you can about who he is and where he came from." He looked down at the empty vial in his hand. "If there are any more like him."

"Yes, my Lord," Briton said.

"But you will do so in the tower. He is too valuable to leave with the others, where anyone can reach him. I want guards stationed at his door at all times."

Carmine turned to the Curor. "Typher, you will personally administer his blood draws. Three times a day. No more than he is able to reasonably handle. We need him alive and healthy."

Typher bowed. "Yes, my Lord."

Carmine looked back at the lands that stretched out in rolling hills under the gray sky. This was his family's domain. Land that had been under hard times these past years. Land that had struggled to produce enough to match House Carmine's past greatness. That was all about to change.

With one boy.

"This blood is going to save House Carmine."


THE BOY GAZED out the tower window, too exhausted to move from his bed. He had been visited by the Curor twice since coming to this new room, and the blood draws had taken their toll. He lay with his eyes transfixed on the gray sky and the tree-tops spreading out in the distance. The Hidden Wood, as Chancey called it. Chancey, who had been his friend. Even in his delirious state, the boy realized Chancey had betrayed him to the Curor. Now, he was banished to the tower to bleed for House Carmine.

That was the last time he'd make the mistake of trusting someone.

A soft tapping on the door startled the boy. Nausea hit him hard, and his thin fingers rubbed the veins in his forearm. *The Curor is back already?* The boy took a breath and fought back the sickness. He wouldn't give the red-robed demon the satisfaction of seeing his fear.

But the door didn't open.

There was a second tapping on the door, as patient as the first. The boy sat up in confusion. The Curor wouldn't knock.

"May I come in?" The voice was gentle. The boy stared at the door. In all his time imprisoned at the castle, no one had ever asked his permission for anything.

"Who's there?" the boy asked.

"My name is Briton Moonglass," the voice said.

"What do you want?"

"As previously stated, I would like to come in."

"What for?"

There was a moment of silence.

"Perhaps this conversation would be easier had, if not through a three-inch thick wooden door," the voice said with some strain.

This must be some kind of game. If this man got all the way up the tower, past the guards at the door, then he was important enough to do as he wished. Why the act?

"Go ahead," the boy said. "It's locked from the outside anyway." Something he had discovered that night when he built up the energy to crawl from his bed and test the door. Getting back into bed in his state proved more difficult.

The heavy door slid open. The boy recognized the balding man who stood before him. The man from the library. The boy did not know his role, as he wore simple blue-gray robes, but he seemed to move about the castle as he pleased. And judging by the meals he was brought, must be of some status. Plus, there was the look. Something in the man's calm blue eyes looked perfectly at home in the great castle.

"Thank you," Briton said, closing the door behind him. "My old ears could barely hear through the door." He smiled. "As I said before, my name is Briton Moonglass."

The man waited as if the boy were supposed to have an opinion on the stranger's name.

"Do you have a name?" Briton asked.

The boy shook his head.

"What do people call you?"

"They don't call me anything."

Briton nodded and moved forward, stopping a safe distance from the bed. "Well, that won't do. What would you like me to call you?"

"I don't care."

"How about *I don't* for short?"

"What do you want?" the boy snapped. Whatever this game was, he didn't have the energy to play.

"I'd like to talk," Briton said, "If you're not too busy." The old man glanced around the room. The tower room was furnished with a bed—softer than his barracks cot—a chair, a bedside table, and a chamber pot. There was even a window, locked and barred though it was. It was a view of the world the boy feared he'd never set foot in again.

"You don't have a name," Briton said. "Did you have a home before Castle Carmine?"

"I don't know."

"You don't remember?"

"No."

Briton studied the boy as if assessing if he was simply being uncooperative. The boy had nothing to hide from any of them, not anymore. He looked at Briton with both his eyes, he felt the "C" tattoo in full view on his open face.

"What do you remember?"

*Nothing*, the boy was prepared to say. But something in the man's face, in those eyes, worked more out of him.

"I remember trees," the boy said, thinking back through the fog of his memory. "I remember being locked in a wooden box with pain so bad I could barely open my eyes. We traveled for I don't know how long. Days."

The boy felt a chill at the memory. The pain, still so recent, he could feel it in his bones. Was that all he remembered? Every night he had searched for more, some glimpse at his previous life, but nothing came.

"They brought me to the auction," the boy said. "Where I was sold here as a Descendant. That's all I remember."

"Sold as a Descendant," Briton repeated. "You were not a Descendant before?"

"I don't know," the boy said. "I'd never heard that word before."

Briton's eyes sparkled with interest. He lowered himself into a chair beside the bed. The boy instinctively recoiled. It was where the Curor sat to perform the blood draws.

"What do you know of your blood?" Briton asked, his tone sympathetic.

The boy stopped. Unsure why he was talking to this man. He didn't seem the type to order the guards in and force information out of him, though it was surely within his power. The boy had already confided in one person at the castle, and he had learned his lesson.

"I'm done talking."

"I'm sorry," the man said. "Did I offend you?"

"I'd say holding me against my will so you can cut me and steal my blood qualifies as an offense."

The man nodded. "It must be incredibly difficult for you here. While I don't agree with the way you have been treated, there is little in my power to change it. But I will do what I can to make your time here more bearable."

89

"You think a softer bed helps? Better food?" The boy's eyes were welling up now. He hated betraying his emotion, but the strain of hiding it these past weeks was exhausting. "What does a better meal matter when you haven't the stomach to eat? When you have to force food down just to recover enough strength for the next blood draw?"

Tears streamed down the boy's cheeks now. But he didn't hide his face from Briton. He stared at the old man, his defiance all that he had left.

The old man didn't leave, he didn't storm out or order the guards to attack. He simply sat with the boy in silence.

Eventually, when the boy's pulse and breathing returned to normal, the old man spoke.

"I cannot understand what you're going through nor can I stop your suffering." Briton raised his bushy eyebrow so that his blue eyes peered directly into the boy. "But I can arm you."

Before the boy could figure out what the old man meant, the door swung open. The Curor stood in the doorway, glowering. This time his anger was aimed at Briton.

"You must leave," The Curor said.

Briton stood and locked eyes with the man in red. Something unspoken passed between them. It was not friendly.

Briton turned to the boy, "Do you like riddles?"

The boy shook his head, confused. "What?"

"Let me leave you with one. I'll return tomorrow for your answer. If tomorrow you prefer no company, you will not see me again."

The Curor set his case down at the foot of the bed and opened it to reveal two empty glass bottles, tubing, and small blades. Briton's eyes moved over the contents of the case. It seemed to shake him.

"Some of us have real work to do," the Curor said. He pushed past Briton and set the two empty bottles on the bedside table.

Briton backed away.

The boy could feel nausea rushing through him like a river at the sight of the Curor's instruments. He had hardly recovered from the last visit, and already he was here for more blood. The boy turned from the Curor and his blades.

"The riddle," the boy called to Briton. "What is the riddle?"

Briton looked the boy in the eyes with such a confident gaze that it seemed to pass on a bit of strength. "What is the most powerful thing in all the world?"

"The most powerful thing in the world," the boy repeated in a whisper.

"Guards!" the Curor snapped. "Clear the room." The two guards at the door stepped in, unsure.

Briton nodded to the guards and walked out the door. He stopped at the threshold and gave one final glance at the boy in the tower.

"I'll return for your answer tomorrow," Briton said. Then he left the room. The guards slammed the door closed behind him with a boom that rattled the boy's bones.

The boy looked to the window, avoiding the Curor and his work. Small strands of light seeped through the gray clouds outside as the afternoon sun struggled to shine through. The boy kept his gaze on the sky out the window, looking far into the distance, as if he could transport his attention away from this room and the pain that was to come. The metal of the blade clinked as it was pulled from the case, but the boy hardly heard it. He was gone, soaring over land and treetops once more—searching for an answer to the old man's question.

As the blade plunged into his arm and opened a pathway to his blood, the boy held his eyes shut and repeated the question until he blacked out. *What is the most powerful thing in the world?*

*What is the most powerful thing in the world?*

# 8

The old man's riddle consumed the boy's thoughts. In between sleep and the Curor's visits, there was little else to do. Locked away in the tower, it was a nice relief to think of something other than the horrors of his current circumstances.

So despite his weakened condition—and his resistance to the old man's ploy—the boy worked on the question. He settled on possible answers through the night, only to change them in the morning. When he grew frustrated he quit and vowed not to speak to the old man. And when he grew bored, he scrambled for a new answer.

The boy stood at the barred window, studying the distant mountains that rose without end, disappearing into the clouds. Faint footsteps shuffled up the stairs. The boy turned to the door, ashamed at his own excitement.

He crawled into bed and wiped all interest from his face. Then he waited. He started to worry it was another visit from the Curor, when he heard a light tapping on the door.

"Yes," the boy called, too quickly.

The wooden door unlocked and creaked open. Briton Moonglass stepped inside. White hair sprang wild from the sides of his head as if to make up for its absence on top.

"Good day," Briton said, hanging in the doorway. "I don't mean to intrude. If you'd rather be alone…"

"You can come in if you want," the boy said with a forced sigh.

Briton bowed his head and closed the door. He crossed the small room and stopped at the window. He looked out as if inspecting the view for the first time.

"A clear day," Briton said. "Or as clear as you'll find in the north. You can see all the way to the Ghost Mountains."

"Ghost Mountains?"

Briton smiled. "Some superstitions still linger." He turned from the window to face the boy. "Do you have an answer to my riddle? Or should I leave you in peace?"

"Your riddle?" As if he could have forgotten the question he'd repeated to himself a hundred times.

"What is the most powerful thing in all the world?"

The boy stirred in bed. He had gone through many answers, none he was confident in. In the end, he settled on one he thought would suit the old man.

"The Highfather," the boy said.

Briton didn't so much as blink. His flat expression betrayed nothing. "Why?"

"I hear he rules over all the land—even your Lord Carmine. He has the world's largest army at his command, which is greater than any single weapon."

Briton nodded. "The Highfather of the Faith is very powerful."

"But not the most powerful?"

Briton shrugged. "Titles and reigns end. Someone new always rises to power. The current Highfather's appointment has been exceptionally long, but it, too, will pass to another…"

"Fire," the boy blurted out before Briton finished. If the answer surprised Briton with its complete change of direction, he didn't show it. "It's hot enough to melt steel of any sword. It can destroy a village or wipe out an entire forest."

"And it could kill even the Highfather of the Faith." Briton tapped at his chin. His blue eyes studied the boy. "And how do you stop fire?"

"Water," the boy grumbled.

"Water is more powerful then?"

"I guess so. Enough water and you can drown an army."

"And how do you survive drowning in water?"

"You swim," the boy said. He racked his brain for another answer, not wanting to admit defeat. "Love?"

At this Briton did raise an eyebrow.

"Love?"

"Yes," the boy said, annoyed. "I know you'll pick apart everything I say, and I assume this riddle has a moral in the end. So, what? It's love?"

Briton chuckled. "Love is indeed a powerful thing. But you may find in your life that love too can be broken."

"I give up," the boy said, leaning back in his pillow. The game was tiring, and he didn't feel like going round in circles with the old man. "What is the most powerful thing in all the world?"

The old man moved closer and sat on the end of the boy's bed. "The world is full of power. Everything you named can kill a man, even love. But everything can be stopped as well. What is it that defeats each of these powers?"

"No one thing. Each one is different."

"Each obstacle we face requires a different solution. But what gives us the solution?"

"I don't—"

"Stop," Briton raised his voice, catching the boy by surprise. "A thoughtful answer is superior to a quick one."

The boy thought through their discussion and each of Briton's rebuttals. Water puts out fire...a man can learn to swim... *What did they have in common?*

"Knowledge," the boy said, finally.

Briton nodded. "Very good. Knowledge is the most powerful

thing in all the world. The knowledge of how to swim can transform dangerous water into a peaceful lake. It can teach you to build armor to deflect arrows or the plans to outmaneuver a larger army. It can keep you warm, keep you fed, and it can even overthrow those in power."

The boy thought about this for a moment, searching for holes in Briton's answer. In the end, he relented. He realized with his loss of memory, he also suffered a loss of knowledge. Maybe that was why he felt so powerless.

"Where do you get knowledge?"

"Lots of ways," Briton said. "Books, teachers…life. If you have a curious and hungry mind, you can learn something from every person and situation you encounter. Even while trapped in a tower."

"What's the point of learning if you're to spend the rest of your life in a prison."

Briton nodded solemnly and looked around the room as if taking in the full weight of the boy's situation before answering.

"Books can take you far from here. Let you experience the world when you can't leave your room."

"But why does it matter if I have knowledge? My life is pretty much planned out for me."

The boy saw the vision he feared most: himself as an old man, still trapped in this tower room, his blood taken from him by Curor after Curor. His blood spread out all over the world, flowing inside of strangers while he remained forever imprisoned in the castle. This was his nightmare. This was worse than death.

"Knowledge can be a powerful weapon," Briton said. "If you have the wisdom to wield it. Every problem has a solution. One need only discover the answer."

Briton leaned forward, his blue eyes looking directly into the boy's. "Never rob yourself of the chance to learn."

*There it is*, the boy realized. *The point of his riddle at last.*

"And you want to…what? Be my teacher?"

"If you wish," Briton said. "I served as teacher for Lord

Carmine when he was your age. Though some might hold that against my record." The old man smiled to himself. "There is much I can teach you, but only if you are willing to learn. A man cannot fill an overturned bucket."

The boy thought this over. This must be some kind of trick. Everyone wanted something.

"What is in it for you?"

"You are of great interest to me. I have been studying the history of your people for a long time. There is still so much we don't know about where you came from or the source of your blood powers. The Faith would have us believe it is simply a blessing from Hemo, that it has lost its power over generations because of man's sin. But I believe there is a different answer. I know you don't remember your past, but perhaps we can find the answers together."

The boy considered the old man's words. As much as he didn't want to let Briton in, the old man's gentle demeanor had a way of breaking through his resistance. Perhaps the boy could use him; learn what he can from the old man without fully trusting him. Besides, it wasn't like he had anything better to do.

"Who is Hemo?" the boy asked.

One of Briton's eyebrows rose into a bushy white arch. "You've never heard of Hemo before?"

"I've heard the name but...I don't remember."

"Interesting," Briton scratched at his chin. "Hemo is said to be the Lord of all. An invisible ruler who created man and Descendant and who watches over us all. According to the Faith's doctrine, he created the Descendants as vessels to heal his people. And only the worthy among us will receive the "good blood." And since the blood is controlled by those in power, their high placement must be a reward from Hemo."

"You don't believe it."

"Faith is a tricky business. Especially when it is distilled by those in power."

The boy tried to make sense of it all. Gods and the Faith and different kinds of blood. It was all so confusing, but if everyone believed it, from the Highfather who ruled to the Descendants in the castle's kitchen, it must be true. Right?

The boy was about to ask Briton more when the old man's blue eyes shot wide in sudden surprise. "Oh!" he exclaimed. "I almost forgot." He reached into a pocket of his blue robes. "I brought you a gift."

The boy's eyes darted to the pocket as Briton pulled out a long scroll and handed it to the boy. The boy carefully unrolled the stiff paper to find pictures drawn in tiny detail over the length of the scroll. It took him a moment to recognize symbols for mountains and rivers, and there were castles and villages with names beneath them.

"Now, I know you already have some basic reading ability, but I thought it best to start with—"

"It's a map," the boy said, his eyes scanning the image. There was so much to take in. And everything seemed to have a name. Not just the cities, but the mountains and forests.

"Yes, it is a map of all the known world."

"And this is us," the boy exclaimed, pointing to an area on the upper left side of the picture.

Briton leaned over the map. "How did you know that?" he asked.

The boy pointed below the square drawing of a castle. "It says House Carmine."

"And this?" Briton asked, pointing to the far right of the scroll to a circle symbol with lines crossing through its center.

"North, East, South, West," the boy said.

"Where'd you learn to read?"

"I…I don't remember." Like the rest of his memories, it was lost in the fog of his past. He could recognize written words like he was able to speak them; he thought nothing of it. But from the look on Briton's face, this must be unusual.

"What's wrong?" the boy asked.

"Few men outside noble houses are taught to read," Briton

said. "And I've never heard of a Descendant who could read." The old man's eyes looked to the window and some invisible distance as if his mind were a thousand miles away. When he came back he looked directly at the boy, his voice hushed. "Tell no one else of this. Do you understand?"

"Yes," the boy said. Like he had casual conversations with the guards stationed outside his door. "What does it mean?"

"Something I suspected since the moment I saw you," Briton said, his face alive with excitement. Or was it fear? "That you are special."

The boy looked down at the map. The large world of land and oceans and cities. "But where am I from?"

"I don't know," Briton said, his eyes falling on the map as well. "Perhaps one day we'll find out."

Briton stood up, his bones cracking from the sudden movement.

"I must go now," Briton said. "Study this map. I will bring you more books when I can."

Before Briton got to the door, the boy called out to him. "You said knowledge is the most powerful thing in the world. But what if the problem is too big. What if it's impossible to solve?"

Briton's eyes moved around the tower room, taking in the chair, the barred window, the brick ceiling. Then his gaze fell on the boy. "Every problem has a solution. Whether we are wise enough to discover it or not."

And so the boy's lessons began.

CARMINE STOOD to address the table, the formal dress cape of House Carmine hanging from him like a flag. The seven noble lords of the west stared back at him. Some faces held interest, others bitterness at having been convinced to meet by someone they still considered a boy. Even Briton couldn't say when the seven houses had last gathered in one place. But Jonathan

Carmine had done it. And all it took was a small sample of the boy's blood.

"Thank you all for coming," Carmine said. "I know many of you have traveled a great distance, so I extend my deepest gratitude on this historic day. For generations now, the western houses have been beset by—"

"Get on with it, Carmine," Lord Chamberlain called, twisting in his seat. The old lord's rock of a face stretched into a frown. Carmine could forgive the lord's impatience; the great house Chamberlain was not used to being at someone else's bidding. Still, Carmine had played this meeting out in his head and was annoyed to have his rehearsed speech interrupted. "Are the stories true?"

"I can't imagine you would have made the journey yourself, Lord Chamberlain, had the blood not proven that of the highest quality."

"Too high to be believed," Lord Fautus interjected. "Blood alchemy is a dangerous game, Carmine. Whatever trick you managed with that sample will bring the interest of the Temple. And the last thing we need is the Faith's eyes in the west."

Grumbles of agreement filled the room. The western realms had lived for generations under their own system and laws. As long as they sent their tithes to the Temple Fathers, the Faith stayed out of their affairs. Carmine knew that the presence of the boy would upset that peace. That is why he needed to bring the lords of the west together.

"It is not alchemy or magic," Carmine said. "I have found a source of the purest blood on record."

Carmine waited as the lords looked around at one another. Each had been sent a vial to test as they pleased. The glances around confirmed that each one had come to the same conclusion.

"I'll admit it was like no blood I had ever seen," Lord Gorgen said, folding his hands over his mountainous belly. Briton had ordered a special chair brought in for the enormous lord. Carmine smiled, thinking it was now worth the effort.

"But why have you summoned us all here?" asked Chamberlain. "To gloat?"

"To unite," Carmine said. "I will offer you, my neighboring lords, first opportunity to buy the pure blood. And yes, the price will be high, and House Carmine stands to grow very, very rich, but it will be worth the cost to strengthen the western realm. For if we remain loyal to each other, we can stand against any threat from the Faith. With this blood and a united front, the Highfather himself cannot stand in our way."

That was the part of his speech Carmine had practiced again and again, and judging from the silence in the room, he pulled it off perfectly.

After a prolonged silence, Lord Severen spoke. "Going against the Faith? What you speak can be considered blasphemy."

Carmine's jaw clenched as he held the thin lord's gaze. Carmine could understand how a rich lord like Gorgen could succumb to gluttony. But Severen was a bitter man whose contempt must extend to food as well. Seated beside Gorgen, Severen was practically a skeleton.

"No, Lord Severen," Carmine said. "We will keep the peace, even continue our tithe as our duty requires. But with a unified north, the Faith would think twice before seizing what is ours with unlawful acts of force."

"The Faith makes the laws, therefore what action they take *is* lawful."

"But it isn't right," Lady Rune spoke up. "How many times have the Faith bent the law to serve themselves? Taken what they wish and claiming it Hemo's will? We may rule our lands, but we are not free."

"I see no reason to make enemies of the Highfather," Lord Fautus said. "We are alive and wealthy."

"We may rule our lands but we are not free," Lady Rune

said, her voice confident. Lord Rune had died over a decade ago, and since then, Lady Rune has not even considered marriage proposals. The last thing she seemed interested in was another man in her way.

"That is why I call upon your support," Carmine said. He clapped twice. At the signal, the hall doors opened, and servants entered carrying bottles of blood. They set a single bottle on the table before each lord; the vibrant red blood shifted inside. What sat on the table was a week's worth of draining the boy. It was the entire supply of his blood.

"Join the western alliance and this blood is yours," Carmine said. He watched as each lord studied the bottles of blood before him, each of their minds filled with visions of what they could do with blood that healed any wound or sickness—that made their soldiers invincible. Carmine saw the hunger in their eyes and smiled. Greed outweighed any fears of the Faith.

"For the simple price of one thousand shrines," Carmine said.

"For a single bottle of blood?" Lord Chamberlain scoffed. "You're mad."

"As I said, you get first choice. If you refuse your share, I will simply offer it to the lord seated next to you. If there is no alliance, think of what it will be like knowing the noble house that borders your own has the power of this blood in their hands."

"And if we all refuse your price?" Severen asked, but his voice was without its bite as he eyed the bottle before him.

"Then I will offer the blood up to the lords of others realms," Carmine said. "Once they discover how powerful it is, the blood will sell. Even at double your price."

"You wouldn't," Fautus said. "Not to those eastern barbarians."

The room filled with murmurs as the lords conferred with each other. Carmine leaned back in his chair, feeling suddenly taller. His plan was working. How could one of them refuse when their neighbor would gladly take their share? Carmine suddenly saw the future of House Carmine laid out before him. A future that was brighter than any his father could have imagined. With the descendant boy, Carmine held the most valuable thing in all of Terene. And that boy was going to make Carmine a very wealthy man.

"So, my lords," Carmine said with a smile. "What'll it be?"

# 9

The table at the boy's bedside was stacked with books left by Briton. Over the past week, the boy had read a great deal on a wide variety of subjects, but nothing interested him as much as history. How could he remember math and science, and yet so much about culture and history felt new? It was like his memory loss had extended to not just his identity but particular areas of study as well. When he was awake and recovered from his blood draws enough for the room to stop spinning, the boy read through stories of the Descendants in Terene and mankind's Blood War with the Royals.

Although Briton's lessons were a welcome distraction, escape was never far from the Boy's mind. While feeling the weight of a particularly thick book, *Foundations of the Faith*, he fantasized about knocking out the Curor with the old tome. If he hid behind the door, standing up on the bedside table, the book could do some damage. But then there was the matter of getting through the guards at the door and however many guarded the tower.

This was followed by the scaling of the castle walls and outrunning an army of Carmine guards through a land he only knew from a map and the view out the tower window. With the heavy clouds, that view consisted mostly of the thick treetops of the Hidden Wood. The boy imagined roaming through the forest, far from the reaches of the Curor and Carmine guards. If he thought of anything more than his lessons with Briton, it was escaping this place.

There was a quick knock, and then the door swung open. Briton stepped in carrying two new books under his robed arm. He stopped when he saw the boy standing by the window and closed the door behind him.

"You're up," Briton said. "That's good. Your body needs the exercise. It'll deteriorate stuck in bed all day."

"I haven't much choice," the boy said, nodding his head to the tiny tower room. "Can't exactly run laps in here, even if I did feel up to it."

The boy placed the *Foundations of the Faith* back on the bedside table and sat down, resting.

"I've brought you a book on the Royals, as you requested." Briton placed the book on the bed. "It's from my own personal collection. So be careful with it."

Briton gave the boy a look as if he knew the boy contemplated using books as bludgeons. The boy dismissed this; he was being paranoid. The old man was wise but he couldn't see into his mind. The boy had spent a lot of time with the teacher over the past weeks. He'd learned a great deal and had grown to look forward to their time together. Still, the boy could not trust him. As friendly as he acted, Briton served Lord Carmine.

The boy picked up the book and examined its cover. The book was so old its title was too faded to read. He gently flipped through its first few pages, once again lost in the upside down world of the past.

Long ago, mankind once lived as slaves and servants while the world was controlled by the Royals, the powerful ruling class of Terene. Men outside the Temple lands lived lives as peasants and farmers, never able to rise above a certain class because of their inferior blood. Now, centuries later, everything had changed.

"I still don't understand," the boy said. "If the Royals were so powerful, how were they defeated by Raw Bloods?"

"Because it was Hemo's will," Briton said. "That is what you will find in the history books at least. The Royals grew prideful and unworthy. So Hemo chose Drusas and mankind who, despite their suffering, still held to their faith."

"But that's not what you believe," the boy said.

"I agree that it took brave, heroic men, to go up against the Royals."

"But how did they win?" The boy held up the book. "If it's true what the accounts say about the Royals. That they were stronger and faster than Raw Bloods. That they could be cut down in battle and rise to fight moments later."

"We had the numbers," Briton said, his blue eyes turned to gaze out the window, to the land beyond. "Mankind spread all over Terene, growing to keep up with the workload demanded by the Royals. Generations later, the workers found there were ten times as many of them as there were masters."

The boy imagined the Temple siege during the Blood War, pictured thousands of people flooding the Temple walls. He saw the farmers and servants falling at the hands of the trained Royal soldiers, yet still coming.

"The stories of the Blood War never sat right with me, either," Briton said. "But I'm starting to understand that the Royal king was conflicted on how to handle mankind. Division among the Royals may have proved their weakness." Briton sighed. "After the victory, the Faith killed every Royal they found. They were afraid to let any live."

"But some did live," the boy said.

"A few Royals were eventually found and rounded up. Imprisoned in the Temple dungeons and drained of their blood. Once people saw what the blood could do, it became the most valuable substance in the world. The demand was so high that the Royals were bred with common servants in order to create more blood vessels. The blood of the half-breeds wasn't as strong, but it still healed. Eventually, the Royal line disappeared altogether, and what we have left now, centuries later, is only the pale glimmer of the bloodline that once was."

"The Descendants of the Royals."

Briton nodded. "Until you."

"What about me?"

"Yours is the purest blood we've encountered."

The boy shook his head. "But how can that be? I don't feel any stronger. I can barely stand up without passing out."

"We don't know how the blood works, exactly. We don't even know where the Royal blood came from. There's nothing on the surface different between our two people. It's just your blood."

*Special blood.* That explained why Lord Carmine kept him locked away in this tower—why the blood draws had increased. And because of his blood, he would never get out of this place.

The boy's eyes dropped down to the second book, still cradled in Briton's arm. "What's that book?"

Briton looked down as if he had forgotten the book was there. "Oh, this. This is today's assignment."

The boy groaned. With the image of himself trapped in this tower for the rest of his days, his appetite for lessons vanished. Briton, however, continued unbothered.

"Today you have an important assignment," he said, a smile breaking out as he set the book beside the boy. "Today, you will pick a name."

"A name?"

"It's a little impractical to keep calling you 'boy' forever." Briton's eyes twinkled. "Most men have no choice in their names, but you do. Your assignment is to find one that calls to you."

"But," the boy stammered, caught off guard. "How will I know I've picked the right one?"

"A great man defines a name, not the other way around. This book and all these others are filled with stories of great men whose names will be remembered throughout history. Maybe one day, yours will be, too."

The boy flipped open the book. Listed inside were genealogies of the different houses, names upon names stretching far back in time. The boy glanced at the names—given names and house names. He didn't know exactly what he was looking for, but he knew the name couldn't be common. He also didn't want the name of a famous king or knight. He wanted the name to be his own.

He turned to the back of the book and flipped through the lineage of lesser noble houses, but few jumped out at him. And any that did, he'd soon find the person's life was riddled with either feuds or scandals, even incest. Under Briton's patient eye, the boy moved on from the house genealogy to other books on the bedside table, playing with names in his head and combinations of words. But nothing called to him.

Late at night, the boy had often sat awake wondering what his real name was. He had to have had a name at one point in his life, but it had faded into the dark pool that was his memory. As he searched through the books, the boy secretly hoped he would stumble upon it, and he would finally remember who he was. But nothing came to him.

Briton said nothing as the boy's search stretched into hours. He simply sat on the bed and opened a square medallion necklace he had hidden under his robes. Inside, he pulled out a tiny book and began reading. His brow furrowed in frustration.

A meal came for the boy, brought in by one of the guards, and the boy took a few bites as he scanned through a book on the history of the Faith. Still, Briton didn't rush him to make a decision.

When the Curor came for a blood draw, Briton stayed in the room. He watched from the corner, a sick look on his face until the Curor had finished his business and left with the bottle of blood.

While the boy was recovering and too sick to read, Briton read through Carmine's family genealogy, adding his own biographies of the stated person, most of whose names he agreed after reflection would be unfit to carry on.

The two of them spent the day together talking and reading. There was a sense of security in having Briton there. The boy almost didn't want to find a name if it meant the teacher would leave him.

The daylight was fading when the boy turned to the scroll map Briton had brought to him that first day. If the names of famous men were tainted, perhaps he would choose the name of a city or a mountain. Over the past weeks, the boy had returned to the map more than a few times in search of the area where he had been found. He held out hope that it would be a key to where he had come from. He knew it was a few days journey to the Temple in the back of that cart and over rough hilly terrain.

The boy went back to the locations he had previously searched at the very top of the map near the Ghost Mountains that marked the end of Terene. That's when he saw it. The name was spelled out along a thin crooked line. It was a river that ran like a vein from the northern mountains south through the valleys and forests. The boy pulled the map closer to him, re-reading the small word scrawled in faded ink. *The Arathan River.*

"Briton," the boy called.

The old man snorted awake in his chair, his back cracking at the sudden movement and his tiny book falling to the floor. "Hmm? What? What is it?"

"Are there books on the history of rivers?"

"History of rivers?" Briton thought for a moment. "I'm not sure there are any. What river is this concerning?"

"This one," the boy spread the map out on the bed and pointed to the top section. "Arathan."

"Hmm," Briton said as he studied the map. "Odd for such a

small river to be named on a map. There are rivers much larger without names here."

"Have you heard of it?" the boy asked.

"Not that I remember. I've certainly never ventured so far north. Few men have." Briton nodded approvingly. "Small and mysterious. It certainly fits."

The boy looked down at the map and the river that twisted through the upper region. It didn't bother him that people believed the northern lands were haunted. In fact, he liked the idea of a name that made people afraid.

"I choose Arathan," the boy said.

Briton nodded. "A strong name, indeed." He smiled as if the boy had passed some test set before him. "Though, if I might make a small suggestion."

The boy tilted his head.

"Ara for short."

"Ara. I like that."

"Then Ara it shall be." Briton reached out his hand. The boy looked at the old man and then back to the outstretched hand. As much time as they had spent together, they had never touched. The boy reached out and Briton's warm hand closed around his own.

"Nice to meet you, Ara," Briton smiled.

"Thank you." The words spilled out, surprising the boy. It surprised him even more that he had meant it. As guarded as he was, he felt a sudden gratefulness to the old man, even though nothing had changed. He was still locked away in the tower, a prisoner to Lord Carmine. But the name gave the boy a new sense of weight. Like he was a real person. Not some forgotten ghost.

JONATHAN CARMINE WAS deep at work, studying House Carmine's finances. He wrote in the most recent sale: an order from House Chamberlain that was so large it would take a week of the boy's blood to fulfill. Just a week ago, the northern lords had seemed resistant to his offer, now the orders were coming in so fast he couldn't keep up. People were finally understanding the value of House Carmine's good blood.

Carmine smiled as he added up this month's profits. Accounting was much more pleasant with bigger numbers.

There was a quick knock and a creek as the study door opened further.

"Sir," the servant's voice called.

Carmine held up a finger as he wrote down the final tally. His father had never come close to numbers like this. A year of this and Carmine would be the richest lord in all of Terene.

Carmine looked up from the ledger, annoyed that the moment had been interrupted. "Yes?"

"We have company coming up the road," the servant said.

"More buyers. Word travels fast." Carmine grinned, imagining the eastern lords panicking to get a taste of the good blood. Carmine was fair; he wouldn't deny lords because of petty politics. *If* the price was right. "Who is it?"

"It's, um, a rather large caravan."

Carmine put his pen down. Something in the servant's voice. Nervousness. Fear.

Carmine moved to the window.

"They sent no word they were coming," the servant said.

The air caught in Carmine's throat as he saw the flags and banners of white. The caravan that marched up the road toward his gates would not fit within his castle walls, even if the entire courtyard were cleared. Carmine stared wide-eyed at the large ornate carriages rolling up the road surrounded on all sides by an army of Temple guards.

The Faith had come to Castle Carmine.

"Send for Briton," Carmine said, turning back to the servant. "And hide the boy!"

# 10

---

*"We have been given a great gift and what have we done with it? Built monuments to ourselves."*

---

The carriage doors opened and Aeilus Haemon, Highfather of the Faith, stepped out onto the dirt of the courtyard as if it was unworthy of his feet. Briton had seen much of the world in his travels as advisor to House Carmine and had been inside the Faith's Temple on numerous occasions. Only once on those visits had he seen the Highfather in person. But now here he was, the most powerful man in all of Terene, with his perfect white robes with gold trim and the red miter atop his head. Suddenly, Castle Carmine seemed so very small.

Two other Fathers stepped onto the courtyard from their carriages, in similar white robes of the Faith, but the man who caught Briton's eye was the Highfather's personal guard—Bale, the Blood Knight. Standing a full head above any of the Fathers, the knight's black eyes took in Castle Carmine and its people like a hawk scanning a field for mice.

To Briton's right, Jonathan Carmine took a breath and stepped forward to greet the Highfather.

"Highfather Haemon," Carmine said with a bow. "What an unexpected surprise. Had we known of your coming, we would have organized a formal welcoming party."

The Highfather looked Carmine over and nodded slowly.

"It has been too long since I visited our western lands. I trust we have not caught you at an inopportune time."

"Not at all, we are honored by your visit. You are welcome to stay as long as you wish, of course."

"That is very accommodating of you, Lord Carmine. But I do not wish to burden you. I know House Carmine has had difficulties since your father's passing."

Carmine's face showed no reaction to the Highfather's words. Briton was proud of Jonathan. The Faith's sudden appearance had obviously been intended to shock, but the young lord was handling this situation with the dignity befitting his title.

"Perhaps some wine is in order, my Lord," Briton suggested.

"That would be wonderful," the Highfather said, a slight smile creasing his wrinkled face. "The west has a great reputation for the potency of their blood wine."

"Right this way." Carmine led the way to the castle. The Highfather was followed by two Fathers and four Temple guards. Briton fell in behind the Fathers, staying the appropriate distance away for an advisor—far enough to not be intrusive to the conversation, but within earshot if a question arose. This would be a true test for Carmine and the game he had begun to orchestrate. The Highfather of the Faith did not make courtesy visits. Which meant that someone had told him about the blood; the Faith knew about the boy. Briton did not know how this would play out. It was time to trust Jonathan and follow his lead.

Briton stopped at the castle doors and looked back at the crowd of Temple guards in the courtyard.

"I don't like this," whispered Nathaniel, the head of

Carmine's guard, as he approached Briton and shared the view of Temple guards. "They come with an army of white shirts, and we open our gates to them."

"It's only a show of force," Briton said. "The Faith have never moved against a noble lord without provocation."

"There's always a first time."

"Let's hope their etiquette outweighs their greed. Still, see that your men stay with Carmine at all times."

Nathaniel nodded and headed into the castle after the procession. Nathaniel was a good soldier, and his worry was not unwarranted. Guarding a noble lord was difficult, especially one as stubborn-headed as Jonathan Carmine. One whose own parents had been assassinated.

Memories of that awful day flooded back to Briton, fresh as ever. The guards returning from the woods with James' and Maddie's bodies slung over their horses. The long climb to young Jonathan's room to tell him the news. A boy forced to be a lord, long before he was ready.

Briton was brought back to the present by a black shape crossing the courtyard like a shadow moving from the caravans. The Blood Knight marched in long determined strides toward the Descendants' quarters.

Carmine stepped through the archway into the rooftop gardens. For so long this had been his sanctuary, his place of peace. But now it took on a different feel. As if vipers had slithered into the bushes.

"I'd heard stories about House Carmine's amazing garden, but I am still impressed," the Highfather said as the company stepped into the gardens. "This must take a great deal of your time."

"Thank you," Carmine said, unsure if it was meant as a compliment. "It was first started by my mother."

"Yes, a lovely woman," the Highfather said. "It's only natural that she would seek to surround herself with more beauty."

"You knew my mother?" Carmine asked in surprise. His parents were not fervent followers of the Faith and seldom traveled to the Temple. The only time he could remember his parents mentioning the Highfather was when complaining about tithes.

"Both your parents, on numerous occasions. I regret I have not traveled west as much as I once did; age has its limits, I'm afraid. But House Carmine has long been a strong leader in the west and loyal to the Faith. If not for the support of our noble lords, the Faith would be unable to do the good work we do in Terene. And I would hate to see what became of a world without the Faith's guiding hand."

"Hemo forbid," a Father muttered from behind.

"We try to do our part, of course," Carmine said, moving through the garden. Flowers stretched their petals wide, trying to lap up what sunlight peeked through the stone-gray sky.

"These are troubling times, Lord Carmine," the other Father said, jumping into the conversation. "The bloodline has been dwindling for generations, we have inherited the weakest crop, and the people of Terene are afraid. It is imperative that whatever blessings great Hemo grants us be shared by the Faith."

Carmine eyed the Father. A younger man than most of the Fathers but he still carried the somber expression of all Fathers, as if he was weighed down by higher knowledge. Carmine never understood why someone would pursue a life of Fatherhood. But then again, not everyone is born a noble lord's son.

"Certainly, whatever blessings come from Hemo would be granted to the worthiest of us, Father. In which case, the Faith has no need to fear."

The young Father's face flushed red. "It is not up to outsiders to interpret Hemo's will."

"Outsiders? I believe House Carmine contributes greatly to

the Faith and has so for generations. Surely such devotion has not been misplaced."

"We all give in what way we can," said the other Father, tilting his large head into a slight bow. Unlike his companion, his face was solemn. Devoid of emotion. "Sharing Hemo's blessings is one of our highest callings."

"Is it sharing if it only goes one way?" Carmine glanced back to Briton. A look of concern hung on his old teacher's face. Briton would surely advise restraint when dealing with the Faith, but Carmine would not put up with being pushed around—not here in his own castle. *If they wanted to tax me and keep my House down to pay for their Temple and fancy robes, I'll have them acknowledge it openly.*

The younger Father didn't hide his scowl. His voice rose an octave as he stammered. "Why…you…you can't speak to us like that!"

The Highfather stopped and raised a hand, cutting the Father off. "Lord Carmine and I shall talk alone for a moment. I trust this castle offers even more wonderful sights that would make the Fathers glad for the visit?"

Carmine nodded to Briton, and the advisor snapped back, clapping his hands together. "Our library! It is quite lovely, I'm sure learned men such as yourselves will appreciate our many collections."

The Fathers grumbled as Briton escorted them out the garden's archway and back into the castle. A handful of guards accompanied them, but two stayed behind along with two of Carmine's own. Nathaniel watched the two Temple guards uneasily, sizing up weapons and armor.

"Shall we?" the Highfather asked, motioning forward once the company had gone.

"As you wish, Father," Carmine said, and the two of them walked deeper into the garden after signaling their guards to stay behind.

"Father," the Highfather repeated the word. "It is an old title that dates back to the foundation of the Faith over twelve hundred years ago. The first leaders of the Faith were not Fathers as we know them, nor were they Curors who had a studied knowledge of the blood. Back then the responsibility for the communities fell on a few leaders to do what was right for their people—their children."

The Highfather stopped at the koboto tree. Carmine almost shouted when Haemon reached up and touched the rare fruit that after so many years, had almost ripened. The Highfather caressed the fruit with his bony fingers.

"A father will do anything to see that his children do not suffer. Even if it calls for a sacrifice."

With a harsh pull, he ripped the fruit from the tree, taking a portion of the branch with it. He studied the fruit in his hands.

Carmine gritted his teeth. "As long as the sacrifices are made by others."

The Highfather looked at him, a small smile crossing his face.

"We all have our place, Carmine. Let us not reach beyond our grasp. For we may come up empty."

With that, the Highfather casually tossed the koboto fruit over the edge of the castle wall.

"On what grounds do you come here and threaten me?" Carmine snapped. "House Carmine pays its tithe each season, though it cripples our growth. We support the Faith as the law calls for."

The HighFather's face turned dark and withered, causing Carmine to take a step back. "Nothing goes on in Terene that I don't hear about," the Highfather said. "You think you're safe here behind your little stone walls? This world belongs to Hemo and everything in it."

Carmine held his breath but did not turn away from the darkness that passed over the HighFather's face. The viper had revealed its fangs, and they were sharper than Carmine could have imagined.

"We'll see," Carmine said, holding the Highfather's gaze. This was Carmine Castle after all; he wasn't going to let anyone come in and threaten him, no matter how powerful they thought they were.

"Yes," the Highfather said, his wrinkled face reshaping into a grin that was no less threatening. "You will."

The Highfather swept back through the garden, his white robes flowing in the wind. He disappeared through the arched doorway, and his Temple guards followed behind.

Carmine breathed in relief, steadying himself on the ivy wrapped wall. Briton would not approve of how he handled this meeting. Still, it felt good to stand up to the Highfather. He just hoped he had the power to back up his words. He turned and looked out over the large company of horses and soldiers that filled his courtyard. As large as it was, it was nothing compared to the full force of the Faith. *Will the western nobles stand with me? Will it be enough?*

Carmine leaned over the stone wall. The koboto fruit lay far below. A faint red smudge, already covered with dirt.


BALE DIDN'T UNDERSTAND why Haemon insisted on playing games. The Highfather knew of the Descendant boy Carmine had in his possession, and with the army of Temple guards at his command, Haemon could sack this castle and take the boy at any time. Bale could do it himself with a few of his own men, and the Highfather wouldn't even have to leave the Temple. But politics interfered, as they always did when those that ruled preferred the illusion of order.

Bale looked around the stinking room of the Descendants' quarters. Unlike the Temple where the Descendants were kept locked away in dungeons, Carmine's Descendants moved about the grounds, performing the menial tasks of servants. He treated them as if they were people. This was another reason the soft lord would fall.

Before he had examined the barracks, Bale knew the boy was not there. He'd found no resistance to his trespasses. Even the foolish Carmines wouldn't leave a possession as important as this boy unguarded.

Bale left the empty room and continued down the castle hallway. He pushed through a doorway and stepped back outside into the castle courtyard. The eyes of the locals fell on the tall knight in his black armor and then quickly shifted elsewhere. A stablehand coming Bale's way gasped and then changed his path, hurrying to the other side of the road. Bale had grown accustomed to the fear in the public's eyes as stories of Bale the Blood Knight spread throughout Terene. He didn't discourage it. It made his job easier.

Bale looked up along the castle walls, studying the building and its defenses. Guards walked the ramparts and peered out of the parapets upon the army of Temple guards below. On the four corners of the castle rose towers. The boy was in one of those. It was the right choice. Bale crossed the courtyard to the western tower, the farthest from where Carmine had escorted the Fathers.

Bale couldn't help wondering at the rumors of this Descendant boy. Though the information had come from a trustworthy source, it still seemed unbelievable; a Descendant with blood like the Royals of old. As skeptical as Bale was of this, a part of him hoped it was true. It could finally prove an answer to the sickness poisoning his heart.

At the front door to the tower stood four Carmine guards. A large number for an innocuous tower. The guards shifted uneasily and exchanged troubled glances as Bale approached.

He had guessed right.

It wasn't until Bale was right upon the men that one guard stepped forward, putting himself between Bale and the tower door.

"Can…can we help you?" the front guard asked.

"You can step out of my way," Bale said.

"I'm sorry, sir. This part of the castle is off limits."

"Nothing in Terene is off limits to the Highfather's personal guard," Bale snapped.

"We have our orders," another guard added.

"And my orders are to see to the Highfather's safety, along with the other Fathers of the Faith. Now, you are clearly unfamiliar with the Fathers' visit and routines so I will excuse the confusion." Bale moved forward, and the guard put a hand to Bale's chest.

That was a mistake.

Bale seized the hand and twisted it away until it snapped. The guard fell back with a shriek, clutching his broken wrist. The other guards reached for their swords but did not draw, unsure how to proceed.

"The next one that touches me loses more than his hand," Bale said.

They were in a standoff. Bale wasn't supposed to capture the boy, only discover his location. His hand moved to his own broadsword. But, as long as he was here…

"Oh look, a member of the Temple guard," a voice called from behind. Bale turned to see an old man with blue-gray robes approaching. The fool was smiling.

"You must be searching for the Fathers," the man continued. "They're still talking business, I'm afraid. Politics can be so tiresome if you ask me. Come along, I will take you to them."

"I am where I need to be," Bale said.

"Oh, talking shop are we?" the old man looked to Carmine's guards. If he read the distress on their faces, he didn't show it. "I always thought the Temple guards wore white armor. Yet, here you are draped in black. That must get hot."

"Who are you?" Bale asked through gritted teeth, his hand still on his sword.

"My name is Briton Moonglass, chief advisor to Lord Carmine. I pray our men here are treating you with the utmost courtesy on your visit." Briton shook his head at the guards. "I would hate to have to report otherwise to Lord Carmine and the Highfather."

Before Bale could react there was a small trumpet sound from across the courtyard. Time to leave already? The talks with Carmine must not have gone well. Good. That meant the game of politics was over.

Bale stepped away from the door. He had all the information he needed. There was no need to start a fight before the Highfather ordered it. Bale lifted his hand off his sword and sneered at the old man. "Briton Moonglass. I won't forget your...hospitality."

"My duty and honor," Briton said with a bow. "Now shall I escort you back to—?"

"I can find my way," Bale said and fixed the old man with a final icy stare before staggering off. It took great self-restraint not to slice the old man in half for his interference and condescending tone. But Bale took comfort knowing the time would soon come when this upstart house would crumble. And when it did, Bale would see to Carmine's advisor—personally.

## 11

—————

The Moon Tavern was conveniently located a mile from Castle Carmine. It was an old building whose doors and windows never went a full year without needing replacement from a drunken brawl. Just off the main road, it presented stables and lodging for travelers with business at Castle Carmine. It was also a place of escape for those who worked at the castle. Whatever their varying purposes, patrons were united in one thing, a loyalty to generous servings of ale.

One such mugful slid across the bar into Geyer's hand, foam splashing over the brim.

"Never seen you move so fast," Clover, the barman, laughed. His jovial face was covered in brown freckles as if he'd leaned over a wagon wheel spinning in mud.

"I save my energy for when it's really needed," Geyer said. He downed half the mug and belched. Then he looked around the crowded room. The Moon Tavern was busy on most nights —he should know since it was a nightly stop for him after his guard shift ended—but tonight's crowd was filled with unfamiliar faces. Geyer recognized the uniforms of a few men in the corner as belonging to House Rune. Another table wore the purple sigil of House Gorgen. There were still more in plain clothes that Geyer did not recognize. Something was going on at Castle Carmine. Something big enough to bring the Faith.

Geyer didn't dwell on it long, as there was still more ale that needed drinking. He was tired from his long day at Castle Carmine; it was amazing how boredom could be so exhausting. These days his body was stiffer after a day of standing in place than it ever was from his days of riding or competing in tournaments.

Two men beside Geyer grew louder with each glass of ale. Their conversation was now right in Geyer's ear.

"You didn't!" the younger man exclaimed, his voice surprisingly high for his size.

"That's right, I saw the Highfather himself," said an older man with a beard so thick it nearly reached his eyes. "He walked right by me when I was feeding Carmine's horses."

"The Highfather of the Faith walked through the stables?"

"No, you halfwit! I saw him out the window. It was him alright—pointy hat and all."

"I'm surprised the Temple guards didn't cut your eyes out just for looking on the Highfather," the younger man shook his head.

"Baaa. Ain't no sense in that. Even for Temple guards."

"Since when do white-tins make sense?"

"Ha!" the bearded man laughed hard, striking Geyer's elbow in the process. Geyer gripped his mug to keep it from spilling. "Careful with the insults, boy. You know they got eyes and ears everywhere."

Geyer looked around the tavern again. The drunk man was right; there were plenty of strangers still around tonight. It wasn't farfetched to believe that the Faith had left a few men behind.

"Why did the Highfather come all the way out to Castle Carmine in the first place?" the young man asked in a lower voice.

"On account of the magic boy."

"What do you mean magic boy?"

"I heard it from a gal in the kitchen. Carmine's got some special Descendant boy whose blood can heal anything. Just yesterday a noble begged Carmine on behalf of his blind grandfather. A few drops of magic blood in his eyes, the old man could see again!"

"That's impossible," the young man's voice cracked and he shook his head.

"I'm telling you the truth. That's why everyone's coming to Castle Carmine when no one cared two licks about us a week ago, especially not the Highfather of the Faith."

"Magic blood…" the younger whispered in amazement, his glazed eyes staring up at the ceiling.

Geyer was familiar with tavern rumors; drunk men were prone to exaggerate stories to top the story before it, so a tale—no matter how astonishing in truth—left the tavern doors ten feet taller. But something different was in the air tonight. It had been different around the castle for the past few weeks and, even posted away from the action, Geyer had sensed it. But whatever was happening, Geyer would be the last to know.

Geyer's eyes fixed on a table in the corner of the tavern where a man sat by the window, alone. The man had slick dark hair and a scar across the side of his face that could only be made by a blade. A worn black travel cloak covered what Geyer was sure were hidden weapons. He had been around enough bars in his time to recognize a cutthroat when he saw one. The man ignored the tavern festivities. No drink at his table, eyes fixed on the window—he was here on business.

"You there," a hand tugged at Geyer's shoulder. He turned to the bearded man beside him breathing in his face. "You're a castle guard, aren't you?" The man looked Geyer over skeptically. He had removed his armor but still wore the gray and red shirt. Geyer's scraggly beard was in violation of guard standards, but Geyer didn't care about such standards. It was ignored because the powers that be didn't care about Geyer. Not anymore.

"If it gets me a drink, I'll be Lord Carmine himself," Geyer said.

"Are the rumors true?" the younger man asked, leaning forward. "About this Descendant boy?"

"You shouldn't believe everything you hear in a tavern. You'll end up trading your horse for a vial of *magic blood*."

"See, I told you," the young man said to his companion. "You're playing with me."

"You two deny it all you want," the bearded man said. "But don't be surprised if things start changing around here. Mark my words, House Carmine is on the rise."

The man sipped his drink. Geyer did the same, happy the two had stopped barking in his ear.

Geyer caught movement from the corner of his eye. He turned in time to see Scarred Face slip out the back door. That's when it came. The itchy feeling in his gut—the one all these years of drinking was supposed to have gotten rid of. *It's not your job*, he told himself as he turned back to the bar and picked up his mug. *You're just a lowly guard now. And a crippled one at that.*

*It's not your job.*

After a few more swigs, the feeling in his gut was replaced by the one in his bladder. Geyer slammed the mug on the bar. "This better not be empty when I get back," he grumbled to Clover.

"Going to the privy to make more room?" the barman asked.

"When it comes to ale, I always have room. Even for this piss you sell."

"I could sell piss, and you'd still be back every night for more."

"But I wouldn't be nearly as pleasant to be around."

Geyer pushed away from the bar, his good right leg taking most of his weight. He limped across the busy tavern to the back door.

The night was dark with the light of the moon choked behind heavy clouds. Torches along the ramparts of Castle Carmine glowed in the distance. Even from this far away vantage, it looked as magnificent as the night Geyer first saw it. A young knight riding into town, in search of glory. What a fool he'd been.

The privy was a shed not thirty paces behind the Moon Tavern. Geyer walked the other way, into the cover of trees. He liked pissing in the open air. It brought back memories of traveling the open road, camping beneath the stars. A life that felt more and more like a stranger's.

Geyer was about to relieve himself when he heard voices ahead in the trees. His fingers moved from his belt to the handle of his sword, and he stood still as the night.

The faint voices came from deeper in the darkness of trees. The itching in his gut returned. Ignoring his better judgment, Geyer crept toward the low voices.

Forest ground made silent movements difficult, as every dry leaf or twig sent alarm bells to the trained ear. But Geyer took his time and even with his bad leg, moved to within earshot of the voices. He leaned against the cover of a thick tree and peered into the darkness until his eyes adjusted enough to spot the two figures.

He'd have recognized the cutthroat from his crooked figure, even if the scar wasn't plain on his face. The man stood hunched as if guarding great secrets under his cloak. His head darted around like a raven on a corpse. Geyer couldn't make out the second man because his back was to Geyer. The man was tall and like his companion, wore all black. But unlike Scarred Face, this man stood still as the trees.

Geyer closed his eyes and focused his ear. He could only make out fragments of their hushed conversation.

"…Three hundred shrines."

"Better not fail…most displeased."

"I can do my job…ready when I…the castle wall."

"The wall…then on your own…I trust that you can…one boy."

"It won't be a problem."

Then there was the jingle of a coin purse handed over. Geyer strained his ears but their words still escaped him, and he dared not move closer.

"…Other half…night when it is finished and you hand him over. If you fail, I'll come for you and your men myself."

"I don't need your threats," the voice Geyer took to be Scarred Face's grew loud and clear.

"They are promises," the other man said, his voice also rising. "If anyone hears about this, if you or your men brag about this job, even months after it's done…"

"I wouldn't still be in this profession if I blabbed about every job I took."

"Just remember what's at stake."

Another jingle of the coin purse. "I'll remember."

Then footsteps—coming toward Geyer. Geyer leaned back against the tree as if trying to press himself inside the trunk. Leaves cracked under approaching steps. The man would be upon him in seconds and even in this darkness, he couldn't miss what was right in front of him. Geyer grabbed the handle of his sword and felt the wave of sickness that always came before a fight. Geyer cursed himself and his curiosity as his heart thumped in his chest. He knew even if he got the cutthroat by surprise, the tall man would be on him in a second.

*Dying for coming out to take a piss. And with a full mug of ale waiting for you back in the bar!*

The man's black boots came around the tree, and Geyer inched his sword out of its scabbard.

"Wait," the tall man called.

The black boots stopped. Geyer watched them unblinking, holding his breath. His sword partly drawn. The cutthroat just behind the tree. Close enough to smell.

"Don't go back to the tavern. Too many eyes there and you cutthroats and your black cloaks are much too obvious."

"You'd like me to wear prissy armor instead?" Scarred Face said.

126

"Tomorrow I would. And get your hair cut while you're at it."

The boots turned back, crossing in the other direction. Geyer still did not breathe.

"I know the plan, I don't need any more of your advice. If you could still do this type of work yourself, you wouldn't have had to call me."

With that, Scarred Face walked the other way. Relief flooded through Geyer as the sounds of two sets of feet trailed off in different directions.

After the sounds had faded completely, Geyer pushed his sword into its scabbard and slid down the trunk of the tree to the forest floor. He swallowed the night air in full deep breaths until his heart settled. He rubbed his bad leg, but it was only out of habit. His body was still too numb from fear to feel any pain.

What had he been thinking? He was just an old castle guard now, past his prime. He had no business getting caught up in this kind of trouble. He had no business following his old instincts. Hadn't he seen enough in his lifetime to know the world had no room for fools playing hero?

*Fates*, when would he learn?

Geyer remained on the ground for a while, looking up at the starless night. When he finally got up and stretched out his stiff leg, he walked right past the Moon Tavern and the drink Clover had waiting for him.

For the first time in a long time, Geyer wasn't thirsty.

## 12

---

Geyer strained to keep up with the captain of the guards as he marched the Castle ramparts. Guards stood at attention as they passed.

"So let me get this straight," Nathaniel said. "You were out drinking last night and while stumbling through the woods, you ran into some men you can't identify who were plotting something but you don't know what. Do I have that right?"

Geyer sighed. "I couldn't understand exactly what they were saying, but they were plotting something against the castle, I'm sure of it."

"And you couldn't understand because you were drunk?"

"No, because they were whispering."

"Oh, so you hadn't been drinking?"

"No, I was drunk. But that doesn't mean I can't identify a plot when I hear one."

Nathaniel stopped and waved nearby guards at ease. He then aimed his hard face at Geyer. Nathaniel had been at Castle Carmine a long time, he was one of the few who knew Geyer from before. Nathaniel was the reason Geyer still had a position here, small as it was.

"Listen, Geyer. You drink too much, your dress and manner

cry out insubordination, and I highly doubt you currently meet the minimum physical requirements of a castle guard—even without your leg. Now, I made a promise that you'd always have a place at Castle Carmine, but that doesn't mean I have to put up with your lack of discipline and crazy drunken visions. You are assigned to guarding the northern tower for the rest of the week."

"Someone was threatening to attack Carmine. You can't ignore that."

"*Lord* Carmine's safety is always our concern. What would you have us do that we aren't already doing? Build the walls higher? He is accompanied by guards at all times—guards that are much more fit and ready to serve than some…" Nathaniel caught himself.

"Some washed up drunk."

Nathaniel frowned, his voice dropping to a whisper. "I know you still blame yourself for James's death. But you weren't the only one with him. You did everything you could…"

Geyer shook his head, cutting Nathaniel off. He didn't need some hollow reassurance. He knew better than anyone how he'd failed. "Forget it. It's probably nothing. I know Lord Carmine is in good hands."

Geyer read the concern in the younger man's eyes. Was he worried about Geyer or was he worried he could end up as old and broken himself one day?

"My offer still stands, Geyer. If you ever want to clean up your act. We could use a good swordsman to train my men. Most haven't ever seen any real battle. They could learn a lot from you."

Geyer lowered his head and spun the wheel of his pommel. "That part of me is gone, Nathaniel. There's no getting it back." He stood up straight, chest out, in his best show of attention. He raised a flat hand to his brow in salute. "Just keep your eyes open, will ya?"

Nathaniel returned the gesture. "Always."

The captain of the guards moved down the castle wall, inspecting his men and their stations. Nathaniel had an attention to detail that was necessary for a leader. It was something Geyer never had. Perhaps if he had been more attentive, things would have worked out differently.

Geyer headed back along the castle ramparts, his bad leg shuffling behind. Guards snickered and jeered as he passed, but he continued on toward the northern tower. As much as he despised working at the Castle, there was nowhere else for him to go. Traveling town to town in search of adventures was a young man's game. And if Geyer still possessed anything from his younger days—it certainly wasn't his youth.

THE HIDDEN SUN hung low over the fields when Briton caught up with Carmine. He was outside the castle walls watching the field hands finish their day's work. With the orange haze lighting his face, the young lord looked more than his twenty-six years of age.

"Master Briton," Carmine said. "I hadn't seen you today. I'd thought you were ill."

"I apologize," Briton said, crossing the hard soil to Carmine's side. "I was caught up with—"

"Entertaining our young guest. I know."

Briton ignored Carmine's tone. If the lord could understand what the boy meant, the answers they could discover... "He's like no Descendant I've ever seen. Not just his blood, he's—"

"They are amazing creatures, aren't they?" Carmine interrupted without taking his eyes off the field. Briton followed his gaze to where the workers toiled. Nearest to them were the field Descendants. Low bloods digging up the ground with picks and shovels as guards stood over them. "We run their bodies ragged all day, and, in the morning, they wake up good as new."

"I don't think it's that simple, my Lord," Briton said. "The

Descendants are more like us than most like to believe. Pain takes its toll, only slower."

A crunch rang through the air as a nearby Descendant swung a pickaxe, breaking up the rocky terrain. The man was old but strong, his skin darkened by years of work for House Carmine. Though his body moved, his eyes were as vacant as those of a horse ridden well beyond its years.

"When I was a boy, I had a maid named Pearl. A silly name for a Descendant. Pearl used to draw my bath…sweep my room. She showed me a silent kindness and affection my mother never had." Carmine's eyes drifted to the horizon and the setting sun. "One day, when I was seven years old, my father took me to the courtyard just outside the Descendants' barracks. His men had caught a runaway in the Hidden Wood. I almost didn't recognize her when I saw her; her clothes were torn and her hair was down in wild tangles. She was on her knees, sobbing—not begging, just sobbing like she knew there was no changing what was to come. My father made me watch as the guards beat Pearl with broom handles."

Briton did not remember this moment. Though beating of escaped Descendants was common, even at Castle Carmine, for James Carmine to force his seven-year-old son to watch…*Where had I been that day?*

"I still remember the sound of her bones snapping," Carmine continued. "I thought they killed her. She was just a lump of dirt and blood when the guards dragged her away. I hated my father in that moment. I cried for a long time, unable to get the image of the beating out of my mind. I cried again that night when a new woman came to fill my bath." Carmine kicked the dirt in front of him and scoffed. "Then, a few days later, I saw Pearl again, sweeping the hallway outside my room as if nothing had happened."

Carmine turned to Briton. "That's when I realized what my father was showing me. As much as they look like us, the Descendants aren't people."

"I beg your pardon, my Lord, but that isn't true."

"Yes, it is Briton. You just don't want to see it. While your sympathy is an admirable trait, it is not good for business. Think of what any other noble lord would do if he had this boy. What the Highfather would do."

"I know what they'd do," Briton shuddered. In other castles, Descendants were kept chained in dungeons, fed just enough to keep them pumping blood. Never seeing the light of day. "That compassion is what separates House Carmine from the others. This is a place of cooperation, not slavery."

"Don't be naive, Briton. We give them better clothes and food than most and feel good about ourselves—but that doesn't change what it is. And if House Carmine is going to survive the coming time, we first need to accept the truth."

The bell rang from the castle tower signaling the end of the day. The Descendants in the field stopped their work, gathered their tools and trudged back to the castle. Their weary heads stayed low to the ground. They kept their distance from Carmine and Briton.

"Your time with the boy is over," Carmine said. "Tomorrow he will be moved to the Curor's lab, permanently. Typher will take as much blood as he can for as long as he can."

"Jonathan, you can't!" Briton exclaimed. "He's just a boy. He can't survive that kind of life!"

"He'll survive. That's what they do." Carmine sighed and looked down at his advisor. "Remember your role, Briton. It's time you put the needs of House Carmine above that of a single Descendant."

With that, Carmine crossed back toward the castle gate, his guards following behind.

Briton stood alone, looking over the quiet fields that stretched out from the castle to the Hidden Wood. He thought of young Jonathan as a boy, disobeying Briton's commands and running through the fields toward the woods. A noble lord with the finest food and comforts imaginable and all he wanted was to run free.

As the light disappeared behind the cloudy horizon, Briton could not shake Carmine's words because of the truth that lay within. A truth that despite all his teaching and philosophical debates, he'd never admitted to himself.

He'd done nothing. He preached compassion for the Descendants but still lived a life that relied on their suffering. These were the actions of a hypocrite. This was the life of a coward.

Briton lowered his head thinking about the road ahead—the fight Jonathan had picked with the Highfather and what it would mean for the future of House Carmine. Win or lose, it would bring out the worst in all of them.

As he walked back to the massive stone castle, Briton Moonglass found his concern drifting away from Jonathan Carmine, to the fate of another boy.

GEYER HAD GONE NEARLY a full twenty hours without a drink and it was taking its toll. His head ached with the unfamiliar sensation of prolonged sobriety. The darkening sky signaled he was nearing the end of his shift. Down below, vendors packed up for the day; the sounds of carts and horses echoed up to where Geyer sat, slumped against the tower's dirty bricks.

*So this is it. This is what I'm worth to Castle Carmine.* Geyer had to chuckle. Here he was, marooned on a far tower with nothing to guard but an abandoned bird's nest.

Geyer sighed and looked at the sword in his lap. He had removed it since it was uncomfortable to sit with a four-foot piece of metal strapped to your waist. The sword lay sleeping in its leather sheath. And how many years had it been since Geyer saw any more than the hilt? He'd heard it said that the best sword a knight could have is an unused one. The saying was meant to extol diplomacy, however, not laziness. Though the sword had been at Geyer's side for over twenty years, he'd never given it a name. He had always thought it silly when knights named their swords.

*Deathbringer* and *Honorblade*—it seemed so childish. A sword was a tool, no more. Blacksmiths didn't name their hammers, did they? Still, he did have some affection for the weapon that had saved his life on more than a few occasions.

Geyer's mind wandered down the shadowy alleys of the past as he spun the circular pommel at the end of the handle that marked the weapon's only adornment. His pommel was shaped into a wheel with six spokes. It was meant to remind Geyer of the wheel of one's shifting fortunes—though it seems like his own had been permanently stuck at the bottom.

With a grunt of pain, Geyer pulled himself to his feet and stretched his stiff leg. He leaned on the tower's edge and looked out on the night. Lanterns from the Moon Tavern glowed in the distance, the faint sound of lively music that carried on the wind made Geyer smile. Perhaps he would visit tonight after all. Just for the music, of course. Maybe a drink or two as long as he was there. There was no need to be rude.

Geyer was about to quit a little early when he saw movement below. A guard was crossing Lord Carmine's garden toward the western tower. Geyer hadn't seen anyone in the garden all day, except for Semus watering the plants. A single guard strolling through the lord's prized garden looked out of place.

Geyer squinted to get a better look. There was something else. Something odd about the guard's gait. The man didn't walk with the monotonous rhythm and straight-lined efficiency of a Carmine guard but seemed to slink through the night.

Geyer's stomach began to tingle.

Just before the guard disappeared into the arched doorway leading to the western tower, he glanced back over his shoulder. Though it was a good distance away, and Geyer's eyesight not being what it once was, he could have sworn he saw, running the length of the man's face, the line of a scar.

## 13

Night had fallen, but Ara lay awake, staring at the ceiling. He slept in bursts following the Curor's visits. Food and sleep restored him faster, so he slept and ate as often as he could to be alert for Briton's lessons. He had learned a great deal from his teacher over the past weeks, but he was still no closer to finding an answer to his most immediate problem. Ara turned his head to the barred window as he let himself drift off, closing his eyes to his reality.

Footsteps ascended the stairs outside. Ara's stomach tightened. The Curor was back already? It had been less than two hours since the last blood draw and he was already coming back for more?

But instead of the Curor's quick entry, there were voices. The guards spoke to someone. Were they arguing?

Steel clashed outside. Quick and harsh coupled with unnatural groans and the thud of bodies hitting the floor.

Ara shot up in bed. His eyes held on the opening door.

The man standing in the doorway was not the red-robed Curor. He wore the armor and red bird sigil of House Carmine, but his face was out of place. A scar ran along the man's cheek and over dark hungry eyes. Blood dripped from the wet dagger in his hand. The bodies of two guards lay at his feet.

"Time to go, boy," the man said, raising the blade.

"Who are you?" Ara cried. "What do you want?"

"You're coming with me." The man stepped into the room, returning his dagger to his belt. He grabbed Ara's arm and yanked him out of bed. Ara's head spun, and he tried to steady himself as he was dragged toward the door. He was still weak from the blood draw, resisting was out of the question.

"Quickly now," the man said. "I'd hate to spill that precious blood of yours."

"Wait, I don't understand."

The man dragged Ara out of his room and over the bodies of two guards. Blood pooled around their throats. *What do I do?* Ara's mind raced for an answer as they moved down the spiral staircase. Still in his sleeping garments, Ara's bare feet flinched at the chilly touch of the stone steps. His captor pushed him to hurry and Ara lost his balance and almost toppled down the stairs.

When they reached the fourth-floor level, the man pushed Ara away from the stairs down a hallway. Moonlight seeped in as the hallway opened to the rooftop garden. Ara's teeth chattered, the cold night air attacking his thinly covered body.

"Where are you taking me?" Ara demanded, digging his heels into the ground. "I'm not going another step until you tell me—"

The man shoved Ara forward, sending his frail body crashing onto the stone steps of the garden floor. Cold pain shot through the bones of his elbow from the impact. Ara felt to see if his arm was broken.

The man's scarred face twisted with anger as he stormed toward Ara. "Get up or I'll throw you off the roof and pick up the pieces later."

"You're in an awful hurry."

The man spun around toward the direction of the voice. A

Carmine guard stood in the garden's arched entrance. The guard looked familiar. Where had Ara seen him before? Then he remembered the disheveled guard he'd found sleeping in the hallway on his first day delivering meals. But now the man stood tall, hand on the hilt of his sword, eyeing the scarred face man.

"You know, I don't recognize you," the guard said, walking from the archway. "And I know and hate most of Carmine's guards."

The scarred face man drew his dagger and pointed it down at Ara. "Stand back or I'll kill the boy."

The blade hovered over Ara, still red from the blood of the guards he'd killed. The scraggly guard didn't flinch. "He's not worth anything dead." He straightened his helmet, pushing back strands of shaggy blond-gray hair. "I mean even you aren't stupid enough to come all this way just to kill him."

The clomping of boots echoed from the hallway behind the guard. He grinned. "Looks like the cavalry has arrived."

From the arched doorway appeared not Carmine guards, but three men dressed in black cloaks, swords in their hands. The smile faded from the guard's face. "Fates."

"Not stupid enough to come alone," the scarred face man said, turning his dagger to the guard.

"Well, that's a shame," the guard said. He drew his sword from his side scabbard and limped away from the archway toward the garden wall, keeping both the scarred face man and the three swordsmen in front of him. The men moved in on the guard.

"Kid," the guard said, raising his sword up in a defensive position. "This would be a good time to run."

Ara didn't need any more convincing. He rolled along the stone ground into a high shrub just as the scarred face man turned back to him. Ara kept rolling, pressing his body under the bush, its branches scraping his skin.

"Get back here," the scarred face man cried and swung his dagger, slashing at the shrub. Fire shot through Ara's calf. The blade caught him. Ara crawled on, pulling himself through the shrub and out the other side. He climbed to his feet and took off running. Behind him, the clang of swords filled the night.

Ara raced ahead, fear creating strength where there had been none. He zigzagged through the maze of plants, staying low and out of sight. Behind him, his pursuer hurled angry insults. "Come back here! I swear I'll chop you to pieces!"

Ara slid behind a potted tree and bent over stopped, his lungs stinging and his heart pounding at the thin wall of his chest. He touched the wound on his calf and felt the warm blood that left a trail behind him in the moonlight. Ara looked around for cover. Ahead of him stood the small glass house. He held his calf to stop the bleeding and slipped inside the warm room, closing the door behind him.

The red flower had grown since he last saw it. Taller now, it drooped limply in the center of the crate of sand as if sleeping. Ara carefully squeezed behind the crate and the glass wall, thankful for his thin frame. He held the rim of the crate for balance, and a drop of his blood dripped into the sand. The Blood Flower straightened up, spreading its petals wide. The boy pulled his hand away, remembering Semus's warning.

"There you are," a voice snapped. The man stood in the doorway, eyes on Ara. "Glass doesn't make a great hiding place you know."

Ara squeezed down into the small space behind the crate. As he did, the flower turned toward him as if following his scent. Ara closed his eyes as if he could simply wish this all away. He realized the clang of swords had stopped. The attackers had made quick work of the old guard.

"I haven't time for games, boy," the man said. He reached a hand over the crate, grabbing the boy's hair. Ara's scalp burned as the man lifted him from his hiding place. Ara fought the man's hands, trying to pry his fingers loose, but the man's grip was too strong. He pulled Ara over the lip of the sandy crate. The Blood

Flower opened fully, leaning toward his face like a blind predator.

"No," Ara grunted. He grabbed the man's hand again but instead of pulling away, he went with it, pushing forward and down toward the flower. The move caught the man off-balance, and his arm fell into the sand and against the flower's stem. The Blood Flower twisted and latched onto his arm, its red petals digging into his exposed wrist.

A shrill scream echoed in the glass house. The scarred face man released Ara and reached for his arm. Blood gushed from his wrist into the sand as his hand disappeared in a pool of blood and petals. The flower wrapped its stalk around the man's arm like a serpent, as its petals expanding to enclose his hand. The screams increased. The man yanked back and fell away from the crate. His hand was gone. He grabbed at the bloody stump in horror.

Gagging, Ara scrambled back. He pressed against the glass wall, trying to get away from the horrible sight. *The flower ate his hand!*

With a smash, the glass shattered behind him, and Ara toppled out into the cold night air. The old Carmine guard stood over him, sword in hand.

"Never seen that before," the guard said, grimacing at the flower in the pool of blood.

Outside the glass house, the scarred face man pressed the stump of his hand against his chest. His eyes fell on Ara. He unleashed a wild cry as he charged at them. But the guard's sword was too fast. It drove into the man above the chest-plate, bringing the screams to an abrupt halt. The man's body fell to the ground in cold silence.

The guard reached down and pulled Ara to his feet.

"What about the others?" Ara asked, looking around for the three attackers. "Where are they?"

"Lucky for me they don't make assassins like they used to."

"Assassins?" Ara still didn't understand. It was all happening so fast. And where were the rest of Carmine's guards?

"Ara!" a voice called. Ara and the guard turned to see Briton hurrying toward them, a pack slung over his back. Briton took in the mess around them—the broken glass, the bloody body of the assassin. Then his eyes stopped on the Carmine guard with a look of surprise. "Sir Geyer? Thank you."

An alarm bell rang from the eastern tower. Voices called out from the courtyard and along the ramparts. Windows came alive with torchlight.

"We have to go," Briton said, more to himself than the others. "We have to leave, right now."

"If there are more of them, the garden will be the safest place," the guard said. "We can see them coming through the archway, and there are places for the boy to hide."

"No," Briton said, his brow wrinkling as if his thoughts wrestled in his head. "We have to leave the castle."

"What are you talking about?" the guard asked.

"The boy is not safe here. The Faith will not stop until they have him, and even if they don't…" Briton looked the boy over, his face clearing. "This place is a death sentence for him."

"You're going to help a Descendant escape?"

"I know who you are, Sir Geyer," Briton said. "I've served at this castle longer than anyone else. I know what you've done and sacrificed. I'm calling on you now, not as a Carmine guard, but as a knight, sworn to justice and the protection of the weak. We have to help this boy."

"I'm no knight," Geyer said. "Haven't been for a long time." He slid his sword back into the sheath on his hip.

"Then if you won't help us," Briton said, stepping behind Ara and placing his hands on his shoulders. "Please, don't stand in our way."

"You don't know what you're doing."

"You're right," Briton said. "But I have to try."

The boy couldn't believe what he was hearing. He'd nearly

been killed, and now Briton was talking about escape. Was he serious? Could it be done?

"Come on." Briton pulled Ara through the garden toward the archway.

"Thank you," Ara said.

"You can thank me if we get through this," Briton said.

"Briton," Geyer called. They stopped under the archway. Ara's breath froze in his chest. But the guard did not move to stop them. "I hope you live to regret this."

"Me, too," Briton said. Then he and Ara hurried down the castle stairs.

"WHAT'S GOING ON?" Carmine asked, striding into the hallway. He had been awoken by voices and movement outside. Now the alarm bell was ringing. Three guards stood outside his door with swords drawn. The look on Nathaniel's face snapped Carmine awake.

"We may be under attack, my Lord," Nathaniel said. "One of the lookouts was found dead."

"Where?" Carmine couldn't believe it. Carmine Castle had never been under attack. Not in all his years.

"The west wall. You should return to your room my Lord, until we're sure the castle is secured."

"The boy," Carmine said, panic setting in. "Send your men to the tower. They're coming for the boy. If they get him, we're done for."

"We will, my Lord. But you need to go to your room, now."

A scream sounded down the hall and then was cut short. Silenced. Carmine couldn't believe it. Someone was attacking the castle.

"Go," Nathaniel said. "Lock the door."

Carmine turned back into his chambers and pulled the heavy bar down, sealing the room. He stood listening through the heavy wooden door, trying to understand what was happening. Who would dare openly move against House Carmine?

*That old fool*, Carmine fumed as he stepped back into his room. *Underestimating me like I was another noble under his boot.* As long as Carmine had the boy, he had supporters. And they would not stand for this treachery. If Aeilus Haemon wanted a war, then a war he would get.

Something stirred in the room. Carmine turned to see his window open, the curtains flapping in the night air. When had he left his window open?

The darkness in the room grew. A tall black figure slipped from the shadows. Carmine froze at the sight of Bale, The Blood Knight.

"You…you dare?" Carmine stammered, backing away. "The other nobles will not stand for this. This is an act of war!"

"Your castle was attacked by unknown assassins," Bale said. "With you flaunting the boy to every noble in Terene, there's no way to tell who hired them. With you dead, it'll be only right that the Highfather and the Faith look after the boy."

Bale pulled a long sword from his back and crossed toward Carmine in slow strides. Carmine tripped, slamming into the ground. He scrambled back on the palms of his hands. "No, you can't. You can't touch me. I am lord of this region."

"But you forgot who reigns over this world."

Carmine's back smacked into the door. There was nowhere left to run.

"Lord Carmine," Nathaniel called from outside the room. "Are you okay?"

Carmine looked up at Bale who was now only feet from him, sword spinning in his hand. This was the end. Not just of him and his plans, but the end of the Carmine family line. No glorious end, leading his army into battle; not even a fight in the woods like his father. Just Carmine alone, groveling on the floor of his chambers.

*No. Not like this.*

Carmine rose to his feet. He leaned against the door as he faced Bale. "The Highfather will die someday. He can't live forever. Even with the boy."

Bale shook his head. There was no remorse in those awful black eyes. No hesitation. "It's nothing you need to worry about," Bale said. He plunged his sword into Carmine. The black blade went through his stomach and through the door behind him. Carmine lifted his feet off the ground, pinned like an insect.

"Lord Carmine!" Nathaniel yelled, pounding on the door. Vibrations ran through Carmine's bones. He grabbed at his wound, trying to hold himself in place, but blood poured through his fingers, pooling on the floor. So much blood.

"And so ends House Carmine," Bale said. He ripped his sword free, and Carmine crumpled to the ground.

Jonathan Carmine lifted his head. On the stone wall above him hung the Carmine family sigil—the cardinal, bright and majestic. *Father…please.* Carmine choked on the warm blood that filled his mouth and streamed down his chin. The taste was not so foreign.

CASTLE CARMINE WAS alive with sounds of panic: shouting voices, footsteps of people running, clanking armor of guards scrambling in different directions. Ara stopped on the stairwell and caught his breath, no longer able to keep up with Briton.

"I can't," Ara steadied himself against the stairway wall. His garments were torn and speckled with blood. His bare feet stung from the cold.

"You must, Ara," Briton said. "You won't get another opportunity."

Ara listened to the chaos around him. Castle Carmine was in an uproar. If this was his only chance at freedom, he would find the strength, even if killed him. Ara grabbed onto Briton's pack as he led him down the stairs. A travel pack? Had Briton prepared for this?

They reached the bottom floor by the kitchen and the Descendant's barracks; the place Ara spent his first months at the castle. Leaning on Briton, they headed down the hallway leading to the courtyard.

"But what about the gate?" Ara asked. Even if they got outside and reached the gate, there was no way they'd get through the guards and archers on the wall.

"We'll figure it out when we get there," Briton said. The old teacher was breathing heavily, his movements more labored. There's no way they could outrun Carmine guards. But, there was no point in turning back; if he went back to the tower, he'd be trapped there forever.

Briton stopped. Between them and the door stood a red figure. The Curor looked shocked at first, and then realization lit across his face.

"I knew it," the Curor said, his lip curled into a sneer. "I knew you put your own interests above those of House Carmine, but I never thought you would stoop to such treachery."

"Out of the way, Typher," Briton said. But Ara felt the hopelessness set in. It was over. They hadn't even made it out of the castle.

"So you can run off and have the boy all to yourself?" the Curor scoffed. "I can't wait to see what Lord Carmine does to you when he finds out."

"I can't sit back and watch you torture this boy again and again."

"Oh, you won't have to watch," the Curor said. "Because you will be rotting the final years of your miserable life in the castle's dungeon, you treasonous—"

His speech was interrupted by a loud crack. The Curor collapsed to the floor in a pile of red robes. Behind him stood a short round figure holding a broomstick.

"Wow, that felt good," Chancey said, looking at the unconscious Curor at his feet. "I've wanted to do that for a long time."

"Chancey?" Ara called. "What are you doing?"

Chancey frowned as he looked at Ara. "I'm helping you get out of here."

As mad as he had been at Chancey, as much as he blamed him for his time in the tower, it was good to see his old friend. "Thanks, Chancey."

Chancey beamed. He threw down the broomstick and pulled off his shoes. He handed them to Ara. "Here, you'll need these."

Ara slipped on the shoes. They were too big but would be better than traveling barefoot. Chancey stepped forward and wrapped his coat around Ara's skinny frame.

Voices sounded down the hallway behind them.

Ara pulled the large coat tight and put his hand on the boy's shoulder. "Come with us, Chancey."

"I can't. I'll only slow you down."

"But Chancey, they'll kill you for this," Ara pleaded.

Chancey looked down at the Curor at his feet. "If you get away, then it was worth it."

"Ara," Briton said, moving down the hallway away from the approaching footsteps. "We need to go. Now."

"Ara," Chancey smiled. "You found your name."

Ara nodded. "I did."

"Now go find the rest." Chancey bent down and picked up the broomstick once again. "I'll slow them down."

"But Chancey…"

Briton pulled Ara down the hallway as the guard's voices grew louder.

"Good luck…Ara," Chancey called. Then he raised the broomstick toward the approaching guards. Five armed men, charging down the hallway.

"There, the boy!" one guard cried.

Ara turned away and ran after Briton. Away from his friend. Away from the shouts and the crack of wood breaking.

*Chancey!*

Ara didn't look back. It took all his strength to stay on his feet as he and Briton raced out the door and into the castle courtyard. The grounds were dark and empty, lit only by the castle windows. Above them, the tower bell continued ringing out the alarm. Ara and Briton ran across the courtyard, past the stables, and toward the castle gates.

The guard at the gate looked from the castle to Briton, trying to understand the situation. "What's going on, Master Briton?"

"The castle is under attack," Briton said, catching his breath. "We must get people to safety."

The guard looked past Briton to the chaos erupting in the castle above. "But we can't let down the castle's defenses."

"Open the gate, son."

"Sir, I'm not allowed to—"

"Stop them," a voice called out behind them. The group of guards charged out of the castle—swords in hand. "Do not let the traitors escape."

The gate guard drew his sword and held it out toward Briton.

It was over. What hope there was had disappeared. Ara grabbed Briton's arm to steady himself. *Back to the tower. Back to the never-ending blood draws.*

The five guards stormed across the courtyard toward them.

Ara had come so close. Now, he would be locked away in Castle Carmine forever, without even Briton's lessons to offer some relief.

*No.*

Ara shot past the guard. He dug his feet into the dirt and pulled on the gate. It didn't budge. He clawed at the wooden plank locking it in place like a trapped animal. The guard tore him away and tossed him to the ground. He drew his sword and held it over the boy. Tears filled Ara's eyes as he lay in the dirt. *I can't go back. I can't.*

Then the stable doors exploded. A stampede of horses shot across the courtyard, plowing straight through the guards. All five fell under the horses' pounding hooves. Two more horses charged out of the stables. The great brown horse carried a rider and he pulled the white horse behind him with a rope. The rider wore the uniform of a Carmine guard, but his helmet had been removed, and his shaggy hair flew behind him in the wind.

It was the guard, Sir Geyer.

"Stop," the gate guard ordered, turning his sword to the approaching Geyer. But Geyer's horse did not slow down. The guard leaped out of the way as Geyer's horse passed and then came to a stop, kicking its front legs up and screeching wildly.

When the great beast's legs came back to the ground, Geyer looked down at Briton and Ara with a crooked smile on his face. "What kind of escape is this? You're not going to get anywhere on foot."

He pulled the white horse forward, tossing the rope to Briton.

"Take her," he said.

"Stop, traitor!" the gate guard yelled. He got halfway to his feet before Ara put him back down with a kick to the head. The guard's helmet spun backward, blocking his vision.

Briton and Ara hurried to the gate. Together they removed the wood plank. Ara dug his shoulder into the gate, pushing it. The heavy gate inched open. Ara pushed, his feet slipping in the dirt, but he kept pushing, inch by inch.

"That's good," Geyer shouted. "Let's go."

Guards called out above them; charging toward them along the castle wall. In the courtyard, two of the guards had recovered their swords and were closing in.

Briton groaned as he pulled himself onto the white horse.

"Your hand," Geyer said, holding out his own gloved hand.

Ara reached up and the guard pulled him up onto the back of the brown horse. "Hold on tight."

Geyer kicked and the horse squeezed through the gate and stormed off into the night. Something whisked by Ara with a swoosh. The sound came again, this time followed by a ding off Geyer's armor, the blow nearly knocking them to the ground.

"Fates!" Geyer cursed, repositioning himself on the horse. "Archers!" Geyer pulled the reins back and forth and the horse cut a zigzag pattern as more arrows whistled by. Ara felt his grip slipping; he was sliding off the back of the horse. With a grunt, he pulled himself up. He wrapped his arms around Geyer's waist and buried his head against his armored back. Ara yelled, but his voice was lost under the horse's hooves racing down the road.

It wasn't until maybe a half hour later, when they were far from the noise of the castle, that Geyer slowed the pace. Ara let go of Geyer's armor and found he could not straighten his fingers.

After a few minutes, they heard someone approaching. Briton's white horse raced up the road and the old man pulled it to a stop, slipping halfway off the saddle. He was panting as loudly as the horse.

"Are you okay?" Ara asked, relieved to see the old man had made it.

"My body isn't," Briton said. "Haven't ridden like that in a long time." He arched his back, which brought a string of cracks and pops. He groaned. "Okay, I've *never* ridden like that."

"Are they following us?" Ara asked. He looked back down the road but saw nothing coming through the darkness.

"They will once they figure out what happened," Geyer said.

"What did happen?" Ara asked. "Who were those men who attacked?"

"Assassins," Geyer said. "Cutthroats hired to come for you."

"For me?" Ara couldn't believe it. All that mess back at the castle—the dead men, the alarms...Chancey...it had been on account of him.

"Thank you, Sir Geyer," Briton said, breathing normally once again. "We wouldn't have made it if not for you."

"You haven't made it yet."

Ara looked at the two men. They had risked their lives for him, but he still didn't know if he could trust them. Did they want his blood all for themselves?

"We can't stay on the main road," Briton said. "It's too dangerous."

"Come daylight, anyway." Geyer looked up at the night sky. "Until then we cover as much ground as we can. Can you ride?"

Briton nodded, with a sigh. "I'll have to."

"Where are we going?" Ara asked. The castle was bad, but at least there he knew what to expect. He knew nothing of this outside world or what lay ahead for him.

"First, we get you safe," Briton said. "Then we'll figure it out."

"Wow," Geyer said. "I feel much better knowing you've planned this out so thoroughly."

The old guard slapped the horse's reins; the tired animal neighed stubbornly but moved all the same. This time, Geyer kept the speed down so Briton could keep up. They rode on, their way lit by what moonlight escaped the clouds. Ara turned in the saddle and looked back the way they had come. Castle Carmine was now but a small light in the distance. Growing smaller.

# PART II

THE ROAD

# 14

---

*"The others say Hemo will not forsake his chosen people. But when I call out in the night, I find only silence."*

---

The mood inside the Temple's outer sanctuary was somber. Believers and Fathers of the Faith came from all over to mourn for the fallen Lord Carmine. Lords from surrounding areas came partly to pay respect in the eyes of the Fathers, and partly to exchange gossip about the circumstances surrounding the young lord's death. The most intriguing stories centered around a magical Descendant boy.

As Bale passed through the sanctuary, he stopped to look at the body. Carmine was hung upside down at the altar. The ceremonial bowl beneath him was nearly full. The last of his blood fell in sporadic drops. Soon the body would be empty of mortal blood, a vessel ready to be filled anew in the afterlife.

To Bale, it was just a rotting corpse.

Guards stepped out of his way as Bale passed through the sanctuary doors and into the main Temple, leaving the soft murmuring of prayers behind. Three floors up, in the Highfather's study, Bale found the mood did not match the peaceful reverence below.

"How could you have lost the boy?" Aeilus Haemon shouted as he swung his arms, knocking the quills and scrolls from his desk.

"It seems Carmine's men were more prepared than we anticipated," Bale said, his voice low. He was not used to reporting failure. "The assassins never made it out."

"You should have done it yourself with your men instead of hiring some cheap cutthroats." Haemon smashed his fist on the empty desk.

"If my men were discovered, it would lead back to you."

Haemon shook his head, winded from his outburst. "How is it your men failed, yet the boy is not at Castle Carmine? Is it a ploy to confuse us?"

"Our reports from inside the castle confirm the boy has escaped with the aid of Carmine's advisor and a guard."

"An old man and one guard made a fool of the great Blood Knight." Haemon fell back into his chair and caught his rasping breath. The old man needed blood. Bale could see how dependent he had become, how weak he was without it. "At least you managed to kill that ingrate Carmine. With House Carmine destroyed, no one has claim to the boy. He will be all ours— once you and your men find him!"

"I will bring you the boy," Bale said, standing to his full height. He detested Haemon's whining and was eager to get back in the field and fulfill his mission. This was twice Carmine's advisor had gotten in the way of his plans. "What do you want us to do with his companions?"

"You mean the traitors who kidnapped the boy and orchestrated the death of their own lord?"

Bale had to marvel at the old man; he seemed to actually believe the lies he spun. As physically weak as the Highfather had become, he was still dangerous.

"You think the people will believe that?"

"They will believe whatever their Father tells them," Haemon said. "You just see to it those traitors are silenced."

"They will be."

Haemon pulled a case of blood vials from his drawer and slid it across his desk. Bale collected the blood. This was enough to keep his blood poison at bay for two weeks if he stretched it. He better find the boy in that time.

"Take as many men as you need," Haemon said, tapping his spidery fingers on the desk. "Turn over as many cities, burn as many villages, do whatever you have to do…it is Hemo's will that we find that boy!"

Bale took the vials and bowed, sweeping out of the room. Outside the Highfather's study, he hurried down the hallway with new energy. With the full army of the Faith at his command, he would find the boy in no time. Then, once the boy was in his possession, perhaps he would do his own little experiment. Find out if he even needed the Highfather and his team of Curors, or if the boy's good blood was cure enough.

If so, the next conversation with Haemon would go quite differently.

THEY'D RIDDEN two days with little rest. Ara finally convinced Geyer to stop when Briton fell from his horse. The old man's body was so locked up they had to carry him to cover. Ara didn't feel much better. As soon as they set Briton down, he walked a few paces and curled up to sleep beneath a tree. Briton forced him to eat something he pulled from his pack, saying the same thing that had been repeated to Ara again and again during their time at Castle Carmine: "You need your strength."

*You need it so we can take it from you.*

Fatigue replaced fear, and Ara closed his eyes, no longer caring if they were caught by Carmine's guards or a whole company of assassins, as long as he could close his eyes for a moment. So, despite the rough ground of rocks and pine needles that hadn't been properly swept away, despite the cold air that seeped into the folds of Chancey's oversized coat, despite the hunger clenching up his belly like an angry fist, Ara slept like a stone.

In the morning, Ara woke to a snort and turned to see the two horses tied to a nearby tree, heads hung in exhaustion, steam rising from their snouts. Daylight leaked in through the thick trees and warmth came with it. Briton slept a few feet away, his skin pale enough that he'd pass for a corpse if not for the steady snoring. Geyer was nowhere to be seen.

Birds chirped in the branches above, not morning songs but what sounded like a warning to the rest of the forest about intruders. Briton's eyes opened as Ara crawled close to him.

"How are you?" Ara asked.

"I feel like I was the one ridden for the past two days," Briton groaned. He tried to sit up, but his body had other plans. "Do yourself a favor, Ara. Never grow old. The pain is not worth the extra years."

Ara helped Briton, leaning the old teacher against the trunk of the nearby tree.

"How do *you* feel?" Briton asked.

When Ara stopped to think about it, he was surprised by the answer. Yes, he was cold and uncomfortable and certainly hungry, but he did not feel as travel-broken as he should. In fact, when he tested his legs, he felt stronger than he had in some time. His blood hadn't been stolen in two full days.

"I feel good."

"Then you can collect the wood for a fire," Geyer said.

Ara was startled to see the figure walking toward them through the trees. No longer wearing his guard's armor, Geyer looked much leaner in his simple green stitched shirt and black pants. His wavy, yellow-gray hair hung down to his shoulder, and his stubble had grown to the beginnings of a proper beard.

"Is a fire wise?" Briton asked.

"Unless you want your breakfast raw." Geyer tossed a rabbit

carcass to the ground. Its dirty brown fur was speckled with blood.

"Only one?" Ara asked.

"You're welcome to try yourself. Took me all morning to spear that one, but maybe you're better with a knife."

"I didn't mean…" Ara began and then fell silent. A third of that rabbit wouldn't go toward filling his empty stomach, but he had no place to complain. These men had risked their lives to save him, and he still didn't know why. "I'll get the wood."

"Careful not to go too far, Ara," Briton called after him.

Ara nodded and looked to the ground for sticks, hoping to make himself useful and do his part. Hoping to make breakfast come sooner.

GEYER DIDN'T GET UP EARLY that morning to hunt rabbit. He walked the woods around their camp kicking himself for getting into this mess and thinking of ways to get out of it. Everyone was looking for the boy, they didn't care about him. It was dark and chaotic at the castle, they might not even know who had helped him escape. If he left now, Geyer still had a chance at freedom. Darker thoughts had also entered his mind. Thoughts of what reward awaited the one who delivered the boy to the Faith.

But, being the fool he was, Geyer had returned to the camp. As he cleared away pine needles to create a bed for a fire, he couldn't help but think where he could be if he left. On his way to an inn. A drink waiting for him along with a much better breakfast than rabbit.

"You're sure he's okay out there on his own?" Briton asked. Carmine's advisor watched the trees where the boy had disappeared to collect firewood.

"There's nobody else around," Geyer said.

"The boy doesn't remember anything before the castle. He's like a new fawn tripping around the woods."

"No memory," Geyer scoffed. "How is that?"

"I don't know. He's obviously suffered some kind of trauma. Something severe. When I first saw him, he was covered in bruises, and his head looked like it had been split open. And that is *with* his healing ability."

Geyer nodded. He'd been around the boy's kind enough to know that their powers varied Descendant to Descendant. Where one could take a sword to the stomach and appear the next day as if nothing happened, others wore the same scars for weeks. It was hard to believe this scrawny little boy was anything special.

"The boy has recovered from the ride, but you haven't. Now, I've never been a proponent of Curors but—"

"No," Briton cut him off. "I got him out so he would never have to give up his blood again."

"I understand. I'm just saying we would move a lot faster if you were at full strength."

"What about you?" Briton gave him a scrutinizing look. "You've had that limp since James Carmine's assassination. Why didn't you fix it when you had the chance?"

Geyer looked down. He'd been rubbing his left leg. "Sometimes we need reminders of our mistakes."

"Mistakes? As I recall, you were outnumbered three to one."

"I never should have let Lord Carmine go hunting in the Hidden Wood. It was a time of war. It was too dangerous a risk, even with four guards." Geyer took in the silent forest that was their new home. "I can't help thinking how different things would be if James was still alive. Castle Carmine would be a much different place."

"What I have learned in my years serving both Carmines is there is no changing a lord's mind when it's set on something. It is just as much my fault as yours not to see an ambush coming. And now I have betrayed Jonathan Carmine. What a family advisor I turned out to be."

GOOD BLOOD

"We all keep our scars," Geyer said. "Even in a world of magic blood."

Geyer pulled the hidden knife from his left boot and began working on the rabbit. As he cleaned it, his mind drifted back to that day in the Hidden Wood; he'd gone over the events countless times in the years since James Carmine's death. James loved the Hidden Wood. Probably more than he loved the castle and its garden. Riding through the forest, they had stopped at the sight of the fallen deer. The animal was splayed out in the clearing, its throat slit. Geyer should have seen it right there at that moment. If he'd acted in time maybe they'd have gotten away from the company of assassins that fell upon them.

Geyer's sword cut through the attackers, but he couldn't reach Carmine. A longsword cut James down from his horse. He was dead before he hit the ground. The killer's dark eyes still haunted Geyer's sober nights. The one who stormed through Geyer's men like they were farmers. Geyer had the chance to avenge James and Maddie right there. He met the assassin's black blade. Geyer, who'd fought for shrines and trophies, now fought for his honor as a knight—and failed. The assassin cut Geyer to ribbons, nearly taking his leg off.

But if Geyer was going to die, he'd take the killer with him. In a final desperate move, he got to his feet and hurled himself at the assassin, plunging his sword into the tall man's chest. The assassin fell, choking on his own blood as his men dragged his body away. Geyer fell to the forest floor beside the bloody bodies of James and Madeline Carmine.

Geyer had blood on his hands. He set the skinned rabbit aside and wiped his knife clean.

"Do you have a plan from here, Briton?"

"Get as far away as we can for now," Briton said. "Both Carmine and the Highfather will have men after us. There's no noble house that will grant us sanctuary. We'll have to stick to smaller towns and villages."

"And when did you last spend time outside a noble castle's walls?"

"Quite some time, I'm afraid. I guess in that respect, you are saddled with two fawns tripping around the woods."

"I already did my good deed helping you escape the castle. I didn't sign on for adventures with the old man and his magic boy."

Briton's face went flat. "Sir Geyer, we'll never make it without you. The boy will go right back to a prison cell, or worse if the Faith gets their hands on him. You must help."

"Playing on a sense of honor only works with the honorable." Geyer stood and dusted himself off. "I'm not a young fool anymore who dreams of having stories written about him. I've found it's better to live to sing the songs of others. Preferably beside a warm fire and with a good ale."

"You're leaving now?"

"I'll help you get moving again first," Geyer said. "If you're lucky, you'll stay ahead of trouble for a few days, maybe a week. But I don't see any way this ends happily for you two."

Briton didn't argue, but simply looked down. Despite spending his life pampered in a lord's castle, the old man understood how the world works.

"Don't tell the boy," Briton said, his voice low. "Not yet. Let him hold onto some hope for a little longer."

At that moment the boy stumbled back toward their camp, a load of thin branches jutting out of his arms at different lengths. A large grin spread across his tattooed face. "I found some wood!"

Geyer shook his head. "Who taught you to build a fire? We'll be lucky if those branches last five minutes."

"I've never made a fire before." Ara studied the sticks in his arms. "I don't think I have, anyway."

"Right," Geyer said. He took the branches from Ara and piled them in the cleared area. Luckily, Briton had packed flint in his bag. He wasn't completely worthless after all. Geyer found a decent log to add to the boy's kindling, and soon the three travelers sat beside a warm fire—the tiny rabbit meat gone far too quickly. No one spoke for a long time. It was peaceful in the woods with no sound but the crackling fire. Geyer could almost forget they were being hunted.

"There's one thing we still gotta do," Geyer said, "but you're not going to like it." Geyer stoked the fire with his boot-knife. The blade was good and sharp, and its metal glowed from the heat.

"What's that?" Briton asked.

"You're conspicuous enough as it is, traveling with a boy. But you've got no chance at blending in while the boy's got the mark of House Carmine on his face."

Ara touched the "C" shaped tattoo on his right cheek.

"It's already begun to fade," Briton said. "He heals faster than other Descendants. With food and rest, it will probably be gone in another few weeks."

"You don't have that kind of time."

Briton stared silently into the dimming fire. Geyer didn't like it any better than he did, but these two had no hope of traveling unnoticed with a big target on the boy's face. Everyone in Terene would be looking for the boy with that brand.

"Maybe we can cover his face with a scarf," Briton offered. "He can be a Santar traveler from the Endless Desert."

"You'd still bring attention to yourselves. Northerners hold as much prejudice against the sand children as they do Descendants."

"But if I kept him in the woods…"

"Do it," Ara interrupted them. "Get it off of me."

Geyer turned to the boy, studying the crooked "C" tattoo.

"I'll have to cut deep," Geyer said. "Below the ink."

"I said, do it."

Geyer pulled the knife from the fire and shook it in the cool air. The tattoo ran along the right side of the boy's face from brow to cheek. It would not be clean. The boy's blood better be as powerful as everyone said.

"I'll need your help holding him down," Geyer said to Briton. "And to cover his mouth."

Briton shook his head but obeyed nonetheless, moving to Ara's side. They laid the boy on the ground so his right side faced the light of the fire. Geyer grunted as he lowered down and knelt over the boy. He didn't have to do this; he could leave now and save the boy a lot of pain. The boy was going to be caught anyway, tattoo or no tattoo. He couldn't hide forever. But as much as this wasn't Geyer's problem, he had to at least leave them with a fighting chance.

Ara winced and held his breath. Geyer gritted his teeth and cut over the boy's screams. It was an awful mess. Geyer didn't know what he expected—perhaps that the special Descendant boy wouldn't bleed like a Raw Blood. But metal cut through his skin like it did through every living thing. Like it had through the rabbit earlier that morning.

The boy was brave and struggled to hold still as Geyer carved around the "C" shaped tattoo, digging his knife deep into his flesh, trying his best to avoid the shaking boy's eye. Briton wept as he leaned his weight on the boy, one hand clamped over the boy's mouth, muffling his cries of pain.

"Stop," Briton whispered. "Please stop." Geyer wanted to. He wanted to step away from the blood and the tortured screams. But he kept going until the job was done.

Afterward, the boy lay on the ground, motionless. A blood-stained cloth covered his face while Briton stroked his hair. Geyer stayed on the other side of the camp, tending to the horses. The screams had spooked the animals, and their ropes needed to be retied. Geyer ran his hands along the brown horse's neck, calming him while he considered his next move. He'd stay until the boy could travel. He could do that much. Nobody would fault him. Fates, nobody would even remember Briton and the boy in a few weeks. People suffered injustice every day, these two were nothing special.

The horse pressed his head into Geyer's chest. "There, there," he whispered. "It's alright." He reached a hand and rummaged through the contents of his saddlebag. At one time, Geyer had been a noble knight, a champion swordsman, a well-paid captain of the guards. Now, all he had left in the world was an empty waterskin, cheap armor, and a long sword that had no name.

# 15

---

"We demand answers," Father Edmund Turney said as the council meeting began. Aeilus Haemon looked down the table at the young Father, who apparently spoke for everyone.

"Answers?" Haemon asked, surprised. "You think I have answers into the inner workings of every noble castle in the land? I'm flattered by the scope of my perceived powers, Edmund, but perhaps you'll find someday that even the position of Highfather has its limits."

Edmund scoffed. "Father Haemon, rumors swirl from all over about a boy with blood the likes of which hasn't been seen in centuries. There are even accusations that the Faith had a hand in the death of Lord Carmine. You claim to have no knowledge of this?"

Haemon gave a long drawn out yawn.

"There are always rumors meant to discredit the Faith and blame all the woes and tragedies of this world on us. So we must take a skeptical view of such stories and not get caught up in blasphemous conspiracies, no matter how sweet the taste." He smiled at Edmund, and before the young Father could respond, he steered the conversation in another direction. "What has been reported is that a certain long time advisor to House Carmine disappeared on the very same night Carmine was killed."

"I have heard that as well," Father Kent added. "Briton Moonglass, a well-respected man among the nobles."

"Well respected, yes," Haemon said. "But no one is impervious to greed, especially one who has sat so long at the side of power."

Haemon turned to Edmund; the young Father met his glare.

"Are you saying Briton Moonglass had something to do with Carmine's death?" Father Loren asked.

"Hmm," Haemon rubbed his pointed chin. "That's an interesting point. The same night Carmine is killed, his advisor flees with a valuable Descendant. Perhaps the assassins were hired to cover his escape and to take Carmine out of the picture. Perhaps this Moonglass plans to sell the boy and finally gain lands and titles of his own."

"That makes sense," Father Claudia said. She steepled her fingers against her chin, thinking through the implications.

The idea spread like fire through the council room. Fathers chimed in to fill the gaps in his story. All except for Edmund who seethed in silence. His plan to turn the council on Haemon was now gone. But he'd try again. These meetings were so boring, Haemon almost looked forward to the challenge.

"What shall we do?" Father Kent asked over the murmuring voices. All eyes turned to the Highfather.

"Order must be restored," Haemon said. "And true answers found. We must find this fugitive and the boy in his possession. With House Carmine in disarray and no heir, I shall personally take control of the castle in the name of the Faith. For do not forget my brothers, the Descendant rebellion will seek to take advantage of a misfortune such as this. As the guardians of Terene, we must be strong and unwavering."

And so it was settled. Hemo's will had washed over the council as surely as it would wash over the rest of Terene. The whole world will soon be looking for Briton and the boy; there will be no sanctuary for them anywhere. Now, if Bale upholds his end, the boy will be in his possession soon enough.

In the meantime, Haemon would return to Castle Carmine and see just how powerful this blood really was.

BRITON GAVE the last of the provisions to the boy. If he didn't recover enough to travel, they would starve anyway. It was now late afternoon, and Ara had not moved from his place beneath the tree. Though Briton understood it had to be done, watching Geyer cut the skin from the boy's face had been excruciating. It was something he could never have done.

Sir Geyer had not spoken since the ordeal. He kept his distance, busying himself with tasks on the far end of the camp. He would occasionally shoot a concerned glance their way, but he did not approach the boy. At least he hadn't left yet. Briton didn't know how he and the boy were going to get by on their own. Back at the castle, he was a valuable advisor and scholar. But what use was he out here in the real world?

Briton finished feeding the boy and stayed by his side, swatting away the mosquitoes that circled the bloody cloth on the boy's face. "Ara," he whispered. "Ara, can you hear me?"

"Yes," Ara moaned out of the left side of his mouth. Briton flipped over part of the bloody cloth to uncover the boy's left eye.

"How are you feeling?"

"Like I had half of my face cut off."

Briton nodded. "Can you see that tree above us? The one you slept under last night?"

The boy blinked. "Yes."

"What type of tree is it?"

"Why does it matter?"

"Do you know the answer?"

"It's a pine."

"And that one beside it, with the larger leaves."

"Is this really the time for lessons?"

"Are you busy?" Briton raised an eyebrow. "Besides, an active mind is distracted from—"

"Oak," Ara grumbled.

"Yes," Briton nodded. "And that one over there."

"Still oak."

"Very good." Briton brushed off the mosquito that landed on Ara's forehead. "And how is it you know the names of these trees?"

Ara fell silent for a moment. "I don't know, I must have learned them before."

"How many desert plants can you name?"

"I have the image of a blood rose forever scarred in my brain."

"Any other?"

Ara closed his eye, thinking. "No," he said finally.

Briton nodded.

"What does that mean?" Ara asked, trying to sit up.

"Wait." Briton tore a strip of fabric off the bottom of his robe and tied it around the boy's head, securing the bloody cloth like an eyepatch. The boy flinched as Briton pulled it tight, but he did not cry out. Briton helped the boy sit up against the pine tree. It was good to see him alert, even if only half of his face was visible.

"You are familiar with trees of the forest but not the deserts of the south," Briton said.

"I have seen visions," Ara whispered. "Of myself flying above the trees. I didn't know if they were images from dreams or memory."

"They are one and the same. You cannot dream beyond what your mind knows."

"But what does it tell us?" Ara's eye bored into Briton, longing for answers. "That I am from the north."

"It is but a piece to the puzzle," Briton said, not wanting to disappoint the boy. "But we must start somewhere. What else have you seen in these visions?"

The boy closed his eye and concentrated. On the other side of the camp, Geyer sharpened the points of sticks with a knife. But Briton could see he was listening.

"I see the sky," Ara began. "But it is not this gray above us. It is bright and warm like a fire spread out across a mountainous horizon."

"A sunset," Briton nodded. He had seen places outside the western lands where the clouds were not so thick. But he'd never seen one as clear as the boy described. Therefore, the boy couldn't be talking about the great northern mountains that ended Terene like a wall; for the sky there was blanketed in gray.

Briton frowned. The pieces to this puzzle didn't fit.

"I did bring some books in the pack if you would like to continue your reading while we still have daylight," Briton said. He climbed to his feet and approached the white horse, happy to be of use, even if it was but a distraction.

"While you two are playing school, I'll see if I can find more food so we don't starve to death," Geyer said as he passed Briton carrying three roughly made spears under his arm. "Perhaps if you find the time between philosophy and tree naming, you could rebuild the fire."

"Of course," Briton said. "If there's anything I can do—"

"I'll go with you," Ara said.

"What?" Briton and Geyer said in unison.

"I'll help you look for food." Ara lifted himself up against the oak tree. "Three eyes are better than two."

"I think you better rest," Geyer said.

"I can be in pain here or in pain out there. At least out there I'll be useful."

"I don't know how useful a one-eyed boy with no hunting experience will be."

"Well, I have to learn sometime if we are to have food once you leave."

Geyer looked to Briton. But Briton was just as surprised. *How did the boy know?*

"You are leaving, aren't you?" Ara asked. He pushed off the tree and took a few tentative steps forward.

Geyer looked down at the three spears under his arm, deciding.

"Come then," he said, finally. "But I won't wait if you fall behind. I'm too hungry for patience."

"You're sure you're up for this?" Briton asked Ara. He secured the bandage in place over the right side of the boy's face. From the little he saw of the underside, the wound had already healed a great deal.

Ara gave him a half smile. "Never rob yourself of the chance to learn."

"Very wise," Briton said, returning the smile. "And much like a student to throw his teacher's words back at him." Briton's smile faded as he thought of a young Jonathan Carmine. As different as their upbringings were, the boy was every bit as sure-headed and stubborn as a young noble lord. "Stay alert."

Ara scampered off through the forest after Geyer, his wobbly legs trying to keep up with the larger man's. Geyer chuckled. A fawn indeed.


"Keep up, I'm not slowing down for you," Geyer said. Ara quickened his pace to match the man's long strides. Even with a limp, Geyer covered the forest ground well. "And walk light, on the balls of your feet, or you'll scare away every animal in the forest."

Ara did as he was told; he checked his footing with each step, avoiding twigs and dry leaves. His face still ached, but it felt good to move again.

"It will be dark soon," Ara said and felt foolish for pointing out the obvious.

"Then we better find something. I'd hate to have to eat one of the horses."

Ara didn't know if that was a joke. The man, Geyer, had an odd sense of humor. Ara wondered how true the stories were that Briton had told him. That Geyer had once been a great knight and Lord Carmine's personal guard. That for a time, he was famous for his skill with a sword and that knights used to visit Castle Carmine simply to duel with the great Sir Geyer. Watching the back of the man in green, Ara had his doubts.

Still, Ara followed the old knight into the forest. For there were some things Briton couldn't teach him.

"You should teach me to use a sword," Ara said, speaking his thoughts out loud.

"Keep your voice down," Geyer whispered. He searched the ground for animal tracks. The forest seemed utterly vacant of life. Aside from the awful grubs they'd dug up, the only living thing Ara had seen was a squirrel scurry up a tree trunk as they approached.

"I need to learn to fight," Ara said, his voice low.

"You're going to fight your way through an army of guards, are you? You can't even lift a sword."

"Yes, I can."

"Uh-huh. Better keep to your books, kid. Your only hope is if Briton can pass you off as a girl." Geyer glanced back, his eyes falling on the boy's covered face. Geyer looked away. "It's good that you want to learn something that's actually valuable in the real world, but I'm no teacher."

"Yeah? What are you?" Ara snapped.

"I'm tired, hungry, and in desperate need of a drink. Now if you don't…" Geyer stopped mid-sentence and crouched to the ground.

"What is it?" Ara whispered, tiptoeing to him.

"Shhh," Geyer motioned him down. Staying low, Ara crept forward until he could see over the bushes. In the clearing ahead were two birds with dark feathers and white heads. They pecked at the ground, turning over dirt and leaves. Geyer handed a stick to Ara. Ara touched the point, surprised at the sharpness of the crudely fashioned spear.

"Stay here," Geyer whispered. "I'll circle to the other side, and we'll attack from two ends. Don't throw until I signal you."

"How do I do it?" Ara whispered, holding up the stick.

"Throw the pointy end at the bird."

Geyer crawled back from the edge of the clearing and then circled around, his movements almost silent. His body had adapted to the injured leg; something Ara would never have to do. Ara's body would carry no scars, no permanent wounds. Only a memory of pain—and for him, even that was uncertain.

Off to his far right, Geyer inched toward the clearing. Ara weighed the weapon in his hand, moving his grip just up from the stick's middle. His grip tightened on the spear; it felt good in his hand. Had he held a spear before? The black birds sauntered around on the forest floor, occasionally diving their pointed beaks into the ground. Ara's belly ached.

To his right, Geyer waited for the right moment.

The bird closest to Ara spotted something it liked and hopped forward, burying its head in the ground. The other bird came near, looking to share in the discovery. Geyer nodded his head once. The signal. Geyer stood up and raised his first spear behind his head. Ara fixed his gaze on the closer bird, drew his spear back and heaved it with all his strength. It flew high and right. Before it hit, however, Geyer's spear struck straight through the second bird. In a blink, the closer bird shot away, directly into the path of Ara's spear. But Ara's shot was not straight. The side of the stick merely knocked the bird to the ground, dazed, and flapping its crooked wing.

"Yes!" Ara cheered.

The bird righted itself and turned toward Ara. Then it charged toward him, squawking, its beak looking suddenly sharper than before. Ara reeled back, tangling his legs in the bush and stumbling to the ground.

Before the charging bird got to the edge of the clearing, Geyer was upon it. He stabbed his second spear through the bird's back, pinning it to the ground.

Ara caught his breath as Geyer raised two spears with two dead birds.

"Well, that went much better than I thought," Geyer said.

Ara laughed in relief, the smile stinging his raw flesh.

Geyer nodded to Ara. "That wasn't a completely horrible shot."

"It was lucky," Ara admitted.

"Even better. We could use the fates on our side."

Geyer looked Ara over, and Ara imagined what a pitiful sight he must be: thin and pale, standing in torn pajamas and over-sized boots, half his face covered by a bloody rag.

But he had hit the bird. Lucky or not, he helped catch their dinner. Tonight they would feast on two tiny feeble creatures, thanks in part to him.

"Come on, Ara," Geyer said. "Let's get back and build a fire before it gets dark. And try to find some decent firewood this time."

Geyer handed Ara the spear with the second bird and then walked back toward camp. Ara stood, feeling the weight of the dead animal on the end of his spear. His belly growled.

"Turns out you're not useless on a hunt after all," Geyer called back. "We can always use you as bait."

THREE BLOOD HOUNDS tore up the road beside the horses. Twice the size of normal dogs, these beasts had been bred for generations with one purpose—to hunt Descendants. Bale had given them a whiff of the bottle of blood recovered from Carmine's storehouse. Now they raced madly down the road with the scent of the boy's blood on their tongues.

Bale had used blood hounds to hunt Descendants before. If a Descendant had open blood in the air, the hounds could smell it from a mile away. Plus, Bale liked having the great beasts with him on a hunt. The very sight of them sent Descendants running for their lives.

The twelve Temple guards riding with Bale had been hand-picked. Even though this mission was approved by the council, Bale's tactics were not. He needed men he could trust. Men who understood that the greater good demanded a necessary brutality.

The company of guards rode two days, stopping for only short rests. Copher, Bale's lead guard, tracked the trail of two horses along the main road from Castle Carmine. The fugitives had stuck to the road for a long time, making their tracks easier to follow, but their distance covered far greater. It had been nearly a week since the attack on Castle Carmine, but unless they flew away on the backs of eagles, Copher could track them.

Copher pulled his horse to a stop, and Bale raised a hand for the men to stop. The blood hounds growled, searching the road's edge with their snouts to the ground, slobber hanging from their fangs. Copher dropped from his horse and walked back a few paces, his eyes to the ground. Bale did not speak or question the tracker. It was only a matter of time before they found the old man and the boy. But the Highfather was an impatient man. And Bale's blood supply wouldn't last forever.

"They left the road here," Copher said, pointing to a space where the trees parted. The tracker's long braid of hair swept against his back. "They're in the forest."

They had turned off the road before Denfold, avoiding the eyes of the nearby city. Maybe the old man was more than a castle-raised twit, after all. Or maybe they didn't travel alone. Though there were only two horse tracks, there were reports that a Carmine guard helped them escape. A deserter.

"Then they couldn't have gotten much farther," Bale said. He followed Copher into the wood as a wind whipped through the trees.

Copher swept pine needles aside to reveal circular hoof

prints. He was about to speak when the hounds perked up. The two beasts moved ahead, sniffing at the wind as it whistled, blowing dry leaves along the ground. One of the blood hounds raised its head and bellowed out a long howl. The other three followed, howling and barking toward the trees.

Blood was in the air.

"They have his scent," Copher said, standing up in surprise. The hounds fought at their chains, the scent driving them into a frenzy.

"Go get 'em," Bale yelled and unhooked their chains. The hounds charged ahead, their monstrous bodies tearing through the forest.

"Ya!" Bale commanded Smoke, and the great gray horse kicked forward, bounding after the blood hounds. The twelve guards raced to keep up.

This was it, they'd found them. Riding through the forest with the wind against his face, Bale could almost smell the blood himself. Blood he would taste before the day was through.

# 16

The morning was warm enough for Ara to ride without Chancey's heavy coat. Geyer led them through the forest on the white mare, and Ara sat with Briton on the bigger brown horse, talking through the day's lesson. Being outside the castle walls, on the run for their lives, hadn't stopped Ara's schooling in Briton's mind.

At least it passed the time on the long rides.

Ara recited the four main languages of Terene back to Briton, something Briton had explained to him just the previous day. Briton always reviewed past material to make sure Ara had not forgotten. Ara's memory was very good. He had plenty of space available, as Geyer put it.

"Dalcati, or the common tongue, is the dominant language of Terene," Ara said. "It is used throughout the known world and by all nobility and Fathers of the Faith. Next comes Biconda, spoken in the eastern shore. Cramna, the native tongue of the hill people of Clyda. And finally Sanstat, the desert language of the south."

"Very good," Briton said. "And why are there different languages?"

"People are separated by mountains and rivers and great

distances. Over time, each formed their own language. The Faith spoke Dalcati, and so over the centuries, it has become the dominant language under their rule. The other languages are now practiced only in the fringes and by those outside the Faith."

"Almost word for word," Briton said. "Your memory is even more of a gift than your blood, Ara. And what does this tell you of your past?"

"I speak Dalcati, therefore, I come from a Faith-dominated region."

"Let's say, *Faith influenced.* Many tribes not with the Faith still speak the common tongue."

"Dalcati has been around a long time."

Briton cocked his head. "Why do you say that?"

"It's the language of that old book of yours." Briton touched the chain around his neck. Though Briton claimed it was simply a diary from long ago, the old teacher still carried the tiny book with him.

"Good observation. Yes, Dalcati was the language of the Royals."

"What answers has that book taught you about the source of the Royal blood?" Ara asked.

Briton sighed. "Very little, I'm afraid. Either the source of the bloodline was a mystery, even to the Royals, or it was so commonly known that the king had no reason to give an account."

Morning light streamed through the cracks in the canopy above. From underneath, the thin leaves seemed to glow.

"Is Hemo real?" Ara asked.

Briton didn't answer.

"I know the Faith isn't the holy order they claim to be, since they want to hunt me down and torture me and everything, but both the Raw Bloods and the Royals believe in Hemo. They fight and die for him. So, is it true?"

Briton rode in silence for a moment, weighing his answer.

"There's nothing I've read or seen that proves he exists, or if he did exist, that he's still with us. But our very existence is a great mystery. We had to come from somewhere, the world and everything in it. I'm afraid it's likely a problem to which we'll never discover the solution."

That sounded like the kind of answer Ara would find in a philosophy book. It didn't tell him anything. "But do *you* believe in Hemo?"

Briton sighed. "Honestly, Ara, I don't know. If he does exist, I can't imagine him condoning the practices of the Faith, or wanting the Descendants persecuted in his name. And if he does, he's not someone we should be building monuments to."

The white horse stopped ahead of them, and Geyer turned in the saddle. His eyes searched the forest behind them.

"What is it?" Briton asked.

Geyer held up his hand. Ara couldn't hear anything through the wood save the occasional bird overhead. It had been so long since they encountered another person, he'd almost forgotten they weren't the only people in this part of the world.

A ferocious cry sounded in the distance.

"What is that?" Ara asked.

Fear spread across Geyer's face. "Blood hounds!" He looked to Ara and cursed himself, "Foolish clot!" He turned the surprised horse around and rode back, stopping alongside them. He ripped the bloody bandage off of Ara's face. It came loose with a tear. Ara's hand covered the stinging side of his face. He blinked, his right eye suddenly stabbed with gray light.

"They can follow the scent of his blood," Geyer said to Briton, holding up the cloth. "Ride on. Fast. I'll join you when I can."

The hounds howled in the distance, the dark call drawing closer.

"Ride!" Geyer shouted. Briton kicked, and the great brown horse charged forward with such speed that it nearly sent Ara to the ground. He clung to Briton's robes as they sped through the forest. Geyer rode off in another direction, the bloody cloth held out in the air.

They rode as fast as Briton could push the horse through the thick wood. The horse's hooves threatened to trip multiple times and send them toppling, but each time it caught its footing. Ara clung to Briton's waist so hard he feared he'd crush the old man. The howls of pursuit kept them moving forward, Briton letting the horse choose its own path.

They came to a rise and took it. The horse climbed, panting heavily. When they neared the top of the hill, Briton pulled the horse to a stop under the cover of trees. They sucked in air in great gasps, trying to catch their breaths.

"There," Briton pointed down the hill. Back in the forest below them, two separate parties of riders moved through the trees. White glinting shapes, forking away from each other.

"They've split up," Briton said. "Half must be chasing Geyer."

"Will they catch him?"

"He's got a better chance than us."

A large animal ran ahead of the horses, tearing up the ground in powerful bounds.

"What is that thing?"

"A blood hound. Used to track runaway Descendants. It must have gotten a hold of your blood."

"Can it still smell me?"

"I don't know. They may just be following our tracks."

The closer party of riders moved through the forest toward the slope. They came to the hill at the same spot Ara and Briton had begun their ascent. Ara got a clear view of what hunted him. Six men on horses. Beside them was a monstrous beast of brown and black fur. It looked like a small bear with a metal collar around its great head. It scrambled up the hill, barking and snarling ahead of the horses.

"No, no, no," Ara stammered at the approaching nightmare.

"Hold on," Briton said. He turned the horse and pushed it farther up the hill.

Ara didn't think the riders had seen them, but the hound had; he felt its eyes on his back now as he reached the top of the hill. He imagined what would happen when it finally caught them, and the beast leaped upon him with those teeth, tearing through his body to get to his blood. Could he heal from that? Would he want to?

The brown horse crested the hill and charged down the other side, picking up speed. The horse wobbled, trying to stay in control and avoid toppling over. Ara didn't care. Falling to his death would be better than dying under the claws and fangs of the hound.

At the bottom of the hill, the trees rose up thick before them. Ara could not see a gap the horse could possibly fit through. They were going to crash. He fought to keep his eyes open, not to turn away from the fate that awaited him.

"Whoa," Briton said, pulling back on the reins. But it was too late; they were moving too fast. The horse reached the bottom of the hill and leaped forward, clearing brush and a fallen tree. Ara felt himself flying through the air, as if in one of his visions. Then they crashed back to land with such force that it unseated him. He clawed for the saddle and hung for a moment on the side of the horse, his left foot stuck in the saddle bag. He looked up; a pool of water stretched out ahead of them.

"Whoaaaa," Briton tried again. The horse slowed, but not in time. They flew into the dark green pool. Water hit Ara like solid ground and ripped him off the horse. He spun underwater, surrounded by the thunderous kicks of the horse.

Ara's head stopped swirling as he finally came to rest, touching a foot to a soft slimy bottom. It gave way as he kicked up, swallowing his boot. Ara flailed his arms until his head emerged from the stagnant water. He gasped for breath and looked around. The brown horse charged still, coming out of the other side of the pool, shallower and shallower. Black leaves clung to its body. The horse didn't stop. It ran riderless through the woods, as if sensing the beast that pursued it.

Voices shouted behind them. Barks and growls filled the air.

Ara swung his arms and legs trying to stay above water.

"Ara," Briton called weakly. The old man's head poked out of the water near the side of the pool. Black leaves covered his bald head. "Your face."

*My face?* Ara stopped his thrashing long enough to reach up and touch his face. He felt a slippery texture. Mud stuck in his wound? He rubbed it but it would not scrape off. He looked down at his hand; they were not leaves. Black worm-like creatures spread flat along his skin, pulsing with life.

The creatures were everywhere, covering Ara's body. He swung his arms, trying to pull them off. He sunk down, unable to stay above water. The more he struggled the weaker he grew. Soon, he could barely kick his legs. It was a familiar weakness, the draining of strength. The pulsing black creatures were feeding on his blood!

"Through here!" a voice shouted over the barking. The riders crashed into the tree line.

Ara splashed frantically to stay above water and to wipe away the tiny creatures. But more and more black shapes floated toward him from all directions, biting onto his skin, sucking his blood, weighing him down. No longer able to stay afloat, Ara sunk under the surface as the creatures teemed on top of one another.

When he hit the bottom, the muddy floor encased him. As the blood left his body into hundreds of tiny parasites, Ara had a realization.

There was no healing from drowning.

GEYER KICKED THE WHITE HORSE, urging her on. A damn fool he had been to leave Ara's blood around. Of course, the Temple guard would use blood hounds to track them. A few days in the quiet of the woods, and he had forgotten what was after them.

Now, the hungry barks closing in reminded him all too well.

Geyer had hoped the pursuers would follow the scent of Ara's blood and leave the slower Briton and Ara, but they had divided ranks. A half-dozen riders chased Geyer with the blood-thirsty dogs. He had seen first-hand what the beasts could do to a man. Something he'd never forget. He kicked harder, cursing the weight of Briton's pack on the horse. *Who brings books on an escape party!*

Geyer raced ahead with no plan but to flee in a separate direction from Briton and Ara. As he cut through the trees, he needed to come up with something fast. The riders would soon be upon him.

A river roared somewhere ahead. Geyer turned the horse toward the sound, descending a small incline to a lower valley with a winding river. Geyer charged down the riverbank, leading the horse into the water. The horse's hoof prints ended at the sandy beach, disappearing as he reached the rock-bottomed river. This was it; he had only minutes before the riders were upon him. He leaped off the mare, splashing into the cold water. The river's current was strong and pulled at his legs. Geyer leaned forward, holding the horse's reins for balance.

"Stay here, girl," he said. Then he let go and strode through the water back to the riverbank, the bloody cloth in one hand. He lifted a small log that had washed up on the bank, careful to keep his feet on the rocks and not mark the sandy shore. He carried the log into the river until the cold water covered his waist. His foot slipped on the slick rocks and he was almost swept down the river. Geyer pressed the cloth through a jutting point on the log, poking a hole in the fabric. Then he wrapped the cloth around the log and released it. The log moved at an angle, and Geyer feared it would wash up on the bank again, but the rapids pulled it into their white channels; the log shot down-river and out of sight.

It worked. Now he had to get to cover. The riders would be upon him any second.

Geyer fought his way back to the horse, who had stayed despite the current's pull. "Good girl," Geyer said. He grabbed the reins and marched her up the river, staying deep enough in the water to not leave tracks. Pushing against the river was like fighting fate itself.

Hooves pounded behind Geyer; the riders were almost there.

*A little farther.* Geyer pressed through rapids to where the river calmed and sprinted around the bend just as the blood hounds reached the sandy riverbank. Barks and angry snarls echoed over the sound of the river.

Geyer bent down under the bank and held the horse still, praying the log trick would work and take the riders downriver. All of them this time.

Geyer's horse whinnied and shook off the cold water.

"Shhh. Quiet, girl." Geyer petted her head and led her to the soft riverbank. Though the rapids smashing against the rocks was loud, Geyer didn't want to take the chance of being heard. He tied the horse to a thin branch and pulled his sword from the saddle scabbard, tying it across his waist. With any luck, he wouldn't need it. The thought of luck made Geyer glance at the wheel of fate on the end of his sword handle. He frowned. He'd been wrong to think he'd hit bottom at Castle Carmine. Fate could always spin him lower.

Crouching, Geyer inched along the bank under the cover of brush. Two great blood hounds sniffed along the spot he had entered the water. The hounds dug their snouts into the sand and rocks coming his way and then circled back around.

Seven riders reached the river's edge and pulled up their horses. They wore the white uniform of the Temple guard over their armor. All except one. Atop a great gray horse sat a tall man in black armor. This was the one people talk about; Bale the Blood Knight, personal sword to the Highfather himself.

Geyer held his breath. His sword felt heavy in his hands. Could he still use it as he once had?

Then the fates shined on him. The blood hounds stood erect, aiming their noses high in the air. They barked downriver and tore off after Ara's bloody rag. The riders followed after them.

Geyer exhaled as the beasts and six Temple guards disappeared down the winding riverbank. But one did not go. The man in black stayed behind, scanning the river's edge.

Geyer crouched lower into the brush as the man turned his way, his dark eyes falling upon him. A cold chill whipped through Geyer's body; his legs froze in place. He'd seen that face before. It came to him on those fitful nights when the alcohol failed to drown out the nightmares of the past.

It was the face of the assassin who killed James and Maddie Carmine.

But that was impossible. Geyer had sent his sword through the man's heart that day in the Hidden Forest. Yet, here he stood. Alive. The leader of the Temple guard. It wasn't possible.

Geyer wrapped a shaking hand around the handle of his sword. He was slow and far from fighting shape. Still, it was Geyer's duty to avenge his old master. The knight's code demanded it. But his legs trembled under him, forbidding him to rise. He dropped lower; a coward hiding in the brush.

Death waited on the riverbank.

Geyer stayed hidden long after the horse hooves had faded and Bale the Blood Knight was gone. Geyer crumbled to his knees. He'd been defeated without even drawing his sword. As much as he hated his life, he was afraid to die.

Behind him, the white horse pulled loose from the tree branch and trotted up to him. Geyer grabbed the horse's reins, his mind coming back to the present—the old man and the boy. By now, they were either dead or captured.

No. Geyer had to know for sure. He pulled himself onto the horse.

*You coward. It is not time to surrender yet.*

The white horse raced uphill, away from the river and back toward where they had separated. Could they still be alive? The Blood Knight and the hounds had followed Geyer, maybe he'd only sent a small party after Briton and the boy. Geyer's hopes faded when he found their tracks. The forest floor was torn up by hooves and paw prints.

Geyer gritted his teeth and forced the white horse on, afraid of what he would find at the end of the trail.

THE BARKING FADED. Briton moved from his cover in the brush and frantically ripped the leeches off his skin and wet robes. One held fast to his neck and bled once he finally tore it free. The riders were gone, following the tracks of the runaway horse. They had not seen Briton or...

"Ara," Briton called. The boy had disappeared under the water's surface. Briton had thought it was to hide. Briton had held his own breath at the sight of the Temple guards and the giant hound, but Ara had not come up again. He'd been under too long.

"Ara!" Briton lurched back into the stagnant green pool. His boots sank in the muddy bottom as he waded out to the spot where Ara's body had submerged. "Ara!"

Briton slipped, his legs buckling. Even if he found the boy, he didn't have the strength to carry him out; he could barely stay afloat himself. He would simply have to find a way. *Every problem has a solution, you old fool!*

The water was up to Briton's chin now, and he held his head up as he waded forward. The dark shapes of leeches moved through the murky green water, but Briton pressed on. He would likely drown himself, but still, Briton pressed on.

His boot struck something solid underwater. Something that gave way.

"Ara!" Briton yelled. Before he could think he dropped down under the water, reaching to the bottom of the pool. Briton grabbed at the body until he caught hold of an arm. The arm was slimy with leeches, but Briton held on, throwing it over his shoulder. His back cried out in pain. Exhaling air through gritted teeth, Briton pushed the boy's body to the surface.

Briton gasped for breath. He maneuvered Ara's head out of the water. The body was lifeless in his hands. Ara did not breathe.

"Ara, please," Briton cried out. His mouth filled with putrid water as he tried to keep his own head above the surface as well as Ara's. Black leeches covered Ara's neck and face; one hung out of his open mouth. "Breathe, Ara. Breathe." Briton kicked, pulling Ara toward dry ground.

Horse hooves beat the ground nearby. The riders had heard his cries. It didn't matter; he had to save Ara. Briton lost his footing, and they collapsed under water. He scrambled back to the surface, choking on the filthy water. Ahead of him, a white horse stood on the water's edge.

"Give him to me," Geyer said, seizing Ara's limp body. Geyer carried the boy out of the pool and laid him on the ground of dry leaves.

"Is he alive?" Briton cried, his voice weak as he crawled his way to the boy's side. Geyer drew his knife and cut leeches from Ara's body; they were fat with Ara's blood. The leeches fell away to reveal the boy's usual pale skin was now a deep blue. "Is he?"

"He's not breathing," Geyer said. He flipped Ara on his side and struck his upper back with the heel of his hand in powerful bursts. Ara's body flopped lifelessly on the ground.

Then, dark water shot from the boy's mouth. He coughed up more, opening his eyes and gasping for breath. Geyer turned him onto his hands and knees and patted his back, gently this time. "It's okay, Ara. It's over now."

"My blood," Ara said faintly, his eyes closed as he rocked back and forth. "They took my blood."

"Leeches," Geyer said, kicking away a few that were crawling back toward Ara.

"That feeling," Ara said, hugging his knees and shivering. His words fell out in sobs. "Never again. I'll die before anyone takes my blood again."

Geyer grabbed Briton's hand and pulled him to his feet. Briton didn't think he could stand but he managed, leaning against a tree and brushing the leeches from his robe.

"What of the Temple guards?" Geyer asked, scanning the forest.

"That way," Briton said. "They went after the horse. They'll catch him soon if they haven't already."

"Yes, we need to move."

"We won't get far," Briton groaned, his back locking like a steel trap. "We've only the one horse."

Geyer looked around, thinking. "They don't know where you abandoned the horse. We should head back to the road. If we follow the same path, we'll be harder to track. If we make it to the road, we head to Denfold and try to find help there."

"What about the blood hounds?"

He looked at Ara's body. Red patches marked his pale skin.

"We keep him covered and hope he heals in time."

Briton nodded. They didn't have much of a choice.

"They were Temple guards, not Carmine's men."

Geyer nodded. "I saw. It was the one they called the Blood Knight."

"Then it's the Highfather who hunts for the boy. Who sent the assassins to Carmine Castle."

"That's not all. He's the one who killed James and Maddie, who butchered my men."

"Bale was the assassin? But I thought he died."

Geyer's face darkened. "So did I."

Briton thought about the implications. The Highfather of the Faith orchestrating the murder of James Carmine. What would Jonathan do once he found out? Did he have the power to unite the western lords to his side?

Briton shook his head. He was still thinking like Carmine's

advisor. He had forsaken that duty when he helped the boy escape. Now he was nothing but a fugitive. A traitor.

Ara's whimpering had stopped. He had fallen asleep but was still breathing. Geyer lifted the boy up and carried him to the horse, tying him to the saddle.

"Ride with him," Geyer said. "We can't stay here."

Geyer helped Briton onto the horse behind Ara, and they set off at a gentle pace, Geyer walking the horse up the hill. It began to rain.

"Looks like we have a little luck left," Geyer said. "The rain will cover our tracks and slow their riding."

Briton pulled his wet robes tighter. He had nearly died, and if they didn't find shelter soon they'd freeze to death. What a sight they made; an old man, a lifeless boy, and a hobbled knight on the run from the largest, most powerful force in the known world.

Briton might have laughed at their chances if it wouldn't have hurt so much.

# 17

It was the same story in every miserable town Cambria and the caravan of doctors visited. Superstitious fools putting their hope in ancient magical cures. This time it was in the northwestern town of Denfold. The doctors arrived and set up their tents; they offered medicine and care for next to nothing, knowing what the poor villagers could afford. And still, the sick and injured of the town did not come. They would rather wait in line for hours outside the Curor shop, hoping blood would solve all their problems, from arthritis to the dry crop season. The northern villages shunned actual medicine.

The three villagers that did venture to their tents that morning suffered the same thing: rashes. The urgency of their burning skin outweighed the stigma of the doctors. Cambria fetched the creams from the tent, and Hannah applied them to the men who reluctantly revealed their skin to the women. Cambria could see the immediate effects of the cooling cream as the men relaxed, the burning itch subsiding. Soon the relief on their faces was replaced with fear.

"What kind of magic is this?" one of the men asked.

"No magic sir, a mixture of simple herbs found in the nearby forest," Hannah said.

"Witch's work," the man said and pulled his pants back up and hurried off with the others without paying, running fast on legs now free of rash.

"The cowards didn't even pay," Cambria grumbled.

"Petar will take care of it," Hannah said. "Besides, it's enough that we helped. They will spread the word, and the town will open up to us."

"Why are they so afraid?" Cambria asked. "I picked the elderweed for that cream just outside the village. The fools walk by it every day."

"People fear what they don't understand. Our work is to teach as much as it is to heal."

Cambria shook her head as she tightened the lid on the cream and put it back on the shelf. Things were much easier south, where people actually appreciated their services. There, a doctor could make a decent living, even stay in one spot and not have to brave the dangers of the road. But in the north where the Faith ruled, blood was the only thing people believed in.

"Next time I'll put some of this elderweed in their drinks and see how they like our witch magic then."

"Cambria," Hannah shot her a disapproving look. "If you know what happens if elderweed is ingested then you know not to joke about it."

Cambria knew. It'd been one of the first things her mother had taught her. It had gotten her hooked on medicine in the first place. The same ingredients that could remedy a rash if applied on the epidermis, would cause projectile diarrhea if given orally.

"I just thought if we were going to teach these people, it would help to first clear out all the feces they'd been fed."

Hannah bit her lip to stifle a laugh and tossed an empty stone tonic bottle to Cambria. "That's enough. Go see if Brim needs any help with supplies."

Cambria stepped out of the tent into the gloomy late morning air. They had arrived in Denfold by night and slept in their wagons. They set up tents at first light; most of the work was done by Petar, Aaron, and Brim, leaving Cambria and Hannah to organize supplies from the two wagons. Aaron was now off trading supplies in town. Cambria hoped he would get some honey cakes. It had been a long time since the travelers had indulged on something sweet. It made Cambria miss her parents even more.

Word of their work had indeed traveled fast as a large group now approached their tents. But Cambria's heart sank at the sight of a red robe. A Curor. Cambria's hand went to her belt, where her knife was hidden.

Before she could call a warning, Petar came out of the main tent and met the men with a smile. "Good health, gentlemen. How can we be of service?"

The Curor stepped forward and looked over their tents and wagons with disgust. "Denfold is a loyal town of the Faith," the Curor said. "This is no place for false healers."

"Then we are in agreement," Petar said. "For we are simple doctors offering help to those in need."

"Witchcraft, you mean!" a man shouted.

"No, only science. My companions and I are well-versed in anatomy and medicine. We reset broken bones and offer natural medicine to the sick. We know no spells or magic potions." Petar chuckled at this, but the others didn't share his sense of humor.

"I am the town Curor," the red-robed man said. "Appointed by the Fathers of the Faith to serve these lands with blessed blood from Hemo."

"And what of those who cannot afford the price of blood?"

"Hemo helps all who are deemed worthy. We have no need for the interference of southern medicine."

With that, the Curor raised his hand, and the men moved forward, brandishing their crude swords; the largest man held an old axe whose loose head slid when he raised the handle. At the sight of the weapons, Brim came out of the tent, and the men took a step back, seeing the size of him. Petar put a hand to Brim. "We want no trouble," he called.

"Then leave now before we cut you and your tents to ribbons," a man called.

Cambria inched closer, her hand on her blade. The men's eyes held on Brim; they weren't paying her any mind. She studied the closest man, noting the places her small blade could do the most damage.

"Alright," Petar sighed. "We respect your wishes." He nodded to Brim. The large man gave no objection but set to work on dismantling the tents he had just finished setting up. The Curor said something to his men and then swept back toward town. Three men stayed behind to watch the doctors.

"That's it then?" Cambria asked, approaching Petar. "We're just going to let these thugs run us off?"

"Our mission is to heal injuries, not to be the cause of them," Petar said. He headed to Hannah's tent; she wasn't going to like the news. A doctor's life was lived on the move, but it'd been too long since they found a friendly town.

When Aaron returned with supplies, the wagons were already packed. "What's going on?" he asked, setting down his small cart.

"Let's get this stuff loaded in the wagons," Petar said. He and Brim grabbed the food and provisions out of Aaron's cart.

Aaron frowned when he saw the three armed men beside their camp. "What happened here?" he asked Cambria, who had come over to inspect the contents of his cart.

"The usual northern welcoming," she grumbled.

"Again?" Aaron whined. "I'm sick of the road." At nineteen, he was older than Cambria but still complained like a child; it betrayed a rich upbringing. He didn't speak much of his past before meeting up with the caravan, but Cambria could tell he'd studied at some southern university. She, on the other hand, had only her parents and the things she picked up from Petar and Hannah.

Petar climbed aboard the front of the first wagon and started the horse moving. Brim followed with the second. Under the watchful gaze of three armed men, they left the town of Denfold. They had treated three men and been run out of town for their trouble. Now they were back on the road heading to another superstitious town wary of real medicine. Cambria leaned back as the old wagon bounced on the dirt road, angry that Aaron had returned without a single treat.

As they traveled down the road, Cambria kept herself busy taking inventory. One benefit of a lack of business was that it kept their supply of bandages and medicine stocked. However, they would need to stop before the next town to gather some elderweed. The recipe was her mother's. Petar and Hannah had been impressed by the fast working cream; so much so that soon after taking Cambria on, it replaced the standard Apothecary's Rose. At the time, Cambria had been lucky to find a company of doctors. She fit right in with Petar, Hannah, and their caravan of lost causes.

After all that time, Brim was the only other one who remained. Though the big dolt didn't know the first thing about medicine, and obviously couldn't work with patients. Petar had saved Brim's life, and Brim had been attached to the doctor's side ever since. Aaron, they picked up a little over a year ago along with three others. They were a group of four young doctors with proper training, who sought to share their new skills with the archaic northerners. Six months later only Aaron remained.

Cambria finished her list of supplies when the wagon slowed to a stop. It was too early to break for a rest. Cambria's heartbeat quickened. She climbed out of the wagon into the gray light, her hand moving to her belt. The blade was small but could do damage in the right hands; hands that knew the body and its most vulnerable points. She crept to the front and peered out of the wagon. Three figures waited in the road ahead. They were a wretched sight and made for strange companions.

A large man in green led the way on foot; he had wild hair and dragged his left leg. A horse carried an old bald man in dirty, gray robes who looked ready to topple over at any moment. In front of that man lay a sleeping boy, tied to the horse. Cambria almost mistook him for a corpse. Cambria let go of her blade. She'd encountered bandits along the road; it was part of the trade. Some had been quite theatrical in their approach—wounded old men, mothers carrying sick babies, a marriage party seeking help for a poisoned bride—but, if this was an act, it was the best she'd ever seen.

"Ho, there," Petar called, stepping down from the lead wagon. "Good health and peace be with you."

"And you as well," the old man on the horse spoke up in a weak voice. The man in green eyed the caravan suspiciously. That was a good sign, Cambria thought. Friendly travelers on the road were usually up to something; those who were harmless would be equally as skeptical of friendliness.

"You look road weary, friends," Petar said. "Can we offer you something to eat, perhaps take a look at the boy."

"No," the large man said, stepping in front of the horse and the boy.

"We mean you no harm," Petar said. "You may pass freely if you wish, but we do have food and medicine, and are trained in administering at least one of them." He smiled that grin of his, the one Cambria warned him about. People on the road were naturally untrusting, she told him. That smile made him look like an accomplished robber.

"You are doctors?" the old man asked. "This far north?"

"People are in need of health everywhere. Even in the north."

The old man considered Petar. Then his eyes fell on the boy before him. "Food would be much appreciated," he said. "It has been some time since we ate or rested."

"No," his companion said. "We must keep moving."

"You are heading to Denfold," Petar said. "We just came from there. I hope your reception is warmer than our own."

The two men spoke amongst each other. The boy on the

horse was still unconscious. What had they done to him? He was obviously sick and malnourished; his skin was pale, almost blue. He would not make it to Denfold. And when he didn't, they would simply believe it was Hemo's will. Cambria couldn't take any more of this superstitious foolishness, especially when it would cost a boy his life.

"If you are seeking the Curor in Denfold, then you are making a mistake," Cambria said, climbing out of the wagon. "The boy will die before you get there."

The old man looked down at the boy; uncertainty registered on his face.

"You'll have to forgive Cambria," Petar said. "A talented girl for her age, but lacking in bedside manner. Though her diagnosis is likely accurate. The boy does not look well."

"We do not travel to Denfold," the old man said. "We only...wish to be off the road, and that is the nearest town. We passed some men in the wood we would like to avoid."

Petar nodded. "We know all too well the dangers of the road. But there is safety in numbers. Come with us. We can provide food and rest, and we will be away from here faster than you would with a man on foot."

The old man looked to his companion. The man in green nodded reluctantly. "We would be most grateful to accept your offer," the old man said. "Tell us your price and we will happily join you."

"That can be worked out at a later time. Tie your horse to the rear wagon and we will find you some room inside. My wife Hannah will tend to the boy."

The man in green would not take a wagon but insisted on sitting up front alongside Petar. He was nervous about something and pulled a long sword from the horse's saddle to carry on his lap as they rode. It was not the simple sword of a villager.

Cambria tried to join Hannah in the rear wagon, not wanting to leave the woman alone with the two strangers—even an old man and an unconscious boy. But it was too crowded, and Hannah ordered her to the front wagon.

"Use gloves," Cambria warned her, thinking of another time she'd met sick strangers on the road. "We don't know what he has."

Hannah gave a gentle nod. "I'll be careful, Cambria. I promise. Now go to the front wagon. I need space to work."

Cambria did as she was told and took her place beside Aaron as the wagons moved once more.

"Was that boy dead?" Aaron asked, looking out to the rear wagon.

"Not yet," Cambria said. "If he can be saved, Hannah will do it." Though Hannah proved her skill time and time again, Cambria couldn't help but feel nervous. It wasn't Gray Fever, but she still hoped Hannah would take every precaution. She couldn't handle losing her and Petar.

The wagon bumped down the road once again. Cambria crawled to the front of the wagon, right behind the man in green. These strangers didn't seem the outlaw type, not the old man and the boy, anyway. But they were hiding something. Petar was a gentle man—it made him a good doctor but a mark on the road. Cambria waited with her eyes open and her knife close. If trouble came, it would be up to her to get them through it.

BRITON WAS RELIEVED when the wagon started moving. He had accepted they would likely die in the forest with Ara carted off to spend his days tortured for his blood in the Temple dungeons. He was surprised to make the long trek back to the road with no sign of the Temple guard. Now, hope began to creep in once again, along with the fear of it being taken away.

"What is the boy's name?" Hannah asked as she wrapped a blanket around Ara.

"Ara," Briton said, looking down at the pale blue figure. The boy had moved in and out of consciousness on the slow ride, but with no food or water, his body looked too weak to heal itself. Not to mention the amount of blood he had lost. With the constant blood draws, Ara's body hadn't been allowed to recover since coming to Castle Carmine. Briton wondered what the boy could do at full strength.

"Ara," Hannah said gently, leaning close to the boy's face. "You need to drink this." She held up a glass of a light brown liquid mixed with leaves. She put the glass to Ara's lips and forced some down in slow pours. Ara coughed as he drank, never opening his eyes.

"Good, Ara, good," she said. "It would be better warm, but, apparently we don't have time to stop for a fire." She turned to Briton. "What happened to him? His skin is freezing."

"He nearly drowned," Briton said.

"And these marks?"

"Leeches."

Hannah shook her head. "Seems like this boy's been through an awful lot of trouble." She hovered her hand over his face, inspecting the scars from Geyer's knife.

"Yes, he has," Briton said.

"Besides being cold and almost drowning, the boy is malnourished. You look like you haven't eaten in days."

Briton nodded weakly. It took great effort just to stay sitting up in the bumpy wagon and not collapse into unconsciousness himself. But he had to stay awake to watch the boy. He didn't know if these people could be trusted. Though, if they meant them ill, there was little he could do about it.

"Here," Hannah said. She twisted open a jar containing strips of dried meat. The smell filled the wagon, and Briton's stomach jumped. "Salted meat to hold you over until we can make a proper meal. Feed what you can to the boy and eat some yourself before you pass out."

"Thank you, my lady," Briton said, taking the meat strips.

"We are indebted to you for your generosity. Few doctors would come to these lands. I know it must be difficult for you."

"That is why we are here."

"Well, the north is better for it."

As they rode on, Briton tore the meat into small bites and fed them to Ara. The boy ate slowly and without opening his eyes, still in the delirium of semi-consciousness. Briton ate as well; his tongue welcoming the salted meat. All the while Briton had one ear on the road outside the wagon, anticipating the sound of horses or the chilling howl of a blood hound. He ate and watched Hannah work, rubbing a cream on Ara's skin. He couldn't help but feel guilty for endangering these people. For when the Temple guard caught them, they would certainly be slain.

But the attack never came. And as day faded into night and they moved farther and farther away from Carmine's lands, it looked like they might just survive another day.

"Did they catch us?" Ara asked suddenly, startling Briton. The boy's eyes opened, and he tried to sit up, looking around the wagon.

"Shhh," Briton whispered, patting his hair and holding him down. "You're safe. Rest now."

They rode on, and Ara's appetite grew. He took full bites of the salted meat and finished off Hannah's herbal drink before returning to sleep. The leech marks on Ara's skin had begun to fade and his color returned to his normal shade. If Hannah noticed, she said nothing.

Though it felt good to be out of the forest and in the care of the traveling doctors, Briton knew they needed to leave. For the scars on Ara's face would soon disappear and the doctors would have questions they could not answer. But for now, Briton could no longer keep his eyes open. He lay down in an empty space in the wagon and slept. Their problems would still be waiting for him when he woke.

· · ·

"IT LOOKS LIKE ANY OTHER BLOOD," Vorrel said, holding the bottle of blood up to his crooked nose. Haemon studied it with a frown. They had raided Carmine Castle only to find a single bottle of the Descendant boy's blood left in Carmine's storehouse. It seems Carmine had used nearly his entire supply in bribing the western lords. This made finding the boy all that more important to Haemon's plans.

"Are you saying there's no difference?" Haemon asked his Head Curor. They met in a hidden lab in the old part of the Temple. Holes of broken stone still filled the wall from the Blood War. Here Vorrel's work could be kept secret from Edmund Turney and the other Fathers.

"Not that the eye can detect," Vorrel said. "But that doesn't mean it is not all that it is claimed to be. Descendants blood looks identical as well. It is only through testing the effects, or knowing the breeding history of the Descendant, that we know if it is good blood or not."

Haemon coughed, pulling a rag from his pocket. He felt more tired lately even as his daily dose continued to grow. How long before blood wasn't enough?

"This blood came at great cost," the Highfather said. "Are you able to replicate it?"

Vorrel shifted nervously. He knew how much Haemon wanted this, needed this. He also knew what had happened to the last Curor in charge of creating a more powerful blood. "We are very close."

"Good," Haemon said. "Our world can no longer rely on Descendant blood. The others on the council do not see it. They think it is the will of Hemo that blood is weakening with each generation, but Hemo has called me to action. It's a fool who sits in prayer while his world collapses around him."

"What about Father Turney? His men search the Temple, they will find this lab eventually."

The Highfather sighed. Edmund had proved a thorn in his

palm. It seemed his ambition rivaled Haemon's own, once upon a time. A good trait in a subordinate, but a dangerous one in a political adversary. If Edmund wanted his chair, it would take a lot more than snooping. He didn't know if Edmund was ready to pay the price as he once had.

"I'll take care of the young Father. Hemo has given us this blood, no one will stand in our way." The Highfather reached out and took the bottle. It was heavy in his hands. But everything was these days. Was this bottle really worth starting a war over? He had to be sure.

Haemon pried loose the cork.

"Father," Vorrel said, "the blood is untested. We cannot be sure of its safety."

Haemon raised the bottle to his lips and took a small sip, just a taste. The blood tasted like any other; no stronger than his daily dose. Had this all been for nothing?

Then a warmth came over him. A wave of relief shifting through his body. Haemon stood straighter; his muscles tightened and his bones hardened. It was as if years had shed like a skin. Then, as quickly as it had come, the warmth receded. He felt his spine curl, and the pain returned to his taxed muscles. Pain that was more noticeable now for having been suspended. It took all of Haemon's willpower not to down the whole bottle.

"I must have more of this blood!"

"Yes," Vorrel said, carefully taking the bottle from Haemon's hands. "We will find an answer, Father. Have faith."

Haemon closed his eyes as the bottle left his hands. "Do we know how the boy came to possess such pure blood?"

"No. But we will find the answers." Vorrel looked around the small makeshift lab and his table of instruments. "It will help once we have the boy himself to examine."

"You will soon enough. Make certain the process is ready. I expect you to be able to replicate the blood on a massive scale as soon as I bring you the boy."

"Yes, Father," Vorrel bowed.

Haemon turned as the coughing came in fits this time. He hunched against the doorway until it was over. His rag was stained red with his own blood. He wadded it up in his fist.

Bale better find the boy. He better find him soon.

# 18

---

The howls grew louder as the blood hounds closed in. No matter how fast Ara ran, the riders in white armor followed tirelessly. No place was safe; the great hounds at their heels could smell Ara over great distance. They followed his scent through rivers and over mountains, thirsting for his blood. His legs slipped on mud, he could run no more. The hounds were upon him. Then Ara found himself underwater. He sank lower, expending the last of his strength to fight away hounds and leeches and Curors, all grasping for his blood. He screamed for help and water filled his lungs.

Ara woke, gasping for air, covered in sweat. He breathed until his heart settled in his chest. The leech marks on his skin were gone. He felt his face and found no traces of the scars that had been there the day before. He felt the power of his blood coursing through his veins.

Despite drowning in his dream, Ara's throat was dry. He climbed over Briton's sleeping body and out of the wagon in search of something to drink. The morning air was cold. Ara shivered, pulling Chancey's oversized coat over his torn night-shirt. Along with his crumbling pants, what he wore could no longer be described as clothes. He would need to find something else to wear. And soon.

The white horse grazed in a field of grass beside two brown horses. All three were tied to long ropes that allowed them to move about. The second wagon was parked near the first, and though the flap was down, Ara could hear the heavy breathing of someone asleep inside. Further on in the clearing stood two small tents that looked surprisingly sturdy for having been set up in the dark.

The crackling of a fire caught Ara's ear, and he moved around the wagon. A large man sat on a rock, warming his hands over the small fire. His dark hair was uniformly short like it was recovering from being shaved. Ara recognized the broad shoulders as belonging to the driver of his wagon. The man watched as Ara took a seat on one of the rocks gathered in a circle around the fire. Then he turned his attention back to warming his big, calloused hands.

A teakettle leaning near the fire reminded Ara of his thirst. "Can I have some?" he asked, pointing to the kettle and nearby cups. The man studied Ara and then the kettle before finally nodding. Ara moved closer feeling the warm fire on his face as he poured himself a cup of the liquid. "Do you want a cup?"

The man shook his head and flipped his hands over, heating the backside now.

Ara came back to his rock and took a careful sip. The drink warmed his insides as if bringing them to life. It was a different drink than the woman had made, plainer, but the warm liquid felt good on his throat. Ara drank until the cup was empty.

"Thank you," Ara said, still holding the empty cup in his hands.

The man didn't respond. He kept his eyes on the fire.

It seemed not everyone in their party shared Hannah's welcoming demeanor. Ara stood to leave, not wanting to upset the large man when one of the tent flaps opened. A man with straight blond hair stepped out and stretched his thin arms in the air. He looked at Ara and then to the big man by the fire. He grinned at some unspoken joke. The thin man approached the fire and put a hand on the big man's shoulder.

"You making our guest feel at home, Brim?" the man asked, his smile growing even bigger as he turned to Ara. "You'll have to forgive Brim; he's not great at conversation. It's good to see you up and about. Hannah must have worked wonders on you."

Ara became aware of how he must look this morning compared to yesterday, his blood having healed him, but the man did not press the issue. His face was anything but accusatory.

"My name is Petar," the man said.

"Ara."

"Welcome, Ara. I hope you were able to get some sleep on the road the past couple days. Your friend in green was adamant that we keep moving." Petar looked around the grass clearing. "But if we hadn't, we never would have found this lovely spot. Beautiful isn't it?"

Ara scanned the forest. He'd grown tired of trees.

"So much green in this part of the world." Petar smiled, taking in the morning. "We have nothing like this in Seren."

"Seren?" Ara asked. "Is that where you're from?"

"Yes," Petar said, sitting down on a rock beside Ara. "My wife Hannah and I worked as doctors there before making the venture north. Brim here is a northerner. Aren't you, Brim?"

Brim nodded slightly.

"He's been with us the past five years now. Cambria for three, and we picked up Aaron just last summer."

"What are doctors?" Ara asked.

"Ha, we really are in the north," Petar laughed. "Doctors are trained to help and heal people using science and medicine."

"So, you are like Curors."

"Quite the opposite. We believe the recovery of one shouldn't come at the suffering of another. There are many ways to heal our bodies without the use of old blood cures—as you already saw from Hannah's work."

Ara thought of the tea and the liquid she rubbed on his body.

"How are you feeling today?" Petar asked.

"Much better, thank you. I just needed some rest."

"You were certainly a rugged bunch when we found you on the road. I hope your friends were able to get some sleep. They seemed quite on edge."

With that, Geyer came limping from the forest. The former knight looked as run down as before, and Ara wondered if he had slept at all over the past two days.

"Morning, friend," Petar said with a smile.

Geyer nodded. "What is your plan, Petar?"

"The plan is breakfast. The horses still need a little rest, as do we all, after the last couple days. We should be ready to head out again by late morning if that works for you."

Geyer nodded, looking into the fire. "Yes. Fine."

"Did you say breakfast?" Ara asked, his stomach leaped at the word.

"We have some fresh bread and oranges from Denfold if you are hungry."

"Yes! Thank you." He was starving.

"Later," Geyer said. "Ara, come with me."

Ara looked at him confused. What could be more important than breakfast?

"We're taking a short walk," Geyer said to Petar. "We'll be back soon."

"We'll have breakfast ready," Petar said. "Right, Brim?"

Brim looked at Geyer, but didn't say a word. It was clear he didn't like what he saw.

"Ara," Geyer called. Ara got up and reluctantly followed Geyer through the grass clearing toward the wood where he had come.

"Where are we going?" Ara asked once they were out of earshot.

"What do you think of our new companions?"

"They seem very friendly," Ara said. "They're doctors."

"Hmm. Friendly travelers on the road are like honorable knights—they're told in many tales but rarely ever encountered."

"Are we going to leave? Can we at least wait until after breakfast?"

They walked through the wood for a while to where the trees were spread out allowing room for light to shine down from the gray morning sky. Ara walked softly on the balls of his feet as Geyer had taught him. Finally, they reached an open space where the ground was level.

"You can't rely on these doctors or me or Briton," Geyer said, turning to Ara. "The way to survive in this world is to look after yourself."

Geyer's face was serious, his voice missing his usual wry humor.

"You wanted to learn to fight with a sword, but you are too weak to handle one proficiently."

"I can get stronger. I already—"

Geyer held up his hand, and Ara fell silent.

"You may get strong enough to use a sword—one day you may become the greatest swordsman who ever lived, and men may sing of your glory—but the danger is here, now. So, we'll start with a knife."

Geyer reached to his belt, and his hand came away with such speed that Ara hardly had time to flinch as a knife whizzed by and slammed into a tree trunk behind him. The knife clattered to the grass at Ara's feet.

Geyer frowned. "That was supposed to stick."

The old knight pulled a second knife from a hiding place in his left boot, the blade as long as his hand.

"You won't be stronger than your opponent, but you can be faster." He nodded to the knife on the ground. "Go on."

Ara picked up the knife and studied it. He moved the weapon, testing its weight. The leather handle was worn, but the blade was sharp. It felt natural in his hand. Familiar.

"Fighting is all about advantage," Geyer said. "What advantage can you find?"

"I don't have an advantage," Ara said. "Everyone is bigger than me."

"And they will underestimate you. You must use surprise. They can't see you as a threat until it's too late."

"Is that why you have a limp?"

"No," Geyer stopped, furrowing his brow. "I have a limp because someone nearly cut my leg off."

"Oh. Right."

Geyer stepped forward with his knife out. "Now show me how fast you are. Keep the knife tight to your body to strike, and away from your body to defend."

"We're going to practice with real knives? Shouldn't we use sticks or something first?"

"If you want to learn to fight with a stick use a stick. If you want to learn to fight with a knife use a knife. Much time is wasted teaching fighting with wooden swords. Once you move to a real blade, the weight and balance and fear must be relearned all over again. We don't have the luxury of time, but we do have one luxury that will make your training faster than anyone else's."

"What's that?" Before Ara finished the question, Geyer leaped forward, thrusting at Ara. Ara jumped back and swung his knife to defend the oncoming blade. Metal clinked on metal as Ara stumbled backward. Geyer attacked again. Ara blocked the first obvious thrust, and then Geyer swung the blade down and sliced Ara above the knee. Ara screamed in pain and grabbed at the cut.

"Our luxury is that you can heal," Geyer said. "So there's no need to hold back."

"It still hurts!" Ara yelled, holding his knee. He pulled his hand away. It was colored by blood. His blood.

"That's something you need to get used to." Geyer held his knife out, pointing at Ara. "Now, attack."

"But what if I cut *you*?" Ara asked.

"Then the lesson will be over, and you can have your breakfast."

Ara didn't know what he wanted more. He sprung forward, swinging his knife wildly. Geyer stepped back, keeping his distance, not needing to raise his knife. He was quick even with the bad leg. Ara could see how most of the old knight's weight fell on the good right leg, and the other touched the ground behind him for balance. Ara thrust the knife straight for Geyer's belly, and Geyer made a casual backhand swipe that knocked the knife from Ara's hand.

"Grip your knife as if your life depends on it. Because it does."

Ara picked the knife off the ground and gripped it tighter. He swung a fury of attacks, this time deliberately targeting high and low. With each move, he felt more capable, as if the knife was at home in his hand. The steps came naturally: parry, attack, parry, attack. He swung a combination at Geyer's gut, and the old knight nearly tripped as he fended it off.

Geyer looked at Ara in surprise. "You were holding out on me."

"What do you mean?"

"You've done this before."

"Not that I remember."

But, yes, something felt familiar about this. He'd handled weapons in the past. Ara bobbed back and forth, excitedly. This might trigger his memories, help him remember who he was.

Then Geyer attacked. His blows were more fierce, showing he'd only been holding back. Ara weaved and blocked, narrowly dodging Geyer's blade. Their knives met overhead, and Geyer swung his good leg, sweeping Ara's feet out from under him.

Ara fell flat on his back, losing his breath on impact. But he held onto his knife.

"Good," Geyer said. "There might be hope for you yet. If you happen to face an old cripple and not an army of Temple guards, that is."

Ara breathed heavily. He was already out of breath from the short skirmish. His stomach longed for the breakfast waiting back at the fire. Had Petar said, oranges? Plus, Ara felt ridiculous fighting in Chancey's oversized coat.

"Can I take this off?" Ara asked. "It's hard to move in."

Geyer nodded. Ara took off the coat slowly, switching knife hands to get the sleeves off and using the time to catch his breath. The moment the coat was off, Ara flung it at Geyer. Geyer caught the coat as it covered his head, and Ara lunged forward. He swiped at Geyer's bad leg, knowing it would be slower to move. Geyer recovered from the ambush, tossing the coat aside, but Ara was upon him. Ara swung low and nicked Geyer's calf. It was a small scratch, but it tore Geyer's pants and left a sliver of a cut.

Ara stepped back, his knife out in a defensive position. Ready for Geyer's angry reaction.

Geyer looked at the droplet of blood on his leg and then at Ara.

"That was well done. You used surprise and found an advantage. Even the strongest fighter only has two hands."

Geyer bent down and slipped his knife into his boot sheath. Ara kept his own knife ready, not wanting to drop his guard if this was some kind of trick. "You can relax. The lesson is over for now."

Ara offered the knife back to Geyer, but the man shook his head and pulled the second sheath off his belt and tossed it to Ara. "It's yours. Keep it with you at all times."

Ara sheathed the knife and looked down at the rags of his nightshirt and pants. There was nowhere to put it. He definitely needed new clothes. He pulled on Chancey's coat and stuffed the blade in one of the pockets.

"Your wound has already healed," Geyer said.

Ara looked down at his knee. The pants were torn, but the cut was gone. Only the faintest traces of a line remained.

"It doesn't hurt," Ara said.

Geyer shook his head. "Where did you get your training?"

"What?"

"Your defensive stance and the way you move, two feet at a time so your balance is never compromised. It's clear you were taught to fight before."

"I don't…" Ara thought through the dark fog that was his memory. "I don't remember."

Geyer wiped the spot of blood from his calf. "Well, whoever taught you, knew what they were doing."

Ara pondered this as they walked through the forest back to the grass clearing. The weapon in his hand, sparring with a teacher, it somehow felt right. Even the hunting spear had felt oddly familiar. But who would have trained a Descendant?

Ara was thinking about what it all meant when they reached the wagons. Everyone had gathered around the fire. Briton, Petar, Hannah, Brim, a young man of twenty, and a girl Ara's age. The girl had red hair and freckles marked her face. Her eyes seemed to scowl. Ara smiled. The gesture was not returned.

"About time, you two," Petar said with a smile. "I was having to defend your breakfast from these animals. I hope you're still hungry."

At the sight of the loaf of bread split open and resting on a blanket, Ara lost all thoughts except for the one that came from his stomach.


CAMBRIA COULDN'T BELIEVE the boy eating bread beside her was the same boy they had taken in two days ago. He still looked miserable, of course, in his bare feet and thin clothes riddled with holes. But he'd appeared moments from death, and now he was walking around with ease. And she could have sworn he had scars on his face. Hannah was good but she wasn't a miracle worker. Had it been an act? Were these travelers just using Petar and Hannah's hospitality for a free meal? Or something worse?

"Again, we must thank you for your generosity," the old man said. "Without you, we would have likely starved on the road. Now we are sitting here enjoying a warm breakfast. How can we ever repay you?"

"The bread cost about two coppers," Cambria said.

"Cambria," Hannah chided. She turned to the old man and smiled. "We were happy to help. It is good to see you all doing so much better. Ara, I can hardly believe your improvement. You look like a new person."

The boy buried his face in the bread.

The old man stood up, his back cracking louder than the fire. "The girl...Cambria, was it? She's right. We do not seek to take advantage of your hospitality." He reached into a pocket in his gray robes and pulled out a coin purse. He counted out some coins and then rounded the fire and handed them to Petar.

"This is far too much," Petar said, looking down at the coins in his hand.

"Well, if it is alright then, perhaps we will continue on with you for a little while longer."

"Of course. We are happy to have the company. Listening to Brim's stories can get old." Petar laughed at his own joke. Brim met Cambria's eyes. She could tell he was as suspicious of these strangers as she was. Good. They would need a second set of eyes on them.

"Where do you guys come from?" Aaron asked. "I'm curious. You seem such an odd pairing."

No one spoke above the crackling fire.

"As do we, I'm sure," Petar interrupted the silence.

"Of course," Aaron nodded, taking the hint not to pry.

"It's okay," the old man said. "I do think a formal introduction is in order. You've met the lad, Ara." Again, the boy ducked as the eyes fell on him. He had pale skin and tangled hair that matched the bronze color of his eyes. He was in desperate need of a bath.

The old man pointed to the large bearded man in green, who sat farthest from the fire. "And this cheerful gentleman is… Mister Mortimer Marigold."

The boy, Ara, choked on his bread.

"Like the flower?" Hannah asked.

Marigold's teeth tightened into what could only generously be called a smile. "One and the same."

Marigold stood and waved a hand toward the old man. "And this is the boy's great…*great*-grandfather. Benjamin Dullstone."

"Quite right," Dullstone said with a bow. "But you can call me Stone for short."

"Or Dull," Marigold said.

"Well it's wonderful to officially meet you," Petar said and clapped his hands. "Now, would anyone like some more bread?"

After some small talk—mostly by Petar—the fire was put out and the tents packed away. Cambria kept an eye on the new additions to their caravan. Stone and Marigold exchanged some words in a whispered argument while Ara looked around as if in a daze. Cambria didn't know what these strangers' story was, but she knew there was more they weren't letting on.

"You look nervous," Aaron said as the wagons rolled out of the clearing and onto the road.

"I'm not nervous," she said.

"You don't need to worry over everything. They seem like good people."

"What do you know? You've been with us for less than a year. You haven't seen what people on the road are capable of."

"I know, Cambria," Aaron's voice grew low and serious. "I was just teasing. I didn't mean to bring up…" Aaron's voice trailed off as he gave her that look she hated; the look of pity. "But believe it or not, I had a life before you, and on a few occasions even had interactions with people. I have a good feeling about these ones, that's all."

"Yeah, well relax all you want then, but I'm going to be ready in case something happens."

"Like in Minan?" Aaron raised an eyebrow. "You almost cut off that man's hand. Brim had to hold him down to stop him from running away so Petar could stitch him up."

"I thought he was trying to grab me," Cambria said. "He could have just told me there was a bee on my shirt."

"I've never seen Petar so angry," Aaron laughed, leaning back against the wagon's side canvas. "You're the only doctor I've met who sends the patients away worse off than before."

Cambria tried to keep a straight face, but a smile broke through. It wasn't fair. She had helped plenty of people; all her life she worked with doctors—her parents first and then Petar and Hannah. In all those treatments, only a handful were from injuries she had caused.

Still, it felt better to be made fun of than pitied.

Cambria looked out the back of the wagon as Aaron was still chuckling at his own joke. Maybe he was right about these three; Stone and Ara seemed harmless enough, anyway. Maybe life had made her too distrustful. Maybe it was better to live carefree and oblivious to the dangers around her—like Aaron and Petar? But she couldn't do that. She would keep her guard up and do the worrying for all of them.

Cambria couldn't risk losing any more people she cared about.

# 19

---

*"It is my fear that we have underestimated the strength of the Raw Bloods and, in doing so, have condemned ourselves."*

---

Bale cursed as he pulled his horse to a stop in the wet forest. There was no sign of the boy. They followed the river for miles before the hounds found the bloody rag tied to a branch. The diversion had cost them half a day, and now Copher could not pick up their trail in the heavy rain. Markas and his party of guards found only an abandoned horse. Which meant their quarry was down to one horse for a party of three. Yet days of tracking still produced no results. Somehow a Descendant boy, an old man, and a traitorous Carmine guard had outsmarted the Temple's finest. The Highfather would not be pleased.

Bale drank only a quarter of blood from the vial. It cooled the burning in his chest and neck, but the relief would not last; he would soon be out of blood. Since the trail was cold, he would take his men into the nearest town for the night and secure some more blood from the Curor there. It would be weak town blood, but it might hold him over until he found the boy.

The rain had stopped by the time the guards rode into the small western town. Denfold was in the realm of the now defunct House Carmine but didn't seem to notice the change. The political battles of the nobles rarely affect the average man's daily routine. The townspeople on the street at this hour gaped and steered their course away from the twelve Temple guards and the three blood hounds.

Bale climbed off Smoke and handed the horse's reins to the guard named Van. "Get the horses settled in the stable and find us rooms at the inn."

"If there is no room?" asked the tall guard. He shook his wet hair and sniffed through a nose battered from countless fights.

"Then make room."

Bale crossed the street toward the town's Curor's shop, a red heart painted on the front of the wooden door. It had been a long day's ride hunting through the forest, but anger outweighed his fatigue. They had been close. Whatever secrets that dirty Descendant hid had been within Bale's grasp. Now he was gone. Even Copher would have difficulty tracking him after so much time had passed. Bale needed another strategy. But first, he needed blood.

Bale's fist struck the Curor's door so hard it almost came off its hinges.

There was a thump inside the shop. Then an angry voice shouted, "I'm closed."

"Open the door."

The voice grew louder as it approached the door. "Go away before I have you flogged. I am an appointed Curor of the Faith."

"And as such you fall under my command."

There was a pause inside from the now uncertain Curor.

"Open the door before I bust it down and take what I need," Bale ordered.

The door cracked open and the red-robed man's eyes lit up at the sight of Bale in his black armor. "The Blood Kni—" the Curor caught himself, opening the door and stepping back. "Sir Bale, I wasn't expecting—"

"I'm here on direct orders from the Highfather," Bale said, stepping past him into the Curor's shop. "I need blood."

"I...I don't have the strongest blood, being so far from the Temple," the Curor stammered. He shut the door behind Bale and hurried to the knight's side as if to block his attention from the contents of his shop.

"One bottle of your best blood will do," Bale said looking around the shop. It was a mess. Bottles left out and unmarked. Equipment spread about the table, dirty tubes and blades marked with rust. So far from the Temple and the Fathers' eyes had made this Curor careless. Not only that, this man was hiding something.

"A whole bottle?" the Curor said. "Yes, of course, of course." He rummaged around on a shelf behind Bale.

"And do not try to send me off with the pig blood you sell the townspeople," Bale said. "If it is not the blood of Descendants, I will know. And you will lose more than a single bottle."

The Curor gasped, insulted. He looked ready to deny it but then thought better of it and returned to the shelf. The sooner he got the bottle, the sooner Bale would be out of his shop. Specs of dried blood powder dusted the table near Bale. An enterprising Curor. Not only was he selling false blood, he was making illegal blood powder for sniffers; addicts who inhaled the drug.

"You get a lot of blood sniffers this far from the city?" Bale asked as he wiped his black-gloved finger over the table, picking up red specks.

"Of course not," the Curor croaked. Fear mangling his voice. "Desecration of the holy blood is sacrilegious."

"Yes, it is." Bale flicked the dust off his fingers. "But I'm not here to arrest you. I keep no illusions about the morality of the

Faith. I'm looking for someone, and perhaps you can spread the word to your…more desperate customers."

"I would be happy to assist the Highfather in any way I can."

"A Descendant boy escaped House Carmine. I need to find him. Alive. It would be in anyone's interest to be on the lookout for him or any suspicious travelers."

The Curor nodded and handed a bottle of blood to Bale. The glass bottle was cold; he had stored it for some time. Bale doubted this was the special occasion the Curor had imagined.

"There were some travelers who came through two days ago," the Curor said. "They were traveling doctors from the southern realm."

"Doctors? Here?" Bale thought about the last time doctors dared travel in the Faith's lands. He had personally been ordered to…*convert* them. "Where are they now?"

"I ran them out of town," the Curor said with pride. "They took to the road, heading east. They won't find any hospitality in this part of Terene, I guarantee you that."

Bale rubbed at his neck. He craved the contents of this bottle to ease the burning; wanted to down the whole thing right there. But he had work to do. He stuffed the bottle in his pack and headed for the door.

"Spread the word about the boy."

"Of course."

"And if this blood isn't what it should be, I'll be back."

The Curor quickly shut the door behind Bale. Bale walked through the quiet street of Denfold toward the inn. The blood poison burned in his chest. How much longer could he last? He had to find the boy soon. And he better be everything the Highfather claimed. Bale winced and tore off the bottle's cap. He allowed himself one sip, no more.

AFTER FOUR DAYS of traveling east, the wagons stopped at the town of Dal Doran in the realm of House Chamberlain.

According to Briton, House Chamberlain controlled the largest land area of all the western houses. Geyer and Briton had both been wary of venturing into a populated area, but they couldn't prevent the doctors from doing their jobs.

Ara was just happy to be off the road. Days in the wagon with nothing to look at but endless trees had felt almost as much a prison as Carmine Castle. A day in town also meant a break from his lessons. For days Ara had been attacked on both ends, morning workouts in the woods with Geyer that often left him bruised and bloody, followed by constant study and questions from Briton about everything from the currency system of Terene to the religious history of the desert people of Santar. Ara didn't see the purpose of learning either since he would likely never have a shrine to his name, and he hoped to never set foot in the Endless Desert.

As far as the fighting lessons with Geyer, after a few painful sessions, he had regretted ever asking for the old knight's help.

They tied the horses to trees beside an open patch of land on the outside of town. Brim started unpacking the tents. Ara jumped down and stretched his legs. They were still sore from the morning's sparring session.

"Aaron," Petar called. "Find the market and see about trading for supplies. Cambria has made a list of what we need."

"Along with some extra sweets, I'm sure," Aaron said.

"Perhaps I can go with you," Briton said. "There are a few things I need as well."

"Oh, yeah," Aaron said. "I'd be happy to have some company for a change."

Briton turned to Ara. "Are you okay here, Ara?"

"Can I go with you too?" Ara asked. He desperately wanted to explore in town. To see something other than more trees.

Briton shook his head, his blue eyes looking into Ara. "I think it's better if you stay here."

"We'll look after him, Stone," Petar said, carrying a box from the back of the wagon. "We have plenty of work for him to do." Petar gave Ara a wink the boy did not return.

"Very well then," Briton said. "Stay close to Petar and the others."

Briton followed Aaron into town, carrying some bags of supplies for trade, his dusty gray robe disappearing in the street crowd. Ara turned around to see Geyer hopping down from the wagon and following after them, taking his time on his bad leg.

"Where are you going?" Ara asked.

"To see what kind of tavern this town has," Geyer said without looking back.

Ara's first thought was of disappointment that he had been left behind. But his second thought was more worrisome. Though Geyer had changed over the weeks of travel, Ara still feared he would disappear on them. And then where would Ara be? He didn't like feeling so dependent. Especially on the whims of a drunk.

"Ara," Petar called. "You can help Brim set up the tents and then assist Cambria."

Ara sighed. He didn't mind helping Brim. The large man hadn't uttered a single word the entire trip. He just worked, indifferent to Ara's existence. The girl Cambria, on the other hand, openly despised him. She might as well be mute too from the amount that she had spoken to Ara. She communicated mostly with scowls.

As if on cue, Cambria stormed over to have some words with Petar. She moved briskly, her red hair was a stark contrast to the green of the trees behind her. She must have heard him and not liked the idea of Ara helping either.

Ara held a tent pole as Brim pounded it into the ground. He hoped the big man's aim was good. The doctors had looked past his speedy recovery but some smashed fingers that healed in minutes might be a different story.

Across the way, Cambria turned from Petar and shot Ara an

angry look. Well, maybe it was her natural look since Ara couldn't remember ever seeing a smile on her freckled face.

"Find me in the wagon when you're done here," she said as she stalked off toward the second wagon. Brim shrugged to Ara. Then he heaved the hammer and struck the pole so hard it rattled Ara's bones.

He hoped Briton and Geyer would return soon.

GEYER COULDN'T REMEMBER the last time he had gone this long without a drink. Though he hadn't thought of it in some time; running for your life from Temple guards and blood hounds tended to command your attention. But what was the point of surviving if you couldn't have a mug of ale?

Geyer had passed through Dal Doran a few times in his younger days. He knew to avoid the taverns on the main street that sold overpriced ale to naive travelers. He was happy to see the Green Lady still in business. The name came from the faded green building and its proprietor, the beautiful Lady Magdalene. The few shrines in Geyer's pocket would go much further there.

Pushing his way through the crowded street and into the wooden door of The Green Lady, Geyer was hit with the familiar darkness of a true tavern. It smelled of wood, stale ale belches, and sweat. Geyer was home. A few heads turned to Geyer as he came through the door. Geyer didn't stop but closed the door and headed straight for the bar as if a usual patron. The heads soon turned back to their conversations.

Behind the bar was a small man with a thick black mustache that did not hide his boiled egg of a nose. This was certainly not the Magdalene he remembered. The man squinted appraisingly. Geyer took a stool at the bar.

"Good afternoon," Geyer said, setting one of Briton's shrines on the counter. "I'd like as big a mug as this will get me."

The barman looked at the coin and then again at Geyer. He didn't move to take the coin or get a mug.

"Where you from, stranger?" he asked.

"Here and there," Geyer said.

"What business do you have in Dal Doran?"

"My own," Geyer said, annoyance clear in his voice. "Does The Green Lady's business now include prying into customers' affairs?"

The men at the bar beside Geyer turned their heads toward him. Geyer didn't take his eyes off the barman. Finally, the man relented, taking the shrine. "I apologize, but we have been drawing unusual guests as of late."

"My only business is to get drunk," Geyer said with a smile meant to relax the barman and those around him.

"Then you've come to the right place." The barman filled a hefty mug from a barrel and setting it before Geyer. "That's the Green Lady's specialty."

Geyer looked the mug over, the foam falling over the top like an inviting bath. He took a hesitant sip. Then a larger one. The familiar burn of the ale going down his throat washed away the stress of the road.

"Ahhh," Geyer gasped in approval. "That's good. What kind of unusual guests?"

The barman frowned. "Out of towers. Bounty hunters. And an unusual number of Temple guards."

"Temple guards all the way out here. Hmm." Geyer brought his mug up to his lips, partially covering his face.

"Seems some outlaws are on the run in these parts," said an old man beside Geyer. His voice was raspy and he had about three teeth left in his mouth.

"Must have done something pretty bad to warrant all that attention," Geyer said.

"I ain't nothing close to a bounty hunter, but I'd be tempted to take up a sword for the price they're offering for those three."

"Three?"

"Two men and a boy." The words whistled out of the empty cavern of the old man's mouth.

"An outlaw boy? Doesn't sound worth all the fuss."

"I heard he's a sorcerer," said the bald man beside him, who couldn't be much younger than his toothless neighbor.

*Sorcerer.* Geyer could just imagine the same daft conversations happening in bars all over Terene. The boy's legend growing and growing. Perhaps they'd even embellished Geyer's role. The traitorous guard who chopped his way out of Castle Carmine with a sword that has slain men by the hundreds. It was one way to get stories told about you.

"Enough with that talk, Anson," the barman said, shaking his head at the older gentleman. "Ain't no such thing as magic sorcerers."

"You tell that to my brother, Charlie," the bald man said. "Some devil on the road put a hex on him. He don't remember much of nothing since. Not even his name."

"Charlie drinks even more than you do," the barman said. "That isn't to say I'm not grateful, now. You Barrett brothers keep the Green Lady in business."

"Haha!" croaked the old man with missing teeth. He slapped the bald man on the head. "It's true, it's true."

Geyer finished his mug and considered another. He still had one shrine he'd stolen from Briton's pack. If the doctors were going to spend the day helping the infirm of Dal Doran, Geyer couldn't think of a better place to pass the time. But the idea of leaving Ara nagged at him. The boy was trouble, and he had somehow become Geyer's trouble. And now Geyer couldn't enjoy his drink in peace knowing every cutthroat in Terene was looking for him.

*It's not your problem*, Geyer reminded himself. *The world's a lousy place for most everyone, why should the boy be any different?*

He'd seen suffering and injustice in every town he'd ever been in. When he was young and foolish, trying to play the part of a knight, he might have tried to do something about it. But he'd learned long ago that you can't help everyone.

"Another drink?" the barman asked.

Geyer played with the remaining shrine, pushing it back and forth between his hands. He watched it roll along the scratched wooden bar like a slowly turning wheel.

THE FIRST PATIENTS had come before the tents were even set up. There was a steady stream of people coming to see the doctors. Ara waited outside with Cambria. Her job was to greet the new patients, evaluate their condition, and then send them to the proper tent. Most people were sent to Hannah's tent.

The worst cases were sent to Petar's tent. Brim had to help carry a few of these patients as some couldn't even walk. There was desperation in the faces of these people. Ara got the feeling they were seeing the doctors only as a last resort. Even the ones with simple injuries had such hopeless broken faces they could have been Descendants.

Ara returned from fetching Hannah more bandages to find Cambria with a man dancing on one leg. His foot was red and swollen. Cambria was not impressed. "It's only a spider bite. Keep it clean, and it'll be gone in another day or two."

"But it's already been two days!" the man said, pointing the foot closer.

"And it'd be gone by now if you'd bathe once in a while," she fanned her hand in front of her nose and leaned back.

"There's nothing else I can do for it? I want to see one of the real doctors."

"Real doctors?" Cambria's voice rose. She looked about to explode when she saw Ara and caught herself. She took a breath and smiled at the man. "Honey will help it heal faster. One drop of honey on the bite just before rinsing in a bath will do the trick."

"Thank you," the man said. He turned and hopped away, boot still in hand.

Ara turned to Cambria. "Won't the bath wash the honey away?"

"Of course it will," Cambria looked at Ara like he was an idiot. But he didn't take great offense because she seemed to look at everyone that way.

With no one else waiting, Cambria walked over and leaned against the wagon.

"How many patients do you usually treat in a day?" Ara asked. He moved close enough to the wagon to talk but not quite join her.

Green eyes studied Ara from behind a freckled face as if deciding if he was worth acknowledging. "It depends on the town," she said finally. "This one has been busier than most. The Temple guards came through and created some business for us."

"Temple guards?" Ara tried to contain his fear as he looked toward the town and the busy streets—he hadn't seen any white uniforms. His mind went to Briton and Geyer in town. Were they in danger?

"They tore up the town two days ago, according to some of the injured patients. Searching for Descendant outlaws."

The reality of the outside world came rushing back. These villagers had been hurt because of him.

"Do the guards ever come after you?" Ara asked. "Br…Stone says the Faith doesn't like doctors."

"We've been run out of towns and even detained under false charges, but those cases are rare. The Faith may not like us, but there's nothing illegal about helping people. We're not much of a threat to them anyway."

"Why do you do it? Help other people, I mean. Most people struggle enough just looking out for themselves."

Cambria looked off into the distance as if she didn't hear him. Then she spoke with a gentleness that caught him by surprise. "My parents believed that helping others was the reason we are alive in the first place. And if more people shared that belief, the world would not be such a bad place. I don't know, sometimes I wonder if they had cared a little bit more about themselves they might still be here."

"What happened to them?"

Cambria's eyes darted to Ara as if she forgot who she was talking to. "They're gone," she said simply. She jumped off the wagon and walked into Hannah's tent.

Ara thought of his own parents who he did not remember. What had happened to them? Were they gone too? Or had they simply abandoned him? After all this time he still could not remember.

A figure approached the doctor's camp. He walked at a slow pace, carrying something in his arms. It was a small boy. Something was wrong with the child.

"Cambria," Ara called. "Cambria!"

"What?" she yelled coming out of the tent. She stopped at the sight of the man and the boy. "Get Petar."

Ara raced into Petar's tent.

"…stopped the bleeding, so stay off of it as much as possible for the next few—" Petar looked up from his patient. "What is it, Ara?"

"There's a boy. He looks bad."

Petar nodded and patted the man he was patching up. "You're going to be fine."

"Thank you, doctor," the man said and dropped two shrines into an offering bucket. But Petar was already out the tent door.

"Bring him in here," Petar called.

The man carried the boy into the tent and set him on the makeshift table. The previous patient gasped at the sight of the unconscious boy and hurried away. The boy was maybe five years old and nothing but skin and bones. Black sores covered his arms and neck, sinking in below the skin-line. Petar cut the boys shirt, revealing more on his chest. Ara winced. Petar's face betrayed nothing.

"How long has he been like this?" Petar asked.

"It came with the new year," the man said. "But it wasn't like this at first. Only a red rash."

Cambria slipped into the tent, her eyes widened at the sight of the boy.

"Petar…" she started.

"Get the bezal cream," Petar said to her. "As much as we have. And tell Hannah to prepare an elmroot tea."

"Petar it's—"

"Go Cambria."

Cambria backed out of the tent.

"Is he going to be okay?" the man asked, but there was no hope in his voice as if he had already accepted the inevitable.

"The sickness has eaten away at his body for a long time," Petar said, frowning as he pulled his gloves up higher. He reached down and touched two fingers to the boy's neck. "He's already well on his way."

"I tried to get good blood for him," the man's voice was flat, exhausted. The skin around his eyes was rubbed raw as if he had no more tears left to cry. "I saw the Curor nearly every day and begged him. But I couldn't afford the price. I couldn't afford…"

He trailed off, and Petar grabbed him by the shoulders and helped him to the corner of the tent. "Stay here. I promise you we will do everything we can."

Petar handed Ara gloves.

Ara looked at the doctor, confused. But he put the gloves on.

"I need you to talk to him," Petar said.

"What do I say?"

"Anything. Let him hear your voice." Petar called for Brim, and the big man was in the tent in an instant, filling up the small space. "Hold him."

Brim knelt over the boy and put a giant gloved hand on his waist and shoulder. The boy's eyes were shut, his chest wasn't moving. Was he already dead?

Petar pressed a flat, spoon-shaped metal tool against a black spot on the boy's arm. It sunk in as if the dark skin were mud. A slight groan escaped the boy's lips.

"Talk to him, Ara."

What could he say? He didn't know this boy or what could help him. The boy's father stood in the corner, broken. Watching his son die.

Ara leaned down, his head close to the boy's.

"My name is Ara," he whispered into the boy's ear. "I know it hurts right now. But the pain will be over soon. Petar is a good doctor. If anyone can help you…it's him" Ara's voice choked up. Petar inspected the hole in the boy's arm; it dripped black ooze. Cambria rushed in with a bottle of white cream and a cup. Petar took the cream and using a tool, wiped it on the wound. The boy groaned but never opened his eyes. Cambria held the boy's mouth open, tilting the contents of the cup inside. Her green eyes were wide with fear.

"You're in a small tent," Ara whispered softly. He didn't have anything to say so he just rambled without thinking. "It's filled with people who care about you. Who are trying to save you… your father…your father is here. I don't know my father or where he is. But you…yours is here with you. It's going to be alright. Drink, drink some more tea. Let your body heal. Let the blood pour through your body. Rest now, let your body work. Rest."

The boy's eyes fluttered behind closed eyelids and then lay still. Ara turned to Petar.

"He's gone," Petar said.

In the corner of the tent, the boy's father threw his head in his hands. "Hemo, why? Why?" His voice trailed off, into sobs that came from somewhere deep within him.

"What do you mean?" Ara asked confused. "He's dead?"

"We did everything we could." Petar set down his instruments and turned to the boy's father. "I'm sorry, the sickness was too severe."

"I should have gotten him blood," the man said. "Even if I had to burn down the Temple, I should have gotten my son blood."

Ara looked at the young boy's lifeless body. How could it just end like that? How was anyone supposed to survive this world with so fragile a body?

"But you, you were supposed to help him," Ara fought back the sickness in his stomach. Sickness and anger. "That's what you do."

Cambria gave him a hard defensive look. "Petar did all he could. We can't do the impossible."

"Prepare a fire," Petar whispered to Brim. "We'll have to burn the body."

The father sobbed. He moved to his son's side but Petar held him back with gloved hands. "Take off your shirt," he said. "Let me get a look at you."

The boy lay on the table, lifeless and alone.

Ara ran out of the suffocating tent, tossing his gloves to the ground. He fled away from the camp and the dead boy. He ran into town, pushing past a crowd of people on the street who stared at him in his tattered rags. Ara turned down a side street and vomited his breakfast into the dirt.

He had done nothing. Sat back and watched the boy die when he could have helped him, given him a little of his blood. It wouldn't have mattered to him. He'd had so much taken over the past months just to make Carmine rich. He could have used his blood to save a boy's life, and instead, he did nothing. Petar and the doctors couldn't do the impossible, but he could.

Ara kicked his foot into a wall, over and over.

*This blood is a curse, whether I use it or not.*

He kicked harder, again and again. The bones in his toes broke. He kept kicking, cracking the wood planks.

"What the hell's going on back here?" a man stepped around the corner. His face grew red when he saw the hole Ara had made in the wall. "You stupid clot! You've wrecked my wall!"

Ara wiped the tears away from his face and limped away; the front of his foot exploded in pain.

"Get back here, boy!" the man yelled. "You're gonna pay for this."

A hand struck him on the back. He flew into the dirt.

"You little brat."

The man kicked Ara in the side. The air left him. The shop-keeper raised his boot. Ara didn't cover up, he just looked at the man with open eyes, waiting for the beating.

The shopkeeper stopped. He stepped back from Ara.

"Go on," Ara said. "I deserve it."

The man shook his head. "What's wrong with you?"

More voices filled the air. A crowd gathered around the scene. The shopkeeper looked around at the attention. Murmurs went through the crowd as they stared at Ara. So many people looking at him, seeing his face.

Hands grabbed under his arms and pulled him to his feet. Ara spun around. "You weren't supposed to draw attention to yourself," Geyer said.

Ara pressed himself against Geyer, wrapping his arms around him. The old knight stepped back, but Ara held tight not letting him go.

"This boy belong to you?" the shopkeeper asked.

Geyer seemed to think about this for a minute. "What'd he do that required a beating from a grown man?"

"He smashed my shop," the man pointed to the broken boards on his wall as justification.

Geyer pulled a shrine from his pocket and threw it on the ground at the man's feet. "Be thankful I don't do the same to you."

The man said nothing. Geyer led Ara away through the crowd. Ara's foot burned with each step, he could barely breathe between the pain in his side and the sobs. But it didn't really matter. He was a Descendant.

"I'm sorry, Geyer," Ara said. "I'm sorry for everything."

"Hush now," Geyer said. "No names. We're being watched."

. . .

BRITON WALKED BACK to the doctor's camp, excited to show Ara the new clothes he'd bought for him. The boy's current outfit was so worn he could be considered more naked than clothed. Briton had bought rugged brown pants and a red shirt that would pass Ara off as a farm boy. But Briton's eagerness wore off when he saw the camp. Though the sun was still two hours from setting, the tents were broken down and being loaded into the wagons.

"Tell me we're not being thrown out again," Aaron groaned by his side. The young man leaned over the wheelbarrow of supplies. "Couldn't we have just one full day in a city?"

The mood of the doctors was bleak as they packed up their supplies. Petar nodded to Briton and Aaron.

"We're leaving already?" Aaron asked.

"Yes," Petar said. "Can you load the supplies and assist Hannah, please."

Aaron didn't argue, perhaps sensing the seriousness in Petar's voice.

"And see if you can find where Cambria disappeared," Petar called after Aaron.

"Is everything alright?" Briton asked.

"It was a hard day, Stone." Petar said. "We lost someone. A young boy. Ara took it pretty hard."

"Where is he now?"

"Just there in the woods."

"I'm sorry, Petar."

"There was nothing to be done. The boy was too far along. I've been doing this a long time. He's not the first patient I've lost." Petar picked up a stack of rags hung out to dry in the sun. "Marigold overheard some hostile talk about our presence in town. He advised we leave as soon as possible."

Briton nodded. "I'm sorry. I know how much these people need you, whether they know it or not."

"We got a good day's work in. That's better than in a lot of northern towns."

Briton nodded and set his bags down in a wagon, careful not to wrinkle the new clothes. He walked toward the tree line. Geyer stepped out, glancing behind Briton to make sure he wasn't followed.

"It's not safe for us here," Geyer said. "Word is all around the city. The Highfather has put a purse on our heads."

"Then we're endangering the doctors by staying with them."

"But it's safer for us. They're looking for a boy traveling in a group of three."

Briton sighed. He didn't want to leave the doctors either. As uncomfortable as the rickety wagon was, it was much better than walking. Plus, he'd grown quite fond of Petar and Hannah. But he knew it was not fair to put them in danger.

Briton looked around the wagons. "Where's Ara?"

"He feels guilty about what happened," Geyer said. "Thinks he could have done something for the boy."

"I'll talk to him."

"Be quick. We need to leave." Geyer scanned the nearby streets. There was a look of worry on the knight's face. More than usual.

Briton walked through the wood. Light grew dim beneath the thick canopy of leaves. He thought of the lanterns in the Carmine Castle library and reading late into the night. It seemed a lifetime ago.

Briton found Ara sitting alone on an uprooted tree, absently drawing patterns in the dirt with a stick. He looked up at Briton's approach and then lowered his head back to the ground.

Briton sat down beside him. "It's not your fault what happened to that boy."

Ara said nothing. He continued moving his stick in the soft ground.

"It is a cruel unforgiving world, Ara. You should know that as much as anyone. People die every day."

"I could have stopped it," Ara mumbled.

"Petar said the boy was past healing."

"I could have tried," Ara snapped. "But instead I did nothing. I just watched him die—because I was scared. Because I was afraid of being caught."

Briton looked at the young boy suffering beside him, wishing there was a way to put some of it on himself. But that's not how it worked. Raw Bloods only took a Descendant's strength, not his pain.

"You have tremendous power," Briton said. "Power you never asked for. And it has caused you more pain than it has helped you. And as strong as you are, Ara, you're still just a boy. It is not your job to save everyone."

Ara stabbed the stick into the ground, and it broke to pieces. He turned and looked up at Briton, tears forming in the corner of his eyes. "Whose job is it then?"

Briton had no answer. He reached out and put his arm around Ara. The boy did not shake it free.


"Time to go," Stone said. Ara helped him to his feet, and the two of them walked out of the woods back toward the wagons.

Cambria stayed crouched in the bushes until they were gone.

She had been suspicious of these travelers, and this secret meeting confirmed it. Ara had called the old man Briton. He had lied about his name. And they were hiding more than their real names. Were they outlaws? Agents of the Faith?

And what was this talk about tremendous power? Ara believed he could have saved the town boy when not even Petar could do that. Cambria had suspected there was something unusual about the boy on that second day when she saw how fast he had recovered from his injuries. But what did it mean? She didn't believe in the northern myths of sorcerers and magic blood. She knew it was the Faith's way of controlling the population. The only thing that healed people was science. There was no such thing as good and bad blood.

Cambria snuck back through the woods, a plan forming in

her mind. She didn't know what their game was, but she knew these strangers couldn't be trusted. She'd have to find out more in order to convince Petar they were dangerous. In the meantime, she'd keep an eye on them.

And keep her blade ready.

## 20

Vorrel's experiments had always interested Haemon. He'd seen living Descendants split open, their organs taken out one at a time. He'd seen limbs hacked off to test what would and wouldn't grow back. Tips of fingers and noses and ears but not whole limbs. Though, if a Descendant had particularly good blood, a severed arm, for instance, could be reattached—the bone fusing together and healing like new. And he'd seen Descendants tortured and killed in as many ways as Vorrel could dream up. Drowned, starved, beaten, burnt, boiled. They were remarkably resilient creatures, but they could be exterminated with just about any method, given enough persistence.

Vorrel's experiments on a good blood replicant, however, were not fascinating. Haemon grew bored, watching his head Curor strain and mix and cook, vials of the Descendant boy's blood as he tried to crack the answer to its power. The table in the center of the hidden lab was filled with vials of failed attempts. They'd already wasted most of the boy's blood they'd retrieved from Castle Carmine.

A guard sliced the prisoner across the chest, cutting a fresh wound over the already marked body. The prisoner cried like a mute dog. His tongue had been removed to keep the noise down. Even in the old part of the Temple, there were ears.

Vorrel lifted a vial of blood to the prisoner's lips. The liquid was dark red and cloudy. He forced it down the prisoner's mouth. The room waited in silence. Vorrel's lips moved as he counted.

Then the prisoner screamed. As much as he could anyway. The skin around the cut dissolved, opening the wound wider. Dark red blood bubbled out of the wound as if eating away at the prisoner from the inside. The prisoner's screams grew higher pitched and he convulsed against his chains, the metal breaking him open at the arms and shoulders. The guard stepped back as the bubbles fizzed in the prisoner's lap, burning his pants. One last whine and the prisoner stopped, his head fell. His chest was open like a hole had been melted through him.

Vorrel sighed. "Put him with the others." Two guards unchained the prisoner, careful to avoid the bubbling blood.

Vorrel shook his head and placed the vial on the table with the others. He scribbled something in his notes. He spoke without meeting Haemon's eyes. "We *are* getting closer."

"How do you determine that?" Haemon asked. "From what I've seen you've managed to turn the most precious substance in all of Terene into poison."

He tapped his quill against the paper. "We learn from every setback. We've identified strains that amplify the blood power, we just need to stabilize it for the Raw Blood body."

"We don't have time to waste, Vorrel. I need to bring the council something more than melting bodies."

"Soon," Vorrel said. "Hemo will give us the answer."

Haemon's loose teeth grinded against one another. How dare this Curor talk to him of Hemo's will. It was Haemon's vision that started this whole project. He would see it through, with or without Vorrel.

There was a knock on the lab door. Haemon's muscles tightened and he immediately regretted the effort. He wheezed, trying to settle the knots in his back. The door opened and a guard stepped inside. Haemon exhaled. It was one of his.

"Father," the guard said. "We found two guards searching the corridors. We believe they were sent by Father Turney."

Edmund. Haemon frowned. The young Father was proving to be a greater problem than he'd anticipated.

"Did they find anything?"

"I don't believe so. I ordered them to the outer sanctuary. Told them they were needed there. But they were reluctant to go."

The Highfather nodded. "Send a messenger for Father Turney. I will speak to him in my study."

"Yes, Father." The guard bowed and slipped out of the door, closing it behind him.

Haemon rubbed at his pointed chin. Some problems required political maneuvering, others you dealt with head-on. He wasn't yet sure which one Edmund was.

"Keep working," Haemon said to Vorrel. "You don't sleep until I have my blood cure."

Then the Highfather strode out of the lab to deal with Father Turney. Gray morning light splintered in through the holes in the stone walls. Their secret lab had been built in the old part of the Temple. A section that still showed the scars of the Blood Wars. The broken ceiling stood as a monument to the last stand. When the Raw Bloods rose up and finally ended the reign of the Royals. To Haemon, it was a reminder of what could happen if the Descendants were allowed too much power.

It was a long trek across the Temple to the Highfather's study. Haemon and his two trailing guards reached the open air courtyard in the heart of the Temple and stopped to catch his breath. His two guards gave him space as he sat on the edge of the Fountain of Absolution. Haemon's lungs burned. He tasted blood in his mouth. His own blood.

When had he grown so old?

"Faith be with you, Highfather," a voice called.

Father Edmund Turney strolled through the courtyard with a single guard of his own. His lips curled into a crooked smile. It was a knowing smile. Like they were peers who held a shared secret that couldn't be spoken aloud. For once Haemon was thankful for his old tired body, for he might otherwise have strangled Edmund right there and then.

"We were supposed to meet in my study," Haemon said.

"I thought this would be easier for you. I know walking can be difficult." Edmund Turney sat down on the fountain's edge beside the Highfather.

Haemon gritted his teeth, imagining what Edmund's panicked face would look like held down beneath the water's surface.

"We learn to deal with difficulties, Father Edmund. Nothing is handed to us." The Highfather's guards had stepped forward but Haemon waved them back. "Even you, the son of a noble lord, must have faced your share of difficulties. It couldn't have been easy renouncing your family's titles to join the Faith."

"I answered a higher calling. It's no more a sacrifice than any Father who takes the vow."

"Yes, perhaps it was a bit easier as a second son."

Edmund's smile remained on his lips, but his eyes gave a different response. His lineage was a sensitive subject. A fact to remember.

"How goes Hemo's work?" Edmund asked, dusting off his robe at the knee. "The pressure must be a lot to bear. With the Descendant rebels still a threat under your watch."

"The watch is all of ours, Father Turney. If you have some insight you believe would remedy Terene's troubles, I hope you aren't keeping them for a more opportune time. People's lives do hang in the balance, after all."

Edmund put a hand to his chest. "I mean no disrespect, Highfather. I can only imagine the complexities of your position. I just hope our resources are aimed at the right target, and not focused elsewhere."

"And where else would they be focused?" Haemon studied the young Father's face. He was getting a feel for the boy. Edmund was adept at the veiled threats of politics but how did he respond when confronted head on?

Edmund did not speak for a moment. He looked past the Highfather to the watching Temple guards. Haemon couldn't read the Father. That was more dangerous than if he saw open hatred in the man's eyes.

"You know, you were the subject of my treatise at Monastery," Edmund said.

Haemon's eyebrows shot up before he could stop himself. "I didn't know that, Edmund. It's interesting that you'd choose something so recent. Most Fathers choose to study Hamada or another founding Highfather, or even General Drusas."

"The Blood Wars are exciting, of course, but I think to be the best Father I can be, it's important to understand the world we live in now."

Haemon shifted on the fountain's stone edge. *Where is this going?*

"It must have been difficult for you after the sudden death of your mentor, Highfather Archaties. You were still so young when called to fulfill his position."

Haemon stared down into the still waters of the Fountain of Absolution. The face he saw reflected was that of an old man. Older than Archaties had ever been.

"It is our duty to serve. If we trust in Hemo and submit ourselves to him, he will give us the strength we need."

Father Turney nodded. "And how did you know when you were following his will and not taking matters in your own hands?"

Haemon sighed. It was a question he'd wrestled with much as Highfather of the Faith. When he was younger, anyway.

"When you silence your personal thoughts and agendas, Hemo will speak to you," Haemon said. He held Father Turney's gaze for a long moment. Then the Highfather pushed himself to his feet; his wobbly legs held up with great effort. But calling to his guards in front of Edmund would be unthinkable. "And, in the end, it always comes down to faith."

"If I am chosen Highfather someday, I pray I have your confidence."

"Hemo rewards the prayer of the humble. Now if you'll excuse me, I have much work to do." Haemon's muscles threatened to cramp after sitting so long on the hard stone but he got them moving. He headed toward his guards, wishing Edmund would go so he could have them carry him to his study and the bottle of good blood that waited for him there. His muscles tightened at the thought of the precious relief.

"Highfather," Edmund's voice rang through the courtyard. Haemon turned his head toward the still sitting Father. "My summons. There was a matter you wanted to see me about?"

Haemon groaned softly. He *had* sent for Edmund Turney. He must be tired from the work with Vorrel. The blood replicant was taking up all his energy. It had allowed the young Father to control their conversation.

Haemon gave Edmund a dismissive wave. "We'll speak another time, Father Turney."

"I look forward to it. Highfather."

Haemon turned his back to Father Turney and walked through the courtyard. The pain in his body dimmed as his mind worked. If he didn't know before, it was clear now. Edmund was dangerous.

THE KNIFE SLICED Ara at the waist. He screamed and stumbled to the ground. He grabbed his side where blood had already formed. His attacker stood over him, shaking his head.

"Good thing you went shirtless," Geyer said. "Or we would have torn up that pretty new shirt Briton bought for you."

"*You* would have torn it up, you mean!" Ara yelled. Holding his side together. The wounds healed faster now. Sometimes it only took a minute for the blood to stop and the skin to start knitting itself back together again. But it still hurt.

"With lazy blocks like that, you're asking for it. Keep the knife raised and your eyes on your opponent's shoulder. That's where the attack comes from first, not the blade in his hands."

"Who taught you to fight, Geyer?" Ara asked. He was both genuinely curious and trying to stall long enough for the wound to heal.

"I had many teachers," Geyer said. "And even more opponents. A swordsman can learn as much from one as the other."

"When did you start studying the sword?"

Geyer laughed. "Studying? You make it sound like a school subject. One does not choose the sword for recreation, Ara. One learns how to fight to survive."

"And how does one become a knight?"

"You have a lot of questions. Are you that winded from some simple sparring?"

"I'm tired of being stabbed."

"Well, learn to deal with it. Healing blood is useless if your opponent does not give you time to recover." Geyer leaped forward swinging his knife down on Ara. Ara blocked the first blow, the metal clang vibrated through the bones in his hand and arm. He rolled away from the second onslaught and popped up in a crouched position, knife outstretched.

"Watch the shoulder now," Geyer said. He bobbed his head left and then struck to Ara's right. Ara flinched right but recovered from the feint in time to block the attack. He countered with a low swipe at Geyer's leg. Geyer raised the leg over the slashing knife and kicked Ara in the stomach, sending him back to the ground once again.

"That blow didn't come from your shoulder," Ara groaned, the wind knocked out of him.

"No, it did not. Remember the knife is not the only weapon. Use it to gain your opponent's attention then strike where he does not expect."

Ara pulled himself to his feet and spit into the dirt. "You know you can give me the lesson before you use it on me." He was tired of being cut and knocked down. He thought some sparring with Geyer during the caravan's break would take his mind off the previous day in Dal Doran, but the guilt still ate at his mind. Made it hard to focus.

"It's easier to remember this way," Geyer said. "I know you have trouble with that memory of yours."

Blood rushed through Ara's body, attacking the pain points. His body healed, but his strength spilled out like water from a barrel full of holes.

"What's the point?" Ara scoffed. "I'll never beat you."

Geyer sheathed his knife. "Is that the goal of your training?"

The old knight pulled a water-skin from his bag, took a gulp and tossed it to Ara. Ara caught it in one hand and drank, sheathing his own knife. The water felt cool and refreshing. He stopped before he drank too much.

"No," Ara said, bending at the waist to catch his breath.

"Then what's the goal?"

"To become a better fighter."

"And are you better than when we started?"

"Yes, it just comes so slow. No matter how much I learn, you still outmatch me."

"And how did I get better than you?"

Ara sighed. Teaching through questions. Geyer sounded like Briton. "You've been training a lot longer than I have, so if I want to get better I have to put in the time." Ara rolled his eyes as he repeated the mantra.

Geyer nodded. "Yes. That is true. But I'm also much smarter than you are." The old knight smiled, and Ara couldn't help but chuckle.

Ara was about to say something when Geyer straightened up. He drew his knife and looked around the forest.

"What is it?" Ara asked.

"We're not alone."

Ara drew his own knife and ran to Geyer's side, following his gaze into the thick forest. Ara hadn't heard whatever sound alerted Geyer. He scanned the green brush, looking for movement.

"Could it have been an animal?" Ara whispered.

Geyer frowned. "Better to be certain. Go back to the wagon. I'll take a look."

"I can help."

"If someone is following us, they won't be friendly."

"All the more reason for you not to go alone."

Geyer kept his eyes on the trees as he moved forward with silent steps. "Stay within eyesight."

Ara split to the left, moving softly through the forest, knife ready as he rounded each tree. Geyer moved ahead, but Ara stayed close enough to come to his aid if someone attacked. Briton and Geyer had told him about the bounty put on his head. Now they not only had to worry about the Temple guards but every lowlife with a sword seeking to make a fortune. It felt like the whole world was after him now.

Something on the ground caught Ara's eye. He bent low and pushed back a green fern branch. There in the dark soil was a footprint. A small footprint. Ara almost thought it was his own until he saw the tread was different than the shoes Briton had bought him. Someone had been close, watching them. Ara was about to call Geyer but Geyer was now far ahead. He didn't want to yell and give away his position if the person following them was nearby. He tightened his grip on the knife and followed the footsteps deeper into the forest.

The mistake Ara made was in focusing so much on the trail of footprints that he did not look up to see where they were leading him. Something hard hit Ara just above the right eye. At first, he thought he'd run into a branch. Then, when the forest stopped spinning, he saw the rock at his feet. Ara's cry of pain was delayed, but it came all the same. "Owww." He grabbed his brow that had already begun to swell. A figure sprinted from a nearby bush and raced away. Anger rushed through Ara; he gave chase without thinking.

"Ara!" Geyer's voice rang through the forest. "Ara stop!"

But Ara didn't stop. He charged after the figure, his knife in hand.

An assassin had found him. He'd put the doctors' lives in danger. Ara couldn't let him get away.

He caught glimpses of his attacker as he weaved through the trees ahead. The figure was small and moved quickly through the forest, but Ara was gaining ground. Blood pumped to his legs, giving him speed.

The figure tripped on something and fell out of sight with a high yelp. Ara charged ahead recklessly.

Could he kill a man? If it meant saving his friends—yes.

The figure was up and running again as the forest began to slope downward. Ara was now close enough to see the figure's red hair. Long red hair.

The figure stopped. If Ara had taken the time to think, he might have realized there was a reason for his prey to stop suddenly. If he had been thinking he might have recognized the freckled face that looked back at him. But at this point, Ara was not thinking, and by the time he recognized Cambria's wide green eyes, he was already flying through the air toward the girl with arms outstretched.

Neither had time to speak before Ara crashed into her and sent them both flying off the cliff. They fell through the air. Then the ground came at them fast and hard. They rolled together down the cliff and through branches, narrowly dodging tree trunks as they tumbled down. Ara let go of his knife and held onto Cambria unsure if the instinct was for his own protection or hers.

Then the ground gave out again, and Ara let go. They fell through the air for a moment and then smacked into cold water. The sudden submersion caused Ara to panic even more. Images of slimy black leaches filled his mind, and he swung his limbs wildly until he broke the surface of the water. Still, he didn't breathe. He kicked and kicked until he was on dry land and frantically slapping at his body to rid himself of the evil bloodsuckers.

"Get them off, get them off." But there were no leeches on the ground or on Ara's body. He looked over both shoulders, feeling his back. There was nothing there.

Cambria crawled out of the pool and coughed up water. "What is wrong with you?" Cambria climbed to her feet and wiped away the red hair matted to her face.

"What's wrong with me?" Ara gasped. "What's wrong with you? You hit me with a rock."

"You were chasing me. With a knife."

"I didn't know it was you. I thought it was…" Ara stopped himself before he said more. How much had Cambria seen? "Why were you spying on us?"

"Because I don't trust you," Cambria said. "And it looks like I was right not to. Who are you guys really?"

"I told you my name is Ara and—"

"Enough with the stories. You're definitely not just poor travelers. I saw what you were doing. You were training to kill."

"No, I was learning to defend myself."

"Yeah? Defend yourself from whom?"

"Carmine guards, Temple guards, Bounty Hunters. Everyone!"

Cambria stepped back, holding his gaze to see if he was telling the truth. "You're them, aren't you? The ones the Faith is looking for."

Ara knew he should deny it, but he couldn't. He'd given it away already, and Cambria's eyes seemed to look through him and see everything. Besides, they deserved to know the truth.

"Yes," Ara said. He fell to the ground in exhaustion. The sand clung to his wet pants. "I'm sorry we lied to you."

Cambria narrowed her eyes at him. "Why are they after you? What did you do?"

"Nothing," Ara started. "I...I escaped."

"Prison?"

"I was being held at Castle Carmine. Briton and Geyer helped me escape."

"Briton and Geyer," Cambria repeated. "I knew their names sounded fake." She shook her head. "Why were you being held? Are you a thief? A murderer?"

"I'm a Descendant."

Ara waited for the shock and disgust to form on Cambria's face. But she just stared at him, weighing his words.

"So you're a runaway Descendant. That doesn't explain why the Temple guards are after you."

"Because they want my blood."

Cambria shook her head. "You northerners and your magic blood. They tear up a village and hurt people all because of a myth."

"It's not a myth. It's true."

Cambria looked at him skeptically. "I've heard the stories, Ara. About a once powerful race of warriors in the north. Warriors that couldn't be killed. Chop off an arm, and it would grow back. And somehow the Raw Bloods rose up and defeated them and now generations later, use their Descendants' blood as a magic healing potion. But that's all it is, a story. A lie people tell to justify slavery and to keep the Faith in power through dependence on false hope."

"You're wrong."

"Am I? I have traveled with doctors for years. I have seen what happens to people who wait for blood to cure them. They die. The only thing that helps is medicine and doctors like Petar and Hannah. And my parents."

Ara picked himself off the wet ground. He was sick of running. Sick of hiding.

Cambria stepped back. "Don't come any closer," she warned.

Ara walked toward her. He held out his hand, palm up.

"What are you doing?" Cambria asked.

"Showing you the truth. Cut me."

"What?"

"The knife in your belt. Cut my hand."

Cambria pulled the small knife. "I'm warning you."

"Do it," he said.

She was about to object, but something in Ara's face told her how serious he was. The small metal glinted in the sunlight. Ara did not lower his hand.

The move was quick and caught Ara by surprise. The blade stung his palm and returned to Cambria's side in a flash. Both of them looked at the red line along Ara's palm. The cut was done with precision. Deep enough to bleed but not to do any real damage. Ara tightened his hand into a fist and squeezed the pain away. Then he walked around the small pool they had fallen in and held his hand up to the dribbling waterfall. The water splashed away the blood. Ara looked at the separated skin and thought of his side and the wound from Geyer's knife. It had already healed. Leaving only a light scar behind.

*Could it heal faster if I focused on the wound, drawing my blood to the spot?*

"Ara!" Geyer's voice called from above.

Both Ara and Cambria looked up to the slope they had fallen down. They couldn't see Geyer through the thick trees and bushes. The cliff was high above. How had they not cracked their heads?

"I'm down here," Ara called back. "I'm alright."

"Fates! What are you doing down there?" Geyer called.

"Uhh, I kind of fell."

"Clumsy fool. I told you to stay within eyesight. I thought you had been taken."

"We'll be up in a minute."

"We?!"

Ara looked to the girl Cambria and then shrugged. "Don't worry. It was just a friend."

Cambria raised an eyebrow at this, perhaps objecting to the

label. Ara walked from the waterfall along the side of the pool. He came to her side. "You may not trust me, Cambria, but I trust you. You and the others are good people. I promise you we will tell them the truth from now on and whatever you guys decide to do we will accept. You have my word."

Ara held out his hand. There wasn't a scratch on it.

Cambria gasped. "How?"

EVERYONE SAT around the unlit fire pit as Briton relayed the entire story: finding Ara, the escape from Castle Carmine, hiding in the forest, fleeing the Temple guards. The doctors fell silent, taking in Briton's account. Geyer watched the faces of the doctors. His hand close to his knife. Whatever trouble it caused, whether it got them sent away or even turned in, Ara did not regret what he did. Telling them felt right.

"When you found us we were desperate," Briton said. "We wouldn't have lasted much longer. We owe you our lives."

"The Temple guards are hunting for you?" Aaron stammered. "They'll kill us if they find out we harbored you, knowingly or not."

"We put you all in danger. I'm sorry we didn't tell you the truth."

Silence fell as the group considered the implications. The truth was like a weight Briton had passed onto the doctors' shoulders. Ara could see them weighted down by the news.

All eyes turned to Petar, who sat on the other end of the fire pit from Briton. Petar scratched at his chin, mulling the information over. Finally, he looked up at the three of them and spoke. "You don't owe us for saving your lives. That's what we do. It doesn't matter who is after you or what you have done, we help those in need."

"But they are outlaws," Aaron said.

Aaron looked to Cambria for support. But she said nothing. She glanced at Ara and then looked away. She had not spoken since they left the pool of water. They had climbed the cliff in silence, and before Ara could tell Geyer what he had done, Cambria ran off back to camp.

"And what laws have they broken?" Hannah asked. "They were rescuing the boy."

"We're in the north! The Faith makes the laws."

"Aaron," Petar said in a calm voice. "We've seen firsthand the atrocities brought on by the cruel religious practices of the Faith. We have nothing against the Descendants."

"But how can we believe them? They lied to us about their names and who they are, and now they're claiming the boy has magic powers. It's ludicrous. Cambria, tell him."

Cambria bit her lip. A war waged behind her green eyes. "I don't know what to believe," she finally said. "I've never believed in the legends of Royals and good and bad blood. I believe in science and what I can judge for myself with my own eyes."

Her head stayed down, her eyes on the cold fire pit. "But what I know of science has no explanation for what I saw him do."

The group fell silent. Ara did not object or offer any defense. They were told the truth, it was up to them to decide what to do. As much as he dreaded being back on foot fleeing through the forest with Briton and Geyer, he would accept whatever decision they made.

"We won't turn you in," Petar said at last. "But we cannot travel together. We will take you as far as the next town. From there you will have to make it on your own."

Briton nodded. "We understand."

Petar took a heavy breath. "I'm sorry we can't do more."

No one spoke for a while. They just stared at the unlit logs. Ara's heart tightened inside his chest. For a few times over the past days, he'd forgotten their troubles. He'd felt some semblance of home. Now, their time together had come to an end.

# 21

The caravan traveled the road at a slow pace that matched their somber mood. Cambria was glad the truth had come out. But she felt a surprising sense of guilt to be abandoning these men. At first, she had been happy to be rid of them and the danger they brought to her people, but as the wagons pushed east, she began to feel the gravity of their situation. They were leaving them to fight the Faith on their own.

"Don't look so glum, Cambria," Aaron said. "Everything will be okay. We'll make it to the next town by nightfall. Then this will all be over."

"I'm not worried about us, Aaron," she said. "We're not the ones being hunted."

"We are as long as they're with us."

Cambria looked out the back flap to the wagon that carried Ara, Briton, and Geyer. Hannah now rode with Aaron and Cambria in the first wagon. She was busy sewing—something Cambria couldn't remember seeing her do before. Even with the shaking wagon, the needle punched in and out of the red fabric with precision.

"There are plenty of people that need help in this world,"

Aaron said. "Think of all the good we can do if we aren't locked away in some Temple dungeon for the rest of our lives."

"The decision has been made," Hannah said. "All we can do now is wish them the best."

*That's not all we can do,* Cambria thought. But she did not say it out loud. In fact, she didn't know where this sudden concern for the strangers had come from. She was the one who unmasked them and caused their departure. Maybe that was why she felt guilty.

It was late afternoon and Cambria must have dozed off because Petar's voice startled her. The horses slowed, and the wagon came to a stop. Had they reached the town so soon before nightfall?

Cambria pulled back the front flap of the wagon's canvas. Two men stood in the middle of the road. They were shirtless and frail; ribs protruding through a thin layer of tanned skin. Their hands were locked in front of them by metal bands, and a chain tied them together at the waist from belt to belt. Ropes stretched from leather bands around their necks to a cart behind them, blocking the road. The two men stared ahead with lifeless eyes. Their sullen faces were marked with tattoos. The letters "CH."

Descendants.

"Hello, there," Petar called, confused. "Good health and peace be with…"

The bushes shook in every direction. Then shouts and the sound of footsteps hitting the road. Lots of feet. It was an ambush. Cambria's hands began to shake. She tightened them into fists and moved to stand, but Hannah pulled her down shutting the canvas flap. She held Cambria's arm and shook her head *no*.

"Hello yourself," a man's voice called.

Cambria couldn't see how many there were, but it sounded like the wagons were surrounded. She shook Hannah away and peeked her head out of the wagon. A man held a bow, the arrow nocked and facing down.

"Any trouble?" Petar asked, his voice shaky.

"There doesn't have to be," the man said. "Tell us what's in the wagons."

"Supplies. We're doctors. We're here to help people."

"Then you're in the right place because we are in need of some help."

"What's wrong with them?" Petar asked. Cambria looked again to the two Descendants tied up and blocking the way. Their faces were void of reaction, like they weren't even there.

"Oh, the blood bags?" The man laughed. "They don't need any help. They're resilient little roaches. No, we just keep them around because we like our blood fresh from the source. No, I think you can help *us*."

"What do you want?"

"Everything you got."

The back of the wagon was thrown open. A large bearded man peered in. He smiled hungrily as he laid eyes on Hannah and Cambria. "Oooh, he was holding out on us."

The man grabbed Cambria by the leg and ripped her from the wagon. Cambria smashed into the ground head first. Dazed, she spat dirt from her mouth. She heard two more thumps and Hannah and Aaron were beside her.

"No! Stop!" Petar's cries were cut short by a sick thud, and he groaned as he hit the ground himself.

"What's the matter big man?" someone asked. "You got something to say?"

Cambria rolled over. Brim was down from the second wagon, standing in the road his fists clenched. Uncertain. He was surrounded by armed men.

"Whoa," said a man with a sword. "You're a big son of a bitch, ain't ya? Gunther, I don't like the way he's looking at me."

From the other side of the wagon, a man let fly an arrow. It struck Brim with a sick *thwack*, sinking into his shoulder and knocking him to a knee.

"Ho! You see that giant take that?"

Brim pulled himself up to his feet. He hobbled toward Cambria and the others, an arrow jutting from his slumped shoulder.

"Don't think he got your message, Gunther."

The bowman drew another arrow and took aim at Brim's back.

"Noooo," Cambria screamed through a dry and dusty mouth.

*Thwack.* The arrow lodged into Brim's hamstring, forcing him down.

"Tough son of a bitch," said the man with the sword. "He didn't even make a sound." He spun his sword in his hand and moved toward Brim. "Let's see if a little steel will get him to sing."

Cambria's heart dropped. She couldn't breathe as she watched the violence unfold before her.

Sword in hand, the man moved toward Brim. A mocking smile filled his face. The other bandits laughed.

Dirty and bleeding, Brim crawled on, his leg dangling uselessly behind him. He didn't even look at the approaching sword. He just kept moving toward Cambria. To protect them.

"No, please," Hannah said. "Please."

But there was nothing she could do. There was no time. The man stood over Brim. "Let's see you walk this one off." He raised his sword high overhead. "Timber!"

But before he could deliver the blow, the man jerked sideways, off balance. He dropped his sword and fell to his knees. He reached behind him toward the knife jutting from the base of his neck. Then he slumped over dead.

"Flin!" one of the bandits yelled.

All the eyes turned from the dead body to the back wagon.

Geyer was already pulling a second knife from his boot.

"Kill that bastard!"

Geyer lodged the second knife deep into a nearby bandit's chest. The man wheezed and grabbed at the blade. He pulled it out—a big mistake. Blood and air fountained from his chest. He fell to the dirt and drowned in his own blood. Geyer ran for his horse, dragging his lame left leg in the dirt.

The bowman drew an arrow from his quiver. He took aim at Geyer while Geyer pulled his sword from the saddle. The bowman had a clear shot, but Brim grabbed the man's ankle, pulling his leg out from under him. The arrow flew into the trees. Brim pulled the man down and was on top of him with all his weight, pounding his head into the ground.

Geyer pulled his sword from the horse and slid behind the wagon.

"Kill them!" shouted a bandit. "Kill them all!"

Cambria looked around at the six remaining men. Beside her, the bearded man grabbed Aaron by the hair and pulled a small hatchet from his belt. Aaron screamed as his head was yanked back, exposing his neck.

Before Cambria could think, she was on her feet and running. She leaped at the bearded man, but he batted her away with an elbow. She hit the ground but did not falter. Her hand went for the blade in her belt. Then it went for the man's heel cord. She severed the tendon with a quick stroke. The man howled in pain and crumpled, grabbing at the back of his bloody ankle.

Cambria watched the man writhe in pain. It was one thing to treat wounds, but another to inflict them. After all her talk of fighting, when it actually came to hurting someone, she felt like the naive girl she was.

She couldn't stop now; her friends needed her. Cambria grabbed the hatchet.

"Quick, under the wagon," she yelled. Hannah, Aaron, and Petar did as she said and crawled for cover.

Behind her, Cambria heard screams and clanging of metal.

Ara was in the middle of the road. He swung his knife, trying to fight off an advancing swordsman. It was clear he was outmatched and wouldn't last long. None of them would.

THIS IS NOT GOING WELL, Ara thought as he deflected another one of the man's blows. The bandit was bigger and stronger, and the last blow of his heavy sword had nearly shattered Ara's knife. *Not going well at all.*

Ara had followed Geyer out of the wagon, despite Briton's warnings. At first, Geyer had said to let the bandits rob them and be on their way, then they shot Brim. They were going to kill him. Geyer was out of the wagon a moment later, and by the time Ara followed, two bandits were already dead.

"Remember your training," Geyer said as he went for his sword. That's when everything went crazy. Brim attacked the bowman, and even Cambria was fighting back. Ara drew his own knife just in time to block the attacks of this bandit. But whatever training there was for him to remember wasn't going to be enough.

The man swung again. Ara ducked under the attack but lost his footing, stumbling to the ground. He rolled away, keeping the knife tight to his body so that he would not stab himself. The man yelled and swung his sword, hitting the side of the wagon as Ara rolled underneath. Ara continued the motion and came out the other side. He got to his feet. He may not be able to outfight these bandits, but maybe he could outrun them.

Ahead of him, Geyer stood over another bandit's body. Two more charged his way. Geyer spun his sword in his hand as if refreshing himself with the feel of the weapon. After all this time, the old knight better remember how to use his sword.

The men closed in and Geyer set his feet in a balanced stance. Patient. He held his ground as the bandits drew near. Too close, Ara thought. There was nowhere to retreat. Then Geyer's sword slashed through the air in two quick strokes, and the men fell dead. Ara had never seen the old knight move like that. It wasn't the speed so much as the smooth efficiency. It looked more like a painter's brush stroke than the wielding of a heavy weapon.

"Ara!" Briton cried from behind him.

Ara turned in time to see the bandit coming around the wagon with his sword raised. No time to run. Ara lifted the knife behind him and threw his arm forward at the charging man. The man ducked his head and raised his sword to block the throw. But the knife never came. Ara had held onto the weapon. The man lifted his head in confusion. Ara charged and dug the blade into the man's belly.

A cry of pain filled his ears as the bandit fell. His hands slid around his wet belly, trying to stop the blood pouring from him. He cursed. Blood bubbling from his mouth.

Ara turned from the sight.

The chaotic sounds of the melee had subsided. Now there were only the groans of pain. Bodies littered the road—dead or well on their way.

Ara ran past them toward the first wagon. He stopped along-side Geyer. One bandit remained; he held a knife to Cambria's throat.

"It's over," Geyer said, lowering his sword; the blade was stained crimson. "Let the girl go."

"You killed my men," the man growled at Geyer, spit flying from his mouth. His face red with hate.

Geyer shook his head. "The choice was always yours."

"As is cutting her throat."

Ara rushed forward.

"Stop, or she dies!" the bandit screamed. Cambria winced as the man drew the blade tighter to her throat.

"Cambria," Hannah cried. She and the other doctors crawled out from under the first wagon. They were alive.

"Geyer, please, do something," Petar pleaded as he got to his feet.

"Everything is going to be alright," Geyer said, keeping his voice calm but never taking his eyes off the armed bandit.

"No, it isn't," the man said, stepping back with Cambria in his grasp.

"What do you want?"

"I want you to die."

"Then let the girl go, and I'll give you that chance."

"I saw you fight, swordsman. No, I think I'll take this little girl with me instead. Follow us and she dies."

Ara's mind raced for an answer. What did he need to do? How could he save Cambria's life?

*Every problem has a solution.*

"Don't do it, please," Briton said from behind Ara. "There's been enough needless bloodshed already. Let the girl go, and you can have your life."

The man looked around. His men were dead in the road; the ambush had failed miserably. Now he was surrounded. His eyes grew wild like a trapped animal.

"You're not taking the girl," Geyer said.

"Stay back," the bandit jerked Cambria's head back. Her red hair matted against the man's sweaty face.

"Stop," Ara said. He raised his hand as if a warning would end the standoff. He needed time to think. To come up with a plan. Even if Geyer had the aim to hit the man with his knife, he couldn't get to the bandit before he slit Cambria's throat.

*What is the answer?*

The bandit took another step back, he was almost to the bushes. Geyer stepped forward, keeping the distance between them short.

"I'll kill her," the bandit said. He twisted to keep Cambria between him and Geyer.

"Cambria!" Hannah called from behind them. Petar caught his wife and held her back.

*Think!* Ara felt the blood pumping in his temples, wracking his brain. Cambria wasn't going to die. No matter what happened here, he wouldn't let that happen.

Then Cambria's eyes met his and locked on, pleading. No —trusting.

"Ara," she winced.

"Cambria," he answered.

"What you say you can do…is it true?"

"Shut up!" the bandit yelled, drawing the knife so tight it cut her skin. A tear of blood ran down her neck. "She's coming with me."

Ara's eyes stayed with Cambria's. He nodded his answer. *Trust me.*

"Geyer," Ara said.

Geyer stepped forward. "You sure?"

The bandit stopped. He looked back and forth between them, confused. Trying to figure out what he'd missed.

Ara breathed, feeling the blood pumping from his heart. Good blood. "Do it," he said.

Geyer leaped forward with such speed Ara thought he might make it before the surprised bandit could react. But the Bandit did react. His eyes went wide, and the knife jerked in his hand. Geyer drove his sword into the bandit's heart, killing him instantly.

Cambria spun away, knocked free from the dead bandit's grasp. She hovered in the road, frozen for a moment, her green eyes searching Ara's. Then they rolled up into her head and blood streamed from her neck as her throat opened. Her small body slunk to the ground.

## 22

There was a moment of complete silence as Cambria's body hit the ground. Ara felt his own heart stop. Then the reality of what just happened set in. Screams followed.

"Noooo!" Petar yelled, running to her.

"Cambria!" cried Hannah.

Geyer pulled the sword from the dead bandit's body. "Hurry, stop the bleeding."

Petar put his hand over Cambria's neck. She gurgled blood. "The wound's too deep," Petar said. He tried to dam the flow; blood covered his hands. "Oh, Cambria."

"Just seal the wound!" Geyer yelled.

Petar looked up at Geyer. Then he looked at Ara. He nodded. "Aaron, get my bag. Hurry."

Aaron jumped into the wagon and came out a moment later with a leather satchel. Hannah ran to Petar's side and tore her sleeve and held it to Cambria's neck as they laid her on her back.

"There's too much blood, I can't see," Petar said, pulling out his needle and thread.

"You can do it," Hannah said. She poured out a water skin onto the wound and Petar went to work stitching.

*I don't know if this is going to work*, Ara thought. *What if she's already dead?*

It didn't matter now. He had to try.

Ara picked up a knife off the ground and wiped the blood off on his pants. Then he rolled up his sleeve.

Geyer grabbed the empty water skin from Hannah and came to Ara's side. "How much will she need?"

"I don't know," Ara said. He touched the blade to his wrist and cut vertically up his arm. "Ahhh," he winced.

"What are you doing?" Aaron cried.

Ara held his wrist over the water skin and squeezed. His blood flowed down into the skin. As it filled up, the familiar nausea returned and Ara's head grew light. He felt like he was back at Castle Carmine as his strength poured out of him.

"That's enough," Geyer said.

"No," Ara said, squeezing his numb arm. "I can do more."

"Ara."

"Just a little more." His grip loosened on his wrist. He struggled to hold on. Spots of blackness formed in his vision. "Have to…save…Cambria."

"It's done," Petar said. "The wound is sealed. But she lost too much blood."

"Save…Cambria." Ara stumbled back. Darkness took over. He collapsed to the ground.

THEIR MASTERS WERE DEAD. For years Dais Mald watched their masters rob travelers on the forest road. Watched them kill and rape. These ones had seemed easy targets. Tied to the cart blocking the road, Dais Mald was ready to watch them die. But instead, the travelers had cut their masters down.

The man in green with the yellow hair and beard knew what he was doing. He handled a sword like no Raw Blood Dais Mald had ever seen. He cut through their masters as if batting away the attacks of children. The big man who Gunther shot had got him in the end, pounding his brains all over the road. And even the young girl had cut Barnum, crippled him. The bearded man had the wits to crawl off into the woods on his injured leg as the fight turned against them. Dais Mald pictured him hobbling through the forest this very moment, in pain and afraid. The tables finally turned.

It gave Dais Mald much satisfaction to watch each one of them die like the dogs they were. But it was what happened after the fight that surprised Dais Mald the most. Before Jamison died, he had killed the young girl.

Or so he thought.

Dais Mald watched as a thin boy filled a bag with his own blood. Then the travelers forced it down the dying girl's throat. What happened next was not possible. The girl started breathing again. The travelers were as shocked as he was. The boy's blood has saved her.

The boy was a Descendant. He didn't have any markings on his face, and he traveled freely in a group of Raw Bloods. But there was no other answer. Dais Mald had seen many powerful Descendants in his life, but he had never seen one do what the boy had done. Not even Spade.

The group carried the unconscious boy and set him in a wagon. The man who had treated the girl came to the big man's aid, removing arrows from his leg and shoulder. The swordsman checked the bodies of the attackers. They were dead except for Barnum, but the swordsman didn't pursue him. Dais Mald hoped wherever he was hiding, his old master was suffering.

It wasn't until later that the old man of the group turned to Dais Mald and Coates as if finally noticing them. He approached with caution, his eyes falling on the straps and chains that held them. Dais Mald felt the pull of the chains as Coates stepped back, but Dais Mald held his ground. He had suffered as much pain as a man can inflict. He would fear no Raw Blood.

The old man gasped. His blue eyes scanned Dais Mald's

body. A body that had been starved and bled dry. "What have they done to you?"

"Careful, Briton," the swordsman called.

Coates and Dais Mald exchanged glances. Unsure of what came next. Were these their new masters? They couldn't be any worse than Jamison and the band of robbers.

The old man reached down and inspected the bands on their wrists. Dais Mald flinched at the gesture. "It's alright," the old man said. Then he reached up and unhooked the rope tied to Dais Mald's collar.

"Is there a key?" the old man asked.

Coates lifted his bound hands toward Jamison's body. The swordsman followed his gesture. He walked back and dug through Jamison's pockets until he found a ring of keys. Then he limped their way, watching them intently. Dais Mald held his gaze.

"We don't want any harm," the swordsman said. "Understood?"

"Understood," Coates said beside him. His voice sounded soft and out of practice. Dais Mald couldn't remember the last time he heard it. Or his own. Their masters had had little need for their talking over the past two winters time. *Two winters*, Dais Mald gritted his teeth at the thought. All this time suffering at the hands of the robbers. Being cut open at night to feed their drunken appetites. Dais Mald grew up at the mercy of House Chamberlain's Curor. At the time he had thought it couldn't get any worse. He had been very wrong.

The swordsman gave Dais Mald a warning look and then unlocked the metal bands. Dais Mald fell to his knees rubbing his wrists. They were a different color from the rest of his arms, pale and thin where the bands had been.

"Thank you," Coates said. Dais Mald shot him a dirty look. *It is a fool who thanks his captors for a bigger cell.* Spade's words came to him now. He would never thank a Raw Blood.

"What do you want with us?" Dais Mald asked the two men.

The words felt strange coming from him; the voice was not the one he remembered. He came to his full height, battered and half naked.

The old man looked at him confused. "We don't want anything. You're free to go."

Dais Mald and Coates exchanged glances. What kind of trick was this? Even if they did not take them for themselves or to sell, it was the law to return Descendants to their rightful owner. The brand on their face said they belonged to House Chamberlain.

"Don't tell the Temple guards you saw us," the old man said.

Dais Mald almost laughed. "We will not be seeking Temple guards."

The old man nodded. "We have food. The doctors can tend to your injuries."

"No," Dais Mald said.

He walked past the old man and stopped at the bushes. He tore off his tattered rags. The woman of the group stepped away, but Dais Mald didn't care. Jamison's shirt was too bloodstained but his pants would do. Dais Mald put on the pants and boots. Coates did the same with Gunther's clothes.

After he had changed, Dais Mald picked up Barnum's hatchet from the ground. He locked eyes with the swordsman and then slipped the hatchet into the belt of his new pants.

"What of the boy?" Dais Mald asked.

"He'll be alright," the swordsman said.

"He belongs to you?"

The swordsman shook his head. "No."

Dais Mald considered this and what he had seen the boy's blood do. What it meant. The girl lay on the ground, her head on a young Raw Blood's lap. Her chest rose up and down. She was alive.

"The boy is special," Dais Mald said, finally.

"Yes, he is."

Dais Mald looked to the wagon where the Descendant lay.

This was not the last he would hear of this boy.

But a chance at freedom was what mattered now. Dais Mald and Coates left the travelers on the road. They walked through the bushes back into the woods. Dais Mald's body felt light. The air was soft on his skin where the chains had been.

After a time, Dais Mald stopped and turned back. He stood there waiting.

"They're not coming after us," Coates said.

The forest was quiet. The sun was sinking lower through the trees.

"No," Dais Mald agreed.

"You saw what the boy did."

Dais Mald nodded.

"You know what he is?"

Dais Mald nodded again. "That can wait."

He turned away from the road toward the bloody trail that snaked through the forest floor. Dais Mald pulled the hatchet from his belt and trudged on. He hoped Barnum would still be alive when they found him.

AFTER BURYING THE BODIES, the party started back on the road. They were not so much in a hurry to get to the next town but to escape the site of bloodshed. Travel was slow and even the horses seemed in shock. At dusk, they set up camp off the main road even though the town of Fallgrove lay only three hours farther. Briton was glad for the stop. It gave Ara a little more time under the doctors' care as his wrist was slow to heal after losing so much blood.

Cambria was still in the wagon. Hannah had stayed at her side until she was certain she would survive. What little of Ara's blood was left over was used to treat Brim's wounds. The big man now sat across the fire ring looking no worse than the rest of them. The camp was silent except for the crackle of the fire. Ara sat staring blankly into its flames.

Briton couldn't imagine where his mind was. Couldn't imagine what it was like to give yourself to another person. He'd recognized that vacant gaze from the Descendants of Castle Carmine. People thought it was mere mental dimness. It allowed men to justify all sorts of things. How could he have ignored the horrors for so long?

"We can take off at first light," Geyer said, breaking the collective silence. "If you don't mind Ara resting with you another night."

"Of course," Petar said. He looked as if he had forgotten their planned departure. "And…thank you for what you did. As horrible as it was, I'm afraid to think of what would have happened if you weren't with us."

Geyer shook his head as he stared into the flames. "We all take chances on the road. I wish it were otherwise."

"We've been robbed before but those men…"

"Got what they deserved," Hannah said, her usual warm expression gone. Fatigue hung heavy on her face.

Briton thought of the bodies in the road, stabbed and gutted. Although he had not taken part in the killing, his hands felt no less bloody.

"What will you do?" Petar asked. His face alternated between Geyer and Briton. The answer held a larger question than what tomorrow would bring. *What will you do with nearly all of Terene on your trail?*

"I don't know," Briton said. "There are western Houses who do not hold loyalty to the Faith. Perhaps we'll seek sanctuary there."

Petar turned to Ara, hesitation on his face. "Ara, your blood…you saved Cambria's life. By all medical knowledge, it isn't possible."

Ara didn't say a word. His hollow gaze stayed fixed on the fire.

"It's real then," Aaron said, shaking his head. "The tales of Descendants and blood magic. We are taught at the university that the Faith are a bunch of superstitions zealots, but they were right all along."

"No," Briton said. "Descendants exist. Traces of the blood of Royals exists. But the Faith is not right. They exploit people for their gain and make slaves of the innocent."

"But all the people that blood could help," Aaron said. "There would be no need for medicine, sickness and disease would be obsolete."

"The Faith doesn't care about helping people. All that matters to them is power."

Ara stood up suddenly, and everyone fell silent.

"Ara?" Briton asked.

"I'm going," Ara said, his bronze eyes reflecting the firelight.

"We should wait until morning," Briton said. "When you have recovered enough to travel."

"No," Ara said. "I'm going alone."

"What?" Briton gasped.

"I don't know who I am or why I am different," Ara said, his voice rising. "Since I was captured, all I wanted was to escape. To no longer be tortured and drained of blood. But now that isn't enough. Being on the run, hiding in the woods, this isn't freedom. So I'm going to find answers."

Ara looked to Geyer and Briton. "Thank you for everything you've done for me. But you can't come with me. I don't want anyone else to get hurt."

"Ara," Briton said. "You can't do this alone. You won't make it. The Highfather's forces are too great."

"There's not much chance of me making it with you either. There's no reason you need to die. It's me they want."

"But Ara—"

"No, Briton. I've made up my mind."

Briton almost didn't recognize the young boy who stood before him. Brave and stubborn. This was not the same boy he had taken from Carmine Castle.

"Then you'll have to change your mind," said a weak voice.

Everyone turned to see Cambria standing in the dim light outside the fire ring. Her throat had been slit only hours earlier. Now, she stood before them, returned from the edge of death.

"Because I'm not giving in to the Faith," Cambria said. "And neither are you."

"But Cambria…" Ara began.

"I gave my pledge to aid people who needed my help. The Highfather and all the Temple guards in Terene can't stop me from doing what is right."

"She's right," Hannah said, standing up. "We can't look the other way when someone is in need. That's not what we do."

She looked to Petar. The doctor scoffed. "Well, if Hannah is in, you know where that leaves me."

"I knew I should have stayed at the university," Aaron said. He nodded his head in agreement. "You guys won't get very far without my skills of gathering supplies and hiding under wagons."

A loud clap startled everyone. Aaron fell off his rock. Brim's face turned red, and he sheepishly lowered his hands. Everyone broke into laughter. Laughter of surprise. Laughter of relief. Briton couldn't believe it. After what they'd just been through and knowing all the dangers that lay before them, these doctors were still with them.

Ara wiped at the tears that were coming fast now.

"And what about you, Geyer," Briton asked. "Now is your chance to leave."

Geyer shrugged, his face twisting with that sly smirk of his. "Not while Ara's fighting is still so piss poor. If word got out that I taught him, I'd never live it down."

More laughter. It warmed Briton's belly like relief from a sickness. For a moment, the day's trouble was forgotten. Brim threw a heavy log on the fire, and it caught quickly, lighting up the circle of faces. A most unlikely group come together. Briton felt better than he had in a long time.

He could almost fool himself into thinking they could win.

# 23

---

*"Power amplifies our effect on the world. A wicked son is the scourge of his family; a wicked lord can decimate a kingdom."*

---

T he stench of Descendants made the Highfather gag. Aeilus Haemon wasn't used to visiting the Temple's cell level. The fact that Father Edmund Turney chose this as a meeting place told Haemon something of the young Father's motives. For if these were normal matters, he would address them in his study or the council chambers. Not in this Hemo-forsaken pit. *What was this little schemer up to now?*

Two Temple guards led Haemon down the winding stairs to the cell level and the door to the dungeon. The smell grew stronger as they moved through rows of dark cells. The hundreds of rotting Descendant's looked at them through the bars with the blank stares of livestock. They sat on the cold stone floor, lacking the strength to stand. Haemon didn't like thinking about where his blood came from. He liked sipping it from a crystal goblet, ignorant of the dark dungeon below the Temple.

Though, it would all change once his men created the replica of the boy's royal blood. Then he would have no need for these animals; they could be exterminated once and for all.

A light glowed up ahead as Haemon moved past the cells toward the Curor's laboratory. The room was enormous as it took dozens of Curors to collect the daily blood toll. Standing by a Curor's table, Edmund Turney looked small and insignificant. A guard stood beside the young Father. Though he wore the white uniform of the Temple guard, the grim look on his face showed he was loyal to Turney.

"Father Haemon," Turney said. "I see you got my letter."

Haemon snorted. The letter contained the meeting place and time followed by a simple message:

I FOUND IT.
 - *Turney*

THE GALL of this traitorous slime almost impressed Haemon.

"And what was so important to drag me down to the Temple dungeon with your cryptic phrase?" Haemon asked in a bored a voice. It took great effort to suppress the anger pumping through his blood. Edmund had called him out.

"I believe you understood the message, otherwise you wouldn't be here."

Haemon gritted his brittle teeth. "This sounds like a conversation better had in private."

Edmund looked at his guard and nodded. *Confident as well as smug.* The guard slipped past Haemon and out of the room along with Haemon's own. They shut the door behind them, leaving Haemon and Edmund alone in the great lab.

"What's this about Edmund?" Haemon asked. He was tired from his long walk down to the Temple's dungeon. Forty-eight stairs. He'd counted every painful step. The thought that

Edmund might have chosen this meeting place for that purpose angered Haemon even more. "What did you find?"

Edmund smiled like a cat who'd finally cornered a slippery mouse. "I found your secret lab."

"My what?"

"Don't try to deny it, Aeilus. I found your blood lab in the old part of the Temple. You have Curors working day and night on a blood replica."

Haemon looked the young Father over, his anger boiling. To dare address the Highfather of the Faith by his first name like some kind of equal!

"Such a thing would be blasphemous…" Haemon began but trailed off. There was no point in lying anymore. If it was Edmund's goal to get Haemon overthrown, he would have gone straight to the council with the information. Not to an underground meeting place. Haemon's eyes wandered around at the Curor's lab. The empty bottles on the shelves. The tools spread out on the table. "What is it you want, Edmund?"

"I want your position, of course. I want to be appointed Highfather of the Faith."

"That much has been clear since you joined the council. Is this how you plan to get it? By turning me in?"

"No," Edmund smiled. "Although I have garnered favor on the council, I am still a junior member. There are many who have a more substantial claim. And I'm not going to sit and wait for my time to come any more than you did."

"And what do you think you know of the details to my ascension?"

"Everything," Edmund said. The young Father's face changed. The greed he'd kept hidden from the council table all these years was now revealed. "I studied your life, remember. I know about the death of Highfather Archaties. I must say, it was masterfully played."

"If you really know what I did to take power, then you know what I'll do to keep it."

"Yes, I do. Which is why I come to you with a proposal."

"Blackmail you mean."

"Call it what you will. You will keep your chair for the time being, but at year's end you will announce me as your successor."

Haemon frowned. "That is not a lot of time."

"More time than you'd have if I went directly to the council with your heresy. You'd be executed, buried with the blood still in your body. A full vessel unable to be filled anew in the after-life." Edmund took a breath. His tone softened. "This way you will go out with your legacy still intact. Besides, how much time could you really have left?"

Haemon ran his finger along the surface of the Curor's table. "And what would you have me do with my small remaining time as Highfather?"

"Finish what you started," Edmund said, excitement on his face. "Eradicate Spade and the Descendant rebellion. Let it be the final triumph of your great rule. Then I will step in to run a new era of peace. Thanks to you."

"And what of the Descendants' dwindling bloodlines? How will you preserve the Faith when the blessings of Hemo have dried up?"

Edmund narrowed his eyes at Haemon. "Is that what you tell yourself your pagan blood experiments are for? To preserve the bloodline for the benefit of the people? You are only after that boy to save yourself."

Haemon's whole hand now rested on the surface of the lab table. He leaned on it for support, his clean robe draping on the messy table. "It is true, I wish to go on living. But it is for the benefit of Terene. I can't imagine what chaos this world would slip into under the rule of a pompous upstart like yourself. I won't let it happen."

Edmund's lip twisted into a snarl. "Then I will take this to the council and have you hung for blasphemy in the Temple Square."

Haemon laughed. Strength surged through him as if he had taken a dose of good blood.

"If you had truly studied my history then you would know better than to meet with me in such a secluded place."

The Highfather's hand closed upon a needle on the Curor's table. In one swift move, he jammed the point into Edmund Turney's throat. The young Father gagged in surprise as blood sprayed from the small puncture hole.

Haemon bent over him. "Archaties was surprised as well. Most Fathers can do nothing more than talk politics and pray. They don't have the courage to act."

Edmund stumbled back against the table, sending tubes and bottles crashing to the floor. The door to the lab swung open, and the three guards ran in with swords drawn. They saw Edmund on the ground, gasping as blood shot from his neck, coloring his white robes red. His tongue hung out as he tried to scream but only choked.

"Thank goodness you came," Haemon said to the guards. "Descendant rebels have infiltrated the Temple. They killed Father Turney. And a Temple guard."

Edmund's guard looked around in confusion. Then the loyal Temple guards drove their swords into his sides, under the armor. The dead guard collapsed on the lab floor.

The two guards then moved to dispatch of Edmund, but Haemon held up his hand. "Let's give the Father a moment. It looks as if he has something to say."

Edmund's face was pale as the blood drained from his body, covering him and the lab floor. His mouth opened and closed as he gagged on his own blood.

"What was that, Edmund?" Haemon asked as he kneeled down beside the dying man. His old knees would regret the move. He would need to drink an extra portion of blood to recover. But it was worth it. He wanted to savor his moment.

Edmund reached a bloody hand toward the Highfather. "Aeeeh, Aeeeilusss," he wheezed with the last of his breath.

"Edmund," Haemon whispered over the dying Father. "You will address me as Father."

Aeilus Haemon stayed crouched on the floor of the Curor's lab, enjoying the painful final moments of Father Edmund Turney's life.

## 24

———

"But how were the Royals defeated if they were so much more powerful?" Ara asked. He sat in the grass field with Briton as the day's lesson shifted once again to questions of the past.

"According to the Faith's account, men had the numbers," Briton said. "And they had a purpose—to overthrow the oppressive Royals. When people find a purpose worth dying for, even the impossible can happen. Plus, General Drusas came up with a military strategy that would work against the Royals."

"What was that?" Ara asked.

"First, they surrounded the Temple and cut off all food supplies. Then they unleashed a constant stream of attacks. Men poured against the Temple walls in steady waves, giving the Royals no chance to heal from battle. The siege lasted seven days. Thirty men fell for every one Royal."

"Then what happened?"

"Once the Raw Bloods took control of the Temple, they slaughtered every Royal they could find. All the Royal leaders and officers. The few that escaped that day were later caught and enslaved. Their blood used to strengthen the people. For generations, people fed off the blood of the few remaining Royals and their offspring. Selling them like property. Breeding was not sanctioned then. Royal blood was mixed with non-royal blood. Now, centuries later, the Descendants have blood that is but a fraction as pure as that of their ancestors."

Briton tilted his head to Ara. "Except for you."

"How?"

"That is the big question. It is possible that a strain of the original Royal blood has manifested itself once again. We don't know what was the original cause that gave the Royals their power. How their bloodline deviated from our own. There is a chance it is happening once again, and you are but the first."

Ara liked the sound of that. There could be more like him out there. If not now, then soon. Whatever made his blood special was happening again.

"So we must find the cause of the blood power," Ara said. "But where do we look?"

"We can start with where you came from. There may be something there, the source for the Royal blood."

*The source.* Ara thought back through the fog of his memories. What had been the source of his power? What in his past had changed him but not others?

"Well, now that your distraction is complete," Briton said, his blue eyes twinkling under bushy gray eyebrows. "I think that's enough for today's lessons."

They stood up and shook off the grass then made their way back to camp. The group had settled about a mile outside the city of Farmount, in the northeastern corner of House Severen's realm. Farmount was a large and dangerous city; Geyer thought it would be easier to go unnoticed there. Ara and Briton hadn't been back at the small camp long before Geyer and Aaron returned. Judging from their faces, trade had not gone well.

Aaron tossed his sack down in the back of a wagon. "We barely got enough bread to last us the day."

"We will make do," Petar said.

"No we won't, we're running out of coin. We weren't making

a fortune as doctors, but at least it kept us fed. Now we have nothing."

"It's too dangerous to set up here," Geyer said. "Maybe in another, smaller town."

"We've faced tough cities before, you know."

As they continued to debate, Ara couldn't help but feel responsible. He was the reason they couldn't practice medicine. He was the reason they were hiding in the forest. When they starved, it would be his fault as well. He had to do something.

Ara returned the lesson book to the tent and grabbed his knife from beneath his pillow. He slid the weapon into his belt and covered it with his shirt. Then he slipped away into the forest.

It wasn't until he was almost to the city of Farmount that Ara realized he was being followed.

"Show yourself," Ara said, crouching low, his hand on the knife in his belt.

"Are you really going to try to stab me again?" Cambria stepped out from behind a tree. Her hair pulled back in a simple braid left her freckled face exposed. Though Cambria was self-conscious of the "blemishes," Ara liked the tiny spots on her nose and cheeks. Her high collar covered much of her neck, but Ara could still see the scar that ran across her throat. Would it be there forever?

"I wouldn't need to stab you if you'd stop sneaking up on me."

"I wouldn't need to sneak up on you if you'd stop trying to hide things."

Ara gave her an annoyed look.

"Where are you going anyway?" Cambria asked. "Are you running away?"

"No. I'm going to find us some shrines."

"And how are you going to do that?"

"I don't know yet," Ara said, embarrassed. He didn't have a plan. He only knew they needed food. The others risked their lives every day for him, now it was his turn. He would find food for the group, even if it took selling his own blood. He was tired of eating grubs from the ground, no matter how nutritious Petar said they were.

"Don't try to send me back," Ara said. "We need shrines and you know it."

"I agree," Cambria said, coming to his side. "But since you have no plan—the only way you're going to get some is with my help."

There was no use trying to change her mind; Cambria was as stubborn as a boulder. Besides, she was probably right; he did need her help.

Ara nodded and the two of them walked the rest of the way together. The forest grew thinner, and the sounds of the city came into crisper focus: horses on the road, wagons rolling through the streets, vendors yelling from an unseen marketplace. A distant hammering.

"Have you ever been here before?" Ara asked.

"No," Cambria said. "We've stayed clear of Farmount."

So far Ara had seen only two kinds of populated areas. The poorer decay of the outskirt towns and the great buildings of the Temple square. Farmount was a mix of both. A castle rose up through the middle of the city like a stone dagger. It was surrounded on all sides by buildings of considerable size, but they carried the tarnished look of structures that had weathered too many storms without upkeep. The city was shell of what it must have once been.

As they walked the road into town, Ara could see the people of Farmount held much the same weathered look. Two men on horseback shot Ara and Cambria dark glances as they passed. No children ran the streets, and the women Ara did see looked the kind that could handle themselves. If Cambria was intimidated, she didn't show it. She strode on, leading the way through the city.

"Maybe this was a mistake," Ara said. "Maybe we should have brought Geyer."

"You scared? You're the one that can't die."

"I can too die," he whispered. "And I'd rather not test out exactly how."

Ara hurried to keep pace with Cambria. She walked with eyes forward like she was on a mission.

"Where are we going?" Ara asked.

Cambria nodded. "toward the noise."

The yelling and hammering grew louder as they followed the flow of traffic through the streets. Yelling and cheers filled the center of town as people formed a ring around some unseen space. The crowd jeered; paper flapped in waving hands. The jingle of coins trading hands caught Ara's attention. "They're gambling."

Cambria's touch startled Ara. She held onto his shoulder for balance as she slipped off a shoe and poured the contents into his hand. Ara caught the coins. Three shrines.

"For emergencies," Cambria said, putting her shoe back on and taking the coins. "Let's see what game they're playing."

"Do you know anything about gambling?"

"It's better to win."

Another clanging sounded; half the crowd cheered while the other half groaned. An eerie chill shook through Ara as he realized the hammering sounds weren't from construction. They squeezed their way to the front of the circle; their gasps of horror were drowned out by the screaming crowd. Below them stood a fighting pit. Two men circled each other with clubs, their bodies battered and bloodied. Each bore an "S" tattoo on the right side of his face.

The crowd was betting on Descendant fighting.

Cambria signaled to Ara to leave, but before they could escape, the crowd erupted, pressing them forward against the pit's metal railing. A cry of pain filled the air; below them, the smaller Descendant's arm dangled, bent the wrong way. He swung his club with his good arm, but the fight had left him. The bigger Descendant heaved his own club back and with an animal roar, caved in his opponent's head. Blood splattered against the spectators on the other side of the pit. The crowd broke into a frenzy. The spectators cheered and licked up the blood.

A sickness erupted in Ara's belly. They were using Descendant lives for sport. Ara wanted to strike back, to take his knife to these horrible people. A hand grabbed his arm. He turned to find Cambria pulling him. "Time to go. Now."

They started to move back through the crowd when a loud voice called out. "Now for the grand event!" A thin man with a curled mustache and sharp eyebrows waved a stack of papers to get the crowd's attention. "This runaway Descendant was caught in the forest. In all his mercy, the gracious Lord Severen has agreed to stay this criminal's execution."

Boos and jeers came from all around. The speaker smiled beneath his wavy mustache then waved the crowd quiet before delivering the punchline. "*If* he can defeat…Honey."

The crowd went crazy pushing Ara and Cambria forward once more. A bar dug into Ara's back as he was squeezed against the pit railing. Below him stood a Descendant with lash marks crisscrossing his back. An "S" tattoo snaked across the Descendant's face. His eyes were full of fear as he stared at the pit door. A roar echoed and the door shook.

"How many minutes will the Descendant last?" the speaker called. "Place your bets!"

Throughout the crowd, men with paper held up their hands, and people raced to place their bets; coins traded for written receipts. All around Ara, people pushed toward the speaker with their shrines.

"Odds on two minutes?"

"Three to one," the mustached speaker answered.

"Eight shrines."

"Two minutes, ha. Honey will get him in the first."

"Two to one odds on that," the speaker said.

"He can barely stand as it is."

"Five shrines."

"Seven!"

The betting continued as Cambria reached Ara again. "Let's go."

The man leaned against the wall of the pit beneath Ara, stepping as far from the door as possible. A few broken weapons were scattered about the pit floor along with puddles of blood.

"We have to do something," Ara whispered. "They're going to kill him."

"There's nothing we can do," Cambria said. "Let's go before someone recognizes you."

The Descendant was so close, Ara could almost touch him. In a minute he would be torn apart. The helplessness that filled Ara turned to anger as his mind raced for a solution. The pit door shook, and a snout poked out, sniffing at the flesh that awaited it.

"Bet your shrines," Ara said, handing Cambria the coins. "All of them."

"On what?" Cambria asked.

"On him winning."

"What?!"

Ara dropped to the ground and grabbed a discarded mug. He shook out the remnants of ale then reached into his pocket for his knife. He slit his finger with the blade.

"Ara," Cambria whispered above him. Ara squeezed his finger and droplets of blood fell into the mug.

"Final call," the speaker yelled. "Place your bets."

"Three shrines," Cambria's soft voice said.

The mustached man laughed. "And what minute would you like, little girl?"

"What are the odds on him winning?"

"Winning?"

Ara squeezed harder. The blood filled only the bottom of the mug. It wasn't enough. Of course, there was likely not enough blood in his entire body to help this man survive. But he had to try.

"That's right," Cambria said.

"Even I would feel guilty taking a little girl's coin."

"Are you afraid of the bet?"

"Not *that* guilty," the speaker said. "Twenty to one on your three shrines. And sorry, lass, Farmount isn't a land of miracles."

The crowd's impatience grew as the people chanted: "Honey. Honey. Honey." People hungry to watch a Descendant be torn to pieces. Ara could feel the bloodlust and it made him sick.

The mug of blood was only a quarter full, but there was no time left. Ara crawled to the edge of the pit and called down. "Hey. Hey. Up here."

The Descendant looked up as if expecting to be spit on. His eyes locked with Ara's, and Ara saw defeat had already settled in. "You can do this," Ara said, but he was not sure if his words got through. The man looked up at him with pity—pity for the boy didn't understand what was about to happen. Ara held the mug out over the railing. "Drink this."

Ara released the mug. The man caught it.

"Alright, all bets are in," the speaker called. "Let's see the Descendant criminal fight for his life against Honey."

The crowd cheered and pressed forward. Ara fought his way to his feet and leaned against the railing. Below him, the Descendant looked down at the mug of blood then up at Ara. Ara nodded. *Please. Drink it.*

The Descendant drank the blood.

The effects were instant. The man stood taller, his bent back now straight. He looked around the pit as if seeing it with new eyes. When he turned to Ara, his gaze was sharp and clear. The fear was still there, but there was something else as well. Life.

"You can do it," Ara yelled, his voice drowned out by the crowd.

"Release Honey!" the speaker called. A man above the pit

pulled a rope that lifted the bar locking the door. The door flew open, and an enormous brown bear charged into the pit. The beast stood on its hind legs, its head nearly reaching the top of the pit and let out a ferocious roar. The crowd thundered in applause and cheers. "Honey. Honey. Honey."

"Start the count," the speaker yelled.

Cambria came to Ara's side, the paper receipt in her hands. "This is your plan?"

They turned their eyes to the pit.

The bear made the pit look suddenly small. It dropped to all fours and fixed on the Descendant. It snorted and growled, showing a savage array of teeth. Then it charged. The Descendant moved with a sudden burst of speed. He dodged the bear's claw with a roll then backed to the other side of the pit. Cheers and groans echoed from the crowd.

The bear stood against the wall and swiped at the people in the crowd. The mighty paw was not two feet from Ara's leg. Finally, the bear turned back to the Descendant and charged again. The Descendant faked right and ran left, this time his escape was narrower. The bear's claw caught him on the shoulder. Blood dripped down from the scratch.

"He's not going to make it," Cambria said over the cheering crowd.

*Come on*, Ara thought, willing the Descendant on. *Fight.*

The Descendant shuffled along the ground toward an ax-head. He picked up the weapon and heaved the metal. There was a loud *thwack* as the blade dug into the bear's hide. The animal roared but did not fall. Its anger only increased as it swirled around toward its prey. The Descendant picked up a broken sword and pointed its jagged tip at the bear.

"Two minutes and still standing!" the speaker yelled. Then he looked down at Cambria, no longer as sure of himself.

The Descendant bounced around on the balls of his feet. His face had changed from hopeless to determined. He was ready for the bear. The enormous beast charged. The Descendant held his ground. As the bear drew close, the Descendant turned around and ran toward the wall. But there was no way he would outrun the bear or climb out of the pit. The bear reared up, almost upon him. The Descendant leaped up and kicked off the wall, flying back at the bear like an arrow, the broken sword its point. He struck the sword into the bear's chest, and the beast fell upon him. The Descendant disappeared under the mound of brown fur.

The crowd fell silent. Beside him, Cambria shut her eyes. The bear stopped moving; it lay in a brown heap.

There was a shake as the bear stirred. Then the man's arms appeared. He pulled himself out from under the bear. The Descendant's torso was stained red, but he managed to stand. He looked defiantly to the crowd. The bear, dead at his feet.

Gasps sounded from the crowd, but no one spoke. Not until Cambria tapped the speaker on the arm and handed back her paper receipt. "I believe that's sixty shrines."

The man's lip snarled under his mustache, but he counted out the coins and handed her enough to fill both hers and Ara's pockets.

"Stick around and we'll see if your luck runs out," the man snarled.

People eyed Ara and Cambria as they tried to find enough places to stuff their small fortune. Ara's clothes sagged under the weight of the coins. He lowered his head, nervous at the attention they were receiving.

"Now can we go?" Cambria asked.

"Yes," Ara said.

The speaker gave them one last grimace then turned to face the Descendant in the pit. The man stared directly at Ara; the look in his eyes was a mixture of gratitude and bewilderment.

"As the generous Lord Severen has decreed, this man will not be executed," the speaker said.

The crowd groaned its displeasure.

The speaker waved them to silence. "He shall live to fight tomorrow!"

The crowd erupted in cheers and applause.

"You can't," Ara said. "You promised his freedom if he survived."

"Where are you from, boy?" The speaker laughed. "He's a Descendant. There is no freedom."

Cambria pulled at Ara's arm, and this time she did not let go. Ara could feel the stares on them as they moved. A hooded figure pushed toward them through the crowd. Ara caught a glimpse of a scar on the man's hidden face.

"This way," Ara said. He pulled Cambria away from the hooded figure's path.

They escaped the crowd at the pit and hurried down an alley, clinking with every step. They reached the street and headed toward the direction they had come. Ara turned several times to make sure they weren't followed, but it was hard to tell with the crowded streets. As soon as they crossed the tree line, they broke into a run, moving as fast as they could under the weight of the shrines.

*I should be happy*, Ara thought. He set out to get some coin for food and ended up with enough to feed them for months. But he couldn't get over the horrors he had witnessed. Descendants beaten and killed for sport. He had seen the mistreatment of Descendants before, but this was something else completely. *How could people live with such cruelty?*

Ara stopped and looked back. The forest behind him was empty though he could not shake the eerie feeling of being followed. Maybe he was still unnerved by what he had seen at the fighting pit. He ran and caught up to Cambria. Neither said a word until they were back at the camp.

"Where have you been?" Hannah's worried voice called as they crossed the grass toward their companions. "We'd thought you'd been abducted."

"I'm sorry," Ara said. "We…went into the city."

"Ara!" Briton rebuked. "Farmount is a dangerous city. You could have been killed. Both of you."

"I'm sorry," Ara repeated. He couldn't think of anything else to say. It was dangerous. He could have been caught and thrown to the bottom of the fighting pit—torn apart for people's entertainment.

"What were you thinking?"

"I…we needed food. I wanted to help. I…"

Cambria cut him off by opening her pockets. Shrines rained down onto the ground. Hannah and Briton looked on with open mouths. Ara reached into his own pockets and poured out an even larger share. Everyone gasped as the gold piled on the ground.

"If it makes you feel any better," Cambria said. "Dinner is on us."

ARA HADN'T FELT this full since…well…as long as he could remember. Geyer had taken some of the shrines back to Farmount and returned with fresh meat, bread, potatoes, carrots, onions and, though it wasn't on the list, a jug of ale. He even found a dish of sugar sweet bread, a special request by Cambria and Aaron. Hannah cooked up the food over a fire, and they ate enough for a group twice their size. Trepidation disappeared along with their hunger, and the mood lightened. It was one of the first pleasant evenings Ara could remember.

After enough of the ale had disappeared, Geyer was even coaxed into telling the story of his first tournament.

"Garmond the Gray," Geyer said. "Big as an oak tree and with an intelligence to match. I was seventeen and entered the tournament as soon as I could afford my first sword. I had to duel in borrowed armor. Nervous as I was, I didn't even try it on before my first bout."

Geyer took a long chug from his mug and wiped the ale from his chin with a satisfied gasp.

"They kept calling my name, thinking I had lost my nerve. Ha! I was with the stablehand, fastening rope to keep the armor from slipping off. What a sight I must have been coming out in front of Lord Broming and most of the eastern realm, swimming in a bigger man's armor."

Everyone laughed at the image. Except for Cambria. Sitting across the fire from Ara, she seemed agitated. Her eyes drifting off into the dark of the forest.

Geyer drained the last of the mug.

"Garmond refused to fight me. Said it would only blemish his reputation to sully himself with someone so far below his station. But tournament rules said nothing about the shape of a swordsman's armor, and Lord Broming ordered him to get on with it. Ha! I think my clumsy attire distracted him because I bested him inside of three minutes. Half blind with my helmet sliding over my eyes with every parry. It took old Garmond years before he showed his face at another contest."

Cambria quietly rose and slinked off into the woods. Geyer finished his tale, and Briton began dissecting its historical inaccuracies. By then Ara couldn't take it anymore; he stood up and followed after her.

The moon was high and full making it easy to move through the trees. Hiding out in the forest these past months, Ara had rarely stopped to notice its beauty. The trees sparkled as if the light came from within their own leaves. The darkness was no longer the home of hidden danger but of mystery. Even the chirping of the insects sounded more welcoming this night.

Ara found Cambria bathed in moonlight, staring off a cliff's edge.

"It's your turn to sneak up on me now, I suppose," she said without looking his way.

"How did you do that?" Ara asked. He had kept his distance and stepped on the balls of his feet with practiced silence.

"It was the silence that gave you away," Cambria said, turning toward him. "The crickets stopped chirping near you."

"And how'd you know it was me?" He stepped closer. Into the moonlight.

Cambria simply gazed back at him. Her hair was combed back, freckles scattered on her face like dark stars.

"I saw that you left," Ara said. "Is everything alright?"

Cambria shook her head. "How can it be? After what we saw today. After what I've seen my whole life. Sometimes I wonder if it's worth doing what we do."

"Don't say that. You and the other doctors help so many people."

"For what purpose? We stitch them up only to get cut again. Heal their sickness only to starve from a lack of food. And that's just Raw Bloods. What you Descendants go through…"

"It's horrible and it's wrong," Ara said with conviction. "I know that long ago, life under the Royals was cruel and unfair. But this cannot be any better. Why must one race always live atop another?"

"Because they're afraid of you. What you can do."

"They should be." Ara shook his head, looking out into the night. All the pain he had suffered these past months…he now understood the Descendants' hatred for Raw Bloods. He could even understand the rebellion's attacks. "I've never felt like a Descendant, I didn't even know what that word meant. But if that's the side I'm on, then I will fight for it."

"No. That's what people don't understand. It's not one side against the other. The world is comprised of individuals. Each one is capable of good or harm. It comes down to what we choose to do." Cambria's eyes sparkled in the moonlight. "You are not defined by your blood."

"That's how the rest of the world sees me. And I don't understand why. Are we really that different?"

"No," Cambria said. "We're not."

Cambria sat on a large round rock near the cliff edge, and Ara joined her. Sounds of a river in the forest below reached up to them. Water that started in the mountains far away and passed them only this brief moment on its way to the other side of the world.

"As a young girl, I thought my suffering was unique. But the more I traveled the more I saw I was just like everyone else." Cambria stopped for a moment, listening to the rolling water below. "I was playing in a river when my parents were killed."

Cambria fixed her gaze on the forest below. A full minute passed before she spoke again. "We met some sick travelers on the road. My parents, of course, offered to help. My mother sent me to the woods to pick elderweed for lotions. I was searching in the forest, and when I heard the sound of a river, I dropped the elderweed and ran to the water. The day was hot, and I played by the water losing track of time, dipping my feet into the current. Splashing. Throwing rocks."

Cambria stopped for a moment as if weighed down by the memory.

"When I returned my parents had already been infected."

"Infected?"

"Gray Fever. They hadn't taken the proper precautions when treating the travelers. They didn't expect to encounter death."

Ara gasped.

"It works fast. One of the travelers had already died, his chest caved in as my father was inspecting him. The others began panicking, trying to run. My father had to contain the disease. He couldn't let it spread. In all that panic, he did what had to be done. He acted like a doctor should, clinical without emotion." Cambria gulped down the lump in her throat. "I didn't know he was capable of that. Or what came next."

She closed her eyes with a deep sigh. "My mother was sobbing when I got back. They were standing over the bodies. I had the elderweed in my hands, my hair was still wet from the river. I saw that something was wrong. At first, I thought they were just mad at me."

"What did you do?"

"Nothing. They wouldn't let me get close to them. I told

them I could help; I begged them to let me try. But there's no cure for Gray Fever.

"We said goodbye. Then my father made me promise to burn the bodies. All of them."

They were silent for a long moment. There was nothing Ara could say. The crickets' song grew louder in all directions. Though they were roughly the same age, Cambria had always seemed more mature. Always taking control. Now, alone, speaking in a soft, close voice, Ara realized how small she really was.

"I was careful," she said. "I took every precaution. If there was a chance they had touched something—supplies, the wagon —I burned it too. It took me all day, but I cleaned the site of any contamination. My father would have been proud."

Cambria wiped her face and looked up.

"I survived on my own in the town of Caldesh for a month until I found Petar and Hannah. I've been with them ever since."

"I'm sorry, Cambria," Ara said.

She nodded. "I haven't told anyone else that story aside from them. Not even Aaron, though he's pieced much of it together." Her eyes turned back to the forest below. "You don't know how many times I've wished to go back. To that morning in the river. Just a little girl playing in the water, not knowing what awaited her. I think it was the last time I was truly happy."

Ara imagined Cambria as a young girl. Her somber face replaced with a carefree smile. "I don't have any happy memories. Not one."

"You really did lose your memory?"

Ara nodded. "It's as if everything started over when I woke up in that hunter's cart. Stuff must have come before because I know things. Only I don't know how I know. I get pieces sometimes but they don't mean anything."

"Like what?"

Ara sat down on the rock beside her.

"Like I'm in the sky, looking down."

"You fly in these memories?"

"It's more like I'm a cloud. I'm just there, above everything. Looking down on trees and mountains and…a river." Ara's voice trailed off as he pictured the scene from his visions.

"What? What is it?"

"It's the Arathan River. I've seen it before, in my visions. I'm sure of it."

"What does that mean?"

"It means that I come from up north. That is where I will find the source. The source of the royal blood."

Ara stood up as he pictured the river on Briton's map the day he chose a name. Something had been familiar then, and now he was sure the river had the same shape as the one in his visions.

Ara was so excited by the hope of an answer that it took him a moment to hear it. The silence. All the crickets in the forest had stopped. Cambria leaped off the rock and spun around, blade already in hand.

"Easy girl," a voice said. A figure stepped from the darkness into the moonlight along with six others. They all had scars on the right side of their faces.

"You're not the one we want," a man said. "We're here for the boy."

## 25

B riton held the lantern away from his face as he peered into the dark forest. He wasn't worried at first when the two kids had snuck off. It was clear they'd grown closer over their time together, and Briton was happy Ara could find some connection in the midst of all this terror. But then they heard Cambria's scream.

"Cambria," Petar called out somewhere to Briton's right. "Ara."

The group had spread out into a search party, scouring the woods. It was unlikely they'd gotten lost; even without a lantern, there was enough light to get by. Briton moved through the brush, his stomach twisting in fear of what he'd find.

A figure raced past him. Briton turned the lantern in that direction and followed, wondering if he should be carrying a weapon. Not that it'd be any use to him. All those years of study and he never once learned how to fend for himself.

A soft moan cut through the silence.

Briton stepped into a clearing by a cliff's edge. Brim sat on the ground, cradling Cambria's body. The girl moaned as the big man rocked her and stroked her hair. Briton held the lantern close; specks of dried blood dotted her hair and the side of her face. Someone had given the poor girl a good crack.

Briton leaned down over the girl. "Cambria?"

Cambria's eyes opened and recoiled from the light. Briton pulled the lantern back. "Cambria, what happened?"

"Ara," Cambria said, trying to sit up and failing. Brim held her tight, stopping further movement.

Briton's heart raced in his chest as he glanced toward the cliff edge. It was a long drop. "Where's Ara?"

It was silly to fear for one who can heal from anything. *Nearly anything*, Briton reminded himself at the sound of water moving below them. Still, he worried. Despite all his power, despite how far he had come these past months—Ara was still just a boy.

Briton asked again, "Cambria, what happened to Ara?"

Cambria looked around, fear and panic taking hold. "They took him."

ARA WOKE IN DARKNESS. His hands were bound tight. His head was covered by a cloth that blocked his vision and trapped his hot breath against his face. He twisted in panic, but ropes scraped his back, holding him in place. The ground shifted beneath him in sync with the clopping sound.

*I'm tied to a horse.*

Ara focused on the clopping hooves around him but couldn't get a count of how many there were. Five? Ten? He thought back to the attack. It had been hard to see in the darkness. He remembered being grabbed, he remembered...

*Cambria!* Ara fought against the ropes. He remembered her knocked to the ground, unmoving.

"Cambria!" Ara yelled into the hot cloth. The horse jumped into a gallop. Ara struggled against the rope, loosening it enough to slip part way off the horse. His feet dangled in the air.

"Whoa," a voice called, and the horse came to a stop. Hands

grabbed Ara. The ropes loosened, and he was thrown down. His left side smacked against the hard ground spilling the air from his lungs.

"That's a good way to get trampled."

Ara climbed to his feet and spun around blindly. He shuffled a few feet left, a few feet right, a few feet left, waiting for the men to attack. But no one did.

"Let's see how far he gets before he cracks his head on a tree."

"Ha. Then we'll see how good his blood really is."

Ara stopped, catching his breath. He reached up with his bound hands and pulled the hood off his head. He blinked away the sudden rush of morning light. There were seven figures before him, five men and two women. They wore dark clothes of brown and black. Scars marked the right side of each of their faces.

Descendant rebels.

"What do you want?" Ara asked.

A tall man with black wavy hair and tanned skin stepped down from his horse and approached Ara. The man was handsome despite his scars, and there was a kindness in his sly smile. Two swords were strapped to his back, the handles crossing behind his head. He held his hands up as a sign of peace.

"My name is Taro Kine," the man said, bowing his head. "We mean you no harm."

Ara fumed. "You have a funny way of showing it."

"I apologize for the crack on the head. We were in a bit of a hurry and didn't have time for explanations."

"In a hurry to kidnap me, you mean."

Taro Kine stepped closer.

"I know this must be hard for you to understand, but we are here to help you."

"Help me?" Ara looked around at the faces of the rebels. He recognized one of the men. It was one of the Descendant prisoners traveling with the bandits. They had set the man free, and now he had returned the favor by kidnapping Ara.

"Spade sent us to find you," said Taro Kine.

*Spade? The rebel leader.* Ara had heard Descendants in Castle Carmine tell stories of the great Descendant rebel. Recounting his attacks on Raw Bloods.

"What does he want with me?" Ara asked. "To take my blood for himself?"

A soft chuckle broke out among the rebels. Taro Kine smiled. "To bring you home."

*Home?* Ara looked around at the faces of the Descendants. Did they know about his past? Who he was? Where he was from?

The mountain path stretched into the distance without cover. Ara couldn't outrun them, especially on foot. And now, his fear of being captured by the outlaws was fading behind the opportunity to learn what they knew.

Ara narrowed his eyes at Taro Kine. "You know what I am?"

"You're a gift," Taro Kine said. He held Ara's gaze for a long time and then turned to the other Descendants. "Let's stop here."

"But there are Temple guards in the area," a woman said. Her blonde hair was cut short like a man's, and she had a grimace that rivaled Cambria's. "We should keep moving."

"We'll be slowed if we have to keep chasing after the boy. He's entitled to some answers."

"It would be easier if I cracked him on the head again."

Taro Kine smiled and approached Ara. "Come, you must be thirsty. Let us rest and I will answer what I can."

The company moved into a covered part of the forest and tied their horses. Without discussion, two men took their place at the perimeter with eyes on the road while the rest sat and ate from their packs. Taro Kine offered Ara his waterskin, and Ara drank liberally, surprised by his thirst.

"You are the Descendant rebels," Ara said after he drank his fill.

"So we are called by the Faith," Taro Kine said. "Those who

seek freedom from oppression are called outlaws and rebels by their oppressors."

"How long have you been free?" Ara asked.

"Many of us have been free for years. Others, like Dais Mald here, were released more recently." Taro Kine gave Ara a knowing grin.

Ara looked to the Descendant they had released from the bandits. He had a fresh scar on the right side of his face where his tattoo had been. *He must have reported me to this Spade.*

"Why do you still have scars?" Ara asked Taro Kine. "Wouldn't they have healed by now?"

"We recut the scars to remind us why we fight. We will keep the mark until all Descendants are freed."

"But isn't it harder to pass as a Raw Blood?"

"We don't want to be one of them," the woman said. She sat behind Taro Kine, a bow in her hands, a quiver of arrows on her back. "They are monsters."

"But you kill people, too. I've heard of rebel raids, the slaughter of villagers."

"Faith lies used to drive hatred against our cause."

"Okay, Bree Sai," Taro Kine said, waving her to quiet. He turned back to Ara. "We have done violent things in the name of the cause. But we are in a war, with a very powerful enemy."

"Bree Sai, Taro Kine," Ara said, something sounded familiar about the rhythm of the words. He'd heard names like that before. "Those names…"

"Are taken from the time of the Royals. Once a Descendant is freed, he chooses his own name, after the Royals of old."

"I see," Ara said, remembering the list of Royal names in Briton's book. So much of what the rebels did was modeled after their ancestors. Ancestors they held up as gods. Would they think differently if they really knew them and what they did?

"What is your plan?" Ara asked. "I mean, what does the rebellion hope to accomplish?"

"To free our people from tyranny," Taro Kine said. "We will

not rest until every last Descendant is released and allowed to live by his own blood."

"And then what?" Ara asked. "You live in peace with the Raw Bloods?"

"Never," Bree Sai said.

"It is hard to see peace when feelings are strong," Taro Kine said. "But the world is big. I believe there is room enough for both of us. I hope one day we face that problem."

Ara looked down at the empty waterskin. The water and rest already working in his body. Sitting still, he became mindful of his blood flowing through his veins, strengthening his muscles.

"And what does Spade want?" Ara asked.

"Peace," Taro Kine said.

But Ara knew there was more to it than that. Even if Descendants were freed, they couldn't coexist with Raw Bloods in the same lands under the same laws. The divide was too great. Then he thought of Cambria's words from the previous night, how the world is filled with individuals. Maybe it is possible for people to choose peace.

"Our blood does not define us," Ara repeated her words aloud.

"It certainly does," Bree Sai said, her lip curling into a snarl. "It is what makes us special."

They rested for another few minutes then Taro Kine agreed it was time to move on. It felt good to get some answers, even if it wasn't about his own past.

They loaded Ara onto a horse behind a young Descendant. His hands were no longer bound, and his eyes were left uncovered. They traveled away from the main road down a narrower path that led up toward the mountains ahead.

Ara and the young Descendant rode in the middle of the other six rebels. He didn't know if that was to protect him or keep him hostage. Ara realized that his desire to escape had lost its urgency. A part of him wanted to continue with these rebels, to meet the one called Spade and learn what he could about these people and the source of his powers.

But another, larger part of him, thought of his friends. Briton and Geyer and the doctors. His friends who had all risked their lives to help him. And not because they wanted what he had. Ara might not be one of them, but they were more his people than these warriors—despite what his blood said.

THEY TRAVELED THROUGH THE DAY, riding single file as the path narrowed up the mountainside. A single scout rode ahead of the others while the group kept a steady pace. Few words were said among the Descendant rebels, hand gestures and nods were sufficient communication. These people were used to moving with speed and stealth.

Ara held onto the belt of the young Descendant rebel in front of him. To his left, the ground ended with a steep vertical cliff. A river snaked alongside the mountain far below. Rivers connected Terene, flowing from region to region, sometimes rough, sometimes placid. Here, where the land was steep, the rapids pounded angrily.

As they rode higher into the mountain lands of the north, Ara could see the hazy blue wall of the northern boundary. The Ghost Mountains spanned sea to sea. Ara had studied the mountain wall on maps, but neither the drawings nor Briton's lessons could prepare him for what he saw. In the distance, the blue mountain walls rose into the clouds with no end. These mountains marked the edge of the world.

Gazing at them, the troubles of one boy felt small and insignificant.

The horses slowed. The lead scout stopped ahead. Tension spilled through the group of rebels. Hands adjusted belts, bringing weapons within reach.

"What is it Solvan Ra?" Taro Kine asked as they approached the scout.

The scout nodded ahead to the next ridge. Ara followed his gaze up the path ahead. There was movement. White armor sparkled in the sun.

"Temple guards," said Solvan Ra.

Taro Kine waved his hand in a small arch, and the rebels pulled their horses into a small alcove where the path widened. They waited in silence behind the rocks, watching the movement up ahead.

Four Temple guards waited idly atop the next ridge, their horses searching the rocky ground for grass. There was movement below the horses. Ara stiffened at the sight of a bloodhound. The large beast paced between the horses, its snout dragging on the ground.

"Steady," Taro Kine said.

"There's only four of them," Bree Sai said. "And we have the element of surprise."

"It needn't come to that. We wait for them to pass."

Bree Sai shook her head in disgust. Her hand gripped her bow.

Ara looked down to the knife holstered on the hip of the Descendant rider before him. It sat loosely in the sheath for quick pulling.

"They're leaving," Solvan Ra whispered.

Up ahead, the Temple guards were turning away down the other side of the mountain. Soon they would be gone.

Faces filled Ara's head. Briton...Geyer...Cambria...Petar and Hannah. He even missed Aaron's worrying and Brim's gruff silence. Despite the chance the Descendant leader could have the answers Ara longed for, he couldn't shake the faces of his friends. Images of the time spent on the road—reading with Briton, sparring with Geyer, arguing with Cambria.

These were real memories. And they were more valuable to Ara than any he could have lost.

Ara's fingers touched the knife on the Descendant's belt. He raised it slowly from its scabbard, just enough for the blade to show. A glint of silver steel.

Then he ran his wrist across the blade.

Blood came instantly.

"What are you doing?" The young Descendant twisted around. Ara held his wrist into the air. It was deeper than he meant to cut. The blood ran down his arm.

Taro Kine's brow wrinkled in confusion.

Up on the ridge, the Temple guards rode down the other side of the mountain path, out of sight.

Ara held his arm high though it ached to be let down. The blood in his body surged upward to the open wound, spilling out into the air and Ara's strength with it.

Then it came. Echoing through the mountains as if crying out to all the world—a high blood-curdling howl.

"Stars!" Taro Kine cursed.

The bloodhound shot down the mountain ridge, kicking up a cloud of dust. Behind it rode the four Temple guards.

"Arm yourselves," Taro Kine yelled. The Descendants drew swords and knives. Bree Sai nocked an arrow and took aim, pulling back the bowstring with a steady hand even atop her horse.

The bloodhound tore down the path toward them, drool streaming from jagged fangs. Bree Sai released her arrow. It flew just wide of the dog, snapping on the dirt. The beast snarled and charged ahead.

The young Descendant in front of Ara raised his sword. Ara covered his wrist with his hand and squeezed to stop the bleeding that had colored his shirt red.

Shouts from the Temple guards could be heard now as they drew closer, their own swords out and ready. Ara didn't know how the Descendants would hold up to the training and armor of the Temple guards. But he was about to find out.

The bloodhound's barks shook Ara's bones; he gripped the horse's saddle. Bree Sai let fly another arrow. This one found its mark lodging in the bloodhound's shoulder. The bloodhound slid sideways then continued on, hardly breaking stride.

The animal charged through the Descendant's horses and leaped straight for Ara. Ara barely got his hands up. The beast struck him like a boulder. They flew off the horse, crashing onto the ground. The bloodhound's jaws clamped on Ara's arm.

"Aaahhh," Ara screamed as the bloodhound's fangs tore deeper into his mangled arm. Ara fought away but the beast held on, shredding Ara's arm. The hound was ravenous for Ara's blood.

The bloodhound yelped and released him. Ara kicked on the ground, separating himself from the beast. The young Descendant rebel pulled his sword out of the hound's dead body. "You asked for this."

"Attack," Taro Kine shouted.

Bree Sai had time to fire one more arrow that unseated the lead guard. Then the Descendant rebels charged out of the rocks and met the guards' swords. Clashing of metal and armor echoed through the mountains. The clamor was intensified by the cry of the colliding horses.

Knocked to the ground, the guards fought the rebels on foot. The fighting was not the elegant footwork of Geyer's lessons, these men fought for their lives in frantic bursts. The Temple guards were no match for the speed of the Descendant Rebels. Taro Kine wielded two swords at once. He swung his sword low and lopped off a guard's leg at the knee and driving the other one through his back. Bree Sai took a sword to the shoulder, letting out a scream before bringing her dagger up, finding unguarded flesh at the armpit of her attacker.

Though the pain was excruciating, Ara dragged his mangled arm up and held it tight to his chest. He stumbled to his feet and ran from the melee.

"The boy," one of the guards shouted. "Get the boy."

Ara ran up the mountain path without looking back. He didn't care who won, he wouldn't be the prize for either side.

Far below, Ara could see the roaring rapids foam white as they beat against outcropping rocks. His body was spent, but fear granted his legs flight. He tried not to think about his mutilated arm and if it would ever heal.

*Where am I going?*

Ara stopped, catching his breath. He couldn't outrun either party. They were on horses, and he was a small weak boy. And he was alone.

As brutal as the fight had been, it was over in minutes. Taro Kine struck both swords into the final guard who crawled for his life. Then all eyes turned up the path to Ara. These were not the faces of friends. Ara didn't know what the rebels were going to do to him for bringing this fight upon them, and he didn't want to find out.

Taro Kine sheathed his swords and leaped on his horse. He rode after Ara.

Ara turned around, searching around him for an answer. The narrow mountain path continued up the hill along the cliff's edge. There was nowhere to run. He couldn't escape them.

"Ara," Taro Kine called and brought his horse to a stop. He no longer wore the easy smile from before. "Get on the horse. We're leaving."

"I'm not going with you," Ara said.

"Yes, you are. You may not see it yet, but you belong with us. The Highfather won't stop until he has your blood. And when he does, there will be no stopping him."

Taro Kine believed what he said, Ara could see that. He looked at the blood running down his fingers, dripping in the dirt. Wasted. Each drop meant power for someone and pain for someone else. If the Faith got his blood, they could strengthen their army of guards, ending any chance the rebellion had. But Ara couldn't let the Descendant rebels have his blood either.

He was nobody's weapon.

Briton's words came to him once again. *There's always an answer.* But he never said anything about liking it.

Ara took a deep breath and faced Taro Kine. "Then I must make sure the Highfather doesn't get it," Ara said. Then he stepped off the mountain cliff.

"Nooooo!" Taro Kine's voice faded as Ara sailed down through the air. He knew this was suicide. If he didn't crack his head open on a rock and bleed out, he'd drown in the river.

Ara didn't care.

*Let this blood spill from my body and wash away. Let me be rid of it.*

Ara lifted his arms out as the wind whipped against him. For a moment it felt like he was flying. Ara closed his eyes and once more faces flashed through his mind. Briton...Geyer...Cambria...and then...another. A man with a neatly trimmed gray beard and bronze eyes that matched Ara's own. It was a face from his past. In that instant, Ara felt the fog of his memory begin to clear as if parted by a great wind. *Who...?*

Then he hit the water.

# 26

*"No side is innocent; it is clear to me now. We fight enemies of our own creation."*

It had been three weeks since the boy escaped Bale at Castle Carmine. Three weeks for the boy to disappear farther into the many shadows of Terene. The trail was now cold. Bale had pushed so hard he was hardly able to stay atop his horse. The blood poisoning had spread its deadly tentacles ever wider across his body; he could feel it eating away at his insides. It would not be long now.

He gave his Blood Knights orders to spread out and continue the hunt, but he knew it was feeble. Bale leaned Smoke west and hung on as the great horse carried him back to the Temple.

The journey was long, and Bale took it at a slow but steady pace. His skin burned from his neck down his left shoulder to the bicep. When it became too much to bear he stopped at a river and waded out until the cold water lapped over him. But the relief was only momentary. Bale rode the rest of the way without his armor and at the greatest speed he could stand. He wouldn't allow himself to die on the road; for some traveling peasants to find Bale the Blood Knight fallen from his horse, lying dead in the dirt.

He craved a worthy end as much as he craved healing blood.

The ride was long and Bale had time to go over his final mission again and again. How he and the great forces at his command had failed to find one simple Descendant boy. They tore every western town apart, and still, they found nothing but rumors and false leads. The Descendant rebels must have gotten a hold of the boy. That's the only thing that could explain his disappearance. Rats hiding underground.

Not that it mattered anymore. It was too late. Bale could feel his damaged heart held together by a string on the brink of snapping. He had been dying since the Carmine guard stabbed him all those years ago. He was living on borrowed time thanks to the Highfather's blood supply, but that time was over.

The sight of the Temple's domes over the tree line brought both relief and dread. Relief for his bones that the ride was almost over. Dread for what awaited him. Bale's grasp slackened as he rode through the Temple square, leaning on Smoke. Heads turned at the sight of Bale the Blood Knight but did not look away as they once had.

Under the shelter of the stables, Bale fell off his horse. Smoke screeched, kicking his legs up into the air. Bale grunted and fought against his muscles, forbidding them to quit. Climbing to his feet, he grabbed the shocked stablehand by the collar and lifted him off the ground.

"Not...not a word," the stablehand stammered. Bale set him down, and the man took Smoke's reins, hurrying out of sight.

Bale passed under the statue of General Drusas that stood just outside the Temple. The legendary warrior's broad-sword pointed up to the heavens as if challenging Hemo himself. Bail spat blood into the dirt.

It was a long walk through the outer sanctuary and through

the Temple halls. Guards and Fathers whispered as he passed, but Bale dared not stop for fear his legs wouldn't start again. One thing drove him forward. Something he had decided on the road and that pushed him on through pain and fatigue. The Blood Knight's final act. One that would be remembered long after his heart burst.

When he finally reached the Highfather's chambers, a guard told him he was not in.

"Well, where is he?" Bale snapped.

The guard was about to turn him away until the look in Bale's eyes changed his mind. "I'll take you to him."

They crossed through the old part of the Temple that still showed scars from the Blood Wars. The guard led Bale through a hallway filled with stone rubble to a hidden doorway. Bale stepped inside to find a laboratory. Red-robed Curors stood around a center table, huddling over something Bale could not see. Beside them sat Aeilus Haemon, the Highfather. Bale couldn't believe the old bastard was going to outlive him.

The heads in the room turned at the sight of Bale. Haemon's face showed no surprise.

"Bale the Blood Knight has returned, which must mean you've found the boy." Haemon looked around the room, mocking him. "I don't see him."

Bale leaned in the lab's doorway, saving his strength.

The Curors stepped back, distancing themselves from Bale and Haemon. A small part of Bale still held onto the hope that Haemon could save him; that the Highfather of the Faith would fulfill his promise. But if there was one thing Bale had learned in this life, it was how little faith was worth.

"You don't look so good, my son," Haemon said. "Come closer."

Bale shuffled into the room. He felt his heart beating lower in his chest, the string that held it weighed down and tearing.

"I did not find the boy," Bale said. "I...ran out of time."

Bale collapsed against the lab table. Bottles wobbled. Vorrel gasped, stepping back beside the other Curors. Haemon didn't blink.

"Time," the Highfather sighed. "A war none of us will win, filled with battles worth fighting just the same. The boy was your weapon against time as much as he was mine."

"I failed us both," Bale said. Grabbing the table's edge, he pulled himself closer. Blood dripped from his mouth, running down his chin. He moved closer.

"Yes, you did. I can see it in your eyes, Bale. The blood poison leaks through your body. Can you feel death coming?"

"It's been riding after me for a long time."

Haemon nodded, looking at the bottle the Curors left on the table. It wasn't blood inside. The liquid was dark, black as oil.

Haemon nodded to the bottle of black liquid. "All the resources in the world at our disposal and we still couldn't replicate the Descendants' blood. After centuries, Hemo has taken away that great gift. There is no fighting his will."

Bale pushed off the table, standing up straight. One hand rested on the table, the other free. "You justify every action as Hemo's will. It can't be that you simply failed?"

He was close enough now. One move to his sword it would be over. He wasn't fast—he could hardly stand. But he didn't need to be. He had the strength left for this.

"Hemo guides my steps, as he always has." The fool stepped closer, sympathy in his eyes. Bale swallowed back the blood forming in his mouth. "Let him help you, now."

Bale scoffed. "How?"

Bale stopped short. The fire that consumed his body, clenching every muscle, held for a moment. Bale looked at the bottle of dark blood before him.

"That's right," Haemon nodded.

"You said it doesn't work."

"I said we haven't been able to replicate Descendant blood."

"This is better," Vorrel said. He stepped toward his handiwork, his eyes bulging like a reptile's. "I have amplified the trace elements found in good blood. The strands that have dissipated with generations of impure breeding and contamination. Biologically, this is the most potent blood we were able to create. It is simply untested."

Bale turned from the slithering Curor to Haemon. "And you want me to test it?"

"I want to save your life."

*Do it now*, Bale told himself. *Don't listen. Draw your sword and cut out his crooked tongue.*

But Bale *was* listening. After all his bravado, his fearlessness in battle, here he was at the end, grabbing onto any shred of chance.

"You're dying," Haemon said. "Vorrel designed this not just to heal, but to make one stronger than before. Imagine an unlimited blood supply. All the sickness and death in this world and we could hold the cure. The ability to heal anyone without the need of Descendants." He waved a hand toward the bottle of dark blood. "This may be Hemo's answer. We need only the courage to find out."

Bale winced, gripped the table's edge with both hands. The fire coursing through his body was unbearable. Bale gritted his teeth. *You coward.*

He tore the cap off the bottle, staring into the dark liquid. He threw his head back and took one great gulp. It ran down his throat, thick as oil. He gasped and caught his breath, waiting for the usual cooling relief to come. But nothing happened.

The Faith's Curors had failed.

"It is worthless," Bale snarled. "You bastards and your empty promises…" He tightened his grip and the bottle shattered in his hand. Dark blood spilling everywhere.

"No!" Vorrel cried. "Save the blood!"

A nearby Curor rushed forward. He dropped to his knees, scooping up the dark blood in his hands.

Bale reached to draw his sword; then it came. Not relief, but pain. Fire erupted in Bale's chest. The string holding his heart snapped. Every muscle in Bale's body seized up at once. He staggered, bent over in pain. His muscles tore loose, splitting his shirt up the back.

"Aaaahhhh," Bale howled in pain.

"Great Hemo," Haemon gasped and stepped back, a chair clanging on the ground. Something was wrong. Bale felt it all over his body as it shifted uncontrollably.

"Stars above!" someone cried.

Bale looked at his arm. His veins turned black and bulged out as if filling with oil. Cracking bones sent him convulsing back and forth; the bones were rearranging themselves inside his body, expanding. He screamed louder as his vision turned red, the world submerged in blood.

He heard another howl of pain behind him. The Curor who had touched the dark blood.

"Mitus, too! What is happening to them?"

"Stay back!"

Bale's hands exploded with pain; his fingers curved into talons. He writhed on the floor, digging into the stone.

"What did you do to me?" he growled, his voice like thunder in his ear.

The voices of the others came to him from a distance, a place Bale had left behind.

"Vorrell, what is happening?"

"Don't touch it. Don't touch the blood."

Someone ran by him. Bale caught the man's leg. He felt bones crumble in his hand like dried bark.

"Ahhh!"

"Great Hemo!"

"Should we kill them, Father? Give the order!"

"Hemo help us, what have we done?"

The last thing Bale heard was the Highfather's voice shouting to the heavens. "Glorious Hemo, thy will be done!"

## 27

Ara woke with his face half buried in wet sand. He gagged and coughed water from his lungs. No part of his body didn't hurt; it felt like a heavy log as he rolled over in the shallow water. He looked up at the sky and breathed in the air. He was alive. Somehow, he was alive.

The water was calm, not the roaring rapids of before. Nor were these the same mountains. He must have lost consciousness on impact and been carried far down the river. How had he not drowned?

Ara tried to stand, but his left arm gave out, and he collapsed onto the wet sand. His arm was still in tatters. The flesh was torn to the bone where the bloodhound had seized him. He had lost a lot of blood. He could feel the emptiness, his body like a hollow well. At least the self-inflicted wound on his other wrist had already gone. He used his right hand to tear some of the tattered cloth from his shirt and did his best to wrap his left arm.

It was quiet except for the trickle of the river beside him and the call of passing birds. There was no sign of the Descendant rebels, but he still had to move. They'd find him eventually.

But where would he go? With some help, he could possibly return to Farmount, but he knew it was unlikely he would find his friends there. Maybe that was best. Ara didn't have the courage to leave the group when he should have. By staying, he had put their lives in danger. Now at least they would be safe.

Ara would go the rest of the way on his own. But the rest of the way to where? The source of his blood power?

*There is no source.*

Ara saw the source for what it was—an idea Briton created to keep him going. The illusion of hope.

Briton was wrong. Not everything had an answer.

Ara climbed to his feet. His clothes heavy with mud and water; his boots were lost to the river. This would make travel slow. But that wasn't a problem since he had nowhere to go.

Ara limped across the sandy shore, cradling his injured arm.

There was movement in the trees ahead. Voices speaking.

Ara looked around the open beach. There was nowhere to hide, and he didn't have the strength to run. He stood watching as a shape pushed through the trees. It was a man in ragged brown clothes. He carried a sack on his shoulder; a flower's long white petal shown out the top. The man stopped in surprise at the sight of Ara. His head shot up, revealing the "G" tattoo on the right side of his face.

A Descendant.

The two stared at each other for a long moment. There was no expression on the Descendant's tanned face.

"Kayto?" a second voice called. "Where'd you go? I said to stay within sight—"

A man in silver armor with purple trim stepped out of the trees. His hand went to his sword, but he did not draw it out.

"Who are you?" the armored man asked. "And what are you doing in the lord's wood? Poaching for wolf-orchids?"

These weren't Temple guards nor Descendant rebels. Maybe they wouldn't recognize Ara.

"I got taken by the river," Ara said. "I didn't know where I was."

"And what happened to your arm?"

Ara looked down at the bloody cloth. The wound hadn't had time to heal, not in Ara's exhausted state.

"Smashed it on a rock," Ara said.

The guard frowned as if he doubted Ara's story.

"I don't mean any trouble," Ara said with a slight bow. "I'll be on my way."

Ara turned to go, but the armored man stepped forward. "You'll stay right where you are." Without taking his eyes off Ara, the man turned his head and yelled behind him. "Semus! Semus, get over here."

A moment later, a third man stepped out of the woods, carrying a sack of his own.

It took Ara a moment to recognize the man from what seemed another lifetime. It was the gardener from Carmine Castle.

"Is this one of the Kendall kids who keep sneaking off with the lord's property?" the armored man asked.

Ara kept his head down, hiding his face from the man. Hoping he didn't recognize him.

"Definitely not," Semus said.

*He remembers.*

Ara met Semus's gaze. The gardener held a stunned expression. Ara didn't know if that was good or bad. Should he risk running? He couldn't fend off the guard, not in his condition. Ara sighed in tired surrender. Just like the river, he'd let this latest problem take hold of him and run its course.

"Lord Gorgen is going to want to hear about this right away," Semus said. "We've found something much more valuable than wolf-orchids."

CASTLE GORGEN WAS BUILT into the side of a cliff. Stone pillars jutted from the cliff's own rocky side. At once the castle looked both a natural piece of the mountainside and an absurd construction that disregarded the laws of physics. A waterfall spilled down the length of the unscalable cliff, just outside the castle's rear wall. Where Carmine Castle had been simple in its design, this castle flaunted its every framework. They passed through gates made of bronze and shaped with flowery designs. The path toward the castle was flanked by stone pedestals and statues of naked men and women.

The Descendant, Tayko, watched Ara the whole way back to the castle. The fact that the man rode his own horse led Ara to believe this Gorgen treated his Descendants better than many lords. Perhaps Ara could survive here yet. Cold hungry nights in the forest had actually made Ara miss the comforts of his tower bed.

The castle grounds were even more majestic than the view from outside. A maze of gardens stretched out before the castle, open for all to see and wander through. The people Ara passed were dressed in fine attire and rich floor-length dresses as if everyone was a noble. In the background, adding a soothing ambiance, was the constant splash of the waterfall that fell down the cliff face just outside the castle's inner wall.

Ara was taken into the castle and led into a large room on the first floor. The walls were lined with portraits of stout subjects. Ara guessed these were the lords and ladies of the castle over the years. He felt for the artists who had to interpret their likeness.

"Stay here while I summon Lord Gorgen," the armored guard ordered. Then he hurried off, excited to personally report their find to Lord Gorgen. With him gone, and the Descendant off to tend the horses, Ara was left alone with Semus.

"How is it you are here now?" Ara asked the gardener in a low voice.

"Castle Carmine is no more," Semus said. "The Highfather's men seized the place and took what they wanted. Everyone left. When Lord Gorgen offered to take me on as his house gardener, we transported what we could from Carmine's garden and began again here."

Castle Carmine, the assassin attack. It seemed so long ago.

"What of you?" Semus asked in a low whisper. "How did you escape? There were rumors, but no one knew for sure what had become of you."

Ara didn't know how much to tell or how much to trust the man. Semus seemed to understand this for he shook his head as if dismissing the question. "Probably best not to say," he said. "But tell me this much at least. Is Master Briton still alive?"

The thought of Briton made Ara stop. He clutched his wounded hand to his chest, picturing those piercing blue eyes that seemed to wink even while staring directly at you. There was genuine concern on Semus's face. Briton had meant something to this man, as well.

"Yes," Ara said.

Semus smiled with relief. "That old bat. I knew he had it in him."

They were interrupted when the doors swung open. An overly obese man in a purple shirt with gold lacing tottered into the room. He had sagging eyes and a wide nose that rested above his numerous chins. Ara had never seen someone so fat; he felt sorry for the Lord's flattened shoes. Lord Gorgen raised a wrinkly brow at the sight of Ara, as if he hadn't believed his guard's report was true.

The guard at his heels pointed to Ara. "Lord Gorgen, I give you the magic Descendant boy."

"Magic Descendant boy?" Gorgen said with skepticism.

"Well, that is what they call him," the guard backtracked, no longer as confident. "Semus identified him. He's the one who claims to—"

"That will be all," Gorgen said, cutting the man off with a thick hand. "Leave us."

The guard hesitated but one look from Gorgen and both he and Semus exited the room. Semus gave Ara one final look before he left, but Ara couldn't interpret its meaning. The doors shut, leaving Ara alone with Lord Gorgen.

"Welcome to House Gorgen," the round man said. "I cannot imagine what you have been through these past months."

Gorgen waited for the boy to react, but Ara said nothing.

"Do you have a name, boy?" he asked.

"My name is Ara."

"Ara, very good. Well, Ara, I'm glad you made it safely to my castle. I must admit, when I heard you had gone missing, I sent some men of my own to look for you. I'd hoped they would find you before the Temple guards, though I didn't think it possible." Gorgen nodded to the closed door and rolled his eyes. "Especially not someone like Duncan."

"He didn't find me. The river brought me here."

Gorgen looked Ara over. "What happened to your arm?"

Ara raised the injured arm. It still stung though it had stopped bleeding and begun to scab over. "A bloodhound."

A worried spread across the folds of Gorgen's face. "The Temple guards? Are they nearby?"

"I lost them somewhere up the river."

"The wound still looks bad," his brow drooped into a frown. "I thought with your good blood you could heal from anything?"

"When my strength is gone, it takes longer to heal. I've had no food or rest." Ara didn't know why he was explaining this. Perhaps the pain made him delirious. He wanted so bad to be off his feet that he considered lying down right there on the marble floor.

"Then I will see that you get both. And I'll send over my Curor to look after your arm."

*Curor.* Ara flinched at the sound of the word. All those nights with Carmine's Curor came back to his mind, along with the sickening feeling of his blood being drained.

"Don't worry," Gorgen said. "He'll only tend to your arm."

Why was Gorgen was being so hospitable? Ara was in his possession. He could throw Ara in a cell and drain all of his blood and there was nothing Ara could do about it. What was Gorgen's game?

"You are my guest in this castle, Ara," Gorgen said, moving to the door. "Get some rest. I'll come to see you when you're healed."

With that, Gorgen left. A moment later the guard, Duncan, returned. "Come with me, boy."

Ara followed Duncan through a long hallway. A wide stairway rose up to the floors higher up the cliffside, but Duncan stopped at a door on the first floor. The room they entered was the farthest thing from a dungeon Ara could imagine. A large four-poster bed sat against the back wall; drapery of purple silk hung from its spiral wooden posts. Light shone through the stained glass window, bathing the room with a warm purple glow. Through the window, he could see the outline of the waterfall.

"You are to stay here and rest until Lord Gorgen calls on you," Duncan said, and Ara could see the disapproval in the man's face. Descendants were not supposed to be treated this well.

"Do not get the sheets dirty," he added looking at Ara with an upturned nose.

"How am I supposed to do that?" Ara asked, gesturing to his filthy, bloodstained garments.

Duncan did not answer, only pivoted and walked out the door. Ara looked around the elegant room. There was a second door that led into a private washroom with a wooden bathing tub. After all his time on the road, sleeping on the forest floor, this felt like a palace all his own.

Ara curled up on the rug at the foot of the bed and drifted to sleep. He was asleep only a few minutes when there was a knock on the door. A man in red robes stepped into the room. Ara jumped up and backed away at the sight of the Curor. The Curor was tall with round owl-eyes. He took in Ara with a couple blinks then set his bag on the bed and opened it to reveal a large assortment of tools. Some were the blades and tubing of Carmine's Curor, but others matched some of the instruments the doctors had carried in their bags.

"Alright, let's take a look at this arm of yours," the Curor said.

Ara reluctantly held out his arm. The pain had subsided a great deal, but when the Curor peeled back the cloth strips, the full scope of the wound was apparent. Bite marks were circled with red skin and yellow pus. From his days with the doctors, Ara could see it was badly infected.

"That was quite the animal that got you," the Curor said, poking at his arm. "You're lucky he didn't tear it completely off. Your kind doesn't heal from that, you know. I've seen it."

The Curor released his arm and zipped up his bag. "Before I bother wrapping the wound, it needs to be cleaned." He looked Ara up and down. "All of you does."

The Curor picked up his bag and left the room. Ara was confused. Since passing through the gates, everything was backward. Ara was so turned around he almost wondered if he had hit his head in the river and was just imagining all this.

But the pain in his arm told him otherwise.

There came another knock on the door, this one soft. Ara waited but nothing happened. The knock came again, only slightly louder this time.

"Oh," Ara said. "Come in."

The door creaked open, and a young girl stepped into the room. Her hair, straight and golden as sunshine, fell down her back almost to the floor. The girl carried a bucket of steaming water that must have weighed close to as much as she did. Ara ran to help with the bucket, his right hand grabbing the handle alongside hers.

The girl looked up timidly. Her hair fell back from her cheek, revealing a small "G" tattoo. What kind of monster could do that to a young girl?

"I am to draw you a bath, sir," the girl said. Her voice was what a frightened finch would sound like if it could speak.

"Let me help you," Ara said. The two of them carried the bucket through the room and dumped the hot water into the bathing tub. It filled only a few inches of the wooden tub.

The girl took the bucket and left the room to get more. Ara followed but the girl stopped him at the door.

"Please," she said.

"I can help you," Ara said.

"It would be better if you didn't." Something in the girl's voice made him step back. She disappeared out the door and returned minutes later. Ara helped her once she reached the doorway. It took six trips until the water was high enough to bathe in.

"Is there anything else, sir?" the girl asked, her eyes at Ara's feet.

"Are you…okay?"

The girl looked up, confused. "Of course, sir." She bowed and turned for the door.

"Wait," Ara called as the girl hurried from the washroom. "What is your name?"

The girl looked at him as if he'd spoken Sanstat. Without another word, she slipped out the door.

Ara wished he could have gotten more out of her; some clue as to what was going on at Castle Gorgen.

His eyes grew heavy. Standing upright was taking all his effort. He closed the door to the washroom and undressed. The stiff clothes came off like layers of skin. The hot water stung as he stepped inside, and lowered himself down in segments. The water was already brown when he dipped his injured arm in. Ara's muscles soon relaxed, and he lay in the warm water for a long time, feeling months of grime crumble from his body. He dunked his head underwater and held his breath. He wasn't sure what new troubles awaited him, but for that moment in the warm water of the bathing tub, Ara allowed himself to forget about the future.

## 28

They searched for three days with little sleep and no sign of Ara. Cambria had gone over that night again and again in her head trying to come up with details that could give them a clue on where to look. The men hadn't been armored, and though it was dark, Cambria had seen the scars on their faces.

"Descendant rebels most likely," Briton had said upon hearing Cambria's account.

"You're sure they weren't Temple guards?" Aaron asked.

"If they were guards, she'd be dead," Geyer said.

But at least if it had been Temple guards, they'd know where to look. No one knew where to find the Descendant rebels; the full weight of the Faith had been trying for years.

On the night of the attack, they scrambled through the forest blindly, searching for Ara. Eventually, they were forced to wait until daylight to look for tracks. Cambria hadn't slept. She kept picturing Ara in the hands of those cutthroats. Ara, who had saved her life. Ara, who she had grown close to these past months. Ara, who she had spoken to about her parents, and who she felt...what? Indebted? Friendship?

*Ara.*

Then morning had greeted them with more disappointment.

Cambria was up at dawn. She found Briton and Geyer already at the site of the attack on the cliff's edge. Even in their hurry, the Descendant rebels had masked their tracks. Footprints led in multiple directions—then backtracked on each other—then appeared to fade into the normal shape of the forest.

Geyer cursed and stomped the rock with such force that it tumbled off the cliff and crashed through the trees below.

The group had left Farmount far behind. As the day wore on and there was no sign of Ara or the Descendant rebels, the futility of their quest began to set in. At first, everyone had the decency to leave it unspoken. A small hope remained in Cambria that they would get lucky and turn a corner to find Ara waiting for them. That embarrassed smirk on his face.

But with each corner they turned, only empty forest awaited them.

Little was spoken at night. Briton went over a map by fire-light, straining as if it was a puzzle to unlock. Geyer took Ara's abduction even harder. He sat away from the fire, keeping watch; he wouldn't let anyone relieve him. Cambria knew he felt guilty for not watching after Ara the night before. In a rage, Geyer had smashed his jug of ale until every last piece was buried in the ground.

Cambria brought Geyer some bread and set it on a cloth beside him. Unlike the others, she did not try telling him to get some sleep.

"We will find him," Cambria said. "I'm sure of it."

Geyer didn't nod or even acknowledge the bread. He kept his eyes on the shadows of the forest.

Later that night, as Cambria settled into bed, she overheard whispers from Hannah and Petar's tent.

"How much longer can we go on?" Hannah asked. "The boy is gone."

"I don't know," Petar said. "It's not for us to say."

"But it is, Petar. These are our wagons, our horses. I feel terrible for Ara, but we have lives to think about as well. What if we did catch up to these rebels. Then what? You've heard stories of what they do to our kind."

"I know. I know."

"We must do something, Petar. Say something."

"Tomorrow. Let's give it one more day. Maybe we'll get lucky yet."

But luck had never been on Cambria's side. Days of searching proved fruitless, and the defeat showed openly on their faces. Even the horses trudged slower with their heads low as if they could sense that hope was lost. Despite Briton's best guess, none of them knew if they were traveling closer or farther away from Ara.

On the fourth day, as the sun began to dip behind the forest's canopy, the caravan stopped to let the horses graze. It was Petar who finally gave voice to what many were thinking.

"We can't keep going like this," Petar said to Briton. "You can't keep up this pace."

"I must," Briton said.

"We don't even know if we're going the right way."

"North," Briton said. "They must have gone north toward the Ghost Mountains. It is the least charted area, farthest from the eyes of the Faith. That is where the rebels will be. That is where we'll find Ara."

"You don't know that," Hannah said. "We don't know where they took him."

"I must keep looking," Briton said, pain scratched his voice. He looked as if he'd aged much these last few days; the thin strands of white hair hung limply from the sides of his head. "I have to."

"But they don't," Geyer said. He stepped off the wagon and approached the gathered circle. "This isn't their fight."

"We're not saying that," Petar said. "Of course we care about Ara. But what can we do?"

"I didn't mean it as an insult, Petar," Geyer said. "You and your people have done more than enough for us and for the boy."

"Well...perhaps...we can give it one more day," Petar stammered. He looked at Hannah, head bent.

"No," Briton said. "I'm sorry. Geyer's right. It would be foolish for you to keep going."

"We can't just leave you."

"You've already done so much. Without you, the Temple guards would have had us long ago."

Petar lowered his head and kicked the dirt off one of his shoes.

"What are you going to do now?" he asked.

"I'm going to continue north," Briton said. He put his hand on Petar's shoulder. "Thank you, my friends. All of you."

Farewells were said, and despite Briton's refusal, the shrines were divided evenly between them and the doctors. It was enough to fund the doctors work for months without collections.

"It makes me happy knowing you will be out there helping people," Briton said. "This world certainly needs you."

"Maybe we'll meet you on the road again someday," Petar said.

"Maybe," Briton agreed.

As they readied to go, Cambria did not board the wagon. She had remained silent during the whole discussion. Peter's logic was sound. They couldn't find Ara; Terene was too big. They weren't trackers or soldiers, they were doctors.

She still couldn't bring herself to board the wagon.

"Cambria," Aaron called.

Cambria's feet remained on the ground as if pulled down by some unseen weight. Helping had been her life. Even before she met the doctors, her parents had raised her to aid others. To apply her knowledge and training to save those who suffered. The doctors were leaving to do just that, but everything in her heart told her to stay.

"I'm not going with you," she said, finally. "I'm going to look for Ara."

The doctors were stunned.

"No Cambria," Hannah said. "It's too dangerous."

"I can't leave him behind. He needs my help."

"I know it's hard. We can't bear to think of Ara suffering either. But we have a mission. Think of all the good you can still do."

"I am," Cambria said.

They each tried to talk her out of it, but her mind was made up. No one could convince her otherwise.

Petar suggested they all continue looking another day or so, but Cambria refused. She said this was best for everyone. She thanked them for the years of looking after her; it felt silly to say. They were her family when she needed family the most. How could words possibly be enough? Tears streamed down Hannah's face as she hugged Cambria.

"I can't believe this is the same little girl we found in the streets of Caldesh," she said, her face a mix of worry and pride. "You take every precaution, you hear?"

Cambria nodded. "I will."

Aaron approached her, but they didn't embrace. He kept a few feet distance digging his foot into the soft ground. "You know how boring travel is going to be without you? Plus, there will be nobody to threaten our patients."

"Goodbye, Aaron," she said. "Don't eat too much sweet bread."

"I never liked the stuff. I just bought it for you."

Brim lifted Cambria up in a big hug and squeezed so hard Cambria thought she'd snap a rib.

"Okay, okay," she said, gasping. "I'll miss you too."

Lastly, Petar put his hand on her shoulder. "You're the strongest person I've ever met. And you're a great doctor." Petar's face was grave, as if he were delivering a terminal diagnosis to a patient. "We'll never save enough. But we do all we can." He squeezed her shoulder and forced a smile. "One life may make all the difference."

After a few more goodbyes, the company split ways. The wagon rolled off; faces peered out the back to catch one last glimpse. This had been her family. She might never see them again. Cambria felt the urge to run after the wagon. But she stood in place, watching her old life disappear down the road.

When the wagons were gone, Cambria took a deep breath and turned to Geyer.

"What's our plan?" she asked.

"Plan?" Geyer snorted, spinning the wheel on the hilt of his sword. "He's the thinker. I just wing it."

Cambria rolled her eyes. Briton gave a faint smile and patted the white horse. It shook its head and snorted softly. "First, I'd suggest we purchase some horses. We won't get far with just the one."

"Well, what are we waiting for?" Cambria pushed past the two men. "Let's get moving."

Cambria led the way north toward the next village. For Ara to have any chance, she'd have to take charge of this rescue party.

"Hmph," Geyer grunted behind her. "How do I always get stuck traveling with kids?"

# 29

Ara awoke to the smell of food. Breakfast sat waiting on his bedside table. He crawled out of the thick purple sheets and pulled the tray onto his lap. He was still starving, even after the previous night's meal. He began devouring the boiled eggs, porridge, and peeled orange. His time in the forest had impressed upon him the uncertainty of a next meal.

He was finishing up the last of the fruit when someone knocked on the door. Lord Gorgen squeezed into the room.

"Good morning, Ara," he said. "I hope you find the accommodations to your liking."

"Yes," Ara said. "Thank you."

Gorgen smiled and took a seat at the foot of the bed, the frame creaking under his weight.

"Good, good. I want you to feel at home here because I want you to stay as part of House Gorgen."

Ara looked at him, not understanding.

"I can only imagine what you've been through, what you've had to endure. I can protect you here. Give you warm meals, even let you roam freely through the castle. If you like this room, it is yours."

Ara glanced at the giant bed. He had not slept like that for days. Sleep had come so easy that his arm was fully healed. Small marks of off-color skin were the only indication there had ever been a wound.

"As payment, I ask for only a small measure of your blood each day."

There it was. Gorgen's real agenda. Like everyone else, he wanted Ara's blood.

"You speak as if I have a choice in the matter," Ara said.

"You do. I want my Descendants to feel at home here, as much as can be. If you are unhappy then you will try to escape, the penalty for which is very high." Gorgen frowned as if the matter was out of his hands. "But I want us to work together, Ara. Here you can live in relative luxury. A life safe from the outside world."

No more nights on the cold ground of the forest. No more empty gut, hoping for scraps of the occasional rabbit. No more running for his life.

"You think you can fend off the Highfather and the Temple guards?" Ara asked.

"This castle is one of the most fortified structures in Terene. There is only one point of access, and my men can hold it against any force. Plus, with your cooperation, your blood would help fund my realm, adding to your own protection. That is the deal I am offering. But if you have a better option…"

Ara thought this over. He had dreaded life at Castle Carmine and had sworn to never allow his blood to be taken again. But so much had changed. And this, after all, would be his choice. Wasn't giving a piece of himself a small price to pay?

"My friends," Ara said. "They are out there, looking for me. Could they…could they come here too."

A smile rolled across Gorgen's face. "Of course. They are welcome here and will fall under my protection as well. Once word gets out that you are here, I'm sure they will come to you."

Ara nodded. The deal made sense, especially since Gorgen

had the power to lock him away and get his blood if he refused. Then why did Ara feel such a sickness in the pit of his stomach?

The bed creaked with relief as Gorgen climbed to his feet.

"You may think it over," the Lord said. "I will leave you to explore the castle. My gardens rival Carmine's, and there is a library in the upper building. Though, it's a bit of a climb."

*A library!* Ara's heart leaped at the thought of unfiltered access to books. Briton's words filled his mind. *Never rob yourself of the chance to learn.* He grew happy at the thought of Briton sharing this place with him—walking freely along the garden grounds and studying in the library. Ara couldn't believe his luck. To think he could have easily drowned in the river. Instead, the waters brought him here.

"I'll have fresh clothes and shoes sent to you," Gorgen said. "Enjoy this day. The Curor can wait until tomorrow."

GEYER LED the group along the smallest hint of a path. The last few days were spent traversing rocky mountain terrain. Though Geyer doubted they would find any inhabited land this far north, he pushed on for Briton's sake. The old man was a wreck. Twice Geyer had tried to force him to rest, but he would not relent. Not while Ara was getting farther away.

Throughout all their trials over the last few months, Geyer had imagined how much better his life would be without the boy. He had been wrong.

Geyer glanced back. Briton was slumped on his horse, half asleep. The old fool was going to get himself trampled out in the middle of nowhere. Then they'd really be in trouble.

"Briton," Geyer called. "What do you know about the Ghost Mountains?"

"Huh?" Briton shook his head, clearing out the sleepiness. "Oh, the wall. It's been there since the beginning of recorded time. I read a centuries-old journal from the first expedition that reached these mountains. They called this place, 'The Edge of the World.'"

"And the stories of ghosts descending from the mountains to snatch people away?"

"Stories, I suppose. Brought on by the fog. The gray sky." Briton gazed at the distant rock wall. "As far as anyone knows, the mountains have no top."

Cambria scoffed. "You northerners and your superstitions." She rode a pony they had bought before fully testing him out. It had been a rough few days for the young doctor. Though Geyer couldn't remember ever seeing her in a good mood. "You fill each new generation with nightmares of ghosts and magic spells."

"This coming from someone who didn't believe in magic blood," Briton raised an eyebrow.

"Well, there's a difference between Royal Blood and ghosts or mountains without end."

"So what's beyond them then?"

"Ocean, I suppose."

"And beyond the ocean?"

Cambria frowned. "More ocean," she murmured.

"So, mountains without end are farfetched, but oceans without end…"

Cambria shot him an angry look and kicked her pony out ahead of the two men.

"Careful not to upset her too much," Geyer said. "She's tougher than she looks."

"She looks pretty tough to me."

They rode on at a slow but steady pace. As daylight dwindled, an uneasy feeling grew in the pit of Geyer's stomach. The feeling of being watched. He squinted up at the rocky hills again, but saw no one. Even though this was the barren north, he suddenly felt too exposed. *Best stay on your guard.*

Cambria was out of sight around the next bend when she called out. "Up here, quick."

Geyer kicked his own horse and sped around the rocky hill-side. He never should have let the girl go off ahead. If anything happened to her...

He found Cambria waiting for them, trying to hold her pony still. Geyer sighed in relief as he pulled up beside her. He followed her gaze to a small village in the valley below. There was life this far north, after all.

"You know this place?" Geyer asked when Briton caught up to them.

"No," Briton said. "We're going down there?"

"Looks like we are. Keep your guard up. The only reason to live this far north is if you don't want to be found."

The three of them rode down the hillside to the village below. It was a small town, composed of a cluster of huts and only a few actual wooden buildings. The streets were quiet except for the occasional farmer. A man stopped pushing a wheelbarrow to stare at the three strangers. His expression was not welcoming. Heads popped up behind windows then darted down again. Geyer stopped in front of one of the main build-ings. A wooden sign hung over the entrance, its name painted in red letters: *The Last Drop.*

Geyer climbed off his horse and tied him to a post.

"We're stopping at a tavern?" Cambria asked.

"Best place to get information," Geyer said.

"Is that true?"

"Best place to get a drink, anyway."

Briton shrugged to her, and the two of them dismounted. Cambria's pony let out a loud whinny that sounded through the town. With their horses tied up, the three of them entered The Last Drop.

The place was quiet; there was no music or loud drunken conversations you typically find in a tavern. The bar area was small, leaving room for the open dining hall and rooms on this floor and the one above. But with a name like The Last Drop, they were bound to serve drinks.

The few heads in the inn turned to the three intruders. After getting a long look, people went back to their private conversations, though their eyes never truly left them. Geyer counted seven people, including the woman behind the bar. They were a ragged bunch. From the dirt on them, they looked like farmers, not cut-throats. Still, Geyer was glad he had brought his sword.

The patrons looked to the woman behind the bar to see how she would handle the situation. Expecting her to be wary of outsiders, Geyer was startled when he heard her warm confident voice.

"How can I help you?" she asked with a pleasant smile, walking to the end of the bar. Her hair was cut short and muscles defined her tan arms. She looked as if she was no stranger to outdoor labor, and that she could handle herself in a rowdy bar. The other patrons grumbled at her welcoming tone, but it didn't seem to bother her.

"We'd like some water, please," Geyer said, taking a seat at the bar. Briton raised an eyebrow, but Geyer ignored it. He felt embarrassed enough ordering water, he didn't need the old man's opinions on the matter.

The woman didn't object to the request. She grabbed a jug and poured three even glasses, with the precision of someone who takes pride in the small details of her work. "You've traveled far."

"Do we look that bad?" Briton gave a tired chuckle.

"Everyone who gets here has traveled far," the woman said.

"What is this place?" Briton asked. "The village. Does it have a name?"

"You won't find it on any map. Just some people who want to live in peace, away from the troubles of the world."

Briton held up his glass in salute. "There are plenty of troubles to get away from." He sipped his water.

The woman studied Briton for a moment then turned to Geyer. There was activity behind the gaze; she was sizing up this odd trio that had stumbled into her establishment. Geyer was glad to have Cambria with them. Traveling with a young girl took away some of the perceived threat.

"We don't get a lot of visitors," the woman said, resting her hands on the bar. Strong, calloused hands with blisters on the knuckles, new and old. She was not just a barkeep. "Can I ask what you're doing this far north?"

Briton's hesitation lasted only a moment. "We're looking for our friend," he said. "We believe he was headed this way."

"I'm sorry, but you're the first new people to come through in a long time."

"You're sure about that?" Geyer asked.

"It's a small village. No one goes unnoticed."

"I expect you're right," Briton said. "It was a long shot. Still, we have traveled far. And haven't had a bed and a proper meal in some time. Does your lovely establishment have open rooms for the night?"

Chair legs scraped the floor behind them. Geyer's back was to the room. He didn't like it.

"Maybe it's not a good idea," Geyer offered. He touched Briton's arm. "Our friend is clearly not here, and we've got enough daylight left to cover a bit more ground today."

Briton caught the mood of the room and nodded. "Yes, I'm sure we can put off a meal a little longer."

"Whatever you feel is best," the woman said.

Geyer was thankful that for once Briton didn't argue with him. There was something off in this place; he couldn't put his finger on it, but he knew they'd be better off far away from this village.

Geyer stood and pushed back from the bar when Cambria's voice called out.

"It's him!" she screamed. Her finger pointed to a man who had just come from a back room. The man looked up in surprise, revealing a scar on the right side of his face.

"The one who took Ara," Cambria said, anger filling her voice. "It's him."

The man looked from them to the women behind the bar. She eyed the three visitors in a new light.

"Oh," she said. "You're looking for *that* friend."

Geyer drew his sword. The patrons followed, jumping to their feet with weapons pointed in their direction. Eight blades, including two held by the newcomer.

"Where is Ara?" Cambria demanded.

The scarred face man stepped forward, his swords ready. They were good weapons of polished steel, not the cheap excuse for weapons held by the other patrons. This man was a Descendant rebel.

Geyer turned toward the Descendant. "The girl asked you a question."

The man looked Geyer up and down and smiled. "You only have one sword between the three of you."

"One's plenty." Geyer wasn't intimidated. Two swords were solely for show. The man probably practiced twirling them in fancy arcs before a mirror, too.

"You want me to get rid of them?" the Descendant rebel asked the woman behind the bar. So she was in charge of the situation. While the other patrons shook with the rush of a possible fight, she remained calm. She was definitely not just a barkeep.

Briton whispered to Geyer in a low voice. "Tell me you can take all of them."

Geyer looked around the inn and the circle of swords closing in. "Would you feel better if I lied to you?"

"Maybe."

"Everything is perfectly fine," Geyer said. He stepped closer to Briton and Cambria as the armed men slowly advanced. "We're in no trouble at all."

THOUGH HE WAS free to search the castle grounds, Ara was not alone. Two guards trailed him like distant shadows. They did not disturb him, but every time he looked around they were somewhere to be seen.

Castle Gorgen was breathtaking. Ara couldn't fathom how much work and care must have gone into the castle's intricate design. Lord Gorgen must employ a full-time staff of artists and carpenters and cleaners. High windows were cut into the walls every few feet, lighting the castle with the warmth of the afternoon. The library matched Carmine's own in the number of books but surpassed it in design. This one actually appeared used. People sat at tables reading and writing on parchment. A few looked up as Ara entered the room but went back to their studies. Briton would love this place.

Ara was eager to sit down and search for books on the Royals, but a servant appeared and beckoned him to follow. As he walked through the castle halls, Ara was ready for this charade of hospitality to come crashing down. Ready to be thrown in the dungeon without a moment's notice. So he was surprised when the servant escorted him to an outdoor table filled with a variety of food; some of which Ara had never laid eyes on.

Lord Gorgen came around the corner and took the large seat at the table's head. "Please, join me for lunch."

A bald man in purple robes took a seat beside Gorgen; his eyes took in Ara with none of Gorgen's amusement.

"Are you finding my home to your liking?" Gorgen asked as Ara took a seat across from the bald man. The rich smells on the table filled his nose, making it hard to concentrate on anything else.

"I've never seen anything like it," Ara said after a moment. *As far as I remember, anyway.* "It's not like Castle Carmine at all. It's so much...cleaner."

"Ha!" Gorgen laughed, his mouth full of food. "I certainly hope so. House Carmine was a great house for a long time, but the Carmines were always so drab and somber. What's the point of having wealth if you don't surround yourself with beauty?"

The patio overlooked the dark forest below. The castle gates separated Ara from endless hidden dangers. From men hunting Ara with beasts that sought his blood.

A servant appeared with a pitcher of water, a "G" was tattooed across the right side of his face. Ara studied the Descendant as he poured his glass. The man's face was shaved and his hair was cut short, not like the usual tangle of knots you find with most Descendants. Ara wanted to speak to him, but the Descendant kept his head bowed, avoiding eye contact.

"Where do they live?" Ara asked as a Descendant took away his finished plate.

"Who? The servants?" Gorgen frowned as if he'd never thought of this. "They have a building behind the gardens, separate from the rest of the castle."

"How many are there?"

"Woodrell," Gorgen said and spooned another bite into his mouth.

"Eleven," the bald man spoke slowly as if to a child. "Not all of them have good blood. But the low bloods still find work here, of course."

"Everyone has some value," Gorgen agreed, chomping on a chicken leg.

Ara thought about the Descendants' barracks at Castle Carmine. The dark room with beds packed so tight you could hear the breathing of the person beside you. The whimpers at night. The smell.

"You don't have to worry about any of that though," Gorgen said, setting down the chicken bone and licking the grease from his fingers. "You're not like them. You're special."

The Descendant returned to fill Gorgen's glass. Again, Ara watched him, hoping to get some sign or communication. The Descendant's eyes locked with Ara's for the briefest of moments then flinched away causing him to spill wine on the table.

"Careless bastard," Gorgen exclaimed.

"I'm sorry, my Lord," the Descendant stammered, setting the

wine bottle down and reaching for a rag to wipe Lord Gorgen's clothes.

A guard stepped forward and knocked the servant to the ground. He put his boot on the man's throat. The Descendant winced in anticipation of coming blows.

"Enough," Gorgen said, raising his hands, smiling. "It was an accident."

The guard stepped back to his position behind Gorgen. The Descendant picked himself up and bowed to Gorgen. Then he hurriedly wiped the wine from the table.

"Wine?" Gorgen asked.

Ara shook his head. "Water is fine."

For the rest of lunch, Gorgen talked about the many features of his Castle built into the cliff face. Woodrell chimed in to correct the lord's facts now and again. Ara nodded without speaking. He'd lost some of his appetite, but he cleaned his plate nonetheless.

After lunch, Gorgen had business to attend to, leaving Ara alone to explore. Ara walked down to the castle's garden, hoping to get a look at the Descendants' barracks. Since the garden had only one entrance and exit, his two shadows stayed outside, which allowed him to roam freely without eyes on him. With a full night's rest and three enormous meals, Ara felt better than ever. Walking didn't tire him; he felt a reserve of strength unlike any he could remember. Not only were his wounds completely healed, but his frail arms had started to fill out a bit. A month at Gorgen Castle and he would look more like a young man than a sickly boy.

Walking east through the garden, the sound of the waterfall grew louder; its water fell from the cliff face like a river in the sky before colliding with the pool far below.

In the garden, Ara passed strange trees of different colors and shapes. He stopped to inspect the thorns on one's yellow trunk. He'd seen nothing like it, even in Carmine's garden. Bushes throughout the garden were carved in different patterns, and in the center of the garden stood a giant stone "G" with a rainbow of flowers lining its sides.

The castle was amazing and Gorgen had been nothing but generous. Still, Ara couldn't stop thinking about the Descendants—the servants who brought him food and cleaned his room and fetched his bath—did his blood really make him better than these people? Could he live in luxury while they suffered?

Ara stopped suddenly. There, in a glass container in the corner of the garden stood the blood rose. Lord Carmine's prized possession. The flower Ara had seen take a man's hand now hung limp, its stem folded over as if hunched in prayer. Though it had grown since he last saw it, its petals were faded and lifeless.

"It's dying," a voice said.

Ara spun around to see Semus leaning on a shovel.

"We've done everything we can for it," the gardener said. "Kept it enclosed and warm—even fed it live critters. But nothing has worked."

Ara turned back to the flower. It drooped so low it was almost laying down in its bed of sand. "What's wrong with it?"

"It's not meant to be here. As much as we try to recreate its home." Semus shrugged at the exotic garden around him. "This is no desert."

"What are you going to do with it?"

"Not much I can do. These things are said to live for up to fifty years in the desert. Fifty years. This one will be lucky to see the summer through."

Ara stepped forward and touched the glass container. He didn't know why but it saddened him to see the flower like this. Trapped and wilting. It had been carried across the world to be placed in a cage.

"I hear Lord Gorgen has offered you a deal," Semus said, his voice soft despite the fact that they were alone in the garden.

"Yes."

"Are you going to take it?"

Ara frowned. "I don't know."

Didn't he though? The castle offered comfort and protection from the violent world outside. From the Highfather and the bloodhounds and a life locked in the Temple dungeon. Was there any reason not to accept?

Semus scratched the back of his tan neck, his face wrinkled like he was wrestling with a thought. When he spoke, his voice was so soft Ara strained to hear over the waterfall. "I know what Briton gave up to help you, and though I may not understand it, he must have had his reasons. He's a much smarter man than I am." Semus glanced around the garden, his voice dropping even lower. "All I gotta say is if you're planning on leaving...don't tell Gorgen. Don't tell anyone. Just go."

Semus grunted and threw his shovel over his shoulder. "You see Briton again, you tell him old Semus is doing right." With that, the gardener lowered his head and walked out of the garden.

Ara stood alone beside the dying blood rose. Beyond him rose the great castle built into the cliff. It was filled with well-dressed and well-fed people immune to the problems of the world. Like the serene waterfall cascading behind it, this place was out of touch with the violence below.

But Ara couldn't forget the cruelty of the world. It was the only memory he had.

## 30

S he was first in line for the night's blood draw. She was tired from the day's work, but her body tensed fully awake when the Curor's door swung open. The guard grabbed her arm and pulled her inside the cold dark room.

"Ah," the Curor said with a smile, his eyes wide as moons. "Excited to get started are we?"

The girl didn't move. Her legs had stopped, not wanting to go into the chilly lab. A guard shoved her forward.

"They go through this procedure every night and still, every night they fight it," the Curor said, shaking his head. "Do they really think we could forget about them? Or decide we have enough blood?" He wiped a blade with an old rag. "There is no such thing as enough blood."

The girl climbed into the chair. It was better to turn the mind off for this part, to simply move through the steps. It made the process easier. It made life easier.

"You know, I think you're old enough now," the Curor said. He untangled a foggy tube and placed one end in a new jar. "Old enough to start making Descendants for your lord."

The guard strapped the girl's wrists to the chair. "I'm sure her fellow Descendants will be happy at the news," he said. Then he ran his dirty fingers through her perfectly yellow hair. "Then again, the bloodline is already so diluted…"

"Hold her still," the Curor said. He gripped the blade and pulled up the girl's sleeve.

She closed her eyes and imagined she was home. Back before all this. Before the castle and the auction. When she had a family. It hadn't been that long ago yet she struggled to remember those days. Each day erased her mother's face more and more. Each day she became less a person and more a vessel for blood.

The blade descended; the girl closed her eyes and tensed her arm. Then a commotion erupted in the hall outside, voices arguing. The sound of metal being struck.

"What was that?" the Curor asked, leaning back from his work.

"Bloody animals," the guard drew a wooden club. "I'll teach them a lesson they'll never forget."

He stormed to the door and flung it open.

"Alright you—" *Crack!* A shovel smashed into the guard's head. The metal clang was so loud the girl tried to cover her ears, but her hands were fastened to the chair. The guard collapsed to the floor.

"Great Hemo," the Curor yelped.

The new boy, the one who's bath she had filled the previous night, stood in the doorway, a shovel in his hands. "It's alright now," the boy said to her.

"You!" the Curor spat. "Gorgen's new pet. You'll pay for this. I warned Gorgen about playing his games with a filthy Descendant. Now you'll get what's coming to you."

Three Descendants stepped past the boy and into the lab. Their angry eyes were fixed on the Curor.

"Get back," the Curor shouted. "All of you. Get back right now."

The girl couldn't believe they would dare attack a Raw Blood. Earlier that day, Kainen had received ten lashes for spilling wine in Lord Gorgen's presence. What would they do when they found a Descendant had struck a guard and threatened the Curor!

But the men didn't seem to care. They stepped over the guard's body. The Curor staggered back, holding out the blade; it suddenly seemed so small. "I'll see you hanged. Every last one of you."

The Descendants didn't flinch. The Curor swung the blade twice then dropped it, covering himself against their blows. He let out screams of pain as they struck him again and again. Years of anger and pain put into each swing.

"Don't look." The boy was at her side, untying her wrists from the chair. But she did look. She listened to his bones snap, watched their heavy boots stomp the Curor's red robes brown.

"Come on," the boy said. "It's time to go."

"Go?" She looked at him, confused. "Go where?"

"Somewhere they can't hurt you."

Who was this boy? He was a Descendant who had been treated like royalty, who then turned around and beat a castle guard. Now he was talking about leaving. It didn't make sense.

She took the boy's outstretched hand and he led her out of the Curor's lab. Behind them, the Descendants continued beating the guard.

"WE HAVE TO HURRY," Ara said to the gathered Descendants. Some paced at the door to the barracks jumping at every sound, while others sat on beds as if they couldn't be bothered. Ara had thought he was doing an honorable thing by not leaving without them—one person had far better odds of sneaking out of a castle than twelve. A few of the Descendants had been quick to join him, realizing it was their best chance of escaping. But not everyone saw it that way.

"Why should we listen to you?" a man said, looking at Ara

from his bed. "We don't know you, and there's a lot worse than Castle Gorgen. I can assure you."

"The choice shouldn't be where to serve your captivity," Ara said. He couldn't believe his ears. He was offering them a chance at freedom. What was there to debate?

"He's right," said a younger man at the door. He held the guard's sword and kept a lookout for anyone coming. "This is our shot at freedom. We should take it."

"Somebody's been fed too many rebellion stories," a woman said. "You're going to get us all whipped, or worse. I'll have no part in it."

The argument went back and forth with voices growing louder. Each moment they wasted decreased their chances.

"How are we going to escape?" another man asked. "Taking down the Curor and a few guards is one thing. But Gorgen has an army of soldiers protecting this castle. There's no way we can get through them."

Everyone turned to Ara, waiting for orders, waiting to be told what to do. They'd been trained with fear their whole lives. Now they were like dogs who wouldn't venture out even with their leashes removed.

"They protect the castle from the outside," Ara said. "Their force is focused on the gate because it is the only way in. But it is not the only way out."

"The cliff?" someone said. "You're crazy."

"It would take days to scale," another added. "If it could be done at all."

"We're not going up the cliff," Ara said. "We're going down the waterfall."

The room fell silent. The Descendants exchanged looks of disbelief.

"We'll drown."

"It's possible," Ara said. "But if it's a chance at freedom, I'm taking it. By the time they realize what's happened, the river will have carried us far away."

"If we don't drown first."

Ara nodded. "If we don't drown first."

They still weren't convinced. They had never lived outside castle walls, never felt the power of their blood when it was not seized from them. The world outside these gates was unknown, and it scared them more than a whipping or the Curor's blade.

"I'm not telling anyone what to do," Ara said. "You don't know me and you may not trust me. But you were all meant to do more in this life than carry dishes and give up your blood to make them rich. And this is your chance."

His words hung in the air. The gravity of their situation was hitting everyone. Ara was about to turn and leave on his own when a small voice spoke up.

"I'm going." It was the girl with golden hair. She stood and walked to Ara's side. "I'm going with you."

"Me, too." Ara recognized the Descendant who had served him lunch earlier that day. The frail man slowly climbed to his feet, wincing as he stood up straight. "I don't know if I'll survive the jump, but I know I don't want to survive here any longer."

Out of the eleven Descendants, only two stayed behind. The rest put their lives in Ara's hands. He hoped he was doing the right thing.

The night was still and quiet. The moon bathed the castle grounds in a ghostly light. Ara ran from the barracks and the Descendants followed. It was a short distance to the back wall. As they drew close, the powerful sound of the waterfall made Ara's stomach tighten. This plan had worked in his head, but hearing the waterfall's thundering force up close was another thing altogether. Ara hid his fear and gave a reassuring nod, pointing to a tree along the castle wall. "We go over here."

Ara expected to hear the ring of alarm bells and shouts of pursuing guards. But there was only the thunder of the waterfall. Ara jumped up and caught the first tree branch, pulling himself up. The girl was hoisted up next, and he pulled her beside him. They climbed to an upper limb, the tree bowing under their weight, and crawled onto the castle's outer wall. Ara scooted down the wall's narrow width to make room for the others. Water sprayed around him in a mist, soaking his clothes. He wiped the water from his face and looked down. The waterfall cascaded down the cliff face into the darkness below. The fear of drowning returned; Ara pushed the thought from his mind. *Be strong for them.*

Soon everyone was on the wall, huddling against the blast of cold water. Nothing Ara said would be heard over the roar of the waterfall. This was just as well; he had nothing to say.

Ara stood, balancing on the slippery stone wall. Beside him, the girl took his hand. He squeezed it tight, and together they leaped out into the waterfall.

Twice now Ara had escaped by jumping to his possible death. This time he did not lose consciousness. Ara held onto the girl's hand as long as he could, pushed down, tumbling in the waterfall's grasp. The impact was hard and abrupt. It tore them apart and spun Ara end over end. What air was left in his lungs exploded from his body. Still, he did not lose consciousness, nor did he panic or fight. He gave in and let the water take him. Even as his body was thrown against rocks, he felt a kind of peace; this struggle would soon end. It was then that he understood the true power of his blood. That every moment, no matter how painful, was temporary.

Pain had no more control over him.

Ara broke the surface and gasped for air. As he breathed, his head whirled around searching for others. The ferocity of the water had subsided. Ten feet away, Ara saw a tangle of golden hair floating on the surface. He kicked his feet and swam to the girl. He pulled her head above water; she gasped, flailing her arms.

"Relax," he said, holding on to her. "It's over. It's over."

Her frantic strokes slowed, and she caught her breath. Ara turned up the river, squinting into the thick, silvery mist at the base of the waterfall. At first, he didn't see anyone. Then heads began to pop out of the water, gasping for air. Nine in all.

Ara couldn't help but smile. They had followed him. Every one of them.

After they came together and everyone was accounted for, the group paddled on in silence. They stayed to the middle of the river, letting the waters carry them away from Castle Gorgen toward whatever lay ahead.

# 31

---

The carriage bounced up and down, increasing Lord Gorgen's discomfort. He couldn't believe he was up in the middle of the night in pursuit of ten escaped Descendants—one of whom could very well be the most valuable thing in the world. And his guards had let him slip out of their fingers. How hard was it to look after a boy and some workers?

"Is he trying to hit every bump in the road!" Gorgen yelled loud enough for the carriage driver to hear.

Woodrell, the Lord's advisor, leaned forward in the cramped carriage with a calming look. "It's a rough road along the river, my Lord. Not built for a carriage."

"Well, I'm not riding a horse," Gorgen said. "Those beasts don't like me. I'm not risking a fall just because our stable master can't properly train a horse."

"Of course," Woodrell said. "Though, I'm surprised you came at all."

"This boy is important to the future of House Gorgen, Woodrell. After our guards let him escape, I had to see this was done right."

Woodrell nodded slowly and looked out the carriage

window. In the bouncing lantern light, his bald head looked like another moon.

"What is it?" Gorgen asked. He could tell when something was on his advisor's mind.

"I just can't help but wonder if this could all have been avoided, had we not played games with the boy."

"I did what was best to keep him long-term," Gorgen said. "You know what happened at House Carmine. The boy needed to think he was staying by his own free will if we were to have a chance of keeping him when the Highfather came. I have no idea why he would turn down our offer."

"Descendants are an untrustworthy bunch."

The carriage lurched to a stop, and Gorgen hit his head on the lantern hanging from the roof. "Stars! Is this man blind? Did he just run into a boulder?"

"We've stopped," Woodrell stated the obvious. He poked his bald head out the window and into the darkness.

Gorgen groaned and felt his forehead. There would be a bump there, he thought. Just his luck. He'd take it out on his Descendants when he caught them. A lashing they'll not soon heal from. And the boy…Gorgen had shown him every kindness imaginable, and the clot had spit in his face. Once he was back at Gorgen Castle, the boy would see what happens to disobedient Descendants.

"What's going on?" Gorgen asked, still rubbing his head.

"There's something in the road ahead," Woodrell reported.

"Did we find them already?" Gorgen's hopes of returning to his bed rose. Woodrell was right—adventures like this were not suitable for a noble lord. Not even one as brave as himself.

"I don't think so," Woodrell said.

"Must I do everything myself?" Gorgen pushed open the carriage door and squeezed out of the tiny structure. *Why don't they make carriages the proper size?* Gorgen squinted in the darkness trying to make out the shapes in the trees ahead. Then he realized those weren't trees. Countless riders blocked their path. The shape of the foremost rider looked all wrong in the moonlight—full of strange black angles. Light shone off the armor of the other men. White armor.

Gorgen was staring at an army of Temple guards.

"What's the meaning of this?" Gorgen said, storming up the road toward the guards. "Stopping my men in my own realm?"

A rider came forward, he wore the Temple guard's armor but donned no helmet. Gorgen recognized the braided hair and dark skin. He was one of Bale's mercenaries. The tracker. Copher wasn't it? A nasty bunch, all of them. How did the Highfather justify employing such cretins.

"Lord Gorgen," Copher said. "What brings you out in the dead of night?"

"I…" Gorgen stammered, looking around at his men. Outnumbered, they kept their distance from the Temple guards. "This is my land. I do as I please. What are you doing here? And where's your boss, the dour fellow?"

Copher's face might as well have been a stone. "Enough games, Gorgen. Where is the boy?"

Gorgen flinched. "Boy? I don't know what you're talking about?"

"You were smart to take the Highfather's side against Carmine," Copher said. "Don't be foolish now."

Gorgen looked around at his men whose distance from the guard army had increased. Woodrell's bald head peered from behind the carriage.

"I was going to report the boy to the Highfather," Gorgen stammered. "But he escaped before I had the chance. Along with nine of my Descendants."

"Escaped?"

"Earlier this evening," Gorgen said. "According to the other Descendants, they jumped into the waterfall. But we found no bodies at the base of the cliff so we believe they survived. We are traveling downriver in search of them."

"Who are these *other* Descendants?"

"The two who stayed behind," Gorgen gestured toward the wagon cell. "We already flogged them. If they knew more they would have told us."

Copher stood tall on his horse, looking back to the wagons like he owned them. "Bring them to me."

Gorgen snorted. Give a cutthroat a little power and it goes straight to his head. Gorgen considered telling the man to go jump in the river; reminding him of the power of House Gorgen. But it was cold, and he wanted to be back in the comfort of his bed.

He waved to his guards. They hurried to the back of the wagon and brought out the two Descendants. A man and woman. Their skin and clothes were ripped from lashings. A small punishment for their crimes. They hadn't, after all, stopped the others from escaping.

The guards tossed the two Descendants at Gorgen's feet. They squirmed and huddled together, hiding their bruised faces.

"Where did the others go?" Copher asked the Descendants.

"We don't know," said the male Descendant, his voice pleading. "We tried to stop them."

Copher raised a hand, cutting them off. He sighed and leaped from his horse. The Descendants cowered at the approaching Temple guard. "Please."

It happened without warning. Two blades from Copher's belt. He rammed them into the sides of the Descendant's head and then squeezed, tunneling deeper into the man's ears until his skull burst like a watermelon dropped from a castle wall. Blood squirted over those nearby. A chunk of skull landed on Gorgen's shoe. He vomited into the dirt.

And he was not alone.

When the retching stopped, Gorgen wiped his face of vomit and blood. Copher stood over the Descendant woman. Blood covered her trembling face.

"You know where they went," Copher said. "The same place you all go when you escape. And you're going to take us there."

The woman nodded frantically.

"Good," Copher said.

The Temple guard looked to Gorgen with a dark smile. "Come, Lord Gorgen. Let's go for a ride."

THEY HAD LEFT the river behind hours ago, yet Ara still hadn't shaken the cold. He stomped his boots as he walked, trying to warm his freezing legs. Ara followed the Descendants along the seemingly endless mountain terrain, his body calling out for rest. He was already second-guessing his decision to leave his warm bed behind.

"It's not much farther," Thoran said. He was an old but still broad-chested man who walked with the confident strut of a former soldier. Though the whispered details of rebel hideouts change with each retelling, in every Descendants' barracks and cell in Terene, Thoran claimed to have been there himself. "It's not much farther," he repeated to the weary group.

Ara wasn't thrilled about seeking out the Descendant rebels; his previous interaction with the group had not gone so well. But these people needed sanctuary, and there was nowhere else to turn. Once he got them to safety, Ara could set off to find his friends. Though he didn't know where to even begin looking.

They marched on; Ara fell to the back of the party, walking beside the young girl.

"You are now free to choose your own name," Ara said. "If only to give me something to call you."

She looked at him but didn't respond. She spoke little. When faced with the atrocities of Descendant life, silence was often the only appropriate response.

"It is important to have an identity of your own," Ara continued as they climbed the mountain path. "You are not someone's property."

After a few more minutes of silent travel, the girl spoke in a soft voice that almost escaped Ara. "What name would I choose?"

"That's for you to decide. Something you like. The moonlight...a flower...something that brings to mind your yellow hair."

"No," she said quickly. "Not that."

Pain showed like cracks on her face. This poor girl. Ara could only imagine what she had endured at House Gorgen.

"We're here," Thoran called from above.

The group stopped at the top of the hill; they could see a cluster of small buildings hidden in the valley below. New energy came to the Descendants at the sight of the village and the end of their journey. They hurried down the rocky hill by the light of the moon. Ara felt his own steps increase as well—though he didn't know what to expect at the hands of the Descendant rebels; he had not only fled from them days earlier but caused a fight with Temple guards. He didn't foresee a warm welcome.

Two riders met them at the edge of town. Though it was dark, Ara recognized them from the party of Descendant rebels who had captured him. He huddled in the back of the group as Thoran gave an account of their escape from Gorgen's Castle.

"And what of the boy?" Bree Sai asked at the end of Thoran's story. All eyes turned to Ara, and the woman's face lit with anger. She leaped down from her horse and drew her dagger. She marched up to Ara, but Ara did not retreat. He stood still, awaiting whatever came.

Thoran stepped in front of Bree Sai. "He rescued us. If it wasn't for the boy, we'd still be prisoners."

Bree Sai eyed Ara over the point of her dagger. Ara held her gaze. The fear for his own safety had been lost, washed away. He had gotten the Descendants here, gotten the girl to safety—that was all that mattered.

"Bree Sai," the other rider called.

The woman grunted and lowered her dagger. "Come," she said. "Spade will decide what to do with you."

Ara was taken ahead of the other Descendants to a building in the center of the village. *The Last Drop* was written over the door. It was late and the inn was empty of patrons, but light still glowed from lanterns on the bar. Bree Sai pushed Ara down into a chair at a small table and lit the lantern overhead. Then she backed away to the door, guarding his exit. A needless precaution since Ara was too tired to run.

Ara's mind wandered to the other Descendants and what would become of them. He hoped this rebel hideout was safe from those who would hunt them. He wondered what kind of life this secluded place could offer the young girl. Would she be looked after? Put to work? Ara was so lost in thought that he didn't see the woman enter through the back door. It was only when he heard movement behind the bar that he looked up to find the tanned woman with short cut hair pouring a glass of water. She put the glass on a tray with a half loaf of bread and brought it to Ara's table.

She nodded for Ara to take it, and he did not hesitate. He tore a piece from the loaf and ate hungrily, washing it down with a gulp of water. Ara felt the energy ripple through his body like new blood.

"Thank you," Ara said to the woman.

"It was a brave thing you did," the woman said. She sat down in the seat across from him. Ara could feel her eyes studying him, but he didn't try to hide. He tore off another piece of bread. "Why did you help the other Descendants? You could have gotten away easier on your own."

"I couldn't leave them there. I know what castle life is like for a Descendant."

"Do you? I'm told you were offered the comforts of a noble lord. That wasn't enough for you?"

"No," Ara said. "It wasn't."

The woman studied him without reaction, her face betraying

nothing. Ara glanced back at the door where Bree Sai stood. Her face, on the other hand, betrayed plenty.

"Bree Sai doesn't like you much," the woman observed.

"I've noticed." Ara turned back to the woman across from him. There was something about her, the way she sat upright and calm, the way she studied Ara. There were no rebel scars carved on the woman's face, but she was as much a warrior as Bree Sai or any of the Descendant rebels. This was no simple barmaid.

"You're Spade," Ara said.

The woman raised an eyebrow; the first sign of surprise she'd shown. "Why do you say that?"

"You're in charge here. They brought me to you."

"But I'm a woman."

"I've known women tough as any men." Cambria's freckled face flashed in Ara's mind.

"You are right, Ara. I am called Spade. Though it was not always my name."

Ara had heard many rumors of the great Rebel leader. Could she hold the answers he was looking for? Did she know the source of his blood power?

"Your blood…is it like mine?"

The woman, Spade, held his gaze. "No one's blood is like yours."

Ara nodded slowly but couldn't help but feel the disappointment. The more he searched the more he found the questions of his past had no answers.

"I do not lead because of my blood. I lead because someone must."

Ara had heard many stories of Spade in the Descendants' barracks of House Carmine. They talked of the rebel leader like a mythical figure who struck fear into the hearts of the Faith. Who could cut through a battalion of Temple guards single-handed. Ara held little faith in such stories.

"Where are you from?" he asked.

Spade took a deep breath and looked past Ara, as if into the past.

"I was born a slave of House Octavian. My parents were slaves there—until my father was traded. When I was fourteen, my mother tried to escape to find my father. She took me with her, but I was young and slow. Octavian's guards hunted us down in the woods. They beat my mother in front of me. I cried and begged for them to stop, but they kept at it, saying they had to teach her a lesson as they took turns on her. They beat her beyond the point of healing. She died right there in the dirt. They didn't lay a fist on me. I clung to her broken bloody body until they pried me off and dragged me home. They left her there in the forest, left her for the animals. For a long time, I thought if only they had beaten me, too. If I had taken even a few of their angry blows, my mother would have lived."

Spade traced her finger over a knot on the table, digging her fingernail into the wood. Ara could see, even after all this time, the pain was still there.

"I later burned House Octavian to the ground and every Raw Blood in it."

Ara's mouth fell open. Even with help, he had barely escaped House Carmine with his life. Spade had taken down an entire noble house. Eradicated it from existence.

"The other Descendants of House Octavian and I fled and started the underground rebellion."

"To fight the Faith."

"To free our people," she corrected him. "The Faith are free to practice whatever beliefs they want as long as they don't enslave and torture us. So yes, we fight them because they will not accept that. There is no Faith without us."

"And what about me?" Ara said. "Why did you have me kidnapped? Enslaved?" Ara turned back to Bree Sai as he said this. There was no remorse on the rebel's face.

"It was not my intention," Spade said. "It was important that we meet, and my people did what they believed they had to do to bring you here."

"To take me against my will? To injure my friend?"

"Raw Bloods are not your friends, no matter what they say or however nice they treat you. When it comes down to it, everyone chooses their own blood."

"You're wrong," Ara said. "There are good Raw Bloods just as there are bad Descendants. We are not defined by our blood."

Ara held Spade's gaze. He was certain about his friends. It had already come down to it, and with their own lives on the line, they had chosen to help him.

"Then you have met better than I," Spade said with a wave of her hand.

"Why did you want to meet with me?" Ara asked. "To use me as a weapon?"

"If Royal blood does truly flow through your veins, then you have powers beyond anyone else. With the proper training, you could push far beyond your limits. With my help, you could be as powerful as the Royals of old."

"What do you know of the Royals?"

"Their powers extended beyond healing and heightened senses. If you mastered your abilities, you'd be faster and stronger than any man. It is said that during the Blood Warn one Royal was equal to fifty Raw Blood soldiers. "

Ara's heart thumped with excitement. Could it be true? He'd been running for so long—how amazing would it be to finally have the power to fight back?

"But how did I get this blood?" Ara asked, and he heard the plea in his voice. "What is the source? Where did I come from, and how come I don't remember?"

"That, I don't know," Spade said. "Since I first heard of your existence, I have looked for answers as well. I tracked down the hunters who found you in an attempt to trace where in the north they found you, in case there were more like you. In the end, they gave us very little. They found you near the northern border wall. You were so badly beaten they thought you were dead. A day later they found you breathing again, back from the dead. Even then, they had no idea what you were."

"But who beat me? Who tried to kill me in the first place?"

"I don't know. But it explains your memory loss. Head split open, beaten to the brink of death."

Ara shook his head. How had he gotten so far north? Who had attacked him? And who was the bearded man in his vision? With every answer, more questions sprouted up. His past was an unending tangle of vines.

"Tonight you will stay here with us," Spade said, gathering the cup and napkin onto the serving tray. "You need to rest after your long journey. You can decide what to do in the morning. If you wish to leave, we will not stop you. But if you stay here and begin your training, it will bring hope to Descendants throughout Terene. Hope that they now have a fighting chance at freedom."

Many thoughts drifted through Ara's mind. He did not know these people, but he felt indebted to them just the same. He felt he owed something to every Descendant locked away in a castle or fighting for his life in a pit. As much as Ara wanted to see his friends again and hide from the problems of this world, he knew that time had passed.

Ara stood up and weariness weighed down on him—from the night's travels and from his entire journey. Rest was a luxury he had had little time for.

"Bree Sai will show you to your bed," Spade said, shooting the Descendant rebel a commanding look. "Sleep well, Ara. I have a surprise for you in the morning. Three of them, actually."

"Thank you, Spade," Ara said. He moved toward Bree Sai. Even if she led him to the stables to sleep, he knew he would sleep well this night.

But before he took another step, the door behind her flew

open, and a man rushed into the inn. His eyes were wide with alarm and sweat poured down his brow. He looked past Ara to Spade.

"They're here," he stammered out of breath. "The Temple guards. They've found us."

# 32

---

*"The attack is imminent. Our walls will not hold. The Raw Bloods will make ghosts of us all."*

---

Within minutes, The Last Drop was filled with people: the Descendants from House Gorgen, armed rebels, and women and children who looked to play no part in a rebellion. Some huddled in the center of the inn while others, including Ara, went to the windows to watch the approaching army. Ara didn't know how many Temple guards there were, but he could see they were surrounded and outnumbered. Screams carried through the darkness from the edge of the valley; rebels rode out but did not come back.

"What do we do?" a woman shouted from the center of the room, cradling a baby in her arms.

Spade gave quick commands to the rebels around her. Her men didn't hesitate. They raced out into the night and to possible death.

"What of the prisoners?" one of the rebels asked.

Spade glanced in Ara's direction before answering. "They're safe where they are."

*Prisoners?* Had the rebels taken some Temple guards alive? Ara didn't know if that would help them or put them in more danger. All these innocent people…hopefully, Spade knew what she was doing.

"Ara," Spade called. "There's something I need to tell you."

But before she reached him, the front door swung open, and Taro Kine stepped in. Blood ran down the side of the rebel's face, fear in his eyes.

Others must have seen the same thing for a general sigh of grief swept through the room. Taro Kine crossed to Spade. "There are too many," he said in a low voice. "We can't beat them."

"How many are there?" Spade asked.

He looked to the window where the lights could be seen, the battle drawing closer. "Hundreds."

Spade didn't blink. Whatever calculations ran through her head were over in seconds. She nodded, putting her hand on Taro Kine's shoulder. "Get everyone back. We leave together."

"It's too late," someone shouted from the window. "They're here."

Torchlight broke through the dark night in all directions like an approaching fire. Ara turned from the window and looked to the corner of the room where the young Descendant girl from House Gorgen lay huddled. Her face was pressed into her knees and hiding beneath a blanket of yellow hair.

*What have I done?*

Outside, the shapes became clearer. An army in white with a small cluster of purple from House Gorgen. They were beyond count. *These poor people…I led the Faith straight to them.*

Spade fastened a sword belt around her waist. The weapon contrasted sharply with her simple innkeeper's clothes.

"If anyone comes near the door, fire on them," she commanded.

The archers moved to the windows and drew their arrows. Rows of Temple guards assembled around the inn, waiting. They were surrounded; there was no escape.

A long-haired man on horseback rode to the front of the line. "Give us the boy," the man called. "We know he's here. Send him out and we shall spare the rest of you."

All eyes in the room fell on Ara.

"It's a lie," Spade said. "They didn't come all this way just to let us go."

"You can't be certain," a woman said. Her baby let out a cry, and she covered his mouth with its blanket, trying to soothe the child. All through the room people huddled in fear.

"Give him up or we burn this place down and comb through the ashes for those with the blood strong enough to survive," the guard leader called.

Ara turned to the door but his feet wouldn't move. Out that door was the Temple dungeon, where he'd be imprisoned and drained for the rest of his days. Ara couldn't imagine anything worse.

Bree Sai stepped forward. The rebel warrior stared daggers at him.

"Foolish brat. You better be worth it." She kicked open the door and screamed into the night. "Raw Blood scum!"

"No," Taro Kine yelled.

Bree Sai drew her arrows and shot three times in the span of a second. The arrows shot through the night, killing the three closest guards. "Die!" she shouted. Her fourth arrow was halfway out of the quiver when a hail of arrows lit up the doorway.

A stunned Bree Sai stumbled back into the inn. Taro Kine rushed forward and caught her. He cradled her arrow-riddled body in his arms. "Nooooo," he howled.

Windows shattered under arrow fire.

"Everyone down," Spade commanded. "Quick. Get everyone downstairs."

A stampede of panic filled the inn, screams coming from

every direction. A man fell at Ara's feet, an arrow shaft lodged in his head.

"We'll never make it in time," someone called.

"Shut up and move."

Rebel archers shot out the windows, but the constant flurry of arrows kept them back.

*They'll never stop.* Ara stood up. Arrows whizzed overhead. The Temple Army was too strong. They're going to kill everyone to get to him. And even if they did escape, the Faith will never stop hunting them. Not as long as Ara was with them.

"Ara, no." Spade dropped to a knee; her hand moved to her sword. "I can't let them have your blood."

But there was no other choice. *No one else is going to die because of me.*

"It's over," Ara said. "They won."

Ara ran out the door waving his arms high in the air. Arrows pounded into the door behind him. One sliced his shoulder, narrowly missing his neck.

"Hold your fire!" a voice commanded.

The arrows stopped. A line of guards pointed their weapons at Ara, their arms tense, ready to fire. But no more arrows came. Ara covered his eyes from the bright torchlight.

"You made the noble choice," the long-haired guard said. He waved his hand, beckoning Ara to come closer.

The inn door slammed shut behind Ara, the lock clicking into place. It did little to dull the cries inside.

*No turning back now.*

All eyes were on him. Ara walked toward the Temple guards who he had spent so long running from. Each step bringing him closer to his fate. Ara had spent days locked in a wagon cell; he'd been imprisoned in a tower, cut off from all others, but he'd never felt as alone as he did at that moment.

From atop his horse, the guard leader stared down at him. His uniform stained with dirt and blood. "You've caused a lot of trouble, boy. I hunted you for months."

"Well, you finally got me."

"Yes. Yes, I did." The guard leader shifted in his seat, his long braid whipping behind him like a noose. "The Highfather has taken a great interest in you. He believes your blood is something special. Perhaps we should test it first."

The man's boot smashed Ara's cheek. He hit the ground, the bones in his face shattered like glass.

"I'd hate to bring him the wrong boy."

Ara lifted his head. Blurry shapes approached. More Temple guards, their heavy armor and boots thundering with each step. "No…please," he whimpered.

Then, they were upon him.

BRITON AWOKE to footsteps in the inn above. The floorboards bowed under the weight of what must be a considerable gathering. Geyer and Cambria were already up, standing at the bars.

"Something's happening," Cambria said.

Briton straightened from his spot on the cell floor; his back let out a series of cracks. "Maybe they're arguing over the most painful way to execute us."

"No," Geyer said. "They're afraid of something."

Feet shuffled and the floorboards overhead creaked louder. It couldn't be morning, yet it seemed the inn was full of anxious bodies. Briton leaned on the stone wall and pulled himself to his feet. His body cursed him for all this travel. *If I ever get out of this, I'm going to settle down in a library with a comfortable chair and never leave.*

Geyer shook his head. "Only one thing would get Descendant rebels this stirred up," Geyer said.

"Temple guards," Briton said. "Did they follow us?"

"I don't know, but I'm sure we'll be blamed either way."

The cellar door opened, and a man came down the stairs followed by a line of people. Geyer was right; fear was all over their faces.

"What's going on?" Briton called, but the man ignored them. He helped a woman and baby down the cellar stairs. Screams rang out from above. Someone pushed forward, and people toppled down the stairs. An old man cried out as people piled on top of him.

"Slowly," the first man shouted, supporting the woman to the cellar floor. The old man howled in pain. His leg was bent at an unnatural angle. He couldn't stand.

"Let us out," Cambria said. "I'm a doctor."

The first man studied her, and then Briton and Geyer—as if weighing whether or not to let them drown. More people flooded down the narrow stairs; the pandemonium was more than he could handle.

"We can help," Briton said.

The man unhooked the keys from the wall and tossed them across the room. Geyer caught them through the bars.

"We're leaving," the man said. "We need to get these people out of here."

Geyer unlocked the cell door and pushed it open. Cambria raced to the old man's side and felt his leg. Geyer moved to a bench that held their belongings. He tied his sword and belt to his waist.

"I need cloth and something straight for a splint," Cambria shouted to Geyer.

Geyer scanned the room then broke a leg off a stool, bringing her the straight piece of wood.

"What's going on out there?" Briton asked as people filled the small cellar.

"The Temple Army is here," the man said. "Hundreds of them."

This was it. After all their running, the Faith had finally tracked them down. Briton breathed a small sigh of relief at one thought: *At least they didn't have Ara.*

A high wail shook Briton back to the moment. At the top of the stairs, a woman held a baby over her head, the infant screamed, its face burning red. "Hurry," she yelled. "They're going to burn it down. Please, no. They're going to burn us!"

At the far wall of the cellar, Geyer helped the man tear boards from the wall. They were nailed over some kind of passageway.

"Stand back," the man ordered to the crowd pushing against them.

To Briton's left Cambria helped the old man to his feet, taking his weight on her shoulders.

"We'll never get everyone out in time," a voice cried. "They'll kill us all."

Chaos and fear were everywhere, and Briton was useless. An old man who had spent his life studying. What use was that in the real world where people were hunted and babies' lives were threatened by armed soldiers?

Briton had sat safely in Carmine Castle while the world inflicted terror and injustice. He'd been in the throne room as the poor and sick were turned away because they had no worth. He'd lived within the walls that regularly practiced the torture and beatings of Descendants; that tore children from their mothers' arms. And what had he done? What had all his knowledge accomplished?

Briton's body tightened like a fist. Before he knew it, he was climbing the stairs, squeezing past people stuck with no room to descend. The panicked sounds seemed to dim, and everyone's movements slowed as Briton's pushed through. He faintly heard his name called but didn't look back.

Briton stepped up the final stair into the inn above. All around him, people crammed toward the cellar stairs, but Briton found his way through. Descendant rebels stood at the windows with bows and swords ready. Weapons that would be useless in Briton's hands. The rebel that held the door said something, but Briton pushed him away. He was a wave, gathering momentum. If he stopped even for a moment, fear would catch up to him.

He had to buy them time. Even a few minutes could make the difference. Could save another life.

Briton threw the inn door open and stepped out into a night lit by a hundred fires.

The first line of guards stopped, raising their swords to him. The torches in their hands illuminated their white armored figures. They hesitated for a moment, as if deciding what to make of the feeble unarmed figure before them.

Briton gulped, the wave of courage washing away as quickly as it had come. *This would have been better with a plan.*

"Who's in charge here?" Briton called with all the authority he could muster.

A few heads turned toward a dark man on horseback, his hair fell behind his back in a long braid.

"Who are you?" the man asked.

"I am Briton Moonglass, chief advisor to House Carmine. You are carrying out an unlawful raid on northern lands and I demand that you leave these hills at once."

More heads turned toward the man on horseback. This guard leader, whoever he was, beckoned his horse forward. The man's face was hard, unswayed. Briton knew his ploy wouldn't work, but if he could keep them busy, he could maybe buy a few more lives.

*Geyer, you stubborn wretch. You better get these people out of here.*

"House Carmine, you say?" the man called, approaching Briton from on high. "And what authority do you think a member of a dead house has over the army of the Faith?"

"Dead house?"

"Oh, you haven't heard?" The man's grin was even nastier than his hard face. "Carmine was murdered in his chambers. Betrayed, it seems, by one of his closest advisors. That couldn't be *you* by any chance? The same man hiding out in a rebel fort?"

Carmine's breath caught in his throat. *Can it be true? Oh, Jonathan.*

361

"You know, I think it is you. What luck that we get to dispatch of you and these Descendant scum all at once."

"You won't win," Briton said. "You think you have the power; you think you're invincible, but one day your empire will crumble to dust like all the others."

"But you see. We've already won."

The man waved a hand and two guards stepped forward, dragging something in their arms. Briton strained to see the shape in the darkness; then he saw what it was.

"Ara!"

The boy raised his head. His eyes bruised and swollen. Ara hung in the guard's arms, his hands and feet chained. "Briton?"

Briton fought back the defeat weakening his knees and nodded. *I am here for you. I will always be here for you.*

"I'm sorry," Ara groaned. "I shouldn't have let them get me. It's all my fault."

"No," Briton said. "It's not over. You'll find a way. There's always an answer."

"Not today, there's not," the long-haired guard said.

"Let him go," Briton said.

"And why would we do that?"

"Because he doesn't belong to you."

The long-haired guard signaled to a nearby guard. The armored man nodded and strode to Briton.

"No!" Ara kicked and squirmed. The guards hoisted him off the ground.

Briton looked at Ara. His last student. He'd given everything up for him: his title, his wealth, his life. And it had been worth it.

*They got away,* Briton told himself. *Geyer and Cambria, they got all the people out of the building.*

*It worked. It had to.*

Silver light flashed in the darkness. Briton stumbled back. He looked down and saw how dirty his clothes were. Blood poured from his chest, staining the stiff fabric.

"Noooo," Ara cried, and then he was at Briton's side, grabbing at his chest and the hole cut into him. Guards seized Ara, but the boy shook them off, clinging to Briton. Holding him up.

"It's okay," Briton said, blood garbling in his throat. He touched the boy's face; he wiped away the tears. "We…saved them…saved…"

Released, Briton Moonglass fell to the ground, his body laid open like an unfinished book.

BRITON'S BODY lay on the ground, unmoving. Blood pooled from his torn body. Ara's scream came out a choked gasp. His lungs were still recovering from the beating. Guards yanked the chains on his wrists, dragging him away.

"No, let me give him blood!" Ara sobbed, tears running down his swollen face. "Please."

But it was too late. Briton was gone.

"His death was not some noble sacrifice," the long-haired guard said. "He was only the first of many." He pointed to the Descendant inn. "Burn it to the ground. Kill anyone who tries to escape."

Ara went limp. He'd watched Briton slaughtered before him, and now more would burn. His heart could take no more.

"No, you can't." This time the words were not Ara's. Lord Gorgen stepped forward, flanked by his personal guards in purple shirts. "My Descendants are in there. You have the boy, leave the others to me."

"They are rebels and terrorists. Their sentence is death."

"But…they're worth a fortune!"

"You're welcome to go collect, Lord Gorgen," the man smiled. The Temple guards moved forward.

"Please, no," Ara begged. "You have me, let them go. Please…"

Guards tossed torches onto the roof of the inn. Arrows flew from the windows, taking down a few guards, but more rose up to take their place. Flames leaped up, illuminating the night sky. The arrows stopped flying.

The guards tossed Ara into a caged wagon and locked the doors. Hands bound, Ara struggled up to his feet as the wagon pulled away. Through the bars, he watched The Last Drop burn. He thought of the people trapped inside. The Descendants he had brought there. All of Spade's rebel army. All gone.

Then another, horrible realization speared through his gut.

*If Briton was here…then the others…Spade's prisoners!*

"Geyer!" Ara screamed into the distant flames. "Cambria! Noooooo!"

That was it. The last of Ara's strength escaped in a tortured scream of agony. He crumbled to the cage floor, a hollow shell. He wished his memory would disappear once again, taking all of this pain with it. Burying this moment deep underground where Ara could never find it.

Ara lay bent and wilted, unable to think. While all around him, his world burned.

## 33

The distant light of dawn sparked over the mountains, ending a night that seemed to last forever. The final few villagers stumbled out of the underground tunnel; the number of survivors was too small.

Cambria hurried to those who suffered coughing fits from smoke inhalation. Lucky for them, the mountain had plenty of Barthillo root to go around. She mashed the soft root with a stone and mixed it with water in a bowl from her pack. She raced around with the concoction, treating people and trying to keep her mind off what had happened.

But it was no use.

Briton was dead. Ara, taken.

The woman leader, the one called Spade, stood with her people discussing what to do next. Once they looked like a powerful band, but after seeing the Temple forces, it was clear just how small and weak the rebellion was. Down the mountain, smoke drifted from the remnants of their burned village. Slain bodies still lay on the ground, crows pecking at their flesh. The Temple guards had moved on. There was nothing left to destroy.

Cambria finished her rounds then crossed to the far side of the hill. She found Geyer sitting alone. He leaned forward on his sheathed sword, his finger flicking the wheel on its handle. He didn't look up as she approached.

"What do we do now?" Cambria asked. Geyer stared at the spinning wheel. "Geyer."

"There's nothing to do," he said. "It's over."

"You're giving up? After what they did to Briton? They took Ara?"

"These aren't some bandits, Cambria. This is the entire Temple army."

"Yes, and now we know where Ara is."

Geyer grunted. "You don't understand. Look at them." Geyer nodded to the surviving Descendant rebels scattered along the hillside. "Their lives were dedicated to fighting the Faith, and even they know it's over."

It didn't matter to Cambria what the rebels were going to do. Every moment that passed, Ara was carried farther and farther away. She couldn't just abandon him to torture at the hands of the Faith. No matter what the odds were.

"I can't believe after everything you fought for—you and Briton together—that you're giving up. You're going to go about your life drinking in taverns, knowing Ara's in the temple being cut and drained? I can't believe you're going to let them win."

Geyer tapped his finger on the wheel of his sword handle. "They were always going to win. Briton knew that. You can't fight fate."

"You can always fight!" Cambria felt the tears coming to her eyes. Hopelessness suffocating her like a heavy sheet. "Win or lose, you can always fight. That's something a knight should know more than anyone."

"I'm not a knight. Not anymore."

Cambria stepped back as if Geyer's despair was contagious. She'd seen what happened to people who lost all hope. Despair ate at the body like any other disease, sucking it dry until there was no life left. She refused to give up.

"Then I'm going alone," she said.

The old knight didn't try to stop her. That he didn't believe her—that he thought this was the bluff of an angry child—doubled Cambria's resolve. She was sick of being told she didn't understand how the world really worked. Looking around at the broken people scattered on the grass like tombstones, Cambria saw what kind of world people settled for. This was not the world she would live in.

Cambria picked up her pack; she checked her water skin and her medical tools then headed down the hill. She didn't know the way to the Temple. She didn't know what she would do if she ever got there. But she knew to stay here was death.

Halfway down the hill, a voice called for her to stop.

Spade descended the hill toward her. "Where are you going?"

"Am I still your prisoner?" Cambria asked bitterly.

Spade stood tall before her. Despite losing so many of her people, Cambria saw the fight still in the rebel leader's eyes.

"I'm going to the Temple," Cambria said. "I'm going to get Ara back." The words sounded foolish even to Cambria's ears. But there was no look of mockery on Spade's face.

"You would risk your life for him?" she asked. "What does a Descendant's life mean to you?"

"Ara's not…he's…I can't…" Cambria meant to yell, but the words tumbled out in pieces. Tears formed on the edges of her eyes, and she hated herself for it. "Whatever you think he is or can do for you, I don't care. He's my friend, and he would do the same for me. He *did* the same for me."

Spade's eyes showed no pity. It made Cambria feel like an equal; not some upset child.

"How do you plan to get him back?"

"I don't know. But I have to try."

"Yes." Spade reached out and placed a hand on Cambria's shoulder. "And I will go with you."

"Spade," called a nearby Descendant rebel. "You can't be serious."

Spade turned and marched up the hill to the group of

survivors. All eyes were on her, waiting for answers. When she spoke, her voice boomed with the confidence of a true leader.

"How many of our people are in the Temple dungeons? How many of our brothers and sisters? We have lived with their suffering because we told ourselves it wasn't time. We needed to build an army first. We needed to prepare a plan. Well, we can wait no longer. They have the boy. With his blood, their armies will be unstoppable. Prepared or not, now is the time to fight."

"It's suicide," a man yelled. He looked around the group pleadingly. "You saw the size of their army. It can't be done."

"Spade," another man said. "You can't ask us to do this. To throw our lives away."

"I'm not asking you," Spade said. "I said that I would go with the girl. I speak for no one else here. I'm not your leader in this; each of you must make your own decision."

There was a long silence. People lowered their heads, avoiding Spade's gaze. It was then, in their frightened hesitation, that Cambria saw the survivors on the hillside for what they were. Not evil rebel outlaws. Not gifted, magical warriors. These were just people. People born with a different type of blood.

Geyer climbed slowly to his feet. He limped down the hill toward Spade, his left leg dragging stiffly.

"You're mad because you've lost and now you want to go out fighting," he said. "I understand that feeling."

Geyer came to stand face to face with Spade. He fastened his sword to his belt at the hip. "But you should know whoever goes with us is not coming back."

Cambria's heart leaped. Her eyes met Geyer's for a moment. Then he looked away, shaking his head as if embarrassed.

Spade didn't argue; she simply nodded to Geyer. "Everyone dies. Even those with good blood."

The hilltop was quiet as people searched the faces of their neighbors. Most ducked their head, ashamed of their fear. Then a voice spoke up.

"I can't let you have all the glory, Spade," Taro Kine said. He leaped to his feet, and a smile crossed his handsome features. He walked up to Geyer. "Nor will the fall of the Faith come at the hands of some Raw Blood."

Geyer scoffed. "Nothing like going into battle with false-confidence."

"The Temple is where our ancestors fell," the one called Solvan Ra called. "It's as good a place to die as any."

Two other Descendant rebels joined them, though Cambria didn't know their names. The old man whose leg Cambria had mended in the breakout volunteered to come, but Spade told him he needed to stay and lead those that remained.

"You are the last of the free Descendants," Spade announced to those on the hillside. "Go and make a new home for our people. I wish I could say I'll see you again, but I'll fight happy knowing you will live well."

With that, the party gathered horses and supplies and set off for the Temple. Seven riders on their way to challenge the most powerful force in Terene. Cambria hoped she had not talked them all into their deaths.

# PART III

---

## THE TEMPLE

# 34

---

*"We cut them down in droves, but they keep coming, an endless swarm empowered by generations of oppression."*

---

For days, Ara drifted in and out of consciousness. Being awake and remembering was too painful, but sleep brought a pain of its own. Nightmares of Briton's bloodied corpse reaching out to him. Of Geyer and the doctors burning in the inn. His name the last word on Cambria's lips.

The road stretched on, but Ara was hardly aware of time passing. He no longer cared about the fate that awaited him. Cage him, beat him, drain his blood—it didn't matter. His friends were dead. Ara sat in his wagon cell, refusing to eat or drink. There was no healing from this.

A few days later, golden domes glinted on the horizon like setting suns. Ara had returned to the Temple of the Faith.

"Get a good look at the sky," a Temple guard said, riding beside Ara's cell. "Because this is the last you'll ever see of it."

Ara lay down and closed his eyes.

He woke later as the wagon bumped along the cobbled

streets of the Temple market. Lanterns and torches filled the square with light as vendors picked up their carts to go home. No one paid the boy in the cart any mind.

"Get out," a guard shouted as he pulled open the wagon door. Ara didn't move. The guard grabbed him by the shirt and dragged him out onto the ground, slamming his head on the stony street.

Ara awoke sopping wet. He shook water off his face. A guard tossed an empty bucket to the floor of the room. Ara couldn't move. Straps on his wrists and ankles pinned him to a chair. The table beside him was lined with familiar instruments: blades, tubes, and a line of empty glass bottles.

A Curor stepped forward, his sharp nose pointed to the side as if it couldn't bare Ara's smell. His robes were vibrant red with a gold heart emblem embroidered on his breast. He stepped forward and inspected Ara with a frown. "I was told they were bringing me the most powerful Descendant in centuries. And then they bring you." He poked Ara's wrist with a curved metal tool. "A skeleton of a boy who's barely alive."

The Curor bent in close to whisper. He moved the metal instrument gently along Ara's neck, drawing a line down his chest. His eyes were wide with hunger.

"I'd cut you open right now to see the root of your 'pure blood,' but the Highfather has other plans, unfortunately, for you."

Ara would have spit in the man's face if he had the saliva to do so. His body felt dry and rung out. It had begged him for water on the road, but Ara refused to drink. Every drop of blood he produced only strengthened the Faith's hold on this world.

The door swung open. An old man strode in like the room and everything in it belonged to him. He wore immaculate white robes decorated with thin red patterns. On his head sat a high pointed red hat; a ridiculous looking article by itself, it somehow added to the man's aura of authority. The Curor and his attending guards bowed before the Highfather of the Faith.

374

"So this is the famous Descendant boy," the Highfather said, looking Ara over. He too must be disappointed with his prize. "It's no surprise my Curors thought nothing of you at the auction. A gift from Hemo, wrapped in rags. Remarkable."

Ara said nothing.

"Have you begun?"

"Your men left him in terrible shape," the Curor said. "It looks like he hasn't eaten anything in days; it would be like squeezing blood from a stone and would likely kill him."

The Highfather rubbed his chin, puzzling over Ara. "Where do you come from boy? How did you come about your powers?"

Ara said nothing.

"All that running in fear and for what reason? You must have known you'd end up here eventually? Think of all the people who needlessly suffered because you tried to save yourself."

The words were meant to hurt, but Ara had told himself as much over the past few days. Briton, Geyer, Cambria…Chancey. They would all be alive if not for him. He had nothing to say to this man.

"I can get him to talk," a guard offered.

The Highfather held up his hand, silencing the guard. He looked to Ara and sighed.

"I've waited a long time for your blood; I can wait until morning. But know this, boy. I'll get what I need to save Terene. Even if it takes bleeding you to your very last drop."

He turned to the Curor. "We will have the ceremony in the morning before the Fathers. See that he is ready by then."

"Yes, Father," the Curor bowed.

"Tomorrow begins a new day for the Faith," the Highfather said, his wrinkled face warping into a smile. "We finally have the power to shape Terene. All the world will fall under Lord Hemo's will. With this boy's blood, our reign shall prove ever-lasting."

The Highfather left the room, his white robe sweeping

behind him. Ara didn't know what his words meant, but he knew it didn't bode well for him. Or the Descendants.

"What do you want me to do with him?" the guard asked the Curor.

"Take him to a cell in the dungeon," the Curor said. "See to it he gets plenty of food and water, even if you have to cram it down his throat."

The Curor snarled at Ara.

"Get some rest, boy. Tomorrow you'll need all your strength."

AEILUS HAEMON BENT to one knee, something he hadn't done in years. His muscles ached from the strain as he lowered himself down. Getting up would prove painfully difficult, but sacrifice was pleasing to Lord Hemo. And he had sacrificed much to get to this point. Now, all his discipline and piousness was paying off. Hemo had blessed him with not one answer, but two!

Haemon closed his eyes and prayed.

He thanked Hemo for delivering the boy to him. With his good blood, Haemon could reign as Highfather for decades more. With that blood in the veins of his soldiers, his army would be unstoppable. Hemo had also given the Faith another weapon. A weapon that would see the end of the Descendant rebellion and all those who opposed the Faith. With a splash of blood, their enemies could be transformed into what the Descendants were always meant to be—obedient slaves. Mindless creatures to do his bidding. And with their new forms, they would be stronger than ever. Hemo's plan was coming together.

*Forgive my doubtfulness, my Lord. You placed the vision of a great future in my heart, but there were times I lost sight of the path. Times I wondered if I was somehow wrong and all my effort had been for naught. But today you have shone your light on me and my quest. Today, all the things I've had to do as Highfather of the Faith, are justified.*

There were no such things as accidents. Years of work trying to replicate the Descendants blood hadn't ended in failure but an entirely different solution. One guided by Hemo's own hand. At this very moment, the Temple Curors were reproducing gallons and gallons of Vorrel's dark blood.

*Lord Hemo, thank you for trusting me to fulfill your vision of a better Terene. I am now, and will always be, your humble servant.*

Haemon opened his eyes and smiled. Even without the Descendant boy's blood, he felt renewed. Alone on the floor of his study as night reigned outside, Aelius Haemon was stronger than ever. For, the pain in his old body was temporary but his legacy was forever.

GUARDS CARRIED Ara down a stairwell to the Temple's dungeon. He was not alone; shadows moved behind the bars. His eyes adjusted to the darkness but there was no adjusting to the smell. The dungeon reeked of rotting corpses.

The guards dropped him in a small cell; his body slammed on the cold stone floor. A plate of food and jug of water was set beside him. He wanted to deny them, to not fatten himself up for tomorrow's slaughter, but this time his hunger overruled his defiance. He ate quickly and greedily, his movements becoming easier with every bite.

With his meal done, Ara lay alone in the cell. This was the end of his journey. He couldn't help but think of the Highfather's words. How much pain and suffering he had caused because he couldn't accept his role as a Descendant. Did he really think he was better than others? That he deserved freedom? Had he stayed at Castle Carmine, his blood would have made Carmine rich, but it also would have healed people. People dying of sickness and injury. What was his one life compared to all those his blood could have saved?

Now, in the hands of the Faith, his blood would be used to build an army to conquer the world. They would hunt down and defeat every last Descendant rebel. Because of him, his people had no future.

Shapes moved behind the bars of his cell. Ara sat up and peered through the darkness—the strength of his sight already increased from the food in his belly.

"Who's there?" Ara whispered. A shape from one of the adjacent cells staggered toward the bars and sat on the floor nearby. It was a ragged man with bushy hair that stood on end, unmoving. A beard stretched to his waist. He looked as if he had been trapped in this dungeon for decades.

"You are the boy they speak of," the man said, his soft voice coarse from neglect.

"Who are you?"

The man considered Ara's question. His eyes searched past Ara into the light of the dungeon's single lantern.

"My name…was Tar Shen."

"You are part of the Descendant rebellion?"

There was silence as Tar Shen looked away. Had Ara somehow offended the man? Maybe he didn't understand. It was easy to see how someone could lose their sanity trapped in this windowless prison.

"I was…long ago," Tar Shen said. "Those days are gone. I am a prisoner now."

"How long have you been here?"

Tar Shen looked up to the stone ceiling as if the days were written there but beyond count. "I do not know. Time does not exist in the dungeon. You will learn this."

"Has anyone escaped?"

Tar Shen shook his head. "It is not possible."

Ara sighed. So this was to be his fate. Forgotten in the Temple dungeons, with no sense of time or self. Through the dim lantern light, Ara saw that Tar Shen's cell was filled with other prisoners. The cell on the other side was also filled with huddled shapes. How long had these people been imprisoned here? Years? Decades?

*Think!*

Ara looked around, startled.

*What's the problem?* Briton's voice sounded in his head, clear as if he'd been standing over him. Delivering Ara another lesson. But it was but a trick of his imagination. His friend was gone.

*To find the answer, you must first identify the problem.*

"I'm trapped," Ara snapped.

Tar Shen glanced at him but did not speak.

*Trapped from what?* Somehow he could clearly hear his teacher's response in his head. He still had the annoying habit of answering questions with more questions.

"From getting out of here. From freedom."

*Why do you want freedom?*

"So they don't take my blood!" Ara yelled, frustrated with this game.

"He's already going mad," said a woman from the next cell. "That didn't take long."

Ara pulled his knees to his chest and rocked back and forth. He couldn't stay here. He couldn't live his days locked in this darkness, alone.

*Don't quit now, think!*

Ara closed his eyes. "Just leave me alone."

Feet shuffled closer on both sides of his cell. Descendant prisoners come to see him crack up.

"There is no escape from the Temple dungeons," a man said. "There is no escape from the Curor's touch."

*That's not true.*

The muscles in Ara's face tightened as he strained to shut out the voice. The rusted metal bars surrounding him rose up into the stone ceiling. The dungeon had only one door. One exit. And they were buried in the heart of the Temple surrounded by an army of guards. There was no escape.

Briton's voice returned, louder. *What have I told you, Ara?*

"Every problem has a solution," Ara whispered. "One need only discover the answer."

A man scoffed. He pressed tight to the bars, looking in at Ara. Dark rings circled his eyes; his cheekbones threatened to puncture the thin skin. "You think you can do what no one else has ever done?"

"Yes," Ara said.

"What makes you special?"

"Because I believe it can be done."

The man answered in a sickly laugh. "You're a fool."

"Leave the boy alone," Tar Shen said. "Just because we lost hope long ago, don't rob him of his last time with it."

Others came closer to the bars, a crowd of skeletons looking in at the naive boy. Ara didn't care. He wasn't ready to give up yet. If there was an answer he would find it. He had to.

But he would need help.

"I can't escape this cell, Briton."

*What happens if you can't escape this cell?*

"They'll take my blood."

*Will you give it to them?*

"I have no choice. Armed guards will come in the morning and take my blood. I can't stop them."

Ara sat in silence, waiting for Briton's voice to speak to him. But it didn't come. He concentrated, searching his mind for an answer. But it was useless. Briton was gone, along with everyone who had ever cared about him. Ara was lost, alone.

Ara took a deep breath and relaxed. He closed his eyes, imagining he was free. He saw himself slipping like a ghost through the dungeon walls and flying away from the Temple. He rose over the forest, high above the trees to the top of a great mountain peak that overlooked the world below. This was his vision, his old memory. From this great height, the world and its problems seemed so small. The trivial fighting of Descendants and Raw Bloods was lost in the distance—dots on a map. Up here, Ara felt at peace. Here, Ara was home.

The answer struck like a knife into its target. He could imagine that familiar twinkle in Briton's blue eyes whenever he got an answer right. Ara's eyes snapped open. Scores of Descendant prisoners were gathered at the bars all around his cell; their gaunt faces watching him. Ara picked up his empty food bowl. Then, he turned to the old Descendant rebel.

"Tar Shen," Ara said. "Find me something sharp."

## 35

The early morning fog hung like an old sheet as Cambria and her companions crossed the Temple square. The few vendors setting up their carts paid the seven cloaked strangers no mind. They had ridden at a frantic pace for days, and now here they were: five rebels, a lame knight, and a young doctor on the doorstep of the most powerful army in the world.

"This isn't so hard," Taro Kine said as they stalked through the streets unhindered.

"There is little security here because no one would be foolish enough to attempt to break in," Geyer said.

"Then they don't know us," Taro Kine smiled.

Cambria couldn't believe how the Descendant rebel could be in such good spirits at a time like this. They had gotten into the Temple marketplace, but that was easy, it was open to every visitor in Terene. Getting into the Temple itself and, more specifically the dungeon level, was a whole other matter. As was getting out with their lives. Their chances rested on Spade's knowledge of the Temple's interior. The night before they had gone over a map of the Temple that marked nearly every room and floor, including a secret opening left from the time of the Royals. Acquiring the information had cost the rebellion dearly,

Spade explained. And she was happy to finally be putting it to use. For getting in through the main sanctuary entrance would have been impossible.

"Are you sure we shouldn't be doing this at night?" Edwar Kel asked, looking around wearily at the Temple guards patrolling the entrance to the sanctuary.

"The Temple is shut down at night; we'd be spotted," Spade said. "During the day, the market is open, and worshipers from all over come to the sanctuary to pray."

"I still don't like doing this in broad daylight," Edwar Kel grumbled.

Taro Kine put his arm around the man's shoulder. "If I had a face like yours, I'd prefer working at night too."

Spade led the group through a sliver of an alley past small unmarked shops to the back side of the Temple. Unlike the polished white stone in the front, this side was overlooked. Vines hung down its chipped and dusty walls. When it was clear no one was watching them, Spade pulled the map from her cloak.

"Should be up ahead here," she said.

"Why is there a secret passage into the Temple?" Cambria asked. Enormous as the complex was, it seemed unbelievable that the Temple guard would have overlooked this flaw after so many centuries.

"Our information says it was put here at the time of the Blood Wars by Royals escaping the siege."

"Hopefully, it works out better for us than it did for them," Mace Ren said, glancing back down the alley.

Spade ran her hand along the vines, searching for the point of the passageway. Cambria glanced down the alley, praying not to see a Temple guard. Standing in the shadow of the Temple, it finally hit her what they were up against. How did she ever think this was a good idea?

"It's not here," Spade whispered.

"Are you sure?" Solvan Ra asked. "Look again."

Spade pulled back the vines, revealing the shape of a doorway sealed with mortar.

"Fates," Geyer cursed.

"Now what?" Edwar Kel asked.

Spade looked down at her map once more. "There's only one other option."

"Retreat and live out our days fat and happy?" Mace Ren offered.

"Through the sanctuary."

"I don't suppose your map shows a secret passageway in the sanctuary that takes us straight to the dungeon, avoiding the hundreds of Temple guards?"

Spade folded the map and slid it into her cloak pocket.

"Well, as long as we're going in through the sanctuary," Mace Ren said, "we might as well offer up some prayers."

The group came out of the alleyway and crossed the market. More vendor carts were set up, and the first visitors to the market were perusing their goods. The doors to the sanctuary were open with two guards standing on either side of the entrance. Cambria and her companions huddled behind the cover of a shop across the street, waiting for a plan to come.

"We charge in," Taro Kine said. "We move fast and surprise them, cutting our way in before anyone can sound an alarm."

"I'd give that about five minutes," Geyer said.

"Then what's your plan, Raw Blood?" Taro Kine said. "You want to run away too?"

"No, I just want to be realistic about our chances. Thinking we're going to fight our way through the front door without raising an alarm is idiotic. I'd rather be prepared for what will happen."

"And what is that?"

"As soon as we draw a blade within the Faith's sanctuary, a hundred Temple guards will be upon us."

"What are we going to do, sweet talk our way in?" Mace Ren asked.

*This is getting nowhere*, Cambria thought. It was her fault they were here. She brought them all into this dangerous mess to rescue Ara, even though she didn't have a plan or even a sword to fight with. Now it was up to her to figure out how to do it.

"I'll go," Cambria said.

The arguing stopped. Everyone turned to Cambria.

"You'll go and do what?" Mace Ren asked.

"Check out the Temple, see exactly what we're up against."

"It's too dangerous," Geyer said.

"We're not going to get anywhere standing here arguing," Cambria said. "And I'll have a better chance at going unnoticed than you."

"She's right," Spade said. "The guards wouldn't think twice about letting her in, a poor peasant girl coming to pray."

The group looked from Spade down to Cambria. It was the best idea they had. Even Geyer couldn't argue.

The old knight sighed and narrowed his eyes at Cambria. "Okay. But you're just going to look around. Don't do anything risky."

"I wasn't asking for permission," Cambria said. She pulled her hood back off her head and repositioned her pack higher on her shoulder. Then, she crossed the street toward the Temple entrance.

Cambria held her breath and kept her eyes down as she climbed the steps past the guards. She waited for a shout, for a hand to seize her, but no one stopped her. She crossed through the doorway into the inner sanctuary. Cambria exhaled and looked up at the Temple's enormous interior: vaulted ceiling, ornate stone pillars, and colorful stained glass windows that depicted people on their knees in prayer as blood flowed down to them from the clouds. There were already a few worshipers in the pews with their heads bowed. More Temple guards stood at the back of the room, blocking the door that led to the rest of the Temple.

In the entryway beside Cambria, stood a wide basin on a

stone stand. It was filled with a red liquid. A worshiper came up the steps behind Cambria and she stepped back to let the person pass. The old woman picked up a goblet off the stone stand and dipped it into the red liquid. She took a sip and then bowed and went into the sanctuary to take her seat at a pew.

*Blood wine*, Cambria thought. Part of the Faith's religious practice. These people who come to worship don't even consider that there's a life on the other end of this tradition. A Descendant who's cut and drained of blood in order to create their sacrament. Cambria entered without touching the blood wine.

She shuffled to a nearby pew and kept her head down. The fifteen or so worshipers didn't notice her, lost in their own prayers. Cambria glanced at the back of the room, to the guards stationed there. Ara was behind that door. *But how are we going to get through there? And once we do, how are we going to find him?*

Cambria fidgeted in her seat, thinking. It was hopeless; she was a doctor, not a warrior. What was she going to do, fight through the Temple guards with bandages and rash remedies?

More people streamed into the Sanctuary, each one stopped to drink the blood wine. *Using the same cup. That can't be sanitary...*

Cambria sat up straight. It was a crazy idea but it just might give them the cover they needed. She slipped off her pack and set it on the floor beneath her. She quietly opened the pack and searched around in her supplies then pulled out the jar of elder-weed cream. How many times had she warned her patients— just as her mother had warned her—about the dangers of ingesting elderweed? Cambria hoped the warnings had been warranted.

When the coast was clear, Cambria crossed back to the Sanctuary entrance. She stopped and emptied the entire jar of elder-weed cream into the basin of blood wine. The yellow cream disappeared into the dark red liquid. Cambria picked up the goblet and dipped it into the wine, mixing the clump of cream around. Desecrating blood wine in the Faith's sanctuary, what was she thinking? If she was caught…

Cambria returned the goblet to the stand and hurried down the steps, away from the sanctuary—likely cursed for all eternity.

"What did you see in there?" Spade asked when she rounded the corner out of breath.

"Two more guards inside the Temple, guarding the inner door. There are about fifteen worshipers right now with more arriving every minute."

"So much for sneaking in unnoticed," Mace Ren said.

"We can do it," Cambria said. "In a few minutes, everyone inside is going to be distracted."

"What? Why?"

Cambria looked to the entrance where more people filed up the sanctuary stairs.

"Follow me," Cambria said. "And whatever you do, don't drink the blood wine."

Twenty minutes later the group was seated in the back row of the sanctuary, growing restless. The pews were now filled with about fifty people come to worship or offer prayers; each one of them had drunk from the blood wine basin. Cambria began to worry her mother's warnings about the side effects of ingesting elderweed were incorrect. Her companions fidgeted nervously as they tried to keep their scarred faces hidden. They were doing quite well considering they were Descendant rebels in the house of the Faith with two Temple guards not twenty feet behind them.

Cambria scanned the sanctuary. *It's not working.* She sighed. If they were going to act, they'd have to do it soon. They were lucky to slip past the distracted front guards with their weapons hidden under their cloaks. And the sanctuary crowd only continued to grow, filling in beside them. Someone was bound to notice them. In the pew behind her, Taro Kine and Spade were whispering about rushing the guards. If they did that, all hopes of going in unseen were off. They were all going to die because her stupid plan didn't work.

"Look," Geyer whispered.

In the front of the sanctuary, a man stood up holding his stomach and shaking his head. He seized over, his face red, and then sprinted for the door. More people began to shift uneasily in their seats. Someone groaned. Two more headed for the exit. Five rows ahead of them a woman stood up and raced for the door, but she didn't make it. She vomited on the floor. Then the place erupted. People heaved in their seats. The sound of flatulence and retching filled the holy sanctuary as people scrambled over each other for the exits, climbing over pews and slipping in the vomit and excrement that was spreading across the marble floors.

Beside her, Cambria's companions grimaced in disgust; Solvan Ra looked ready to be sick himself. Behind them, the door guards raced forward to control the pandemonium. They cursed at the smell and barked orders under covered noses. They slid around, pulling people off the sanctuary floor, their once white uniforms stained brown.

Geyer turned to Cambria, horrified. She shrugged. Her mother had been right, after all.

"Now," Spade whispered. The seven companions hurried to the back of the sanctuary and slipped through the unguarded doors. A long hallway stretched ahead. They stepped over white stone decorated with intricate patterns. Above them, the vaulted ceiling was so high Cambria could throw her shoe and never come close to reaching it. They had made it into the inner Temple of the Faith.

Cambria's moment of triumph vanished an instant later when four Temple guards came around a corner ahead. The armored men stopped fifty yards ahead, gazing at the cloaked intruders.

Geyer pulled his hood back, revealing a head of wild hair

and a white-blond beard. "Alright," he said, drawing his long sword. "The easy part's over."

Aeilus Haemon woke early and climbed out of bed without his normal dose of blood. Anticipation gave his old body new life. Today would mark the crowning achievement of his reign as Highfather of Terene. With the boy's pure blood under his control, they would no longer depend on the weak Descendant offerings. And Vorrel's dark blood would eradicate the Descendants' threat to mankind while gaining a powerful, obedient workforce. Today, the Faith would usher in a new era of peace.

Haemon donned his ceremonial garb of white robes and his red miter, checking his reflection in the mirror. When had he gotten so old? It seemed not so long ago he had been a young Father of the Faith, working his way up to the council to make a real difference in the world. And now here he was. He stood proud; each and every line in his face had been earned.

Guards waited outside his door.

"Have the Fathers been gathered?" Haemon asked.

"Yes, Highfather," a guard said with a bow. "They await your presence in the inner sanctuary."

"Good." Haemon smiled. Let them wait. He waved a hand dismissing the guard. "Get the boy. See that he's ready."

The guard nodded and marched down the hall. Haemon crossed the other way to the inner sanctuary. Walking was slow and painful, but that would soon end. In a few minutes, he would feel the boy's pure blood pumping through him.

Guards pushed open the heavy doors to the inner sanctuary. Early morning light trickled in through the golden dome above like a heavenly smile. Guards lined the walls of the circular room, while the council members waited in the pews. All but Father Turney, of course.

Haemon walked past the row of pews to the center of the sanctuary. The Curors had already set up a table on the stage.

Vorrel's tools for the blood draw and one bottle of dark blood laid open for all to see its shadowy contents. There would be no more hiding their work from the Fathers. Hemo had bestowed his blessing; their acts were justified.

"Fathers of the Faith," Haemon called. "Thank you for accepting my invitation to witness this historical moment."

"Invitation?" Father Kent scoffed. "We were pulled from our beds by our own guards."

"I apologize for any inconvenience, Father Kent. But the matter could not wait." *Frightened children. Burying their heads in tradition, afraid of the slightest change.* Couldn't they see their current lifestyle was unsustainable? He would show them, make them understand. And if any still refused to see the light…

The Highfather stood upright, addressing the scattered council members.

"For centuries now, people have turned from the Faith, belief in Hemo has fallen. And not just in the outer regions of Terene —the northern hills and the wastelands to the south—but in the Temple city. People whisper blasphemy, claiming Hemo has abandoned his people. And they turn to wickedness."

The Fathers reacted to his speech with tired looks. They'd heard his lectures before, but this time wasn't just talk and prayers. This time he had the answer.

"But today, Fathers, our faith is vindicated. I give you proof that Lord Hemo's blessings have returned."

The Fathers sat up, leaning forward in the pews. Haemon beamed. Then, he raised his hand in a dramatic sweep.

"Bring in the boy!"


WITH A FINAL GROAN, the last Temple guard slid down Taro Kine's swords to the floor. The third level hallway was now clear. Cambria winced at another stack of dead bodies—deaths she had caused by bringing the rebels here.

"You really need two swords?" Geyer asked as they dragged

the guards' bodies from the hallway into an open room. Cambria dropped to her knees and scrubbed blood from the floor with a torn piece of a guard's shirt.

"I am twice as good as you, old man," Taro Kine said, spinning his two blades in his hands.

Geyer shook his head. "Show off."

Spade pulled the map from her pocket and studied as she walked. "The dungeon is through there." Spade pointed to a doorway. They pulled it open, revealing a long stairway descending into darkness.

"Great," Geyer grumbled. "More stairs."

"Hurry, we don't have long before someone finds the bodies."

Racing down the stairs, Cambria couldn't help but be impressed at the Descendant rebels' skills. Geyer, she had seen in action, but the others had dispatched the guards they met in quick aggressive fashion, moving faster than seemed possible. If they were a hundred instead of seven, perhaps they'd stand a chance.

"Does your map show another exit?" Geyer called from behind as he limped his way down the stairs. "We're going to have an army waiting for us if we have to go back through the front door."

"One worry at a time," Taro Kine said. "You didn't think we'd get *this* far."

"Our luck will run out eventually," Geyer said. "Then we'll see if you're still smiling."

"I feel much safer having you with us, Geyer. When the guards come, we all have someone we can outrun."

The light grew dark as they moved down the windowless stairway. They stopped at the bottom, met by a steel door. Mace Ren tried the handle. It was locked.

"Check the bodies at the top of the stairs," Spade said to Solvan Ra. "One of them must have a key."

The Descendant rebel raced up the stairs just as Geyer

reached the bottom, out of breath. Taro Kine punched three hard knocks on the steel door. The sound echoed through the stairwell like a warning bell to the entire Temple. Everyone waited as the ringing metal faded to silence.

"It was worth a try," Taro Kine shrugged.

"Cambria," Geyer said, coming beside her. "Once the fighting starts, I want you to run. Take Ara if you can, but don't wait for us and don't try to fight. Just run."

Cambria wanted to say she wouldn't leave them but she knew she would be of little use in a fight. And she was scared. She hated to admit it to herself, but she was scared.

"Cambria," Geyer said.

Cambria squeezed her hands to stop them from shaking. "I will."

"Good girl."

Geyer raised his sword at the sound of hurried footsteps. It was only Solvan Ra. "Got 'em," he said, holding up a large ring of keys.

On the third key, the steel door unlocked and they pushed their way into the Temple dungeon. Cambria could hardly see in the darkness, but was immediately hit by the smell of feces and rotting flesh. How could anyone survive down here?

Edwar Kel took the single lantern down from the wall and they moved through the dungeon. He held the lantern up to the cell's rusty metal bars, and shapes withdrew from the light. It took a few moments for Cambria to recognize the shapes were human. The prisoners were pale and malnourished, their hair wild and filled with lice. Their healing blood had kept the Descendants alive in conditions where Raw Bloods would have died long ago. Cambria gasped at the sight; there must be over a hundred prisoners crammed into these cells.

"It's okay," she said. "We're not here to hurt you."

The faces that looked back were smeared with dirt and grime. They didn't look human. That was probably part of the Faith's plan. It was easier to justify torturing creatures.

"Ara," Geyer called. His voice brought her back to the mission. "Ara, where are you?"

The group spread out, peering into the cells, calling Ara's name. But there was no answer.

Cambria came upon a small cell between the others. It stood empty while the others were packed with Descendants. The floor of the cell was marked with drying blood. Her heart sank. Somehow she knew it; like the sudden stillness when a patient slips away.

Ara was gone.

EVERYONE in the sanctuary turned to the side door, but nothing happened. Haemon snarled at the moment's loss of grandeur. *Can't those bumbling guards do anything right?* Tension filled the room, and Haemon was ready to charge off the stage and escort the boy in himself when the doors finally opened. Two guards entered, dragging an unconscious shape behind him. Father Claudia gasped at the sight of the lifeless child.

Haemon fumed. *What had they done to him?* The boy had looked bad the previous night, but he had been fed and rested since then. Surely his blood would have healed him by now. Instead, his guards carried a corpse into the Temple's inner sanctuary.

"Who is that?" Father Kent's voice echoed through the domed room.

"This is Carmine's Descendant boy," Haemon said, his bluster fading. "With the blood of…Royals."

The guards lifted the body onto the table. The boy was unconscious; the bones of his rib cage showing beneath a chest that didn't rise.

"Is he even alive?" asked Father Loren.

Haemon crossed to the table and jabbed a finger at the guard. "What is the meaning of this?" he demanded in a low voice. "What did you do to him?"

"Nothing, Father," the guard stuttered. "We found him like this. He was hanging upside down in his cell."

The bones in Haemon's hands cracked as they squeezed into fists. The boy's skin was a pale blue. Fresh scars marked both his wrists and across his neck. *How could he do this? What happened to all the blood!*

Murmurs filled the sanctuary. Father Kent stood in his pew. "We've seen enough, Haemon."

"No!" Haemon barked. Anger twisted his face; brittle teeth scraped against each other. "Sit down!"

More gasps from the insolent Fathers.

*This is my moment of victory. I will take it if I have to squeeze every last drop from this cursed corpse!*

"Cut him open," Haemon said to Vorrel.

"Highfather, if he's even alive…he's too weak…"

Haemon grabbed the Curor by his robe and pulled him close. "Give me whatever blood is left in his wretched body or I'll see you bathed in your own dark blood."

CAMBRIA LEANED against the bars of the empty cell. A Descendant watched her from the next cell over. His face was darkened by dirt and a wild gray beard, but the man's eyes shown clear in the dim light.

"They took him," the man said. "Not an hour ago."

"Where?" Cambria asked. She moved to the man's cell. "Where is he?"

"Cambria," Geyer called. The old knight shuffled toward them, but Cambria did not back away.

"Let us out," the prisoner said. "We will help you."

Geyer frowned at the sight of the man, but there was something there. He must have seen it, too. Some strength beneath the starved body.

"Who are you?" Cambria asked.

"My name…is Tar Shen."

"Tar Shen?" Spade called. She crossed the dungeon toward them. Her eyes wide as she studied the old Descendant. Her face softened and she leaned pressed against the cell bars. "Is it really you? You're alive."

A weary smile crossed the prisoner's face. "Ressa." The word escaped his lips in a whisper. "Still fighting the good fight, I see."

Spade reached in and grabbed the old man's hand, cradling it in her own. "Until it is finished."

"Then let that be today."

Footsteps clattered in the distance. Boots charging down the stairs—lots of them.

"Our friends are here," Solvan Ra called. The rebel ran to the steel door and pressed his back against it. "Tell me there's another way out."

The steel screeched, but Solvan Ra held it closed, leaning against it with all his weight. The other rebels moved to the door, tossing off their cloaks and drawing their weapons.

Geyer and Cambria locked eyes; there was nothing to say. This was the end, and they both knew it. She fell in beside him, pulling the small knife from her belt.

"For Ara," he said.

"For Ara," she repeated.

The door cracked open; angry voices yelled in. An army of Temple guards, packed into the stairs.

"Can't hold it much longer," Solvan Ra called.

"Open the cells," Tar Shen said. "We can fight with you."

"You've been in here too long," Spade said. "You're too weak."

Every Descendant in the dungeon stepped forward to the cell doors. There were at least a hundred men and women. Though their faces were sickly and the rags they wore barely clung to their thin frames, there was something in their eyes. A clearness of focus. A hidden strength ready to explode.

"Not anymore," Tar Shen said.

# 36

Vorrel switched to yet another vein in the boy's arm. The small amount of blood he found dribbled through the tube and dropped to the bottom of the glass bottle.

"What's wrong with your equipment?" Haemon shouted, no longer trying to hide his anger from the watching Fathers. If they had a problem with what he was doing, he would find others to take their place on the council.

"It's...it's not the equipment," Vorrel stammered. "It's as if all the blood has already been drained from his body."

Haemon looked from the boy's blue corpse to the glass bottle. After all he'd spent to capture this boy, he only managed to extract a few drops of the boy's blood. Haemon gripped the edge of the table for support. Somebody would pay for this.

"This is an act of Hemo," Father Shanon shouted, standing in his pew. "He's stopping this...this blasphemous act."

Murmurs of descent rattled around the sanctuary; the Fathers were growing bolder in the light of Haemon's failure.

"You've gone too far this time, Haemon," Father Claudia said. "The council will consider the repercussions of this violation of authority."

"Violation of authority?" Haemon coughed, not bothering

to hide the blood that spouted from inside his deteriorating body. "I am the authority." Anger stirred in his belly, he coughed up more blood. "Cowards. Is your faith shaken so easily?"

There was a knock at the door, and a Temple guard came in and whispered something to Vorrel.

"What is it now?" Haemon yelled. He could taste the blood in his mouth, but he was too angry to care.

"There have been reports of a skirmish in the outer sanctuary," Vorrel said. "Someone may have gotten into the Temple."

*Incompetent fools!* Haemon turned his anger on the guard, "Well, do your job and find them."

The guards nodded and left the inner sanctuary. Father Claudia moved to the door, but another guard stepped in front of her.

"Out of my way this instant," she demanded. The guard held his ground. "Haemon, remove your attack dogs."

"No one leaves this room," Haemon ordered. He lost his balance and a guard came to assist him as if he were an invalid. Haemon shoved him away. "Back!"

"This is madness," yelled Father Kent.

The room spun; a distant ringing sounded in Haemon's head. Everything was crashing down on him at once. His moment of triumph was gone. What had happened? *Hemo, what did I do wrong?*

It wasn't over yet. Haemon seized the bottle from the table and lifted it high overhead. The boy's blood trailed along the glass like a raindrop down the Temple window before finally touching Haemon's lips. One salty sip. All his calculations and sacrifice, all for this. Haemon smashed the empty bottle on the floor. Energy surged through his body. It wasn't much, but it was enough. His old bones hardened and his muscles pulled tight, straightening his curved back. For an instant, Haemon felt younger than he had in years.

The room stopped spinning but the ringing was still there. In fact, it grew louder. The Fathers backed away from the sanctuary doors. Temple guards drew their swords. A shout came from outside the room. The sounds of swords clanging on armor.

*Who would dare?*

The door burst open. Temple guards crashed into wooden pews that were centuries old. In the doorway stood a man with a scar cut into the right side of his face.

"Sorry," the Descendant said. "Are we interrupting?"

The Descendant rebel moved like the wind. He raced forward, blocking the blow of the nearest Temple guard and cutting another down with a second sword. Then more armed fighters swept into the sanctuary. Metal clanged with metal; screams of panic and pain. The Temple was under attack.

The Fathers ducked under pews as the fighting commenced. A woman fighter locked eyes with Haemon; her gaze betrayed her hatred. She pointed her sword and yelled for others to attack. A slew of dirty, half-naked wretches stormed into the sanctuary. They were scrawny and pale, but they moved with great speed and ferociousness. They leaped onto the Temple guards with their bare hands, gaining weapons with each guard that fell.

These were the Temple's own Descendants—free from their dungeon cages and attacking with an impossible strength. Aeilus Haemon turned to the lifeless boy on the table. It was all his fault. Somehow he had given away his blood, given his life to the Descendants so that Haemon would never get it. Hemo's gift, taken away.

The battle spread around the inner sanctuary. Cursed Descendants destroying everything he had built. The Highfather fumed, his newfound strength only fueling his anger. This would not be the end. Haemon would make these heathens pay.

He grabbed Vorrel and pulled him from his hiding spot. "It's time. Unleash it."

Vorrel looked back at the battle tearing up the sanctuary. "What about the Fathers…and our men?"

Haemon yelled to be heard over the noise. "Bathe the entire room in dark blood if you have to. I want these Descendants wiped out."

Vorrel hurried to the rear door. Haemon took one last look at the battle destroying his pristine sanctuary before following with his personal guard. He would be back to watch as the dark blood transformed these vermin. But first, he would make them suffer. For he still had one more weapon to use.

CAMBRIA EXPECTED the blood that came with fighting—she had seen her share of it as a doctor working in the aftermath of a duel or skirmish—but she was unprepared for the noise. Pounding metal and screams of agony echoed through the narrow hallway as Descendants collided with Temple guards. Wounded bodies hit the stone floor and then were trampled upon and tripped over. Movement slowed as bodies filled the tight corridor, but the battle was no less violent. Cambria would have covered her ears with her hands if she didn't need them to fight.

She held a dagger picked up from a dead Temple guard. He had cornered Cambria and tried to run her through when Geyer sliced the man's throat. He told her to hide, to stay out of the way, but he knew she wouldn't obey. Not while Ara was here somewhere. Not while there was even a chance he was still alive.

Cambria climbed over a dead Descendant; the man's intestines had spilled out onto the floor. Up ahead, the carnage converged around an oval doorway. Fighters from both sides flooded in and out of the doors like blood pumping to and from the heart.

Ara was through those doors, she could feel it.

Cambria stuck to the wall and stayed low, ducking under most of the fighting as she moved toward the doorway. The Descendant rebel, Solvan Ra, swung a wide blow, knocking down two Temple guards and creating an opening in the doorway. Cambria sprinted forward, slipping inside.

The inner room was another sanctuary, with rows of wooden pews circling a raised stage. A balcony hung overhead and above that the high golden dome marking the center of the Temple. Bodies piled up in the sanctuary; the wounded on both sides crawled away, toward the corners of the room. Where fighting was slow and awkward in the narrow hallways, here in the open sanctuary fighters had plenty of room to charge and hack one another to pieces. Cambria's eyes fell on the stage at the front of the room. *Ara.* Her heart leaped and then fell just as quickly. His body lay on the altar, unmoving.

*No. He can't be dead.*

Something struck Cambria's shoulder and slammed her against the wall. A guard charged past her. She turned to see Solvan Ra backed against the sanctuary door fending off the attack of two Temple guards. One guard drove his sword into the Descendant rebel's upper leg. Solvan Ra screamed in pain. He raised his sword to block the second guard's attack.

Cambria moved without thinking. She charged forward, plunging her dagger into the guard's side. She twisted the blade deeper into his organs before he backhanded her away. The guard fell to the ground, clutching his side and crying in agony. She'd severed his liver. A sickness rose in her. All this time she had carried a knife and thought of using it on her enemies, bad men who would hurt her and the ones she cared about.

Cambria dropped the bloody dagger. She couldn't take the man's life.

The guard gargled blood and reached for Cambria, seizing her pants. Cambria froze, unable to move as the man's bloody hand pulled her closer. Solvan Ra plunged his sword into the guard and the man's hands fell from Cambria like severed branches.

Cambria breathed, life returning to her body. Solvan Ra's leg gave out and he collapsed. Cambria ran to his side and pulled him away from the door as more Temple guards poured into the hallway. Their swords and armor met the wild attacks of Descendant prisoners, many of whom were fighting without weapons and holding their own.

Solvan Ra winced as she set him against the wall. "Raw Blood bastards," he cursed and looked up at Cambria. "No offense."

"Your quadricep is torn," Cambria yelled over the noise. "I don't think you can walk."

"I can still swing a sword. Help me up."

Cambria tore a strip from her shirt and pulled it tight around his leg, just above the wound. Blood sputtered out, but Solvan Ra let out only the softest groan. Cambria got under the rebel's arm and propped him up against the wall.

"We're doing well," he said, a smile on his face. "We might make it out of here, after all."

With the chaos and bloodshed exploding around her, Cambria couldn't agree. Solvan Ra smiled and said something else but the words were lost as they were hit from behind. Cambria landed with Solvan Ra on top of her. Descendants and Temple guards piled on one another, biting and punching whatever exposed skin they could find. Air squeezed out of Cambria's lungs, she tried to take a breath, but her chest was flattened from the weight. Red spots dotted her vision. She screamed but nothing came out. Then, the fighting rolled away, toppling in the other direction in a mess of screams and curses. On the floor, not two feet from her, a Descendant prisoner dug his dirty fingernails into a guard's eye socket until blood fountained over his hands. Cambria groaned and slipped out from under Solvan Ra's heavy body.

"Solvan Ra." She turned him over. His own sword protruded from his gut. His eyes were vacant. "No!"

A Temple guard stomped over his body on his way through the melee. Cambria stepped away from the dead rebel. She should run, flee the Temple while she still could.

Instead, she ran deeper into the sanctuary, toward the stage. toward Ara.

A guard stood before her, brandishing his sword. Cambria dove to the ground, rolling under the cover of the sanctuary's old wooden pews. He turned to pursue her, raising his sword. Cambria scrambled away, bumping her head on the pew, her eyes locked on the heavy metal blade that was about to chop her in half. She should have run when she had the chance. A knife flew through the air and dinged off the guard's armored back. He spun around to face a charging Spade. The rebel leader jumped into the air, covering the distance between them and coming down with a kick that sent the armored guard flying into one of his own men. Spade landed with her sword raised for more attacks. She turned to Cambria long enough to deliver a message with her eyes. *Get Ara.* Then, she spun around, locking swords with another tangle of guards, moving with speed and grace Cambria didn't think possible.

Fresh blood clung to Cambria's clothes as she crawled along the wet floor under cover of the pews. She passed bodies scattered on the ground. Some dead, some well on their way. There seemed no end to the fighting and the death toll. Cambria kept her head down and crawled until she reached the front row. She was almost there; she was going to make it.

Cambria passed the front pew and climbed to her feet, sprinting toward the stage. She stopped when she reached the altar. The table was empty. Restraints lay untied on the floor beside it. He was gone.

Cambria turned back to the sanctuary and the bloodshed claiming life after life. Only one other time had she felt so powerless.

*Ara, where are you?*


THE SWORD PASSED an inch from Geyer's head. One inch lower and he'd be dead. Such was the way of things. Luck kept some men alive while others died. But there was only so much luck given to a man and Geyer worried he'd used his up this day. He was still alive. The attacking guard didn't get a second chance. Geyer kicked him in the groin and drove his sword up under his chin. One man's luck was another's misfortune. The guard was dead before he hit the ground.

Geyer fell back against the sanctuary wall to catch his breath and take the weight off his left leg. He'd pushed through the pain for so long he was surprised the leg hadn't burst open. The battle raged all around him, with a seemingly endless supply of guards descending on the sanctuary. And for every few guards, there was a Descendant. They fought well, moving with such ferocious speed that the heavily armored Temple guards struggled to land blows. Things were going better than he expected, considering he expected them all to be dead by now.

Spade had brought the best of the Descendant rebels as well. The warriors handled their weapons like trained experts, slicing through one Temple guard after another. As many men as Geyer dispatched, Taro Kine was far ahead of him. The cocky fool and his two swords.

A knife clattered off the wall beside Geyer's head. He turned to see the thrower fall to the ground, Spade's sword in his back. She didn't even give Geyer a nod before she turned to face two more charging guards.

*Stupid*, Geyer cursed himself for not paying attention. He'd have all the time in eternity to rest if he caught a Temple guard's sword. Can't be lucky forever. Now, it was time to fight.

Geyer pushed off the wall and worked his way through the Temple guards toward the center of the sanctuary. Ara's body had been there when he first entered the sanctuary, but it was gone now. Geyer didn't know if that was good or bad, but he refused to believe Ara was dead. Callow as he was, the boy had more sense than to get himself killed. If only he'd trained the boy a little more.

"Descendant clots!" a Temple guard cursed as he fought

away Descendant attackers. Geyer recognized the man. He wore no helmet, his long braided hair flapping around as he cut through Descendants. One of Bale's men who had hunted them in the forest. The tracker. Geyer's heart beat like horse hooves in his chest as he scanned the room. Where was the Blood Knight?

Before Geyer knew it, he was pacing toward the tracker. The guard turned to him, blood splattered against his tanned face. Was he there that day in the Hidden Wood? Did his sword land the blow that killed James or Maddie?

Geyer raised his sword, pointing at the cutthroat turned Temple guard.

A wild roar erupted over the clanging metal and screams of agony. The fighting slowed; heads turned, searching for whatever had made the horrible sound. Above, in the balcony that hung over the sanctuary entrance, stood an enormous black shape. Its eyes were red as blood.

Geyer blinked, the air frozen in his chest. This was the demon of his dreams. The one he faced in the nightmares that alcohol didn't dull. This was the monster who slew James Carmine and Geyer's men. This was Bale, the Blood Knight, in his true form.

The creature leaped off the balcony and descended like a shadow. The floor trembled under his weight. Geyer caught himself, leaning heavily on his right leg. The black armor that covered the creature looked more like a part of its flesh than forged metal. The blades it welded were not daggers, but its actual fingers spread wide like talons. The face was a ghostly gray with black lines running under the skin in dark vein-like patterns.

The demon drew a long sword and in one swing, cut a nearby Descendant in half. He turned and swung again, this time slicing through two Descendants and a Temple guard. His red eyes took in the blood around him, and a smile broke out on his ghostly face. Four more fell dead at the Blood Knight's hand.

Both Descendants and guards fled, toppling over one another, clearing away from the monster.

CAMBRIA SCRAMBLED AWAY from the sanctuary, the cacophony of battle fading with each step. So much destruction and bloodshed. Wounded men and women dying, while she ran away. There was nothing she could do; there were too many. She was just one girl.

And she had to find him. *Ara, please be alive.*

Cambria raced through the Temple hall, expecting to hear a flurry of guard boots chasing after her. But none came. She looked left and right as the corridor split, looking for traces of Ara. He couldn't have gotten far. Even he couldn't have healed so quickly from that amount of blood loss.

A faint thud echoed through the hallway. Down the hall to the right. Cambria sprinted to the open doorway.

Cold air hit her like a wall of ice. She skidded to a stop. Bottles of blood lined the room. The blood of a hundred tortured Descendants. Cambria had seen the Temple's dungeons and the state of its prisoners. All that suffering, to pay for bigger palaces.

Red flashed in the corner of the room. A Temple Curor stood before a large closet of heavy wood that housed his robes and medical equipment. He was bent over, filling a bag with scalpel blades, syringes, swathes of cloth, and transfusion tubes. Tools designed to heal that had been reshaped to harm by the warped practices of the Faith's blood doctors.

Cambria stepped into the cold room, her hands balled into fists.

The Curor spun around, startled. Wide eyes looked down a crooked nose at her. "Stop! You can't be in here."

A golden heart insignia adorned the breast of the Curor's robes. This was the Temple's head Curor; the one that experimented on Descendants. Vorrel.

Cambria stepped forward. "Where is he?"

"You're not a Descendant, are you?" Vorrel narrowed his gaze. "Who are you?"

"If you harmed him in any way…"

"You've come for the Descendant boy, is that it? Well, you're too late."

Cambria stiffened. "You're lying."

Vorrel cocked his head, a grin on his face. Pleasure at another's pain. Curors brought dishonor to everything Cambria believed in; everything her parents had taught her.

Vorrel reached back into his bag and drew his scalpel. The sharp blade looked comfortable in his bony hands. "I'm going to cut you open and watch you bleed out just like one of them."


THOUGH FIGHTING PERSISTED on the outer ring of the sanctuary, those in the center retreated for cover as the Blood Knight killed anything close to it. Its long sword cleaved a Descendant's arm. A Temple guard scrambling away was snatched up, his head caught in the creature's claws; his neck twisted with a harsh snap, and his lifeless body fell to the ground.

The long-haired guard laughed as people fled in fear. "Kill them, Bale," he said. "Kill every last one!"

The Blood Knight's roar shook the sword in his hands, but Geyer held his ground, leaning on his front leg. The ghostly face turned toward him, black lines running like cracks in the ashen skin. Geyer twisted his sword in his hands; the wheel of fate spun at the hilt of his sword. Good or bad fortune, he was done running. If this was his time to die, so be it.

Geyer pointed his sword at the demon before him. "You remember me, assassin?"

Red eyes bared down on him; nostrils flared. Was there the flash of recognition on the once human face? With long knife-like fingers, the Blood Knight tapped its chest above the heart.

"That's right," Geyer said. "Now, I'm here to finish what I started."

The Blood Knight lifted its long sword and charged Geyer with surprising speed. Geyer barely got his sword up in time. The blow rattled the old knight's bones, and he stumbled back, his bad leg buckling under him. Somehow, he stayed on his feet.

Geyer had blocked the blade, and it nearly broke his arm. If the creature made contact he'd be cut in half. One mistake and it was over.

The Blood Knight charged again and swung with savage anger.

*Focus.* Geyer pushed the fear from his mind. *Watch its shoulder.*

Geyer sidestepped the first blow, got his sword up for the next two strikes but could not hold on. His sword flew from his hands. An unarmed Geyer faced the Blood Knight as it brought its sword back for a killing blow.

"Go on. Do it, you ugly bastard."

The black figure roared in pain, barring its fangs. The Blood Knight spun around, a line of black blood running down the center of its back.

"Sorry to interrupt," Taro Kine said, spinning a sword in each hand. He grinned at Geyer. "But I can't let you have all the fun."

The Blood Knight swung angrily. Taro Kine ducked the blow and stabbed his sword into the Blood Knight's chest. A wound that would have killed any mortal man. But the Blood Knight kept coming.

The smile vanished from Taro Kine's face as the Blood Knight swung again and again. Taro Kine blocked two massive blows, but the third knocked a sword from his hand. He raised the remaining sword with both hands against the oncoming blow; the sword shattered to pieces.

The Blood Knight rammed its sword into Taro Kine's side. Then, it swung its claw and batted the Descendant rebel across the room. Taro Kine slammed into the wall and crumbled to the floor, his face matted with blood.

"Nooooo!" Geyer yelled.

The Blood Knight swung its sword back to Geyer. The blade split Geyer at the chest.

VORREL STEPPED FORWARD, the scalpel pointed at Cambria. How many veins had he cut open with that instrument? How many people had this monster bled? She should be afraid. She was that same helpless little girl sitting at the riverside while her parents died of gray fever. Hadn't she learned by now? The world was filled with disease and injustice and so many things beyond her control. But seeing this Curor, this medical fraud who had hurt so many, Cambria was just plain mad.

"That's a wide head blade," Cambria said, nodding to the three-inch blade in Vorrel's hand. "Uncommon in traditional scalpels."

Vorrel narrowed his eyes, studying her. Still, he stepped forward, wielding the scalpel. She was just a little girl. No real threat.

"A fine point scalpel is superior," Cambria continued. "It makes a less obtrusive incision in the patient, allowing for swifter healing after surgery."

A grin spread across Vorrel's face, flashing teeth that pointed in every direction. Poor dental alignment. Something Descendant blood didn't correct.

"If you don't want them to bleed out," he said. "But that's the whole purpose of cutting open a Descendant."

Cambria tensed but didn't move. The lab door was open behind her but she stayed her ground, watching the Curor approach. The room's cold air moving through her lungs.

"You see, these animals are difficult to work with," Vorrel said. "A simple incision starts to close within minutes, and then you have to cut them all over again. A Descendant with particularly good blood, you might have to cut eight times in order to fill a full bottle of blood. This blade, however," he held the scalpel up toward Cambria's face. "A cut with my blade and that wound won't be closing any time soon."

Vorrel swung the blade at Cambria's jugular. She leaned back in time to feel the air of the blow pass by her skin. The Curor grunted and swung again. Cambria dropped to the ground, the scalpel passing high above her head.

Cambria pulled her own blade from her belt and drove it into the exposed skin above Vorrel's shoe. The Curor screamed in pain, his scalpel falling to the ground. He hobbled back, crashing into this desk

"Ahhh! You filth! What have you done?"

"I've severed your ankle cord," Cambria said. She holstered her blade and picked up Vorrel's own instrument. The flat blade was scratched from years of use. "Good thing it wasn't with this blade."

She sliced Vorrel along the torso, tearing his red robe and opening his skin above the navel.

"Ahhh," Vorrel howled and fell back against the closet, lab equipment shattering on the floor. "Now that one will be difficult to seal."

Whimpering, Vorrel reached for a nearby shelf, his fingers searching for a bottle of blood.

"No," Cambria said. She sliced his outstretched wrist. Vorrel grabbed at the wound, blood sprayed through his fingers. "No easy cure."

The Curor's robe was wet with blood, as was the floor beneath him. Three open wounds, spilling him open. His face was already turning pale from the blood loss. The doctor in her wanted to spring to action and close the wounds fast. The rest of her wanted to see this man suffer for his crimes.

"Help me," Vorrel squealed, clutching his wrist. "I'm dying."

Cambria shook her head. "Not if you're treated soon. You seal the wounds and stop the bleeding and you'll live."

Vorrel bent over, gasping as blood continued to pour from his wrist and stomach. His face now a pale mask of fear.

"You're the head Curor of the Faith, surely you can tend to some simple cuts."

Veins protruded from Vorrel's neck as he gritted his teeth. "You dirty clot!" The Curor charged her, but there was little strength in the attack. Cambria kicked him square in the chest. Vorrel staggered back into the closet, pulling his robes down on top of him. He cried in pain. "I need blood. Give it to me!"

Cambria looked to the shelves of blood covering the walls of his room. There was enough here to buy a kingdom. To save one as well.

The price was too high.

"That's not your blood to take."

She grabbed his bag of medical tools and tossed them into the closet with him. "Save yourself."

She locked the closet door.

GEYER GRITTED his teeth and looked down expecting to see himself laid open. But the cut wasn't deep, a single red line across his chest. He was still alive. *Lucky, fool.*

The only reason the Blood Knight hadn't finished the job was because of the Descendants. The freed prisoners hurled knives and shields at the monster, giving Geyer time to recover. The objects hitting the creature didn't hurt it, but did make it angry. The Blood Knight spun wildly, swinging his sword in every direction trying to attack everything at once. Whatever that creature had been transformed into, it didn't come with a lot of brains.

It picked up a shield and heaved it across the room, knocking over two Temple guards who had surrounded the wounded rebel Edwar Kel.

"Stop, you idiot," the tracker said, stepping in front of the creature and waving his arms. "Kill the Descendants."

The Blood Knight turned toward the shouting and lopped off the long-haired guard's head with one stroke. The head landed in the upper balcony.

There was no more time to recover; Geyer had to act now, before the creature killed him and everyone else in the room. He searched the debris around him. His sword lay to his right, at the foot of a shattered pew. *Get up. If you can breathe, you can fight.*

Geyer climbed to his feet. The creature turned toward him, seemingly happy to have a single target. The long black sword swung toward Geyer's head. Geyer saw it coming and slid under the blade. He rolled away from the creature, scrambling on the ground toward his sword.

*Still alive. Keep fighting.*

Geyer reached his sword and spun, holding it out to the Blood Knight. His heart drummed against the wall of his bloody chest. His muscles ached; he could barely breathe. The battle continued to rage on the outskirts of the room. Despite overwhelming odds, the Descendants fought on. Prisoners who had been starved and tortured for years were overthrowing the most powerful army in Terene.

This was the kind of battle they wrote songs about.

Geyer stayed crouched, his sword extended; the wheel on its hilt spinning slowly, deciding where to settle. "I stabbed you in the heart and you didn't die," Geyer said.

"Dieeee," the Blood Knight snarled in a gravely voice.

Geyer reached his left hand back to the boot of his back leg. This was it. He'd only get one chance.

"This time, I won't aim for such a small target."

With a ferocious roar, the Blood Knight charged, its longsword slicing down through the air. Geyer lunged under the blade and drove his own sword up at the creature, but the Blood Knight was too fast; its left hand caught Geyer's sword, stopping it mid-thrust. Black blood dripped from the creature's taloned hand, but it held the sword as if it were encased in stone.

"Eeeat...youuu...heaart," the Blood Knight growled, pulling Geyer closer to its open jaws. Geyer strained to hold on to his sword with his right hand as he was lifted into the air, the fangs now inches from his face.

Geyer stared into the creatures red eyes. Anything human had gone; there was nothing left but mindless anger.

"Demon or not," Geyer grunted. "You still only have two hands."

Geyer swung his left hand up, thrusting the dagger through the Blood Knight's open mouth and into its brain. Rivers of black blood ran from the creature's mouth and eyes. It howled in choked anguish.

Tossed to the ground, Geyer's legs collapsed. The black longsword clattered to the ground. On his back, Geyer faced the sanctuary's golden dome ceiling. The creature hovered over him like a cloud of death. Then, it crumbled to the floor.

Geyer couldn't move; there was no more fight in him. He turned his head to face the creature and saw that it was over. Blood pooled from its ghostly face. The fire in its eyes extinguished.

The clash of swords echoed all around him. Descendants fighting a seemingly endless army of Temple guards. Maybe they could still win, maybe it had always been impossible. Out of instinct, he felt for his sword, but his hand came up empty. He stopped searching and simply lay there, his muscles seizing up, consciousness slipping. He'd done his part. He'd killed the monster. Geyer closed his eyes and let fate decide the rest.

# 37

Ara leaned against the wall for support as he moved down the corridor. His head swam, bordering on unconsciousness, and his legs wobbled like they hadn't been used in years. Still, Ara pushed himself on, surprised he was still alive.

He had made the Descendant prisoner Tar Shen promise to take every last drop of his blood—leaving nothing for the Highfather. They tied him upside down against the bars and slit his wrist first. Prisoners passed around dinner bowls, each partaking in his blood. He felt his strength drain out of him until he could barely stay conscious. Then, Tar Shen had slit his throat.

Ara thought that was the end of it. Then, through the black of nothingness, he heard the Highfather's angry voice and knew they had failed.

Ara didn't open his eyes, even when the doors first burst open and the fighting began. He listened, on the brink of consciousness, trying to interpret the battle raging around him. Descendant prisoners fought against Temple guards.

Then, he sat up and saw Cambria and Geyer. They were still alive, and they had come for him.

Ara had tried to get up, to run to them. He must have blacked out again because he awoke on the marble floor under the table. He touched his throat and felt the small scar where he had been bled out. How had he not died? He needed time to recover, time for his body to make more blood. Then he remembered the Highfather's words about poisoning everyone with this dark blood. His friends and the other Descendants were in danger. Ara needed to stop the Highfather.

Ara crawled toward the back door the Highfather and the Curor had escaped through. His lower body was heavy and useless, like pulling a coat of armor. Eventually, he was able to push off his toes. Ara reached the handle of the back door and tried to pull himself up. He woke on the floor. The sound of the battle echoed around him. His friends, fighting for him. Ara pulled himself to his feet and leaned against the wall, inching his way down the hall.

Voices sounded down the corridor ahead of Ara. He hoped it was not a reinforcement of Temple guards. He was in no position to fight; he could barely stay upright. He held his breath as the voices carried out of sight. Ara pushed onward. He wasn't sure how long he walked or how many times he passed out and woke up on the floor.

The light grew brighter and the corridor opened to an atrium. A large stone fountain stood in the center of the atrium. Letting go of the wall, Ara fell to the ground and crawled toward it. The water was cool in his cupped hands. It hit his lips and his mouth came alive. Water ran through his body like life itself. His muscles tightened, his vision cleared. Ara drank until he was able to stand on his own, his body using the water as fuel. He felt his heart pumping new blood through his body, the veins pouring like new rivers through a dry landscape.

His body called out for rest, his eyes growing heavy. But there was no time. He could walk and that would have to be enough. He had to stop the Highfather.

Ara shuffled through the hallway, leaning on the wall for support. The Temple was enormous. Stone passages opened in every direction. The chances of him finding the Highfather…

Ara stopped. Voices called ahead behind an open door. A chill washed through Ara as he recognized the angry voice.

"Hurry," the Highfather ordered. "Fill it up."

Ara inched closer and peered through the door. The Highfather stood in the middle of the room, barking orders while two Temple guards filled a wheelbarrow with bottles of black liquid. *Dark blood.*

A bottle slipped in a guard's hand and he lunged down, catching it before it hit the ground. The room stood in silence.

The Highfather scowled at the guard.

"Sorry, Father."

"You've seen what happens to those exposed to the dark blood," the Highfather warned. He waved to the wheelbarrow. "Take this up to the balcony and drop it on the sanctuary. I want all those cursed Descendants transformed."

"But what about our men? They're still in there fighting."

"They too will serve as our dark-blooded warriors."

Ara couldn't let that happen. *Think.* He looked around for a weapon, something to fight with. He'd have little chance against two guards in the best of circumstances, let alone unarmed and in his weakened condition. But sometimes you didn't have time to plan. Sometimes, you just had to wing it. Ara stepped inside, steadying himself in the doorway. "I won't let you poison all those people."

"You?" the Highfather snarled at the sight of Ara. "But you were dead."

"Yes." Ara nodded, his mind racing through the problem before him. There had to be a solution. The guards stepped away from the wheelbarrow, circling the boy. The Highfather scowled with such hate, his face as red as his pointy hat, his white robe, no longer so pristine.

"Hemo brought me back," Ara said.

The guards stopped. The Highfather's face contorted, his brow bending under a raging storm. "Blasphemy!"

"You're wrong," Ara said. "You've always been wrong. Hemo

brought me back to tell you. He is ashamed of the evils you have done in his name."

The Highfather's eyes flickered. Ara saw it, written beneath the lines of the old man's face. Uncertainty.

"You lie."

"You said yourself I was dead."

The guards were watching the Highfather, waiting. If there was anyone they possibly feared more than him, it was their Lord Hemo.

"Descendant deceiver!" the Highfather shouted. "Hemo didn't bring you back."

Ara tilted his head, his face questioning. "Who else could? Who else has that kind of power?"

The Highfather's mouth twitched. He looked ready to explode.

*Keep stalling.* He had to buy his friends time. Ara stepped farther into the room, as if the armed Temple guards were no threat to him. His legs wobbled under him. *Steady.* He breathed, willing his blood to his legs, giving himself strength. *Keep him talking.*

"Why do you hate us so much?"

"Why?" the Highfather's eyes lit with rage. "Because I know my history. I know what this world looks like for mankind when the Royals rule; when we were slaves under your boots. I will not let that happen again."

"But you're doing exactly what the Royals did. You're enslaving an entire race of people."

"Better you than us."

"It doesn't have to be one or the other. We could have lived in peace."

The Highfather scoffed. "Then you don't know your history. There is always a dominant power. There are those who serve, and there are those of us destined to rule. The only reason your kind still exists is to serve us."

The words of a tyrant. He used his power to make others

suffer and he had done it under the guise of faith. Ara shook his head stepping forward.

"You've deceived yourself. It's a shame. All this power, all this knowledge at your fingertips, and you can still be so wrong."

The Highfather smiled, his confidence returning. "You think you've won? Because of the small revolt in the sanctuary? Poor boy, your faith is misplaced."

Ara thought of his friends. Briton, who rescued him from Castle Carmine, who died trying to save him. Geyer, who never abandoned him, who fought for him now against the entire Temple army. And Cambria, he smiled, glad to have seen her once more, though, it was for the last time. The odds had always been against them, their defeat assured. But it had been worth fighting.

"You're wrong," Ara said, standing proud before the Highfather of the Faith. "I know exactly where to put my faith."

"Kill him!" the Highfather yelled. The guards drew their swords, the metal reflected the light from the stained glass window. Another second and they'd be upon him.

"You want blood?" Ara breathed, summoning strength from what blood he had left. "It's all yours."

He charged forward and kicked the wheelbarrow. It flipped over hitting the Highfather at the legs and taking the old man down. Bottles shattered open; dark blood splashed everywhere, covering the Highfather and staining his white robes. The Highfather screamed tearing at the blood on his face and in his eyes. More glass crashed as he kicked the wheelbarrow off of him. Dark blood spilled across the floor, running over Ara's bare feet.

The guards screamed and retreated. They ran out the door as a wave of blood swept their way.

The Highfather shrieked. "Help meeeee!"

On the floor, rolling in dark blood, the Highfather's body contorted. Bones jutted out of his skin, bending him in strange angles. Black veins bubbled on his face, and his skin faded to gray. He looked at Ara with eyes that bled.

The guards covered their mouths and tore down the hallway, their boots fading fast.

Ara looked down at the pool of dark blood that covered his feet. Whatever was happening to the Highfather would happen to him to; he could feel it coming, growing inside him.

"Ara!" Cambria stood in the doorway, her eyes wide as she took in the scene. "Get out of there!"

The Highfather's cries of pain shifted to a roar. A clawed hand splashed into the wet floor as he pushed himself to his feet. His skull protruded through his bald, gray head like spikes. "I... I'llll...killlll you...alllll," he growled.

"No," Ara said. "This ends now."

Ara charged forward, splashing through the river of dark blood. He collided into the creature and knocked him back through the stained glass window. The glass shattered under the weight and the Highfather flew into the outside air.

His beastly howl descended from the Temple and then cut short. The Highfather's grotesque form hung impaled on a statue. Black blood dripped down the stone figure's longsword that stuck through the Highfather's heart.

It was over.

Ara collapsed to the floor, sliding in dark blood, his vision darkening.

"Ara!" Cambria screamed.

"Stay back," Ara murmured. "The blood...don't let it... infect you."

But Cambria didn't heed his warning. She charged into the room, splashing through the poison to his side.

"Cambria, no," Ara said, his consciousness fading.

"I'm here," Cambria said. She grabbed Ara by the shirt and dragged him across the room. "I'm right here, Ara. I'm with you."

But Ara could feel the poison blood on his feet. Warm and wet.

Cambria set Ara down in the hallway. She ripped off his shirt and then the rest of his clothes. She wiped his face and arms. Then she scrubbed his feet clean. She was talking to him, but he couldn't make out the words. It was all he could do to stay conscious, to not give into the darkness enclosing him.

Ara tried to focus. Cambria's freckled face hovered over his. Her eyes concentrating on her work. "You came for me," Ara mumbled.

Cambria tore her shirt, wiping Ara's naked body.

Ara didn't even have the strength to blush. If this was the end, he couldn't think of a better way to go.

Then, there was another voice. The speaker stood at Ara's side. "You two pick a hell of a time to celebrate."

Ara opened his eyes. *Geyer.*

"Help me get him clean," Cambria said. "We have to hurry."

Geyer picked up Ara's naked body and carried him down the hallway.

"Geyer, you're alive," Ara murmured. "Does that mean…"

"Yes," Geyer said. "Fate knows how, but we won."

They ran through the Temple halls as fast as Geyer's leg would allow. Ara bounced up and down in the old knight's arms. The bodies of a few Temple guards lay scattered on the floor.

A moment later Geyer dropped him into a fountain, submerging him in the cold water. Hands worked him over as Cambria and Geyer scrubbed him clean with torn clothes. But Ara knew it was too late. He felt some of the dark blood in his body, felt it mixing into his own blood like heavy tar.

They pulled him out and dried him off. Eventually, the world returned to Ara. He could sit up on his own, no longer surrendering to unconsciousness.

"That was a brave and stupid thing you did, Ara, destroying all that poison," Geyer said. The knight tore a banner of the Faith from the wall and wrapped it around Ara. "I've come to expect nothing less from you." Geyer smiled, but there was fatigue on his face.

Ara still couldn't believe it was true. They'd won. It felt

strange to no longer be running. To be sitting in the heart of the Temple of the Faith.

How in the world had they pulled it off?

People passed in the halls; Descendants caring for their wounded. Temple guards marched in a line, hands resting on their heads in surrender. So many had died, was there anything left?

"Spade and the others?" Ara asked.

"She's alive, as is Mace Ren. Taro Kine's in bad shape, but it looks like he'll pull through. The Descendants are sharing their blood with the injured. Solvan Ra and Edward Kel are gone."

Ara nodded and reached his hand out to Cambria who was sitting on the edge of the fountain. She watched him like a doctor, looking for signs of illness. Ara took her hand.

"Thank you, for coming for me," Ara said. "Both of you."

Cambria forced a smile, and a tear ran down her perfectly freckled face. "We're even."

"Well, *we're* certainly not even," Geyer said. "I think that's four times now I've saved your life. I'm still waiting for that to come around."

Ara chuckled. "I thought knights didn't charge for their noble deeds, *Sir Geyer.*"

"Hey now, boy. Just because I lose my mind and do one foolish thing, doesn't give you the right to start calling me names."

They sat in silence for a moment. No one needed to speak. They each knew how close they'd come to losing one another. Ara couldn't help but wish Briton could be there in that moment. It didn't feel complete without him. He supposed it never would.

Geyer grunted and rubbed his left leg. "That's enough sitting around for me. I better go check on that fool Taro Kine. Make sure he's not telling everyone that he won this battle single-handed."

As he limped down the hallway, the old knight seems to stand taller.

Ara stayed with Cambria on the fountain's edge. Her hair and clothes were wet. The boots she'd run into the room with were gone. Her hands lay folded in her lap, slightly trembling.

"How do you feel?" Ara asked Cambria. She'd risked exposure to the blood to save him. If anything happened to her…

"I can't stop shaking," she said. "But I think I'm okay. The blood…I don't think it got on me."

Ara sighed with relief.

"How about you?" Cambria asked, studying him as she would a sick patient. "It was on you. Do you feel any different?"

Ara wasn't sure. He'd felt something on the floor of the room, like a creature climbing into his body. Had it all been in his mind? He wasn't transforming into a monster like the Highfather. Maybe his blood had saved him. Or maybe it just took longer to take hold.

Ara looked down at the banner wrapped around his body. "I'll feel a whole lot better once I get some clothes on."

Cambria laughed. "Me, too."

But neither of them moved. They stayed silent for a long time, the full weight of the past few days coming down on them. They had taken on the Faith and the entire Temple guard and somehow survived. The Highfather was gone, but that wasn't the end of it. Terene was a big place and there was always another noble lord or Father ready to claim his place. Ara and Cambria sat together for a long time, not knowing what came next.

For now, it felt good just to rest.

# PART IV

———————

## THE EDGE OF THE WORLD

# 38

---

*"We live now for future generations. May they learn from our mistakes and shape a better world."*

---

Ara closed *The Last Writings of King Garian Kovar* and rubbed his eyes. Geyer had retrieved the necklace containing the tiny book when he sent for Briton's body to be recovered. Briton had carried the book with them throughout their journey, always hoping to find some secret in the king's final diary, something that pointed to the source of the Royals' blood. But the book was mostly a confession.

In the end, Garian was ashamed of how his people treated the Raw Bloods, and he feared their eventual revolt, which he saw as justice. In so many ways, it mirrored the Descendant rebellion. Maybe the Highfather was right, no matter who was in power, some lessons are never learned.

*Kovar*, Ara repeated the king's name. He leaned back in his chair, trying to grab hold of something hovering in his mind. Light shined through the stained glass windows, bathing the Temple library in a warm, red and gold hue. There were more books on one wall of this library than a person could read in a lifetime.

Briton would have loved this place.

Ara closed the book and locked it in its case. As much as he'd enjoyed his days of study in the Temple library, he grew restless. With food and sleep, his body had recovered—in fact, he was feeling stronger than ever—but Cambria still ordered him to rest. Though his body had needed recovery, he felt guilty reading in the library with all the work that needed to be done.

Spade was busy with the few Fathers of the Faith who had stayed, arguing over the Temple's future and the direction of Terene. The defeat of the Highfather was only one small victory; Descendants still sat in prisons throughout Terene, their blood now taken at a higher rate than ever. Even Cambria had not heeded her own advice; she spent her hours tending to the countless injured from both sides. Those who were lucky enough to survive the Temple siege.

Ara gazed at the books spread out before him on the table. He hadn't found the answers he searched for, but he had found a new question. One that wouldn't go away. His eyes fell on the map spread out before him and he let out a sigh. How was he going to tell them?

Ara was so focused that he didn't hear her approach.

"All this reading is bad for your eyes," Cambria said. Her shirt was stained with dirt and dried blood. Her face looked tired from late nights in the new infirmary, but her eyes had a spark of life as she teased Ara.

"That can't be true, can it?" Ara asked.

Cambria shrugged and leaned her hands on the table beside him.

"You can't just make stuff up when it is convenient," Ara said. "There must be some ethical law against that."

"I'd have to be ethical to adhere to it." She studied Ara's face. "How do you feel today?"

"Better than ever. I can't tell you how good it feels having consistent meals and rest. It's like I'd been running on injured legs for the past year and only now realize what normal feels like."

Ara did not tell her about the black veins that had formed on the heels of his feet. Remnants of the Highfather's dark blood.

Cambria's eyes fell on the map spread out before Ara. "When are you leaving?"

"Leaving?" Ara looked up confused. Cambria's features softened, there was no judgment in her eyes, just a look that could see right through him. "I…I was afraid to tell you." Ara looked away. "I have to find out where I'm from. I have to know…"

"I understand," Cambria said, cutting him off, her words suddenly clinical. "You're strong enough to ride; you have been for days. Make sure to pack plenty of provisions. Your blood can do amazing things but it still needs to be fed."

"Cambria," Ara started but lost the words. She stood before him; the freckled face girl he'd met on the road. They'd both changed so much in the short amount of time together.

"Thank you," he said, finally. "For everything."

Cambria nodded, her doctor's disposition cracking for a moment. "Come back soon, Ara. There's still a lot more we have to do."

"I will," Ara promised. And he meant it.

Cambria walked from the library, and Ara held onto her image for a few minutes longer. Then, he turned to the table and collected his notes and the map for the journey ahead.

ARA PACKED his horse and waited in the Temple square, hoping to run into one more person before he left.

"Pick up the pace!" a voice yelled. "We're not marching in a parade sweethearts!"

Ara smiled. A group of Temple guards ran past the stables in full armor. They huffed as they tried to keep up to their new commander's standards. Ara knew the feeling.

"Don't worry," Ara called. "You've trained worse."

Geyer turned his head and grunted at the sight of Ara. He barked out another command to the guards, "Another lap around the Temple. This time like soldiers." Then, he crossed the square, his left leg dragging behind.

"I don't know how I let Spade talk me into this," he said, shaking his head. "Only I would be dim enough to teach sword fighting to the people that were just trying to kill me."

"The outfit suits you."

Geyer glanced down at his new armor. "A big shiny target is all it is."

Ara grinned. Apparently not even defeating the Faith was enough to change Geyer's attitude.

"So it's true," Geyer said, nodding to Ara's horse and supplies. "You *are* leaving."

"I have to," Ara looked down. "I need answers." He was about to explain about the Ghost Mountains and about Kovar's final words when the old knight cut him off.

"It's about time," Geyer said. "You weren't going to find any answers sitting around the library in your pajamas."

Ara laughed. "It's called reading. You should try it sometime."

"I've made it this long without, no point starting now."

"A friend of mine once said, 'never rob yourself of the chance to learn.'"

Geyer grunted and kicked a rock at his feet. "Sounds like a wiser man than me." He pointed to the knife strapped to Ara's belt. "You remember how to use that thing?"

"I remember what you taught me."

"Good. Keep your guard up out there. The road's not a friendly place."

"I remember that, too."

Geyer looked Ara over, sizing him up. "You've finally put on some weight. I may even teach you how to use a sword when you get back."

"I look forward to it."

Geyer grinned. "You shouldn't."

The guards came trudging back around the Temple and stopped in the center of the square, bent over, gasping and spitting in the dirt.

"What does running have to do with sword fighting?" Ara asked.

"Fates, if I know. Just something to keep them busy."

Ara chuckled to himself as he climbed on his horse. He steered the horse toward the Temple gates but stopped to give Geyer a salute. "Sir Geyer."

Geyer rolled his eyes and shuffled over to the panting Temple guards. "Are you winded? Looks like we need another lap. Pick up those feet, you clinking bedpans!"

Ara rode northwest from the Temple following the map in his head. It felt like he was riding upstream, for the road was crowded with travelers heading in the opposite direction. The Temple was now open to all the people of Terene, not just those of the Faith. Ara nodded to passing riders and caravans. It felt strange to travel out in the open, without looking over his shoulder for Temple guards.

He rode hard and he rested hard. At one point he spent a full afternoon beside the river's edge, watching the horse drink and enjoying the sound of the lazy current. He wondered what Cambria would think of this place. He'd wondered that on more than one occasion.

After four days of travel, Ara came to his destination. The end of the map. As best he could tell, this was where he was found almost a year ago—battered and mistaken for dead at the foot of the northern mountain wall.

Ara climbed off his horse and untied his pack. Ara stroked the animal's course mane. Then he let the horse go. It was cruel to leave it tied up with the chance he might not return.

The Ghost Mountains rose up before him, disappearing into the foggy gray sky of Terene. *So, this is the end of the world.* If there were answers to his past—who he was, where he came from—he'd find them up there.

Gazing into the gray unknown, Ara whispered the line from King Kovar's journal that had started him on this journey. "They will make ghosts of us all."

With a hopeful smile, Ara walked toward the mountains without end, and he began to climb.

# ACKNOWLEDGMENTS

A lot of work went into this book, and not just by the author. Thank you to Kyle Cossairt for your notes and accountability through this whole, long process.

To my first readers: Deb, Christine, Vince, Colin, Bryan, Lauren, Doug, Betsi, Raj, Mom and Dad. To germancreative for the epic cover. To Kerri for creating a map of the world.

And to my wife Janelle for letting me sneak away to the library to work and not rolling her eyes too much when I talked about writing a fantasy book.

# ABOUT THE AUTHOR

Billy Ketch Allen grew up in Fallbrook, California, and studied creative writing at Cal State Northridge. He plays professional beach volleyball during the day and writes books at night.

www.billyketchallen.com

CPSIA information can be obtained
at www.ICGtesting.com
Printed in the USA
LVHW041513020622
720264LV00001B/151